A GENTLEMAN THROUGH AND THROUGH

"Tell me the truth—did he insult you?"

"Of course not." Camilla gave a weak laugh. "No one could be more proper. He is always the perfect gentleman, except when he gets that mischievous light in his eyes and you know he is laughing inside at something ridiculous someone has said."

"Is that what you like in a man—that he is a gentleman? I wonder where that puts me?"

She gazed up at him quietly, sensing his bleak, restless mood, sensing he was casting about for something: comfort, encouragement, guidance. But why: with Brittany in his pocket, what more could he possibly want?

"You're more truly a gentleman than anyone I've ever known," she whispered, unable to play coy, unable to do anything but answer him with the forthright honesty that was so much a part of her. "A gentleman through and through."

"But also a man, Camilla," he whispered hoarsely, his hand gripping her nape. "And you're so very beautiful . . ."

Praise for Jill Gregory

and Her Best-selling Novel

Cherished

"WOW! What a wonderful heartwarming story. I love the characters and the storyline. I could feel the emotions of the hero and heroine—don't miss this one!"
—Rendezvous

"A good Western story with lots of action!"
—Heartland Critique

"This is as good as they get. Ms. Gregory is great at what she does. *Cherished* is a fine tale of the old West."
—Affaire de Coeur

"Read *Cherished* . . . all the elements of the typical Western romance novel . . . an enjoyable way to spend a few hours."
—Book Rack

Dell books by Jill Gregory

DAISIES IN THE WIND
FOREVER AFTER
JUST THIS ONCE
NEVER LOVE A COWBOY
COLD NIGHT, WARM STRANGER
ROUGH WRANGLER, TENDER KISSES

JILL GREGORY

FOREVER AFTER

A DELL BOOK

Published by
Dell Publishing
a division of
Random House, Inc.
1540 Broadway
New York, New York 10036

ISBN: 0-440-21512-9

Printed in the United States of America

Published simultaneously in Canada

April 1993

10 9 8 7 6

OPM

For my mother, Ruth,
and her sister, Mildred,
with love that will last forever after

PROLOGUE

Part I
Paris, 1806

It was nearly midnight. Slick, glossy darkness sheathed the streets of Paris. The streetlights shimmered faintly, casting off beams of eerie silver light that scarcely penetrated the dank mist rising off the cobbles, and offered scant illumination, a mere lightening of shadows among the stately trees and houses. Only a stray carriage here and there broke the silence of the cobblestones—until the horse and rider clattered suddenly down the private boulevard and halted before the marble-fronted town house where upstairs Madame Genevieve Saverne lay dying.

With urgent speed, the liveried messenger swung from his horse and up the steps. He banged commandingly upon the ornately carved door until it was opened by a round-shouldered little woman with ferret eyes and a cold mouth. She held a taper aloft in one pudgy hand.

"Madame Saverne—at once!" he snapped.

"Are you mad?"

"I bear a message from his grace, Monsieur le Duc de Mont de Lyon."

She gasped at the name, her eyes widening. The candle flame sputtered in the sudden breeze that whipped down the street. All the color drained from the servant's doughy cheeks. Recovering herself an instant later, she began to close the door.

"Go away. She can see no one. She is dying."

The messenger put a hand to the door, his strength preventing her from closing it.

"Step aside, madame," he warned. "I have a letter from his grace. Your mistress dare not die before she reads it."

Plump, sallow-faced old Suzette had by now ample time to recover from her shock. She glared at the tall liveried man with the pale eyes, and she vowed to herself that he would not disturb her mistress. Ferocious as a dragon despite her advanced years and diminutive size, she hissed at him.

"Have you no *respect?* Bastard. Go *away.* I forbid you to see her! And as for the Duke, I spit on him. Baaa!"

Again she tried to close the door, again he stopped her. "I warned you once, madame. The Duke has charged me with delivering his letter, and that I will do."

With these words, he thrust her from the doorway, not cruelly, but with great firmness, and stalked into the entrance hall. A resplendent chandelier dangled from the vaulted ceiling, the crystal prisms glittering like dagger shards in the murky light cast out from Suzette's candle. Beyond the entrance hall with its small mirror-topped table and gold-painted walls, an eerie gloom gripped the magnificent town house, the velvet-couched salons branching off the marble-tiled hall shrouded in darkness, the great staircase winding its way upward into the shadows.

Suzette might have screamed for other servants to come to her aid, but she did not. She fell back, glaring at the ducal crest on the messenger's braided jacket with hate suffusing her face. Her eyes bulged half in fear, half in loathing.

The messenger hastened to the stairs and started to climb them.

"Wait," she croaked. She cursed him silently, but resigned herself with Gallic practicality to the inevitable. "I will take you. Come with me." *Bastard.*

Shoulders bent, she led the way.

Madame Genevieve Saverne lay quietly beneath the satin folds of her bed coverings. Her exquisitely beautiful face framed by cascading red-gold ringlets was still lovely despite the ghostly pallor of her skin. The sunken appearance of her once vibrant eyes, and the thinness of the beringed hand that gripped her lace-trimmed handkerchief attested to her debilitating illness. For all that she was past forty and upon her deathbed, the evidence of her exceptional beauty was still uncannily strong. Yet, despite her charms, her wide, sensual lips, lush bosom, and rouged cheeks, her eyes were possessed by a cold, empty quality. They glittered, and not only from the fever that consumed her.

Genevieve Saverne bore the countenance of one whose heart has never been softened by love—love of husband, child, home. In truth of fact, Genevieve Saverne had only loved one man in her entire life, and he had spurned her —cruelly spurned her, in her estimation. The pain of that had turned her needful love into malicious, vitriolic hate, a hate that had dominated her life and nearly all her thoughts for the past nineteen years. Instead of softening her, it had hardened her. Instead of opening her to the tender emotions of a woman, it had sealed the shell of her self-absorption and cunning, and intensified her craving for revenge.

When the Duke's messenger stood before her in the sumptuously elegant crimson and gold bedchamber and stated his purpose, with Suzette kneeling beside her and clutching her hand all the while, she said nothing. She did not even look at the man. But through the fever that burned through her body, consuming it the way a forest blaze devours a twig, she was thinking of Girard.

You know, then, do you, chérie? *That doctor's daughter told you. Ah, so my victory is complete.* Bien.

She smiled to herself, filled with joy. She had made him suffer. And he suffered still. Perhaps he would never find the girl. Never. If only it could be . . .

She was chuckling aloud, a throaty, heartfelt chuckle.

"Madame, madame." The messenger's voice intruded into her thoughts. Vaguely, she stared at him. A strong man, by the looks of him, but he could do nothing. Nothing. "Madame, the letter from the Duke. I will read it now. Do you wish this woman to remain?"

This woman? Ah, yes, Suzette. Genevieve glanced at the tear-streaked face of the woman who had served her faithfully for more than twenty-five years, since she had begun her career as a courtesan. They had begun their respective careers together. Genevieve had been the common-born beauty of great ambition, Suzette the plump, devoted servant who had once been a ladies' maid in the same household where Genevieve's mother had been cook. When they had set up housekeeping in a small establishment all those years ago, neither of them had dreamed of the glittering success to come, of the counts and dukes and barons who would fall at Genevieve's feet

and beg to worship her. Neither of them could have predicted how many nobles and aristocrats would become
slaves to her beauty, her voluptuous body and sophisticated sarcasm, how many would shower her with jewels
and silks and gold and lavish her with all the attention
their poor neglected wives would never know. Suzette
had served her faithfully all these years, loyal only to
Genevieve, discreet, efficient, asking nothing in return,
not even kindness.

Genevieve had granted even less, never bothering with
an appreciative word or glance, but when she died, fat old
Suzette would become a very wealthy woman.

It was only fair.

Genevieve Saverne flicked her cold glance at the messenger. "She may stay," she said indifferently.

She closed her eyes as he began to read the Duke's
missive aloud. The words swirled around her, purple
patches in the deeper blackness that was engulfing her.
She scarcely listened, for she was lost in the wanderings
of her own thoughts.

*Girard, Girard, you are an old man now. Pity I should
die before you. Now I'll never know if you find her. I'll never
know. But you've lost all these years . . . they can never be
regained. You have suffered horribly. That alone makes everything worthwhile . . .*

The messenger's words droned on. The Duke was angry with her. Of course. He wanted answers, he wanted
assistance, or he would seek vengeance in ways she could
not even imagine.

Threats. Useless, idiotic threats. She laughed to herself, her mind drifting back, moving from the young dashing Duke who had shared her bed, to the baby, the innocent round-cheeked baby in its gilt cradle. She pictured
the tiny child, sound asleep, wrapped in a soft blue velvet

robe. No, no, it was the other child, *her* child, who wore the blue robe. Or had it been the yellow one?

Her mind churned with the fever. The messenger's voice droned on, the words blurring together.

Suzette's tears were wet upon Genevieve's hand.

The baby. Two babies. One dead, one alive. He would never find the child now. She was a grown woman, if she was still alive. *And I will not say one word to help* . . .

"Don't weep, Suzette," she commanded. She opened her burning eyes and stared triumphantly into the servant's stricken face.

"It doesn't matter what he says, what he does. Don't you see? I have won. I bested the Duke."

"Oui, madame. *Oui.* You bested him. You bested them all," Suzette whispered fiercely.

But as Suzette clutched her mistress's hand, Genevieve's eyes drifted closed. Fear cut through the old woman. The hand clenched so tightly in hers went lax, and at the same moment, a clock somewhere in the hall chimed midnight.

"She is dead." Suzette stared, then came heavily to her feet. She turned furiously on the messenger, with tears shining in her eyes. "Are you satisfied? Go now and tell your Duke that there is no help for him here."

"I think there is," the messenger said softly. He stepped toward her. "You will come with me, madame. You will answer the Duke's questions, since your mistress cannot."

"I will answer nothing!" she spat, her eyes flashing with hate.

He took her arm. "We will see. The Duke's coach stands outside. Come."

Part II
London, 1806

Lady Hampton's ballroom was aglitter with masked ladies and gentlemen of the ton resplendent in all manner of sumptuous costume. Music whirled around the laughing and drinking guests, lilting and gay as it snatched them into the festively daring mood of the evening. All of London had turned out for Lady Hampton's annual masquerade. There were wood nymphs and princesses, dragons, giants, sea goddesses, and wizards. Sophisticated chatter and boisterous laughter rang through the air, and champagne flowed like nectar from the marble fountain poised at the head of the room between tall silver stands of red roses.

A thousand candles lit the marble-tiled room in breathtaking splendor. The ton danced, and gossiped and laughed, elegant couples whirling and dipping their way across the dance floor, or flirting in corners beside potted palms. The mood of the party as the evening progressed became ever more merry, decadent, and wild.

It was a perfect backdrop for the Earl of Westcott. Dashing in his long black cape, a highwayman's mask partially concealing his handsome face, he cut a commanding figure as he made his way across the crowded ballroom with his distinctive pantherish stride.

The ladies ogled him from one end of the ballroom to the other, longing in their eyes.

"Isn't that the Earl of Westcott?" Florence Persimmons whispered to Lady Brittany Deaville.

Lady Brittany, who had only a moment before finished dancing with Lord Morrowton, and had sent her eager partner off to fetch her a lemonade, watched catlike from behind her Grecian mask.

"Perhaps." Her offhand tone was belied by the intense gleam in her violet eyes as she watched the tall, broad-shouldered highwayman stalk across the room and disappear into one of the anterooms where high-stakes gaming was going on.

She sank into a velvet-cushioned gilt chair, arranging the spangled folds of her white Grecian goddess gown artlessly about her. "I am far more interested in identifying Lord Marchfield among all these gentlemen," she said coolly, but her magnificent eyes lingered on the doorway through which the highwayman had disappeared. "The Earl of Westcott is of no concern to me."

Florence hid a smile. Everyone knew the game that was being played out this season in the drawing rooms and ballrooms of London society. Lady Brittany Deaville was the town's acknowledged beauty, unequaled by any other young lady who had made her debut this season. And dozens of beaux had fallen prey to her statuesque, golden-haired charms, among them the most wealthy, sought-after young men of the ton. The astonishing part of it was that the Earl of Westcott had fallen victim to Brittany's loveliness. At the age of eight and twenty years, the Earl had a dangerous reputation. Known for his reck-lessness and sarcasm, for brilliant duels—and for engag-ing in wicked flirtations, which had resulted in a long line of broken hearts—his pursuit of the dazzling Lady Brit-tany was the juiciest on-dit of many a year, cause for much speculation that the rakish young Earl had at last succumbed to love's ensnaring lure.

Tonight, however, Lady Brittany had virtually ignored him in favor of Lord Marchfield, Lord Kirby, Count An-drei of Prussia, and numerous others. Her careless treat-ment quite obviously had the Earl in a towering if con-trolled rage. Though every other young woman in the room would have gladly danced with him if he'd even been half as wealthy and half as fascinatingly handsome as he was, and though they all tried their utmost to waylay and entice him, he ignored them one and all. He was in an ugly mood. Aloof and furious, he stalked from the ballroom proper without a backward glance.

Lady Brittany, smug with the success of her plans, smiled quietly to herself. The Earl, if she chose to land him, was as good as hooked. The only question in her mind was whether she indeed chose to land him. She was undecided as to which catch she preferred: the Earl of Westcott or Lord Marchfield.

Lord Marchfield, suavely handsome, opulently wealthy, and in possession of a mature, sophisticatedly urbane brand of charm, did not precisely excite her the way the virile, ruggedly handsome Earl did, but he was amusing, and certainly attractive. Philip, though . . . Her pulse quickened thinking about him. The impact of the Earl of Westcott's sizzling gray gaze upon her, the heat of his powerful arm clasping her waist when they danced, the sensual curve of his hard mouth and the lightning bolt of masculine electricity that emanated from him sometimes made it difficult for her even to remember which calculated move she intended to seduce him with next. It was, frankly, hard to think when he talked to her, smiled at her, walked with her. Brittany wasn't sure she liked that. And she absolutely didn't like the aura of scandal attached to the Earl's name. Oh, the Audleys were certainly good ton and were received everywhere but it was commonly known that they had a streak of wildness in them, a recklessness in their bloodline that concerned her—as it did her mama.

Above all else, Brittany wished to make a splendid marriage with a perfect man. She had been raised with an excellent understanding of her own consequence, with an appreciation for the superiority of her background and breeding and her preordained place in society as the daughter of a marquis. She had also been made well aware as she left the schoolroom and entered the years of young womanhood, that she was blessed with exceptional beauty, the kind of beauty so rare and breathtaking that it would bring her what every young woman should wish for: a magnificent match, a splendid future, with any man of her choosing.

She intended to choose carefully—and well.

It seemed to her that the Earl of Westcott, with his wild moods, his unpredictable temper, and his duels, might be a somewhat risky choice. Marriage with him might be a shade unconventional.

Lord Kirby, though, was a prime candidate, and so was Lord Marchfield. Yet she kept thinking about the Earl. It was necessary to frequently remind herself that for all his wealth, his estates, his country seat, and his town house in Berkeley Square, the Earl of Westcott had definite drawbacks. For one thing, he possessed a younger sister and brother for whom he was responsible, and then there was that temper of his. Most disturbing of all—that little incident several years ago involving the sister who died . . .

Scandal. Brittany abhorred it, even a whisper of it. So did her mama and her papa. She was safer steering away from the Earl of Westcott and setting her sights firmly on Someone Else, and yet . . .

He was so handsome, and there was something almost dangerously compelling about him. And it was great fun to twist such an unlikely but magnificent catch around her little finger and watch the great fearsome Earl dangle. . . .

"This masquerade," Brittany remarked to Florence, as a trio of eager suitors advanced upon her, "is positively delightful. I declare I have not been so diverted in a fortnight."

"May I have the honor of this dance?" Mr. Seaton cried as he burst forth ahead of the pack to bow before her. Garbed in a green satin tunic with a bow and arrow at his side, in the guise of the legendary outlaw Robin Hood, his eyes pleaded for her acquiescence. An instant later he was pushed aside by the other young men who descended upon her, showering their compliments, begging for the honor of accompanying her into the grand supper.

"Why, gentlemen, how can a lady resist such charming entreaties?" Brittany smiled as she rose to her feet and bestowed her hand in Mr. Seaton's with the grace of a queen. "I must think before I can make a choice among you—for I truly wish I could sup with you all. Oh, dear."

And laughing, she glided off to dance with Mr. Seaton, leaving the others to exchange polite conversation with the insipid Florence. All the while that Brittany traded banter with her partner and slanted provocative glances up at him from beneath her lashes while they danced, she was planning further ways to torment the Earl of Westcott into making her a proposal—a proposal that she would carefully consider—and then regretfully decline.

I'll be known as the lady who broke the Earl's heart, she thought. *It will be a wonderful triumph.*

Or maybe she *would* marry him—convention be damned. Then she could entertain herself for the rest of her days turning the unpredictable Earl into a most predictable and docile husband.

Either prospect offered its unique charm to an unpar-

alleled young beauty confident of her power to mesmer-
ize and bewitch.

Which should she choose?

The Earl of Westcott was playing faro with reckless
abandon—and winning. A crowd gathered around the
game, expanding as the stakes increased, and with every
shift of luck the rippling murmur of the onlookers swelled
like the hum of insects at nightfall.

Philip's old enemy, Lord Marchfield, who also happened to be his rival for the hand of Lady Brittany, was
proving a challenging opponent. Everyone wanted to
know if the Earl's luck would hold.

Cold fire burned from his eyes as he played. He had
removed his highwayman's mask, and his darkly magnetic
young face was a study in boredom, yet beneath the composed veneer, tension coiled within him, and everyone in
the gaming room, from the greenest young dandy to the
old gout-ridden Duke of Cravy, sensed the mutual dislike
in which the two men held one another.

"I hear that Lady Brittany has consented to go in to
supper with young Seaton," one aging gentleman remarked to another, his words ringing out like bells in the
hushed room. His companion held down a chuckle. Everyone else held his breath.

The Earl's hand froze in mid-air for a moment, then
continued to casually carry his brandy goblet to his lips.
He drank deeply, his eyes molten gray in the flickering
candlelight around the table.

It was Lord Marchfield's turn to choose a card.
Dressed as a satyr in black and silver, he smiled with faint
mockery at the Earl. "Do you care to deepen the stakes?"

"As you wish." Philip met his gaze with cool indiffer-
ence.

Marchfield's smile expanded. "I hear there was a spot of trouble recently at Paxton House. Perhaps your brother told you about it," he murmured in his deep, lazy voice.

Frozen silence. "My brother?" The Earl's voice when he spoke was dangerously quiet.

"Oh, not James." The elegant black lace sleeves of the satyr's velvet coat fell back as Marchfield took snuff. "Your *youngest* brother. Jeffrey, Jedson . . . whatever *is* his name?"

A thrill of tension vibrated through the room.

The Earl hid his shock. He came to his feet. His eyes glinted beneath his shock of silky dark hair. "Marchfield, precisely what is it you are trying with so much difficulty to say?"

"I? Why, nothing. Perhaps it was all a mistake."

Marchfield calmly drew a card.

"Are you still in, my lord?" he asked with great gentleness. "Or have you had enough?"

"That is a question I ought to ask you, my lord," Philip replied softly. "Perhaps you would prefer other sport? Pistols—or swords?"

"My dear fellow." Marchfield raised his brows. "I am perfectly content with the game we are playing. Dueling is for young, hot-blooded fools, not grown men of intelligence and style. Which, I wonder, are you?"

Several men gasped. Count Andrei put a hand on Marchfield's shoulder. "Take care, my friend. I hear he has killed two men in duels," he whispered, but the grin only widened across Marchfield's pleasant features.

"No answer, my lord?" he chided. "Well, let me offer you a proposition. I think you will be most interested. It has to do with a certain lady we both know."

Philip set down his brandy glass. "Take care you do not insult the lady," he warned quietly.

Marchfield feigned hurt feelings. "I? Hurt the woman I adore? Never. I merely wish to issue a challenge to you. Unless you are afraid to hear it."

The tension grew nearly to a roar with these words. At the center of it, Philip Audley held his temper in check with great difficulty. The walnut clock on the wall chimed midnight as he stared down his enemy.

From the ballroom came laughter and shrieks as the unmasking began. Inside the salon Philip waited until the chimes ended before making his reply.

"Afraid, my lord? Not at all." It was his turn to smile, a tight, cool smile that never reached his eyes. "Fools enjoy the sound of their own prattle," he said quietly. "So by all means, my lord, speak."

In a ramshackle tavern miles away to the east, a weary and bedraggled serving girl with tray in hand pushed her way through the crowded taproom. The tavern clock struck midnight at the exact moment that the man in the puce coat looked up from his table, noticed her, and made his decision.

It was the same time that Genevieve Saverne died in Paris. It was also precisely the same moment that Lord Marchfield issued his challenge at Lady Hampton's masquerade. Midnight. And at the last stroke of midnight in the Rose and Swan, the dirty-faced serving girl called Weed put down her tray, saw the thin man beckoning her, and set out unknowingly onto the twisted path of Fate.

It all began when the tall man in the puce coat beckoned her to his corner table in the Rose and Swan and held out a sealed and somewhat frayed paper. "You there. Weed. Isn't that what they call you? How would you like to earn yourself an extra shilling? Two, if you're quick and quiet about it." He gave her a nervous smile. His voice was almost inaudible in the surrounding din of the smoke-filled tavern. "You look like an enterprising girl."

Camilla Brent pushed the stringy copper hair from her eyes. She was a tall girl, rather thin and shapeless beneath her much-mended work clothes. She gave the square of paper only a brief glance, then fixed the man in the puce coat with a penetrating look. Despite the guttering candles, the smoke, the screech of drunken voices in the ramshackle tavern, she could make out his features well enough. Sharp, clever features with heavy-lidded eyes and a weak dribble of a chin. His greasy coat bespoke better days. The cut was good, even though it was now shabby and worn. There was a good deal of liquor on the man's breath. Something unsavory here, Camilla sensed with a little quiver up her back, something better left alone. Camilla was about to shake her head and move on with the heavy tray of drinks she held, but as if reading the refusal in her eyes, the tall man with his strange, heavy-lidded eyes suddenly leaned toward her.

"Three shillings," he hissed.

Three shillings. Camilla had a vision of the new shoes three shillings could buy for Hester, and perhaps a sweetmeat as well, and she nodded suddenly. She was given to quick decisions.

"One moment."

She dodged a drunken seaman who pushed back his chair directly into her path, and hurried over to the table of cheerfully besotted dockworkers who had called for their brew.

"Thanks, lovey," the stoutest among them bellowed, but she nimbly sidestepped the fat fingers that would have squeezed her bottom, swerved past another barmaid scurrying to do a mop-up, and returned promptly to the corner table. Camilla wiped her hands on her apron.

"What do you want me to do?"

"Deliver this to Mr. Anders in the White Horse Inn. Do you know where that is?"

"Yes. It's far. I'll need a gold piece as well, to make it worth my while."

"Don't be greedy, my girl . . ." he began warningly, his oily face flushing.

"Greed has nothing to do with it. I risk losing my job here if I run out now . . ."

"Dibbs won't fire you. You're the only one around here worth her wages."

"Compliments aren't gold, Mr. . . . ?"

"Never you mind."

"Mr. Never-you-mind, find yourself another messenger. I've got to get back to work."

He grabbed her wrist then, not gently. "Take your gold piece then, you dirty little beggar. But go now, and don't say a word to anyone. And don't give this over to a soul 'cept Mr. Anders. You hear? No one but him. He's in Room 203."

Camilla kept her face carefully expressionless. Inside, though, elation was pounding through her. A gold piece and three shillings! She could buy Hester a coat for winter as well as the shoes.

She took the paper and stuffed it into the pocket of her much-mended, ale-stained skirt. "Payment in advance, if you please, sir. There's no guarantee you'll be here when I get back."

The heavy-lidded eyes smoldered. "You have my word on it."

"Bah," Camilla scoffed. She put her hands on her hips in a defiant stance. "That and a bottle of Irish will buy me a fine headache in the morning."

Thin lips compressed. She saw the beads of sweat along his high, narrow brow. Anger touched the lidded eyes. Almost, she felt afraid. But she kept her lip curled derisively, her head thrown back. She knew how to appear staunch.

"The shillings now, then," he capitulated, rasping. "But you'll get the gold piece later. That's my final word."

"Done." Camilla flipped the coins he gave her into her pocket along with the square of paper, and turned on her heel. As she made her way through the crowded tavern, Gwynneth Dibbs shouted to her to see to the customers, obviously referring to a rowdy table of seamen who had already finished off their tankards and were shouting for more, but Camilla kept right on going toward the door.

"Clara'll see to them," she called. "I'll be back soon."

"By midnight, if I'm lucky," she muttered to herself, wincing as Gwynneth screeched her fury. Clara threw Camilla an astonished look, and Dibbs shouted across the room, demanding to know where she thought she was going. Then the din of the tavern was behind her. She was out in the dark, damp street, the mist brushing her face like sticky cobwebs. The October air was cold, and she wished she'd stopped for her cloak, but that might have meant Dibbs waylaying her, forcibly keeping her from leaving on her errand, and she hadn't wanted to risk that.

A gold piece and three shillings! It was a kingly sum of money all at once, and the idea of it caused her to quicken her steps past the harbor and toward the White Horse Inn. Once, she mused, her chin scrunched against her shoulder for warmth, such a sum might have seemed like the merest trifle, but that was long ago. A lifetime ago. Before everything had changed.

She remembered the oft-spoken grumble of Mrs. Toombs, who'd run the workhouse where she'd been sent after her parents' death.

In the blink of an eye, your life can change.

True enough. Thinking of how her own life had changed when she was eight—quick as a blink—for the worse, she gave herself a sudden shake. No use thinking back on it all now. What was done, was done. But that didn't mean she couldn't have her dreams, she thought to herself as she rounded a corner and zigzagged in front of an oncoming carriage, much to the outrage of the driver. Camilla ignored his tirade and hurried on, too intent on her errand and her own plans to let herself be distracted by the heavy traffic. *Maybe my luck is changing for the better now,* she thought hopefully, splashing through a puddle. With the shillings in her pocket, and the gold piece to come, she felt rich—rich and lucky and . . . cold.

The damp chill drifting in off the river sliced right through her skin, making her shiver all over as she made her way through the fog-shrouded city. A horse and rider darting suddenly around the street into her path nearly ran her down. Jumping aside only just in time, she stumbled into a heap of trash. She picked herself up, cursing beneath her breath as she brushed bloody meat bones and rotting cabbage from her skirts. But the horse and rider that had suddenly loomed up had made her remember something, something that made her smile as she hurried once more on her way. She had dreamed of *him* again last night.

It was the same dream as before—only different. This time he came to her upon a black steed, and swept her up alongside him with one powerful arm. He cradled her against him as they rode away into the windswept night. In her dream, she sighed with ecstasy.

Sometimes he came on a ship, like a pirate, other times he appeared magically inside the Rose and Swan Tavern, which was crowded and smoky and horrid as always. He bore her away like a marauder, but treated her like a lady. He took her to a lovely castle and set her down with unexpected gentleness upon a bed sprinkled with rose petals. Always, his face was hidden from her, blurred and shadowed, but it was a handsome face, that much she knew, dark and virile and arrogant. His body was magnificently muscled, lean and bronzed, his back broad and strong. Last night when she dreamed the heat of him warmed her despite the drafty chill of her attic room. She dreamed that together they raced on horseback beneath the cool, white stars, that she was warm and safe and content within the circle of his arms.

At last he slid from the stallion's back and pulled her down beside him in a bed of moss and leaves, and then he covered her with his body and the weight of him pressed her into the damp, clinging leaves, and he kissed her. He kissed her long and hard. His mouth demanded as it moved over hers. His hands explored her body in a way that made fire tingle through her blood. The heat glowed through her, and she tried to ask him "Who are you?" but she couldn't speak and there were no words between them, only deep, hungry kisses and that spreading, melting heat. . . .

And then Gwynneth Dibbs, Will's fat, spiteful niece, had awakened her with a pitcherful of water sloshed over her face—and that had been the end of that.

"Rise and shine, lazybones!" Gwynneth had ordered, setting the pitcher down with a thud on the scarred wooden bureau.

Dripping wet, gasping and shivering in the chill of a bleak gray dawn just beginning to leak through the attic window, Camilla had made out the giant girl's orange hair and bloated freckled face. Ugh, how she loathed that face. Nearly six feet tall and stout as a sea captain, Gwynneth possessed flashing, spiteful brown eyes, jowly cheeks, and a bully's temperament.

With water trickling down her face and neck, soaking her skin and hair, Camilla had at first been too stunned and too chilled to speak, but Gwynneth had been only too ready to unleash her morning tirade.

"If you think I'm going to do your share of the work and my own, you've missed your guess," Gwynneth had shouted, kicking at Camilla's pallet. "Get up and get moving, Weed—or do I have to drag you downstairs by your hair?"

Camilla had finally found her voice. Her thin shoulders

trembling with cold in the early morning air, she had
sputtered, "Don't you ever dare throw water on me
again, Gwynneth Dibbs, or I'll . . . I'll . . ."

"What, Weed? What'll you do?" Sneering contemptuously, Gwynneth had taken a menacing step forward, her
flabby hands on her hips. "You miserable, ugly, scrawny
wretch! Tempt me, and I'll break your arm in two! Just
see if I won't. You don't belong here, with all your fancy
airs and manners—and your genteel talk. Soon as I convince my uncle of that you'll be out, you hear me? Out! In
a twinkling, you will. I don't know why my uncle keeps
you on here—you're so clumsy you break half the glasses
and you sleep past daybreak every damned day. And you
think you know everything, but you know nothing. Nothing! Just who do you think you are? You may have been a
squire's daughter once, but you're nothing now—*nobody*,
and it's about time you accepted that."

"I know what *you* are, Gwynneth Dibbs."

"I'm the one who's in charge of you—and I say *get
moving*. Or maybe I'll break *both* arms, and see how you
like *that*."

She'd have done it, too, Camilla reflected, picking her
way over a dead rat in the street. *She'd have broken my
arms and not thought twice about it*. Grimacing, she
moved past the street corner, and out of the feeble glow
of lamplight, deliberately forcing her thoughts away from
Gwynneth Dibbs, thinking instead of the mysterious man
who haunted her dreams.

If only someone *would* come and carry her away from
the Rose and Swan, from the harsh, dull tedium of her
life, from being under Gwynneth Dibbs's thumb, she
thought yearningly.

No one would, though. She knew that. If she were ever
to get out from under Gwynneth's rule, and from the

unwelcome coarseness of the tavern, it would have to be
by her own doing. She'd been trying, of course. She'd
tried to maintain a position in a dressmaker's shop, in a
millinery, and a flower shop; she'd worked (briefly) as a
ladies' maid and a governess, but none of these efforts
had been successful. Each time she'd been discharged.
Too stubborn, too bossy, can't follow orders, speaking up
to the customers—for one reason or another, she had
failed at each endeavor.

But something, somewhere, would work out. She
couldn't see herself living out the remainder of her days
mopping floors and fetching ale in the Rose and Swan,
being bullied by Gwynneth, yelled at by Will Dibbs, and
smacked on the rump in passing by smelly, drunken
seamen who thought serving girls the same as whores. It
wasn't so much the rigorous work of the tavern she detested, work that left her back and shoulders and calves
aching, but it was the squalid surroundings, the crude
shouts of the customers that rang like derisive bells in her
ears, the harsh scolding of Gwynneth, and the pungent
stench of ale and smoke, which she couldn't seem to wash
out of her clothes or her hair.

Camilla's mouth set in determination as she reflected
on the gritty details of her life, not with self-pity, but with
a cool, thoughtful eye as to how and when she might
make her escape. She'd seen a sign in an apothecary window yesterday for a clerk. Maybe she could try that . . .

Seeing at last that she was nearing the seedy block of
buildings among which crouched the White Horse Inn,
she quickened her pace. This was a neighborhood into
which she seldom ventured. Though she was accustomed
to the poor section of London, this area had a reputation
as a cesspool of thieves and cutthroats and packs of scav-
enging youths with no other way of feeding themselves

than stealing from those unsuspecting souls caught crossing their path.

She made her way warily past the buildings huddled over the street, half-expecting to be set upon at any moment, and she let out a breath of relief when she safely reached the White Horse. It was a run-down two-story building with boarded-up windows and a crumbling front stair. Without pausing to scrutinize its decaying appearance, Camilla went inside past a rotting wood doorway, glad to be out of the chill and the shadowy darkness. Inside, she blinked against the sudden brightness. The inn teemed with men. They overflowed from the garishly lit meeting rooms and parlors, onto the stairs, through the hallways, but they were all too drunk to notice her as she hurried up the narrow flight of stairs, squeezing past several huge and boisterous revelers sprawled across the steps in a drunken stupor. The White Horse reeked of liquor and burned ham, and the noise belowstairs was still a dull roar in her ears. Reaching the second story, where the private parlor and the bedchambers were located, she found it comparatively quiet.

All right, Mr. Anders in Room 203, here's your secret message, and then I'm gone from this place. Camilla peered carefully at the numbers painted on the doors. The narrow hall gave her an odd feeling. She wasn't given to flights of fancy, but something vaguely sinister made the hair on the back of her neck prickle as she moved along the threadbare carpet. The uneasiness persisted even as she searched for the numbers she sought. Unconsciously, she fingered the charm in the shape of a lion that she wore on a chain around her neck. She had had it as long as she could remember, and she had always thought of it as her good luck charm. But it didn't help tonight to dispel the apprehension gripping her.

At last she found 203. She knocked. Silence. She knocked again.

No one answered.

Chewing her lip, she considered what to do if Mr. Anders wasn't here. She had been warned against leaving the letter with anyone else, but perhaps she could inquire downstairs and see if the man she sought was in the taproom or one of the parlors. If she didn't return to the Rose and Swan soon, Dibbs would box her ears, but if she returned without completing her errand she would have to give back the money.

Anxiously, she knocked again, on the chance that he was asleep or intoxicated and hadn't heard clearly the first time. This time she thought she heard something inside the room.

"Mr. Anders?" she called out. On an impulse—Mrs. Toombs at the workhouse had always chastised her for being an impulsive girl—she tried the doorknob and it turned beneath her hand. The door swung open.

"Mr. Anders," Camilla began again, stepping forward into the room. The words choked in her throat.

Her stomach turned over and her hands froze in midair before her. On the floor lay a dead man, a knife stuck in his portly chest. And blood all over the room . . .

Oh, God. As Camilla stared in mute shock, the tall dark-cloaked figure standing over the dead man yanked the knife from the prone body, straightened up to his full imposing height, and whirled toward her all in one fluid movement.

She tried to scream and couldn't.

The vision before her was terrifying.

A black satanic visage leered at her above a dark cloaked body that looked huge and powerful in the ugly little room. A demon, she thought at first, seized with hideous fear. In the next instant reason overcame her first wild impression, and she knew that the man wore a mask, a disguise like those favored by the nobles at their masquerades; black velvet, glittering with diamonds, yet somehow this mask was chilling, demonic, with small pointed horns protruding above the ears and only tiny slits slashed through the velvet for the wearer's eyes. And his eyes were the worst of all. They gazed back at her, strangely blue and bright in the smoky dimness of the room, dancing with lust and madness.

Camilla wanted to scream, but she couldn't. Mute with terror, the sound was locked inside.

The murderer inclined his head toward her in a graceful, almost elegant gesture.

"An unfortunate entrance, my lady," he whispered in a hushed, eerily pleasant voice that was all the more terrifying for its calmness. Especially compared to those mad, dilated eyes.

"Now I'll have to kill you, too."

Her knees buckled. In that blinding instant, the ordinary hours of this past evening seemed to whirl before her. How normal and mundane and tedious everything had been up until a moment ago when she had entered this chamber. *In the blink of an eye, your life can change.*

"This isn't what I had in mind," she muttered hoarsely.

He lifted the knife high.

In that next split instant, the scene before her imprinted itself on her brain: the cheap, grimy furnishings of that seedy little bedchamber, the curtains of dusty burlap, the coarse woolen coverlet spread across the bed in the center of the room, the sour stench of spilled ale and blood and . . . death. In the looking glass directly opposite the door, her own image floated back to her in the wispy candlelight, a gangly dirty-faced figure in scullery rags, hair tucked all anyhow beneath a cap, waiting like a paralyzed fool for a madman to kill her.

She was only dimly aware of all this, yet it made a searing impression on her mind as, for that heart-splitting moment, time seemed suspended. Then her stunned gaze focused on the man starting toward her and, at last, she screamed.

Screamed—and bolted.

He lunged at her the same instant, swinging the knife in a wide arc.

But Camilla was gone, and the blade slashed harmlessly into the thick wood of the door.

She catapulted down the stairs, too terrified to waste her breath screaming again. She ran as if pursued by the very devil himself, which to her mind, was not far from the truth.

The steps rushed up at her in a blur, but she was agile and quick, and she managed them without a stumble, leaping over the drunks without hesitation, staggering through the hall. Then she was surrounded by a wild press of bodies, and frantically tried to shove her way through the boisterous, beer-swigging patrons clogging the route to the door. She screamed for help, but her voice was drowned out by the din of the throng. No one listened to her pleas, no one looked or stopped or cared.

If he grabs me, and carries me upstairs to my death, no one will notice, no one will care, she thought with sudden clarity. She had to get out of here. Fighting her way through the crowd, she burst free at last and stumbled out of the inn and into the fog-shrouded London night.

Inky shadows pressed in upon her. The banks of mist that floated ghostlike over the slickened cobblestones seemed to reach out with grasping fingers to clutch her. Even the murky darkness seemed a living, breathing creature, ready to envelop her in dank blackness and never let her go.

Staring wildly about, Camilla stifled a tiny cry of fear. She didn't have time to be afraid, she didn't have time to pause and think. She knew that he would pursue her, and she knew that if he caught her he would kill her in a trice. She fled for her life.

Zigzagging down the narrow cobblestones past darkened wharves where ships bobbed like shadowy dragons, past taverns and crowded slum shops and mounds of rotting garbage, she dodged knots of ragged beggars and drunkards. Once a toothless old man with evil eyes tried to grasp her arm as she raced past. But she shook him off and fled on. Camilla knew these streets well, and she was young and strong. She ran relentlessly, unfailingly, her work-stained skirts grasped between icy fingers, her hair streaming now from beneath the limp folds of her cap, and always, always, she was listening for the sound of boots on cobblestones behind her, running in pursuit. Once she thought she heard that sound, and she glanced back, but she could see nothing—only the shrouding mist, swirling down through the London night. Her shoulders trembled. An icy chill gripped her heart. He was out there. She felt it.

Gulping in great breaths of the damp, sea-scented air she ran on.

If she could only reach the Rose and Swan. She could slip in the back way so Gwynneth and Mr. Dibbs wouldn't even know she was back and then hide herself upstairs in her tiny attic room. Then she would be safe, she told herself, as she tore around a corner and nearly fell on the damp stones.

She wondered if the man in the puce coat would still be in the taproom. If he was . . .

But she was not to know. For as she neared the corner where the tavern stood across from a dilapidated lip of the pier and beside a row of smoke-belching factories, a horse-drawn wagon collided with a hackney and both vehicles overturned together, spilling people and goods into the street.

The sudden catastrophe rocked the night. Amid the screams of the horses, the yells of the drivers, and the accompanying tumult from running passersby as well as those involved in the mishap, Camilla saw that the street was completely blocked. She stopped short. Leaning against a crumbling storefront, her breath coming in painful rasps that hurt her chest, she watched the chaos only a dozen yards before her in silent horror. She braced herself against the rough brick, trying to draw strength from it. The chill of the night had now seeped into her bones. She felt as though her legs were going to collapse, and every muscle ached, but there was no time to rest, no time to stop, no time at all.

He's right on your heels! a tiny voice screamed inside her brain, and Camilla heeded it.

Some sixth sense told her that the murderer was still out there, slipping through the shadows, drawing closer to her with every passing moment. A sudden image of the bloodied knife in his hand galvanized her. *I can't linger here until the street clears. If I do, he'll kill me.*

Spinning about, she darted sideways to a narrow, broken back street that snaked around the glass factory and toward the commercial district. She stumbled over a sleeping cat, which screamed in fury at her, but after one breathless gasp, Camilla kept right on running.

She knew where to go. Only three streets over and one quarter mile down and she would be safe . . . safe. . . .

She ran on until her breath was gone and her feet

dragged wearily upon the pavement. Her breathing was a horrible, tortured sound in the misty night as she at last reached the three-story stone building she sought. It bore a dark, gloomy aspect, with its creeping vines of ivy and its grim rows of shuttered windows like cruelly closed eyes. There was an iron gate separating the building from the run-down commercial shops and warehouses that surrounded it. A sign nailed across the front of the gate proclaimed: "Porridge Street Workhouse."

Camilla walked inside the fence, then skirted around to the rear as quickly as a mouse scenting cheese. As she knew it would be, the kitchen door leading off the vegetable garden was unlocked.

Safe.

Nearly sobbing with relief, she let herself into the place where she had spent a good portion of her life and stood momentarily in the darkness of that huge, cavernous kitchen. She sucked in long breaths of air to sustain her heaving lungs and let her eyes accustom themselves to the blackness.

Silas and Eugenia Toombs administered this workhouse, which sheltered beneath its roof hundreds of indigent men, women, and children. There were dozens of orphans here—children who otherwise would have found themselves living in the gutters among the filthy, violent bands of young criminals who roamed the London streets, stealing and pickpocketing to maintain their ragged and starving existences. Camilla had lived at the workhouse from the age of eight until her fifteenth birthday. She knew all its rooms, its corridors and stairways, its dark and awful secrets. She had seen and experienced things here that had made a mark upon her for life.

During the course of the years she had seen older children grow up, become apprenticed out to factories or tradesmen or shopkeepers, and she had seen younger children come to the workhouse at various ages, each becoming caught up in the rigorous schedule of household and gardening chores and study and lessons and joyless meals where silence was the rule. She herself had been apprenticed out three years ago as a housemaid to a banker's family in London, but it had resulted so disastrously that she had found herself back under Mrs. Toombs's scowling eyes in a month. Then had come the position at the milliner's shop—this too had ended badly —and scarcely two weeks after she had begun. There had been other positions as well. But it had been close to three years now that she'd been at the Rose and Swan and though the cook, Mrs. Pike, often grumbled and scolded, she was in truth quite fond of "Weed," as everyone called Camilla.

Her given name, which sounded pretty and flowerlike, had never seemed to fit the tall, gangly girl whose legs had always appeared too long for her body, whose neck was thin and straight and bony, who moved at an awkward coltish gate. Camilla should have been small and dainty and blond, Mrs. Toombs had reiterated scornfully a hundred times over the past years, not a lanky reed of a thing with clumpy brown hair that always drooped in her eyes.

Her eyes were her most striking feature, when they could be glimpsed beneath that mop of tangled hair. They were green, river-green, clear and wide and deep. They could sparkle with mischief, or darken with anger to a deep jeweled hue, but always they held an intelligence, a spark, that neither beatings, nor poverty, nor loneliness had ever been able to quench.

Not that Mrs. Toombs hadn't tried. But as Camilla had grown older, stronger, and more resilient, the older woman had given up on taming the "uppityness" out of the defiant country orphan.

Life had been much better, Camilla reflected as she sat down on a bench in the darkened kitchen, and rubbed her aching calves, since she left the workhouse. At least

now she was out in the world, though a rough and tumble
world it was. But hard work, no matter what sort, didn't
trouble her. And that pleased Mr. Dibbs, who was accustomed to lazier sorts. A harder-working, more industri-
ous serving maid the Rose and Swan had never known, he
often declared almost fondly—nor one, he tended to add,
as outspoken. Camilla could not deny this. On a regular
basis she informed her employer that he was in need of a
bath. She told the customers, when she was called upon
to run out and mop up a spill, that they were great clumsy
oafs too drunk to recognize their own mothers. She even
had dared to lecture Mr. Toombs—who with his tyrannical wife oversaw the running of the workhouse, and who
was the sternest, grimmest man ever to cross her path—
that he would never find favor in the eyes of God until he
learned to smile kindly upon the children, and to be more
tolerant of their errors, their enthusiasm for life, and
their noise. Nothing prevented Camilla Brent from
speaking her mind.

At least, nothing had until tonight. The sight of that
dead man on the floor had given her such a fright she had
lost her voice; otherwise, she mumbled to herself as she
paced the kitchen, she might have given that murderer a
lecture on the sanctity of human life.

But perhaps not, she admitted as she turned toward
the corridor opening off the kitchen. It would have done
no good trying to reason with that one. He was mad, it
had been plain to see, and any fool knew a madman could
not be persuaded.

Shivering, she tried to blot his image from her mind.
She was safe now. He couldn't have tracked her here. She
would check on Hester, stay hidden a short time, and
then creep out before morning light the same way she
had come in. By then the madman would have surely

given up his search and it would be quite safe to return to the Rose and Swan.

Suddenly, thinking of the tavern, she remembered again about the man in the puce coat and her reason for being in Room 203 tonight. And she also remembered the mysterious letter she had been given, the letter still nestled in her pocket.

Was the dead man Mr. Anders? she wondered, knitting her brows. Or was Mr. Anders the murderer? And what part, if any, did the man in the puce coat play in what had happened tonight?

She reached into her pocket to be sure the letter was still there. It was.

She drew it out slowly, anxious to read it, yet dreading it at the same time. There was not enough light now, and she didn't want to risk a candle or a lamp and possible detection. The contents of the letter would have to wait until later. In her own room at the Rose and Swan, she would read it and think and decide what to do. *Most likely, I will have to go to the authorities as soon as possible and report what I've seen. Perhaps the letter will help them identify the murderer.*

She felt cold and sick. The shock of what she had witnessed was finally beginning to hit her, now that the immediate danger was gone. Camilla fought against the nausea rising in her throat. Shakily, she grasped a chair back for support. *Hester,* she thought weakly, taking deep breaths. *I'll find Hester and sit by her bed. That will make me feel better.*

The children's rooms were on the second story of the workhouse in the east wing. She knew the passages by heart and did not need even a glimmer of light to show her the way. Every uneven floorboard, every creak in the steps, was familiar to her. Camilla had prowled through

this workhouse for years; she knew all its secrets. If Mrs.
Toombs had once caught her stealing extra rations for the
younger children, or had known how nimbly she slipped
in and out of windows, or how expert she was at shinnying
up and down the tree that overhung the children's quarters, she would have confined her to the cellar for fort-
nights at a time. But she never knew. And tonight, while a
full moon sailed through the murky sky above, peeping in
and out among the clouds, Camilla made her way with
steady swiftness to the large damp chamber abovestairs
where Hester and the other orphans slept.

She eased open the door just enough to allow her thin
figure space to slide past. Any further and it would creak.
Through the darkness of the room, her eyes made out the
neat rows of cots, the peeling gray-painted wall with pegs
for caps and coats, even the little shoes all lined up at the
foot of each bed.

There were perhaps twenty of them.

And Hester's was at the very end of the row, nearest
the window. Camilla made her way to it and stood looking down at the small figure in the bed.

Her heart leaped with affection as she gazed down at
the soft mop of lemon-yellow curls framing the oval face.
Hester's Wedgwood-blue eyes were closed, her cheeks
slack, and her breath came evenly, peacefully, in that frail
little chest. Camilla didn't want to wake her. The poor
thing needed her rest. But even as she sank to the floor
beside the cot, and began to make a pillow out of her
arms, thinking to rest a bit there until she could creep out
again, the little girl moved her fingers, and then her eyes
blinked open, and after only an instant she said on a
breathless little squeak, "Weed!"

"Hullo, pumpkin!" Camilla sat up with a grin and

hugged the child who opened her arms wide with such eager delight.

"Shhh!" she warned as the girl began to speak in an excited voice, and several nearby children stirred in their beds.

"Come along," Camilla whispered, grinning. She led Hester by the hand to the partially opened door. They made an odd sight, the ragged young servant girl and the child wrapped in a blanket trotting beside her, but neither made a sound as they skulked along. They slipped into the hall as lightly as a passing April breeze and then they whisked themselves into the broom closet just outside. The broom closet was a small, square, windowless chamber stuffed with brooms and mops and feather dusters. Camilla kept the door ajar a few inches so that some of the light from the hall window could seep in; otherwise the darkness would have been complete. Settling down in the corner, she wrapped Hester more warmly in the blanket and made a place for the little girl beside her. Through the musty smell and dimness of the closet, she managed to make out Hester's bright eyes and smiling bow mouth, and she felt safe and warm for the first time since she had mounted the broken steps of the White Horse Inn.

"I kept hoping you would come!" Hester snuggled close against Camilla's side. She lifted a hopeful face and whispered softly, "Did you bring . . . any food?"

"Food? Oh, you mean like bread and milk—or a potato?" Camilla tapped a finger thoughtfully against her head. "Sorry, I'm afraid not. Why, I don't believe I've even *seen* a potato in a week but— Well, imagine that! I do happen to have something here, but—oh, dear. It's only a gingerbread man. I don't suppose you would like *that*!" she added in a doubtful tone, which at once gave

way to a giggle as Hester's eyes grew wide with delight.
Camilla smiled broadly as she placed the beautiful brown
gingerbread man in the little girl's outstretched hand.

"We haven't had a morsel besides bread and porridge
and potatoes in the longest, longest time." Hester stared
at the gingerbread man in awe for a long minute, her eyes
shining in the darkness. Then slowly, she lifted the crum-
bly baked treasure to her lips, savoring the anticipation of
that first sweet bite. Suddenly, though, she paused and
with an abrupt jerk of her arm held the gingerbread out
to Camilla.

"You take half."

"No, silly." Camilla gently tugged one of the little girl's
lemon curls. "I had one of my own earlier today," she
lied. "This gingerbread man is just for you."

She watched with satisfaction as Hester devoured the
sweet, which in fact had been a gift to Camilla from Pete
Colpers, the baker's boy, that very afternoon. Pete
Colpers was a short, round young lad with a dimpled chin
and large ears who came by the kitchens of the Rose and
Swan twice a day to see the girl he and everyone else
called Weed. Camilla liked him well enough, but only in
the role of a friend, and she had been resisting all his
efforts to charm her into a kiss. Today, though, she had
accepted the gingerbread man with pleasure, thinking
that she would find a chance to seek out Hester in the
next day or so and give the child a treat. Her visits to the
workhouse were infrequent now, for she worked long
hours at the tavern, and had few moments to herself, but
she tried to make time for the children she had left behind and visited them at least once a month. Of all of the
orphans at the Porridge Street Workhouse, seven-year-
old Hester, with her sunny smile and trusting blue eyes,
was her favorite.

Sitting there with Hester, Camilla could almost forget the nightmare she had been through tonight. Almost. But her ordeal was still affecting her, for Hester, between bites of the gingerbread, looked at her with a worried frown.

"What's wrong, Weed?"

"Wrong?"

"You look scared."

"Don't be silly." Camilla tried to laugh. "What would I be scared of . . ."

"But you look all funny. Pale. And your hands are shaking," Hester insisted.

"Are they?" Camilla bit her lip. Hester was right. Her fingers were ice-cold and trembling, and her heart still pounded with fear. So much for the safety of the workhouse, she reflected grimly. Even here, she didn't feel safe from the madman who had pursued her.

"Oh, it's nothing, silly. It's just that I ran all the way here—I was so eager to see you!" She forced a smile as Hester licked her lips over the last crumbs of the gingerbread man. "How is Sophia? And Tory? Is she quite over that nasty cough?"

Hester opened her mouth, closed it, and swallowed hard. "Tory never did get better, Weed. She took real sick with the cough till she couldn't hardly breathe and then she got a fever and . . ." Her voice trailed off. "She died."

Dear Lord. No. Oh no. Camilla felt a sticky lump of grief rise in her throat.

Little Tory, sad and silent as a winter twig left to shiver in the breeze. How many children had died at the workhouse over the years she had been here? Twenty? Thirty? The ones who took sick rarely ever recovered fully. There were too few blankets, and too many drafts, little medi-

cine and inadequate food, and, most infuriating of all,
indifferent care. But Tory, poor Tory . . . she was so
thin, so lost. And only nine.

Camilla enfolded Hester in her arms. A fierce protectiveness swept over her as she rested her cheek against
the child's springy soft curls. She had to find a way to
earn some more extra money so that she could buy Hester and the other children some new blankets. The one
the little girl had wrapped around her now was nearly
threadbare. And winter was coming . . .

"Oh, I almost forgot," Hester murmured drowsily,
growing warm and comfortable as she snuggled against
Camilla's reassuring shoulder. "The reason I was hoping
so hard you'd come. Not just because I wanted to see you
. . . or wanted a treat." She yawned, then went on in a
sleepy tone, "There was a man here today, a funny
Frenchman, and he was looking for you."

At first Camilla didn't think she had heard correctly.
"For me? Oh no, pumpkin, that couldn't be. You must be
mistaken."

Another yawn. But a note of stubbornness entered
Hester's voice as she roused herself enough to sit up and
peer at Camilla. "You know I don't make mistakes. And,
besides, I heard him plain as could be. He was looking for
a matta . . . mattamoz . . ."

Baffled, Camilla stared at her a moment. "Mademoiselle?" she ventured at last.

"That's right." Hester nodded. "He talked so funny
that it was a little hard to make out _all_ the words. But he
said he was looking for an orphan. Like you, Camilla.
Like me."

Like all the other girls here, Camilla thought, but she
waited patiently for Hester to continue.

"He said this matta . . . matta . . . this orphan was

in position of a charm—a golden lion—just like that one you always wear."

Instantly, Camilla's fingers went to the charm on its thin chain around her neck. "In possession of a charm," she corrected absently. She frowned. Her fingers outlined the familiar shape of the majestic lion carved into a charm no larger than a button. "What else did he say, Hester?"

"Here comes the terrible part. Mrs. Toombs said she never knew any such person or any such charm. She lied, Weed. She knows you always wear that charm. She tried to take it from you once—do you remember how you told me she locked you in the cellar and wouldn't let you come out for a whole night?"

How could she forget? One of her earliest memories at the workhouse was of Mrs. Toombs trying to take away the charm. But it was her only link with the life she had known before her parents' death, her only connection with those gone-forever days before the workhouse, a token evoking memories of the gaunt, sweet-faced man who had been her father, of the pertly smiling, ample-waisted woman who had been her mother.

She had fought with frenzied panic to keep it.

In those first months after her parents' deaths, she had sometimes found it frighteningly difficult even to recall their faces, though her grief for them was sharp and painful as glass. Once she had been the cherished only daughter of Squire Andrew Brent and his wife, Matilda—indulged, even a little pampered, treated with respect by everyone in the village—then, suddenly, she was no one —a pauper, an orphan. But she still had the charm, the charm that proved she had once been loved, cared for, that she had lived in a lovely old stone home in the country, and had a huge featherbed all her own, that her mother had kissed her each night when she tucked her into bed, and her father had carried her about on his shoulders when he walked to and from the village. She had owned seven different dresses at once—one for each day of the week, and she had eaten goose and tartlets and kidney pies for luncheon and supper far more often than potatoes and porridge.

She had once lived, Camilla had thought during those first difficult days at the workhouse, like a princess. And she had never even realized or appreciated it.

So, when Mrs. Toombs had tried to take away her golden charm, the last vestige of her past, she had screamed and kicked and bitten and refused to part with it. Mrs. Toombs had promptly locked her in the cellar, all alone with no candle and the door shut tight so that not even a glimmer of light could penetrate. Rats had scurried over her feet. She had been cold and scared and wretched.

But she hadn't given in. It was Mrs. Toombs, the next morning, who had finally relented, vowing in a most angry tone that she didn't even want the girl's stupid precious charm.

"Keep it, brat!" had come the words through the locked cellar door. Then the bolt had been thrown, and light had flooded down the steps, blinding Camilla after all the hours of darkness. "It's probably nothing but paint, anyhow. But you'd best come up and do your chores or there'll be no breakfast for you—nor supper neither. If you don't do your share of the work, I won't have food nor breath to waste upon the selfish likes of you!"

So Camilla had emerged, dazed and dizzy, but triumphant, and the golden charm had never left its place around her neck in all these years. So why had Mrs.

Toombs denied any knowledge of it . . . or of the made-moiselle possessing it? And who in the world was this Frenchman asking questions about her charm?

"You're quite sure this isn't one of your stories, Hester?"

"Course not. It's true all right and tight. Ask Annie, she heard him, too. We were hiding outside the door together." She yawned again, her voice fading nearly to a whisper.

Camilla lifted her to her feet.

"Well, it's very mysterious and I'm not sure what it's all about—but one thing I do know. You must get your rest. In a few hours the morning bell will ring and you'll have to scurry out of your bed like a sleepy little mouse. So come along."

Hester was already fast asleep as Camilla carried her back to her bed near the window. Camilla stood a moment, gazing down at the peaceful little face. Could Hester be right? A man, a Frenchman, had been looking for her? It was too odd—she couldn't make a bit of sense out of it, but she had the strange feeling that it was true, that there was some secret here she must investigate further. But before she could think past the idea of confronting Mrs. Toombs in the morning, a sound reached her ears. It came from outside the open window and she spun about with sudden dread.

The mist was still thick beneath the treetops, but through its gauzy layers Camilla's eyes made out the dark-cloaked figure approaching the front gate. A man, and he was wearing a mask. Fear clawed at her. His movements and bearing were elegant, she saw, peering past the limp curtain with a knot in her stomach. And then she saw what looked like the silvery glint of a knife in his black-gloved hand.

She stifled a gasp and tried to think. She realized at once that he must be a member of the ton, a wealthy man, high-born—and powerful. Something clicked in her mind suddenly. She remembered—there *had* been a masquerade in London tonight. Word had reached even the east end that Lady Hampton was holding her annual masquerade, one of the most famous balls of the season. So this man, she realized slowly, may have been one of her guests. A guest who had drunk champagne, danced and dined, then left the party, gone to the White Horse Inn— and killed a man.

But, she thought, gripping the window ledge with icy fingertips, he had been seen. He had been caught redhanded by a servant girl.

Me. Why did I have to go the White Horse tonight?

Somehow, he had tracked her down. He must have been close on her heels the entire time, watching her, following . . . even when she thought she had lost him. Now all he had to do was kill her, too, and there would be no evidence, no witness to link him with the murder.

The masked man was peering up at all the windows of the workhouse, slowly, methodically looking from one to one, as if diabolically sniffing out the scent of his prey.

She jumped back from the window, terror clutching at her.

Oh, God, she'd been so certain she'd lost him, but now she had led him straight to Hester, to all the children. Her stomach twisting, making her feel sick, she tried to think. She had to look outside again, to see what he was doing.

With her heart racing in her throat, Camilla inched toward the window and forced herself to peep out.

He was letting himself through the gate. Moving toward the rear of the building. Every movement he made was lithe and deliberate. *Dear Lord,* Camilla thought in horror, *if he tries the unlocked door, he will be in the house, searching, in a matter of minutes.* With that knife in his hand, who knew what mayhem he would unleash?

She darted a frantic glance at the rows of sleeping children. There was only one solution. She had to lead him away from here before he could harm or frighten anyone. There wasn't much time.

With shaking fingers she lifted the window and threw a leg across the ledge. The tree was only five feet away—she had only to leap out and grasp the branches . . .

She embraced them nimbly, and in another instant was lowering herself down the rough trunk with the agility of a monkey. *At least I haven't lost my touch,* she thought. Her skirt ripped on a jutting branch, and a twig drew blood on her neck, but Camilla didn't let this slow her down a whit. She reached the bottom with the softest of thuds and glanced around.

The cloaked man had reached the vegetable garden and was scanning the upper windows once more. She resisted the cowardly impulse simply to run away. Reminding herself of the danger she had led straight to the children, she pursed her lips in a shrieking whistle that would have done a watchman proud.

The trilling signal rang out sharply in the murky night.

She saw the cloaked man wheel about in her direction. Deliberately, she stepped from the shadows and let him see her.

For a full two heartbeats she stood there meeting his masked gaze across a span of three hundred yards and then, as he sprinted forward she whirled and fled into the shadows, scampering through the darkness—running, in truth, for her life.

3

Don't stop. Keep going. He might still be out there.

Camilla forced one foot in front of the other, despite the weariness of her aching muscles. She had no idea where she was. All around her was quiet, but for the faint haunting moan of the October wind. As the night shadows deepened throughout the countryside, a light drizzle began, turning the road to mud beneath her feet. Sinking ankle-deep in ooze with every step, she hunched her chin into her neck against the biting autumn chill. She was on a deserted country lane, heaven only knew how many miles outside of London, surrounded by rolling meadows and farmlands and neat hedgerows dripping steadily with collected rain. In the distance on either side of the road rose plumes of smoke from the chimneys of dimly visible thatched cottages. The damp, peacefully sleepy countryside of England was trying to lull her, but a dogged fear of the unknown murderer kept her stumbling along the seemingly endless road. In the darkness, every shrub and picket fence threatened danger, every creak of a branch

underfoot or sigh of the wind through the leaves made
her heart hammer.

She had been walking for hours now along these deserted lanes, ever since the milk wagon she had hidden in
just outside of London had turned into a farmyard lane.
Luckily, the driver hadn't seen her jump out, or slip away
among the hedges. She was all alone—she hoped.

Maybe she had truly escaped him.

But she couldn't risk stopping. She trudged on. The
wraithes of mist still lingered among the treetops. The
faint drizzle soaked her face and dragged at her skirts as
she walked wearily along, listening to the rustle of wind
through the woods, the steady drip of water from leaves,
breathing in the scent of honeysuckle and rich, moist
earth. The country smell reminded her of a long-ago
time, carrying with it the memory of the homey manor
where she had lived with her parents, of her mother's
pretty, well-tended rose garden, and of the prosperous
little farms that had dotted the village countryside.

Long ago, before she had come to the Porridge Street
Workhouse in the East End of London, in the days when
she had been Squire Brent's daughter, she had smelled
this very same luscious earth smell, run free as the breeze
through verdant meadows, skipped happily along quiet
country lanes like this one. Long, long ago . . .

Suddenly, through the gloom, she saw lights up ahead.
Her footsteps quickened. An inn. It had to be an inn.
Eagerly, she staggered on, grasping the gate with fingers
that trembled from exhaustion, pushing herself by sheer
will across the puddled yard.

The Green Goose Inn was quiet at this time of night,
but the innkeeper's wife, a large-bosomed dour-faced
woman in a crumpled apron, was setting her foot on the
bottom stair when Camilla pushed open the door. The

woman spun about, broom in hand, and her protuberant brown eyes widened.

"You're tracking in mud all over my floor!" she snapped, her heavy brows drawing together in a frown. "Who are you, girl? What do you want?"

Her contemptuous gaze raked the ragged figure before her and her eyes darkened with disdain. Camilla was suddenly intensely aware of her filthy, bedraggled appearance. Her work clothes, never lovely, were now muddied and torn beyond repair, her hair hung like a wet, limp mop around her face, her shoes were smeared with mud, and she was shivering from head to toe. She must look like a drowned rat. Or a beggar, she realized in dismay as the woman pursed her lips in rigid disapproval.

"There was an accident on the road," she improvised desperately. "I need a room for the night. I can pay you well," she said, her fingers closing over the three shillings in her pocket.

"Pay me? With what?" Harsh laughter rang through the dimly lit hall. "Cow droppings?"

"I have three shillings."

"Three shillings? Three whole shillings, is it?" The woman sneered down the last of Camilla's hopes. The expression on the innkeeper's wife's florid face was one of utter contempt. "*Thirty* shillings wouldn't be enough for me to house the likes of you! Not in one of my rooms! Now off with you! Be on your way!"

At that precise moment the stout, bald-headed innkeeper bustled in from the taproom, his belly bouncing before him. He took one look at the ragged girl who'd tracked mud into his hall, and his double chins quivered with annoyance.

"Drat it all, Bessie—who the bloody hell is this?" he demanded of his wife.

"No one you needs concern yourself with, Jeb," the woman sighed, and with a shooing motion she now advanced toward Camilla as if she would literally sweep her out the door. "Get out, girl. Get out! We don't shelter the likes of you!"

"Please! I can pay!" Camilla felt as though her knees were going to buckle beneath her. "The barn," she said suddenly, through chattering teeth, thinking of soft, warm hay, a roof over her head, a corner to hide in. "Let me sleep in the barn and I'll pay you a shilling. I'll be gone by morning . . ."

"This is a respectable establishment. We don't want you here, not anywhere on the premises." The innkeeper's wife grasped her arm and dragged her through the door. "Ladies and gentlemen of quality stop here, girl —lords and ladies," she called out as she pushed Camilla toward the steps. "There's other inns for the likes of you. And stay out of our barn—or the dogs'll get you," she added maliciously as the girl sent her a bleary, pleading look. "Off now, you little tart, you've wasted enough of my time. And don't show your face around here again.

"Brazen hussy," she muttered to her husband as she slammed the door of the Green Goose Inn on the filthy girl and cut off the chill October air whipping through the hall.

"Imagine her thinkin' she could find a room here!" the innkeeper mused in wonderment. Then he shook his head, ordered his wife to fetch her mop and pail and wipe the floor before coming up to bed, and pulled out the leg of mutton left over from supper, which he'd stashed deep inside his pocket. He left his wife to finish her work and devoured the mutton with gusto as he ambled up the stairs to his bed.

Returning to the road, Camilla shivered, her toes and

fingers numb with cold. She hugged her arms around herself as she trudged on through the darkness. There would be another inn, up ahead somewhere, she told herself. Or maybe a deserted shed or cottage, she thought hopefully. She *would* find a place to rest.

She walked on and on, down one lonely lane, up another, vaguely searching for another inn. Her dazed mind and exhausted body cried out for sleep.

She must have fallen asleep on her feet. She never heard the chaise and four barreling down the narrow road, never had a chance to jump out of the way. Before she knew what was happening, the horses were bearing down on her in the darkness, the carriage with its gold emblazoned crest was careening toward her, and she had time to do no more than glance over her shoulder and scream before it ran her down.

The Earl of Westcott bent over the unconscious girl and felt for a pulse. Alive. Thank God. By some miracle he had managed to swerve the team in time to avoid stampeding over her, but one of the wheels must have clipped the chit nevertheless, and knocked her cold.

Idiotic little fool. He turned her in his arms. Why would any sane female be alone on the road at this hour —three o'clock in the morning—strolling like a ninny down Edgewood Lane, nearly killing him as well as herself?

The Earl's eyes narrowed as he did a cursory examination of the slender, filthy creature in the muddied scullery clothes. She gave a soft moan as he shifted her in his arms, but her eyes didn't open. From what he could gather, she was not seriously hurt, though her right foot was bent at an unnatural angle, and there was a nasty cut on her hand.

"Damned bad luck for both of us," he muttered half to himself as he lifted her. She was nothing but skin and bones.

What a night. First there was that damned masquerade, then Marchfield, curse his eyes—and now this. His lips twisting, the Earl wondered what other little surprises Fate might hold in store for him before this night was over. The girl made no more sounds as he lifted her in his arms and placed her inside his coach. He covered her with his own velvet-lined cloak and slammed the door.

He never should have let himself get drunk tonight. Even though he was now stone-cold sober—had been for hours, he thought—he wondered if he might have discerned her sooner in the darkness if he'd had a bit less brandy warming his blood. It wasn't like him to imbibe like that, to lose control—or to let Marchfield goad him the way he had. But it was done now. No use thinking backward, as Fader, his old groom used to say.

Then with no more time wasted he was back upon the seat, galloping the horses toward Westcott Park.

Not many moments later found him turning the team up the long, wide drive, galloping between stately columns of oaks that guarded his ancestral home like ghostly sentinels in the darkness. He peered ahead at the lights glowing softly from within the house. They were waiting up for him then, as he had instructed, though he'd never anticipated being this late.

The chaise passed beneath a tall stone arch, curved around the long avenue lined with oaks, and drew up presently in a vast circular drive brilliantly lit with torches in expectation of his arrival.

Westcott Park rose grandly before him, the old weathered stone gleaming faintly buff in the torchlight, seeming to shine like the legendary castle of Camelot. But it was not a castle, as he had often pretended when he was a youth, it was merely a large, fine mansion in the classic mode, possessing a beautifully trimmed five-hundred-foot frontage and grounds that included a lake, maze, and gardens that were the pride of the countryside. The Earl scarcely gave the place a second glance. The Corinthian columns towering upward to the second story, the mullioned windows and graceful north and south wings, the sumptuous lawns and gardens, which made the estate such an impressive site to guests and neighbors alike, were as familiar to him as his own favorite riding coat, worn and comfortable and sturdy as time itself. Even old Durgess, when he hurried to the front entrance to greet his master, didn't impress him, and Durgess had been chosen by Philip's grandfather to impress. He was the loftiest of butlers, every bit as imposing as the Earl who had first hired him, and in all of his twenty-eight years, Philip had never once seen him smile.

"Durgess," the Earl said casually as he jumped down from the coach and threw back the door, "if you will be so good as to send for Dr. Greves at once—there has been an accident. And I'll need Mrs. Wyeth."

The butler's faded sea-blue eyes widened within their crepey lids as he watched his master lift an unconscious, dirty female in disgracefully torn and mud-caked clothing out of the silk-lined chaise. Shock was something Durgess had thought he had outgrown many years earlier, but apparently not, for ripples of it now tore through him as he saw his master's fine evening jacket smeared with mud from the girl's clothes, and he noticed that there was even a wisp of straw clinging to the Earl's mud-spattered boots.

"Sir—if I may be of assistance . . ." he managed, after one moment of uncharacteristic speechlessness.

The Earl strode past him without a second glance. "I believe I have sufficient strength to carry this young woman upstairs on my own, Durgess. Ah, Mrs. Wyeth." He addressed a tiny, mobcapped woman with graying brown hair and a pointed chin. "I will require your assistance upstairs. I assume my brother and his wife have arrived?"

"No, sir. There has been no word from them." The middle-aged housekeeper stared incredulously at the crumpled figure in the Earl's arms. "Sir, may I be so forward as to inquire . . . "

"An injured waif. I ran her down on the road. Durgess—the doctor, at once." The Earl paid little heed to his astonished servants. He carried the girl through the great hall and up the curving walnut staircase at a quick clip, rounding the bend without pausing to see if Mrs. Wyeth followed him—though her labored breathing behind him told him that she did—and continued with long strides toward the door on his left.

The Blue Room was always kept ready for guests. In fact, it had been prepared with especial care that same day for the Earl's brother and his wife, but the Earl dismissed that consideration. Any other room would do just as well for James and Charlotte.

He waited, his face impassive, while Mrs. Wyeth hastened to turn down the elegant embroidered silk bedspread and smoothed back the French linens. He glanced at the girl who lay so still and fragile in his arms. Hard to tell much what she looked like with the dirt and the bruises and that weedy hair hanging in her eyes, but he'd have bet a thousand pounds that she had the brains of a pigeon. She moaned, and he saw her eyelashes flutter, but she didn't wake up. Damn her. What the devil was she doing in the road?

Mrs. Wyeth, who had been waging a silent inner battle, couldn't restrain herself as he started toward the bed. "Your lordship surely is not going to put that dirty creature in this fine bed?" she nearly pleaded, unable to bear letting such filth invade the beauty that was Westcott Park.

"If I may suggest it, your lordship," she went on coaxingly, as if he were still the small stubborn boy who had insisted on caring for every stray or injured creature he happened to find, "why not allow Durgess or one of the footmen to bring the creature into the servants' quarters? 'Tis a shame to muddy fine linen with the likes of her . . ."

"Adjust that pillow a little higher, Mrs. Durgess," the Earl said as though she hadn't spoken.

Mrs. Wyeth groaned inwardly. She knew that intent expression in his lordship's eyes. He cared for no one else's opinion, gave no thought to propriety . . . in this same way had he as a wild, dark-haired youth ignored her pleas to keep those horrid beasts of his in the stable. No, *he* had kept them in his *room.*

Biting her lip, the housekeeper did as she was bid and watched the Earl of Westcott lower the odious girl onto the cushions. His lordship was always one to be mulish beyond words when he once got an idea into his head. All of the Audleys were like that. Some things never changed . . .

The girl moaned faintly as her head lolled back against the satin pillow. The Earl regarded her in silence for a moment, while Mrs. Wyeth tried to read his thoughts, but as always, it was impossible. That hard, handsome face— who could ever read what he was thinking? Certainly not his nurse, even when he was a child, nor had Durgess ever understood a whit about him. And she, who had seen him grow from a wild, happy boy to a wild, saddened young man, had never been able to understand the moods that drove him. All she knew was that all the warmth and carefree happiness had drained straight out of him after the tragedy . . .

His very own family was terrified of him now, though it didn't used to be that way. Why, these days the Earl had only to glance his way, and poor Master Jared looked guilty as sin, and his cheeks set to flushing—and James barely spoke more than two words when his brother was in the room. Even little Miss Dorinda, poor thing, was frightened of him. He hadn't always been like this, though, Mrs. Wyeth reflected sadly. It was only in recent years . . .

As the Earl moved away from the bed he sent a penetrating glance at the housekeeper. "Do what you can for her before the doctor arrives. Bring her round if you can. I'll be in my study awaiting James and Charlotte. No doubt they'll want some refreshment."

"Yes, your lordship."

He strode out without a backward glance. Alone with the unconscious female, Mrs. Wyeth clenched her hands in frustration. Heaven help them all. The creature belonged in the servants' quarters at best—in a stable most preferably—not in this most charming of rooms.

She loathed the idea of even touching this disgustingly soiled Young Person. Who knew what diseases she might be carrying? The housekeeper had a difficult time keeping from stamping her foot. Why, oh, why couldn't the Earl be sensible just once in his life?

Of course not one in his line had ever been *that*. His father had certainly been a mild, genial man who loved his books and his horses and his dogs, but he'd had an unfortunate weakness for spirits—and for gaming. A defi-

nite wild streak. And Master James, the Earl's younger
brother by two years, had nourished a most unsettling
fondness for the sport of boxing—before his marriage, of
course—since then, Mrs. Wyeth reflected with relief, he
had settled down quite nicely, at least as far as she could
see. Yet Philip was very different from his father and
brother. He didn't have their easygoing nature. Oh, he
wasn't a difficult master, not really, but a body couldn't
help being intimidated by him sometimes, for when he
was displeased, he narrowed those eyes of his and didn't
say a word, but *stared* at you until you wanted to crawl
beneath the floorboards. Small wonder poor Master
Jared, sent down in disgrace from Eton, was so unnerved.
And if the Earl found out about the latest trouble . . .

Mrs. Wyeth shuddered whenever she contemplated the
gossip that flew from country kitchen to country kitchen
by way of the servants' grapevine. The Audleys were discussed more than ten other families put together! And
the Earl himself had certainly come under his share of
scrutiny. All those duels Philip fought, his nasty temper,
the races he won, and the outrageous wagers he accepted.
Common knowledge among all who knew of such matters. And, Mrs. Wyeth reflected, as she stared at the girl
on the bed, then there were the women swooning over
him, trying to catch him . . . but for all the noble beau-
ties who sought his affections, he was known to favor
. . . opera singers!

He was an Audley through and through, no doubt
about it. And now, bringing this ragged miss to Westcott
Park under such distressing circumstances . . . well, it
bordered on the scandalous, that's what it did. Her heart
ached for him, for beneath her disapproving frown, she
loved the boy dearly. What would become of him if he
didn't mend these strange ways?

She approached the unconscious girl with trepidation and growing dislike. Disgusting creature. As Mrs. Wyeth bent over her, a feeble moan sounded from the young woman's lips. Mrs. Wyeth poked the girl's bony shoulder.

"Wake up, girl. Wake up and tell me what it is that hurts."

No answer.

"Wake *up*."

Now there was not even a moan.

"Very well, then." The housekeeper's eyes gleamed with sudden inspiration. "Smelling salts. That'll bring you round."

With malicious satisfaction she took herself off in search of the strongest, bitterest smelling salts she could find. It would serve the loathsome creature right.

Downstairs, the Earl stood lost in thought before the flames of the fire burning in the grate of his study. When voices in the hall alerted him that his brother and sister-in-law had arrived, he shook himself out of his reverie. Tension knotted his neck as he heard his brother request to be taken to their rooms. He took a quick swig of his brandy. He knew his duty was to go into the hall and greet them, yet he felt the greatest reluctance to do so.

Once, he and James had been close, brothers in spirit as well as in flesh, but that had all changed three years ago. Now merely the sight of James brought back all that pain, all the guilt . . .

After what had happened, the bond between them could never be restored. Still, obligation compelled him to go into the hall. Philip took one final gulp of his brandy, straightened his shoulders, and opened the door.

"Good evening, James." He strode across the hall, keeping his expression calm, neutral. "Good evening, Charlotte."

"Philip!" James looked stunned. "You're still up and about!"

"Obviously." Tension tightened all his muscles as the Earl surveyed his brother. To say that James was dismayed would be an understatement. Clearly, James had deliberately arrived at this ungodly hour hoping to avoid seeing him tonight. Something twisted painfully inside him, but his eyes reflected only cool equanimity beneath the golden light of the chandelier. "I trust your journey was pleasant," he said in an even tone.

"Quite."

James Audley was a younger, stockier version of the Earl. At five foot ten in his riding boots, he was a good-looking, clean-shaven young man with an air of weariness about him that was odd for his years. His hair was dark brown, not black, like the Earl's, and he had inherited his mother's diamond-blue eyes, not his father's gray ones, but he and Philip, and Jared, too, for that matter, shared the same strong nose and arrogant-looking jawline, the same firm mouth and determined chin that characterized the men of the family.

"You're looking well," Philip commented, precisely as if exchanging civilities with a stranger in the park, and then moved on to kiss Charlotte's small gloved hand. "Charlotte, delighted," he said perfunctorily, noting the way her eyes blinked rapidly in nervousness when he looked into her flushed, pretty face. "No doubt you would like some refreshment after your travels."

Silence followed his words. Philip shoved his hands inside his pockets and gazed in mocking amusement from his brother's drawn, pale face to the agitated countenance of James's tiny golden bride.

"Come, now, not even a word? Surely, James, you can utter a response of some sort, merely for civility's sake."

"Don't trouble yourself on our account," James managed to blurt out. He started toward the stairs, tugging at Charlotte's arm, then stopped and spun back to face his brother. "I didn't even expect you'd still be up! I mean, it's the middle of the night. Who'd have thought—" He broke off suddenly, flushing at his own outburst. "What I mean," he finished in a stiff, formal tone, "is that it was kind of you to wait up for us."

"Do you think so?" Philip asked softly.

James clenched his fists. "I said so, didn't I?"

"Indeed. But we know, don't we, James, that you don't always speak what you mean."

James flinched as if he had been struck. Charlotte clutched his arm and turned bravely to face the Earl.

"As a matter of fact," she interjected in a low, breathless voice, "we would appreciate some refreshment, your . . . your lordship. You see, the inn where we stopped along the way had its private parlor already engaged, and James didn't feel that the quality of the place was such that we should linger in the taproom. And it was growing so late, James felt it best to press on—he mentioned a fondness for Cook's way with a roasted chicken, and . . . and bread pudding, and thought to find something here that would please him. But if it is too much trouble," she added quickly, flushing a deeper shade of pink beneath her brother-in-law's cold stare, "and if it is too late, we would be quite satisfied with a cup of tea and a biscuit. Wouldn't we, James?"

"Certainly." James said tightly, his gaze riveted upon his brother's hard, mocking gray eyes.

"Durgess," said the Earl, and the butler, who had been trying to bow himself out of the hall unobtrusively, now stiffened to attention. "We require a late supper. Master James is in need of sustenance."

"Yes, your lordship."

"And ratafia for Lady Charlotte in my study."

"Yes, your lordship."

Without glancing again at James or Charlotte, Philip led the way into his study. This was a long, spacious, comfortable room, with walnut-paneled walls and a high, beamed ceiling, the entire chamber furnished in buffs and browns and greens, with a walnut desk in the King Louis XVI mode set before the green draperied windows. Endless rows of well-worn leather volumes filled the bookcases from floor to ceiling, and oil paintings of horses and lakes and hunting dogs gleamed richly above overstuffed leather sofas and chairs.

Charlotte seated herself beside James on the dark green sofa, and clasped her hands before her like a schoolgirl. James reached out and patted her knee in an attempt at reassurance. Both of them looked so nervous and uncomfortable they might have expected to be bitten by a snake at any moment, Philip thought. Almost, he laughed. But it was not a night for merriment, and he was not in a mood even for the kind of cynical humor that was all he knew lately. He hated when he was sarcastic and unpleasant, as he had been with James and Charlotte in the hall. But he couldn't seem to stop himself. He and James would never get along again, they would never bridge the gulf between them. And when he saw James, all that wretched ugliness just seemed to pour out of him.

James looked well at least. As well as a nervous young colt about to be ridden by a brutish master might look, he thought with a bitter twist to his mouth. And Charlotte— she looked as though she would topple off the sofa from fright if he so much as blinked at her. Idiotic chit. *And I am an ogre,* Philip thought. Strange, it had never bothered him before what people thought of him. But his own family detested him now, and that was something hard even for him to swallow.

Did Charlotte know what had passed between him and James? He doubted it. But she was clearly afraid of him. Good. Fear was good. Let them all be afraid. It was the only way he had to keep any of them in line, the only hope he possessed of protecting them from themselves.

The silence lengthened in the study, broken only by the crackle of flames in the hearth, and Durgess sweeping in with Charlotte's ratafia.

Philip reached for the decanter upon his desk and poured brandy into two goblets. Without speaking, he handed one to James.

"How are Jared and Dorinda?" James said at last, fixing his brother with an intent gaze.

Philip tossed back the rich burgundy liquid. "Quite well, from what I can gather."

"What the devil does that mean, Philip?"

The Earl narrowed his eyes.

"Something is troubling you?" he inquired.

"I want to know about Jared and Dorinda!"

"Of course you do. Well, as you must surely realize, I spend most of my time in London. Jared, having been sent down from school, spends most of his time here—as does Dorinda. According to the reports I receive from Jared's tutor and Dorinda's governess, they are each doing well in their studies and are in excellent health."

James and Charlotte exchanged stricken glances. "When was the last time you saw them?"

"I don't seem to remember having to answer to you, little brother."

"Damn it, Philip," James exploded, lunging to his feet, "you behave as if you don't care a fig about them. Dorinda is only eight. She needs someone to take an interest in her. Jared, too! Maybe you're angry with me, maybe you even hate me, but that's no reason to take it out on the others! The least you could do is to spend a little time with them—engage them just once in conversation! Once we were a family, hard as it is to believe! Even with Mama gone, when Father was alive there was warmth and laughter in this damned house! But now . . ."

"Go on," Philip said in a tight voice.

"That's all. I beg your pardon. I shouldn't have said anything."

Charlotte swallowed hard, two bright spots in her cheeks matching those on James's countenance. She reached over silently and clasped his hand, then shot Philip a frightened glance.

He ignored her, however, keeping his gaze fastened on his brother. "I applaud your courage, James, if not your judgment. I shall therefore let you live," he murmured dryly. It was at that moment that Durgess interrupted to announce in dulcet tones that the late supper was ready to be served.

"Has the doctor been here yet?" Philip inquired of him.

Durgess replied that he was upstairs at that very moment.

"Doctor?" A thread of alarm vibrated through James's voice.

"Yes. There was an accident with the carriage earlier this evening."

"Oh, dear," Charlotte murmured.

"I almost killed a girl."

"Good Lord!"

"No need to worry. She's all right, she's upstairs in the Blue Room." Philip paced to the window and stared out at the wet night. "Enjoy your supper."

"But who is she?" James persisted. "Someone local?"

Philip turned back, shrugging his shoulders in a dismissive fashion. "Probably. A servant girl from one of the taverns, from the looks of her. Frankly, I don't know and don't care. She'll be seen to, compensated for her injuries, and sent about her business when she is recovered. In the meantime, I'm afraid I won't be joining you at your repast. I have some work to do here."

As if to illustrate the point he went to his desk and fingered a sheaf of papers. Their relieved expressions did not escape him.

"I've advised Mrs. Wyeth to do all she can to make your stay as enjoyable as possible," he added curtly, and turned away.

"Th-thank you, your lordship. You're most kind," Charlotte managed from the doorway.

"No, I'm not." A ghost of a smile flickered in Philip's eyes. "But how civil of you to say so."

When they were gone, Philip set down the papers, sank into his desk chair, and closed his eyes.

James was lost to him forever, he could see that quite plainly. What had happened could never be undone. His heart was heavy as he accepted this fact, thinking of the brother with whom he had once hunted and fished, who had dogged his footsteps in earlier years and wrestled with him like a carefree puppy in this very room.

Now James was as uneasy around him as he had once been comfortable, and there was no going back. Philip couldn't forget his brother's irresponsible folly, or forgive it, and James knew that. And as for Jared and Dorinda . . . well, Philip reflected with a small ray of hope, maybe when he married Brittany Deaville—and he *would* marry Brittany, Marchfield be damned—she would show him the way to make friends with his younger siblings.

Though he was a master horseman, a splendid shot, and a formidable opponent when it came to the boxing ring, he knew nothing about making this house a warm and pleasant place for children, and he was relying on Brittany to bring her charm and brilliant gaiety to Westcott Park.

He stared into the fire, pondering how best to win her. It still rankled that she had shown no partiality for him tonight at the masquerade, dancing with Marchfield and even Kirby every bit as much as with him, smiling at their jokes, flashing those wondrous violet eyes, behaving exactly as though she had no idea which gentleman she preferred. It made Philip more determined than ever to have her. Her very elusiveness, in addition to the fact that every man in London wanted her, made her irresistibly enticing.

For twenty-eight years he had eluded romantic entanglements—except for the light-skirted variety—but this time he had made a decision. Westcott Park needed a mistress, he needed a wife, and Dorinda needed someone to make her home come alive. Brittany, beautiful, sophisticated, impeccably aristocratic Brittany, was the key. She would know how to run the house with a woman's touch. She would also, Philip thought, his eyes brightening with a hot intensity, know how to warm a man's soul—not to mention his bed. Despite the fact that she was the daughter of a marquess, and that her face and figure held all the poise and refinement that her wealth and lineage would suggest, hers was a sparkling, vibrant beauty, smacking of sensuality, from the full-bosomed perfection of her figure to the rich, throaty sound of her laughter. Blond, statuesque, with those amazing eyes and a seductively shaped mouth, Brittany Deauville epitomized Philip's perfect woman. He had been fascinated with her from the first time he encountered her in the ballrooms of Almack's, and her reign as the unparalled beauty of the ton had solidified his fascination. Marchfield wanted her, Kirby, Piermont, even that upstart Boyington, younger than James, but with a fortune and title equal to Philip's own, they all wanted her. But he would have her.

Love had little to do with it—not from her side, not from his. The Earl knew he did not mistake Brittany's character. She wasn't searching for love any more than he was. Neither of them possessed a romantic bone in their bodies. But they were each attracted to the other. They shared a passion, a boldness of character. They would suit each other admirably.

And they would each provide things the other wanted. Brittany desired a grand match, a life of fashion, unquestioned status, luxury, and frivolity and he would provide her with exactly that. Philip sought an elegant wife, and an heir, and Brittany would provide him with both of those. They both knew the game and all of the rules. Both would triumph if they played their hands properly.

And now that he'd agreed to this bet with Marchfield, there could no longer be the slightest doubt that he would woo Brittany at all costs.

Losing was not in the Earl of Westcott's nature.

The fire burned down. The doctor arrived, bowed himself in and out of the study, speaking in between of the injured girl's condition, pronouncing her not too badly off, needing rest, time—but not a long time—for her sprained foot to heal, and then he was gone and it was quiet again, and Philip rose at last from his desk.

He was tired. James and Charlotte must have long ago retired—or retreated, more properly—to their quarters. They would be staying through Christmas, enough time so that little Dorinda shouldn't forget them—and of course they would be attending the ball.

Every year since as far back as Philip could remember, there had been a grand ball at Westcott Park to mark the first of December, his great-great-grandmother's birthday —a tradition begun by his great-great-grandfather—and no one who mattered in the ton would have considered missing it. Brittany would be in attendance, naturally—so would all of Philip's rivals, but he wasn't concerned about that. He knew, from the way he had often caught her glancing at him when she thought he didn't see, from hints that his aunt Lucretia had whispered in his ear once at Almack's, and from the way she flirted madly with every man in sight when he was near, that Brittany wanted this match as much as he did—this elusiveness was merely part of her game. Well, he could play games too. He was, in fact, a master at them, as she would soon see.

Suddenly, Philip felt better. He left the study and went upstairs, carrying with him a very vivid, very enticing picture of Brittany Deaville melting delectably in his arms.

He passed beneath the gilt-framed portraits of his ancestors in the wide hall without noticing any of them, his thoughts centered on the perfect face and form of the lovely Brittany. As he passed the Blue Room, some impulse checked his steps.

He decided to pay a visit to the injured girl. If she was awake, he would tell her exactly what he thought of her antics.

But when he knocked on the door and pushed it open, the bed was empty, save for the hall light spilling along a silvery path onto the tossed-back satin coverlet.

Philip frowned. Had Mrs. Wyeth moved the girl without informing him? Or was she wandering around the house, dazed perhaps, or, he thought—suspicion darkening his features as he remembered he knew nothing about her—was she trying to steal something . . . ?

Philip stepped inside to check the rest of the room.

Something cold and hard smashed into the side of his head. Pain exploded in his temples.

"Don't come a step further—stay away from me!" a voice hissed as he sagged toward the floor.

"Damn this night to hell," he muttered as the floor rushed up to meet him and the girl hit him again.

4

Camilla swung the candlestick again with all her might, gritting her teeth and putting every ounce of desperate energy she possessed into the blow. But the man she aimed at—and he made a very large target—rolled aside just in time to avoid being hit again, and with surprising agility sprang to his feet in the split second that her aim went wide. Off balance, she could do nothing but cry out as he grasped her arm and with ridiculous ease plucked the candlestick from her fingers.

"Oh no you don't."

"Let me go!" she gasped, and tried to pull away. His strength was far superior to hers, and she felt terror bubbling up as she wrenched futilely backward. In her effort to break free, she inadvertently put her weight on her injured ankle. A shudder of agony spasmed through her. She cried out, and would have collapsed, but the man caught her instantly around the waist. He swept her up into powerful arms with one easy movement. Before she could say a word, he was carrying her to the bed and dumping her, not ungently, upon the satin coverlet.

"Stay there and don't move, you little fool. What do you think you're doing?"

Camilla stared up at him, a lanky giant with silky black hair and satin-edged evening clothes. In the delicate blue room of marble and crystal, he looked immense and very powerful—and as though it would afford him great delight to wring her neck.

A tremor ran through her. Her arms and legs were shaking from the effort it had taken her to climb from the bed and hobble across the room moments ago, not to mention striking out at this man with the candlestick. It was frightening to be so weak, to feel herself so disoriented and dizzy. She fought to steady the whirling chaos of her thoughts, to stem the flood of pain ripping through her ankle.

When she'd awakened and heard footsteps approaching, she'd thought it was the murderer come to finish her off . . . she'd been dreaming of him, and then suddenly, she'd woken up—and someone *had* been there, outside the door, and she'd lurched up in terror. She had forced herself to cross the room, clutching only a candlestick for protection. Hiding behind the door, confused and frightened beyond words, with her ankle throbbing torturously, she had waited for him to come inside to kill her.

But now, gazing up at the man who had so easily subdued her attack and had carried her to the bed, she realized that he wasn't the murderer at all.

Candlelight flickering from the dressing table and spilling in from the hallway beyond the room revealed that this tall, furious man had gray eyes, not blue ones—very dark, compelling, and most of all *sane* gray eyes.

"I beg your pardon," she murmured, her lashes fluttering shut momentarily in relief. Then she opened her eyes again and managed a small, apologetic smile. "I thought you were trying to kill me."

"A tempting notion."

He advanced toward her. For one heart-stopping moment as she met that hard gaze, Camilla's fear rushed back, for he looked as though he'd be capable of murder. He was a very tall man, with raven-black hair, and a face that was hard and handsome. Not at all a pretty face, that of a comely boy with evenly matched features and empty beauty. No, his was a ruthlessly masculine face, striking in its roughly chiseled intensity. He had an aggressive-looking nose, a determined chin, and a decidedly rugged jawline. With his above-average height and broad shoulders, his thick, dark hair and glinting eyes, and the hard, sensuous line of his mouth, he looked like a handsome pirate, she thought with a shiver—indeed much more like a pirate than like the pale, indolent members of the nobility she had glimpsed occasionally through carriage windows. Yet his elegant attire and cool manner left no question that he was a member of the nobility. He wore a frilled white shirt and impeccably knotted cravat beneath his black tight-cut waistcoat of superfine, and his long legs were encased in dark silk trousers. His only jewelry was a ruby stickpin in the lace of his cravat, and a heavy gold signet ring.

"Now why would I want to kill you?" he drawled, his eyes raking her as she braced herself on the bed for whatever might happen next. He made a movement, and she shrank back instinctively, but he only reached for the crystal brandy decanter on the bedside table, his eyes narrowing at her indication of fear. Pouring burgundy liquid into a goblet, then handing it to her, he continued in a tone of deadly calm, "Possibly because you've given me a

lump on my head the size of an egg? I suppose I'm
damned lucky you didn't crack my skull."

"Oh, very lucky." Camilla's voice was only a little un-
steady. She hesitated a moment, looking up at him over
the rim of the goblet.

"I was trying to do just that," she admitted. "But that's
because I thought you were someone else . . ."

"A distinctly unfortunate individual," he retorted.

"A murderer!" she cried defensively.

As he raised his brows derisively and shot her a look of
pure skepticism, Camilla tried to clear her foggy brain
and think. Where was she? Who was this man? But her
mind was full of gauzy shadows and elusive memories.

Vaguely a recollection took form—a recollection of
waking up in this beautiful room with its peacock-blue
satin bed coverings and draperies, the roses on the marble dressing table, the flickering candles revealing lovely
rugs and paintings and twin striped brocade sofas with
pillows of rose and blue velvet. She'd thought she was
dreaming. It was so beautiful, more beautiful than anything she had ever seen before.

Then she remembered a man by her bedside—not this
tall black-haired stranger—a small beak-nosed fellow
with large ears and cold hands touching her, pressing
against her sore ankle with stiff, dry fingers. She groped
to remember despite the surging and fading blackness
clouding her mind.

He had given her some medicine—laudanum, he'd
said, to help her sleep. And the next thing she knew she'd
been dreaming of the murderer and there had been footsteps outside her door and then . . .

This man beside her, watching her with those keen gray
eyes. Maybe this was his house. But how had she come to
be here? Desperately, she struggled against the confusion

roiling through her brain as she tried to sort through the strange events of the night.

Her throat was unbearably dry. She gazed longingly at the liquid in the goblet she held, yet hesitated to touch it to her lips.

As if reading her thoughts the tall man said with a touch of amusement in his voice, "It isn't poison, or even Hollands, if that's what you're worried about, wench. Drink it. It's only brandy."

Could she trust him? Somehow, looking into those gleaming eyes, she did. She took a sip, and it burned its way down her throat in a fiery stream that left her gasping, but feeling a tiny bit stronger. Lifting her head, she gazed up at him, aware that he was watching her every move and expression. Begin at the beginning, she told herself, as she set the goblet down upon the marble night stand.

"Perhaps you can enlighten me." She took a deep breath. "I'm afraid I don't understand—"

"Neither do I," he cut her off ruthlessly. "And if you're whole enough to hide behind doors and attack people with candlesticks, my girl, you're damn well whole enough to explain yourself. What precisely were you doing in Edgewood Lane in the middle of the night? Strolling down the middle of the road, no less. Were you *trying* to get yourself killed?"

The carriage! Camilla lurched bolt upright. Suddenly, it all came clear. The coach barreling down upon her in the darkness, the deafening roar of the horses' hooves, the great wheels spinning straight toward her. Everything clicked into place, like the pieces of a puzzle assembling neatly before her eyes. Eyes widening, she stared at the man before her in instantaneous rage. "That was you?" she cried, weakly pushing the hair from her eyes. Beneath her dirt-smudged skin her cheeks flushed bright with anger. "You were the fool who ran me down?"

"The fool who almost ran you down," he corrected.

"You were drunk, weren't you?" she rushed on in a gasp. "No sober man would have driven at such a mad pace."

"If I *had* been drunk you would surely be dead now."

"I very nearly was!"

"Perhaps you should have thought of that before doing something so foolhardy."

Trembling, Camilla hugged her arms around herself. "Do you think I *wanted* to be out in the darkness walking down that horrid road? I didn't! But—" She broke off, biting her lip, realizing too late that she had probably already said much more than was wise. She would do well to keep her troubles to herself, instead of babbling them to this stranger. She could hardly tell him some wild tale about a man being murdered in London, and the murderer pursuing her. He would probably think her mad. She clamped her lips together and decided that the sooner she got away from this place—from *him*—the better off she would be.

He was gazing down at her with an unfathomable expression. She wasn't sure if it was still anger she saw in his face, or perhaps suspicion or some other nasty emotion. It certainly wasn't cordiality. He held her glance for a moment, his eyes glittering in the dimness, and then he said in a cool, hard voice, "I beg you will accept my profound apologies. I never expected at that hour of the night to encounter anyone in the road. Never mind. It was inexcusable, of course." He went on with icy politeness, "How are you feeling now?"

Camilla sank back against the cushions. "You don't really want to know, my lord," she bit off in a low tone.

"Yes," he said forcefully. "I do."

She was making every effort to keep from wincing at the intense pain throbbing through her ankle, to ignore the ache of her bruised muscles, and to keep her head clear despite the laudanum, which kept dragging her weary mind toward sleep.

"I'm sure I'll be perfectly well able to go on my way in the morning," she told him, trying her best to convince herself as well as him.

"Much as I am loath to contradict a woman, I fear I must. You're going nowhere, I'm afraid."

"But I must! I must leave England! You cannot keep me here against my will!"

He looked amused. "That isn't my intention."

"Who are you?" she demanded. "I insist that you allow me to leave." Sitting up again with great effort as she spoke, she next tried to swing her legs to the floor. But he grasped her by the shoulders and pushed her firmly back against the pillows.

Camilla was too weak to resist, crumpling back beneath his strong warm hands like a leaf. As he held her down, her eyes met his, and she felt a sudden sizzling heat far more powerful than the brandy rush through her.

His hands seemed to burn through her clothes. His eyes, silver-gray and smoky in the candlelight, gleamed with an intense magnetism so potent she could not look away.

Familiar. He looked familiar. Like someone in a dream . . .

Suddenly, she feared she *was* going mad. This was the man in her dream, the man whose face she had never seen. Ridiculous, she tried to tell herself as she lost herself in those relentless gray eyes, as she peered desperately at features so handsome they took her breath away.

She had never seen her dream lover's face. How could she know this was he?

Yet, something inside her flickered and grew hot, a blazing flutter of sensation so powerful and delectable it spiraled from her feminine core outward to every fiber of her being, leaving her flushed and heated and breathless —and quite unable to think.

Laudanum, she tried to tell herself, but her senses melted with a strange fire and her heart gave a curious lurch as he continued to grip her by the shoulders, his face only inches from hers.

Camilla forced herself to take a breath, trying to steady the heady rush of sensation flooding through her. "Please, sir," she gasped, shutting her eyes momentarily against the impact he was having upon her. "I . . . I don't even know your name or . . . or where I am." She opened her eyes again, fixing her gaze upon him with fervent desperation. She had to be sensible. She had to make him understand. "The doctor gave me laudanum and it is wearying my brain, but I . . . I cannot rest easily unless I know my circumstances. Why won't you let me leave?"

Philip felt a reluctant tug of admiration as he studied the girl's pale, mud-streaked face. The determined self-control with which she was keeping her composure under these circumstances impressed him. So did the air of quiet dignity she wore like a mantle about her thin shoulders. He felt a stab of curiosity. This scrawny, bedraggled creature mystified him. She appeared quite plain, with her grimy face and filthy garments and her matted hair straggling in her eyes. She looked like a lowly, tattered chimney sweep, a ragamuffin from the slums of London. But there had been a spark in those eyes—a spark of vibrant green flame, which had gleamed through the tan-

gled curtain of unkempt hair when she looked at him,
and that spark bespoke intelligence, a quick understanding, depth—not the sort of emptiness he had expected in
a servant girl who wandered down roads in pitch darkness. And her voice was a mystery too. It was soft, musical—cultured. She didn't sound like any housemaid or
tavern wench he had ever seen, though her clothes bespoke such a station. This girl was educated. That much
was clear. The Earl's mind sifted through the possibilities,
trying to sort it out. Who the hell was she?

Any other young woman he knew would have wept,
screamed, or had a hysterical fit of the vapors after such
an accident as she had undergone, but this female handled herself with self-control and poise, despite her pallor
and her obvious distress. She was in strange, uncomfortable circumstances, she was hurt and alone, but she behaved with the dignity of someone who would never
lower herself to histrionics.

Philip thought of Brittany. How would she have behaved if she found herself in this girl's position? Thinking
of that spirited beauty, he could imagine her weeping
recriminations, her demands for her mama, for a doctor,
for her maid and her clothes. This poor urchin, traversing
the dark country roads alone and unprotected, apparently
possessed remarkable courage. But it was ridiculous to
compare this ragamuffin to Brittany. He pushed away the
foolish notion and, on an impulse, sat down beside the
girl on the bed.

"Rest assured," he told the bedraggled creature, who
trembled as if she feared he might attempt to ravish her
on the spot. "You are safe."

The last of his anger died away and for the first time he
gave her a genuine, if somewhat rueful smile. It lit and
softened the harsh planes of his face far more than any

amount of candlelight. "Allow me to properly introduce myself. I am Westcott—this is my home. Although it isn't my custom to run down young women in the road, I assure you I know my duty and will certainly make amends for such carelessness."

He saw her eyes widen at the mention of his name and wondered if his title was perhaps familiar to her, but she said nothing, and after a slight pause he went on in his matter-of-fact way. "You will be cared for here at Westcott Park until you have fully recovered from the effects of the accident. My housekeeper can offer you good nourishing food, a doctor's care, and the attention of the staff if you require it. I will also see that you are compensated for any lost wages due to your injury. I assume that is satisfactory?"

A stunned look had entered her eyes. She stammered, "That's very kind but . . . I couldn't possibly impose . . ."

"You don't understand. The doctor reports that your ankle is sprained. You won't be walking comfortably on it for some days. You shan't be able to get about very well, much less go on with your work or your family duties, whatever they might be. So if you will tell me where I might discover your family, I will send word to them and . . ."

"I have no family."

"Surely there must be someone . . ."

Camilla thought of Hester sound asleep in the workhouse. Hester was probably the only person in the world who cared if she lived or not. But chances were high she would never see the little girl again—it might be months before it was safe for her to return to London, or years—or maybe it would never be safe at all.

Philip studied the long spiky lashes of her downcast
eyes.

"No one," the girl stated flatly. She spoke with calm
conviction and no other emotion, but Philip noticed the
tiniest quiver of her lower lip.

He stood up abruptly and paced to the window, staring
out at the cool, wet October night. "What is your name?"
he asked.

"Weed."

He turned. Immediately he was struck by the deep hue
of those river-green eyes fixed so steadily upon him. He
stalked toward her and repeated the word with startled
disbelief.

"Weed?"

She nodded, a sudden irrepressible smile curving her
lips. "That is what they call me in the tavern where I
work," she explained. "Though actually, Mrs. Toombs began it, in the workhouse where I grew up."

"I see." Philip shoved his hands into his pockets. "That
is all well and good, my girl, but I prefer to call you by
your proper name." He said this with great authority, for
he was accustomed to having things exactly as he preferred them, and had every expectation that he always
would. It never occurred to him that a servant girl bedridden in his house—at his mercy—would defy him.

To his amazement the chit responded with perfect politeness in a heartfelt tone: "I understand your feelings
perfectly, your lordship, truly I do. But I do not wish to
give my proper name. My reasons are my own—I cannot
share them—but I trust that as a gentleman you will
honor them."

Philip stared intently into that oddly arresting, earnest
face that gazed so steadfastly back at him. It was as if by
sheer force of will he would coerce her to reveal her

name to him. But he found himself confronting a young woman who showed no signs of intimidation, who gazed back at him with a completely natural self-assurance of her own, and an expression in her eyes of calm resolution.

He let out a sudden laugh. A tavern wench? Absurd. This girl spoke with far too much poise to have spent her entire life mopping a tavern floor. She knew her own mind and spoke it, unlike those who were slavishly accustomed to obeying the commands of others.

Philip said slowly, watching her face, which was mobile and interesting beneath its smudges: "It appears you leave me no choice, for the moment. But I won't call you Weed. I shall call you Miss Smith." He waited a moment, half-wondering if she would voice an objection to this, but since she said nothing, and only continued to stare at him in that earnest, expectant, rather charming way of hers, he went on.

"Who are you? Not your name, but—" He broke off, and his dark brows drew together. "You don't speak or behave like any tavern wench I've ever seen."

"Have you seen many, my lord?" Now her eyes sparkled.

"Don't evade the question."

"Is my presence in this house dependent upon satisfying all of your personal inquiries, then? I thought I was to be treated like a guest."

Philip regarded her, narrow-eyed. Rapier sharp, she was. And toying with him—very prettily, too. His conviction grew that she was no common serving wench or workhouse orphan, despite her ragged clothes. Still, she was right about one thing: her background was none of his concern. All he need assure was her recovery—after that point his responsibility to the chit would be finished.

"You are quite correct," he acknowledged with a slight,

ironic bow, wondering why he had spent so much time
here with her already. For a while he had quite forgotten
about Brittany, and that despicable bet he'd made with
Marchfield.

"Your affairs are none of my concern. I beg your pardon. I will send my housekeeper, Mrs. Wyeth, up to attend to you shortly—however, I do trust you will not attack her with a candlestick when she enters this room?"

"She is quite safe from me, your lordship," the girl
assured him.

He strolled toward the door. "I wish you good night
and a speedy recovery. And of course, I hope you will
accept my profound apologies for the injuries I have
caused."

"I would be most ungrateful if I did not."

When he reached the door he paused and turned back
with negligent grace, one hand resting lightly upon the
doorknob.

"May I make a suggestion for the future, Miss Smith?
Try to stay off the public road in the small hours of the
night. It is far healthier, I imagine. The next person to
run you down might not take the trouble to stop."

With a quick, brilliant flash of teeth he was gone before
she could frame a reply.

But his image flared in her mind, bright as a burnished
sword, for long moments after he was gone. As Camilla
sank back thoroughly exhausted against the cushiony pillow, she felt her heartbeat still pounding at a rapid stac-
cato. Though moments passed, his face remained clear,
his recent presence almost tangible to her, filling her with
a curious excitement.

Westcott. The Earl of Westcott. She had heard of him.
Oh yes, she had certainly heard of him. More than once
in recent months the tavern had been abuzz because of

some wild story about him. In May he had wagered some other great lords that he could ride to Newmarket in under four hours. The news that he had done just that set all of London buzzing, and Fredericka, one of the girls in the Rose and Swan, had boasted that she was cousin to one of the Earl's footmen, and that though he was a very grand and magnificent gentleman he was as wild as the devil himself. Her cousin prophesied that his young master would someday break his neck.

The next time Camilla had heard of him, the Earl had killed someone in a duel. Fredericka had proclaimed that her cousin had predicted how it would end: his lordship would prevail, for he was an excellent shot and a marvelous swordsman, and no one could best him.

The Earl of Westcott. Famed for his wild, rakish character, his horsemanship, his superb skill with sword and pistol. And lately, she recalled as she struggled in the quietude of the lulling Blue Room against the ever-encroaching effects of the laudanum, there had been a new rumor. The Earl would soon be wed, Fredericka had reported with the smug satisfaction of one privy to the secrets of the ton. He was in love with the daughter of a marquess, an elegant and dazzling lady more beautiful than the sunrise, a lady all the unmarried gentlemen of the ton desired for their own.

Yes, she thought, that was exactly the kind of lady the Earl of Westcott would choose. They would go splendidly together.

She remembered the disapproving astonishment she had read in the Earl's eyes when she had told him her name was "Weed," and tried very hard to find humor in the situation. If he hadn't thought her beneath contempt until then, that had certainly decided the matter. But, she told herself, as her eyelids drooped and her heartbeat slowed, her body at last giving way to exhaustion, it didn't matter a bit. In all likelihood she would not even see the Earl again during her stay here. Within a week she would set out for Paris and probably never encounter the Earl of Westcott again.

But in the meantime, she thought hazily, losing herself to the laudanum's insidious pull, this house, Westcott Park, would afford her a safe hiding place far from the White Horse Inn.

Vaguely, Camilla realized she couldn't possibly travel to Paris with her ankle as it was—and that was the only plan she'd been able to concoct during that interminable trek from London—that she would go to Paris and try to discover just who was searching for her. She touched the dull golden charm around her neck with limp fingers, dimly trying to rework her plan. When she did leave the protection of this house she would journey as swiftly and inconspicuously as possible to the coast and find work there until she had earned enough money to pay her way on a packet to France.

Until then, Westcott Park would be a haven. She could rest, heal, and above all else, feel safe.

For the time being, she forgot the nightmare chain of events that had ensnared her during the previous hours. She felt dizzy and weak, and it was a relief to close her eyes and savor the softness of satin against her cheek, of feathery comfort beneath her aching body. For a brief moment she thought of how lovely it would be to stay here forever, surrounded by beauty, waited on by servants, safe from all the dark and ugly things of the world.

And the Earl? Thinking of the tall, broad-shouldered man with the granite eyes and sensuous mouth, Camilla felt a warm flutter inside her. *You fool,* she admonished herself, on a long, weary sigh. *Perhaps if you were still a*

*squire's daughter with a respectable dowry and a pretty new
dress, he would look at you, but most likely not.*

Unless she was far mistaken, this Earl, who could have
his pick of women, would select only the most beautiful,
elegant, and accomplished women to flatter with his attentions.

Face up to it, she told herself coldly, for a moment
longer shaking off the urge to sleep. *You're a nobody to
him. Dream or no dream. Gwynneth is right. You're a nobody to the entire world.*

But not to one person. Not to the man who had killed
in Room 203 tonight. To that person, she realized with a
shudder, she was someone very important.

Someone—she prayed—he would not find.

5

Golden sunshine splashed into the room, awakening Camilla to a warm toasty glow as Mrs. Wyeth flung back the cocoon of silken curtains with ruthless purpose.

"Time enough to sleep later," the housekeeper announced curtly. "Your breakfast will be up shortly."

Camilla lay still for a moment, getting her bearings. Then she struggled up onto one elbow, suppressing a groan. Her body felt as though it had been trampled by oxen. But at least her head this morning was clear. She peered around the lovely blue and cream room, which shimmered in the sunlight, and then turned her gaze to the diminutive mobcapped woman who now stood glaring at her, arms folded across her chest. She remembered Mrs. Wyeth coming in late last night.

The housekeeper had wiped some of the grime from Camilla's face and hands with a clean cloth, removed her filthy garments, and bundled her into the white muslin wrapper Camilla now wore—then spoon-fed her hot soup before leaving her to sleep in peace. Camilla vaguely remembered the woman grumbling the entire time.

"Good morning. I remember you caring for me last night. Thank you. I'm sorry to be such a bother."

Mrs. Wyeth's pursed lips parted with surprise. She hadn't expected such pretty manners from the disreputable-looking creature the Earl had brought in. The girl had been so drugged and drowsy when she'd tended to her last night, she had scarce mumbled a word. Eyeing her distrustfully, Mrs. Wyeth replied with crisp condescension, "I cleaned you up a bit, young woman, but you'll need a bath all the same. There's mud and more mud everywhere, as I've never seen it before. We can't have that in Westcott Park."

"Oh no! We certainly cannot!" Camilla broke into an engaging smile. "I would dearly love a bath," she exclaimed. "One can never be too clean, can one? Thank you for all your kindness, Mrs. . . . Wyeth, isn't it?"

"Yes, miss." The housekeeper found herself inspecting her charge more closely. The chit was actually quite pleasant. Charming, even. Reluctantly, she realized that she must somewhat revise her earlier opinion. The girl was not exactly common after all. And now that she was cleaned up a bit, she didn't look nearly as disgusting as she had first appeared. Though that dirty matted hair certainly needed a good sudsing.

"Kate will do the best she can with your clothes, though there isn't much hope for them, from what I can see." She nodded at the soiled garments folded under the window seat. "After Kate brings your breakfast, she and Lucy will help you with your bath." Mrs. Wyeth added primly, "You know, you're very fortunate that his lordship has taken on responsibility for you. Others might not have troubled themselves so."

Camilla nodded. Once more the Earl's dark face glowed inside her mind. "Yes, he seems to be a very fine gentleman," she said slowly, remembering the strength of his hands upon her shoulders, the way he had effortlessly carried her to the bed. "No doubt you are most fond of him."

"Everyone who knows the Earl is fond of him," Mrs. Wyeth rejoined. "Except—" She broke off, a flush spreading downward from the roots of her graying hair past her thin white neck. Why, she had almost said: *except his own family.* That would have been inexcusable, the height of impropriety. Much chagrined at her own loose tongue, she shot the copper-haired girl in the bed a swift, frowning look as she spun about toward the door. "Don't engage in unseemly gossip about his lordship!" she admonished, all of her former good will toward the patient vanishing. "It is not for the likes of you or me to discuss our betters!"

"No, of course not . . ."

"See that you remember it!"

She whisked herself out and slammed the door resoundingly behind her.

Thoughtfully, Camilla chewed her lip. She couldn't *help* but think about "his lordship." His presence here in this room last night, giving her brandy to drink, demanding to know her name, was still vibrant in her mind.

She gazed around the large, airy room, still having difficulty taking in that she was actually nestled in a feathery satin canopy bed within this delightful bedchamber. Yesterday at this hour she had been on her hands and knees scrubbing the tavern floor, under Gwynneth's spiteful eye. Now she had a murderer after her, a maid to help her with her bath, an ankle that ached like the blazes, and a hiding place in a lovely kingdom ruled by an impossibly handsome lord.

A *temporary* hiding place, she reminded herself. She still must leave England as soon as possible.

At that moment her gaze fell upon the bundle of her clothes and with a flip-flop of her heart she suddenly remembered the note tucked in her pocket—the note she had been hired to deliver to Mr. Anders.

Bracing herself against every piece of furniture she encountered, Camilla managed to hobble across the room and back to the bed, whereupon she sank down in relief upon its softness and stared at the sealed paper in her hand.

Her fingers trembled as she held it. She was both eager to discover its contents and leery of doing so, all at the same time. Even with the sunshine that bathed the pretty blue room in a sparkling glow this morning, flashing diamondlike upon the crystal and marble and gold appointments, some of her fear returned as she looked down at the paper in her hand and remembered the deadly results of the errand she had been sent on. She gazed at the small, spidery black writing for a moment, steeling herself, and then proceeded to do what had to be done. She tore open the seal and began silently to read.

Henry—

Don't take less than a thousand pounds, mate. Tell him this'll be the last time. He may squawk at first, but he'll hand it over sure enough. His lordship don't want no fuss, no more'n we do. Bring the money to the dock—and make sure he don't follow you. After all these years he hasn't found me, and I don't need him findin' me now when I'm ready to let him off the hook.

See you tomorrow, mate. We'll be in the gravy then, both of us, and havin' ourselves a fine old time.

It was signed *Silas*.

Camilla's mind raced as she read and then reread the letter. Blackmail. Was that the reason behind the murder? It seemed apparent that Silas and "Mr. Anders" had been blackmailing someone, and maybe that someone had decided not to pay anymore. Maybe he had become fed up with their threats, had felt he could remove the danger they posed to him by doing away with the blackmailers. She swallowed, thinking of the man in the tavern —Silas. Was he still alive, or had the murderer gotten to him, too? And, she wondered, what knowledge did he possess to pose such a threat? What did he and the now-dead Mr. Anders know about a man that was so damaging they had been able to keep him dangling like a fish on a hook, paying them money in return for their silence?

Despite the warm sunshine pouring into the room, and the puffy white clouds swimming through the azure sky beyond her window, she found she was shivering. Fear licked at her. If only she had never left the Rose and Swan last night. If only she had never taken this note from the squint-eyed man.

Her uneasy reflections were interrupted by the opening of the bedroom door. Camilla jumped, then hastily stuffed the note under her pillow. As she watched wide-eyed, a little girl of about eight years old hurtled into the room, flushed and breathless, a blur of motion.

"Shhh, don't tell them I'm here!" the child ordered, and glanced frantically about for a hiding place.

Rapid footsteps clumped along the hall. Without another word, the little girl dove headfirst under the bed.

She had barely disappeared beneath the silken panels when a thick-waisted and heavy-bosomed old woman burst in, wringing her fat white hands. "Dorinda! Dorinda, you wicked monkey! Begging your pardon, my girl," she flung at Camilla in a whiny tone, all the while glancing about with darting eyes. "Ah, you needn't be so surprised. I've heard about you—the Young Person his lordship struck down in the road. And very lucky you were that he didn't leave you there, as some say he ought have. Well, have you seen a little minx of a child? Tell me quick now. His lordship wishes to see her and if I don't present her to him at once, he'll very likely send me straight away. Well, answer me, if you please. Have you seen the child?"

"Why, no, certainly not," Camilla responded instantly. "Why would a child come in here?"

"She's hiding from his lordship," the woman answered, as if that explained everything. As she spoke, her bulging blue eyes, the pale color of an icy pond, peered all about the room, scanning the armoire, the curtains, the oriental screen concealing the tub. Despite Camilla's protests, she began searching each place, then with a heavy sigh, she knelt down upon the floor beside the bed.

"I would certainly know if there was a child here . . ." Camilla burst out.

"I've got to find her," the fat governess huffed with single-minded determination. She was on both knees now, and starting to inch her head toward the floor. "Drat that child! A wilder, more troublesome brat I never did see . . ."

"There she goes!"

"What?" The governess's head snapped up just as she was about to peer beneath the billowing folds of the bed.

"The child! Did she have black hair and was she wearing a pink dress? She scampered down the hall just now, like a little mouse! That way!"

"Oh, curse her, that one will be the death of me yet!" The governess groaned, and heaved herself to her feet.

Perspiration poured down her jowly face. "Which way did
you say? Oh, toward the kitchens! Well, she'll be in the
pantry no doubt—stealing tarts! It's a wonder she isn't as
wide as an elephant with all that she eats . . ."

And she was gone at last, lumbering from the room
very like an elephant herself, Camilla thought, for she
had once seen a picture of one in a book her mother had
shown her, and she could still recall how huge and
strange a creature it had been. She staggered from her
bed the moment the governess was gone and pushed the
door closed.

The child crawled out from beneath the bed. She saw
Camilla wince as she made her way painfully back across
the room and darted forward with outstretched hands.

"Oh, let me help you," the little girl cried. "You're the
girl Philip ran down in the carriage last night, aren't you?
Does it hurt awfully?"

"It's not . . . so very bad," Camilla gasped with as
much cheerfulness as she could muster through gritted
teeth. Apparently everyone in the mansion knew about
last night's mishap, even this small child. She sank down
upon the bed once more with great relief and gingerly
stretched out her legs. Blocking out the throbbing as best
she could, she turned her head to gaze with great interest
at the fetching little face before her.

Pink and round as a button was that face, framed by
jet-black curls caught up in pink ribbons. The girl had a
bow-shaped little mouth, and a daintily upturned, imperious nose. What struck Camilla most forcibly though were
the little girl's eyes. For the child stared curiously at Camilla with eyes so shockingly similar to the Earl's intense
gray ones that it was almost laughable. Though his were
as dangerous and keen as knife blades in that lean, rugged face, hers were startlingly lovely and innocent, those

of a bright, imaginative sprite who looked at the world through childhood's rainbow. Yet for all that, Camilla saw the same fringe of long black lashes overshadowing them, the exact same shade of deep, glinting gray, and the identical depth that bespoke piercing intelligence in both.

The girl wore a flounce-skirted dress of seashell pink, with an elaborate silk sash and lace yoke that would have dazzled poor little Hester quite speechless. She was petite, with thin little arms and legs, and tiny feet encased in pink and white satin slippers.

"Thank you for helping me!" the child exclaimed. "I don't know what I should have done if Gertie had found me!"

"I expect you would have put in an appearance before your brother," Camilla replied with a smile, arranging the covers more comfortably about her. She saw the girl shudder at her words.

"Why are you frightened of him?"

"He doesn't like me."

"Why, of course he does!"

"No. He only likes horses." The child frowned, crossing her arms. "And drinking horrible stuff—I think they call it brandy—and going to parties. And he likes women —grown women," she added darkly. " 'Opera dancers,' Mrs. Wyeth says, though I'm not supposed to have heard that." The little head tilted to one side, birdlike. "What's an opera dancer?"

Camilla gazed back at her solemnly. "Hmmm. An opera dancer. You know, I really couldn't tell you." She patted the edge of the bed invitingly, and the little girl climbed up beside her. "You know, you mustn't be afraid of your brother," Camilla said, touching her hand. "He cares for you a great deal."

"No, he doesn't."

Camilla looked pensive. "Does he shout at you?" she asked gently, after a moment.

"No."

"Does he lock you in your room without supper?"

"No."

"Beat you?"

"No, of course not." The small, stubborn lower lip pushed out, looking dangerously like a pout. "But he scarcely speaks to me, except to question me about my lessons. Ugh." She made a face. "Or to lecture me about how young ladies of quality do *not* climb trees or take off their clothes and wade in the lake or follow the grooms about bothering them with a lot of pesky questions. Pesky questions, my word! I'm trying to learn all about horses and it's perfectly all right for Philip to know about such things, and for James and Jared, but because I'm a girl they want me only to speak French and wear gloves and learn how to curtsy prettily and never have any fun at all!"

"Curtsy! Do you know how to do that? I think it would be great fun to know how to curtsy prettily." Camilla leaned forward, her eyes sparkling. "When my ankle is healed, will you teach me, Dorinda?"

"You mean you don't know? And you're a girl!"

The child looked so astonished that Camilla burst out laughing. "But no one ever taught me that," she explained. "Well, perhaps my mama did when I was very little, but I can't remember. I can't even remember *her* very well."

"You can't?"

"You see, it's been many years since she's been gone." Camilla gave her head a tiny shake. "I lived in a workhouse after my parents died," she explained, "and we didn't learn things like curtsying there."

Dorinda's eyes widened even further, dwarfing the other features of her face. "A workhouse! Gertie says they are horrid places with rats and fleas and nothing to eat but bread and water, and that they are where wicked children go when their parents don't want them anymore. She said my brother Philip will send me there if I don't behave properly."

"What rubbish!" Camilla stared at her. "Dorinda, he never would do such a thing!"

"Gertrude said Philip told her he would."

"She said that, did she?" Camilla was beginning to understand. Anger rushed through her. She leaned forward, grasping the edges of the coverlet in her hands. "Well, she was lying to you. Listen to me, Dorinda. Your brother would never do anything of the sort, I promise you. I only met him briefly, and he is a bit intimidating, but he is a very fine and decent and good man. Why, he must be, for only see how he is taking on responsibility for me after a ridiculous accident—and he need not, except that his conscience dictates it—and that is very honorable of him indeed. And as for you, his own little sister, I can imagine how much more he feels for you and all that he is willing to do for you! You will always have a home with him, until you are grown up and want one of your own, you may be sure of that." Her eyes narrowed. "Gertie is only trying to frighten you. I know the type of person who does that, because when I lived in the workhouse the woman who ran it always tried to frighten me, but I didn't let her. I learned when a threat was the truth, and when it was made up for the moment. What Gertie told you was made up for the moment, Dorinda. Do you understand?"

"Ye . . . es. I think so."

Camilla studied the sober little face a moment. "Is that why you were frightened to see your brother?" she asked at length. "Because you thought he would send you away if you didn't please him?"

Dorinda nodded.

"Well, Gertie ought to be dismissed for that! To think that *I* was dismissed from Miss Victoria Motterly's employ only because she caught me trying on one of her hats when she was supposed to be out driving in the park!"

That diverted the child's attention away from her own troubles, making her eyes brighten with interest. "Did you really?"

"Well, it was so awfully fetching, I couldn't resist," Camilla admitted with a rueful smile. "It had beautiful lavender colored ribbons and tiny satin flowers with bits of green lace for the leaves, you see, and seed pearls . . . oh, it was certainly the most breathtaking hat I'd ever seen. And I'd never owned a hat like that, only ugly little white mobcaps, like Gertie was wearing, and so one time I just set it upon my head for a moment, and started to tie the ribbons beneath my chin, and wouldn't you know, Victoria Motterly walked straight in upon me and shrieked as if the devil were sticking her bottom with his pitchfork!"

Dorinda laughed, covering her mouth with her hand. "And she dismissed you?"

"After a strong spell of hysterics."

The little girl giggled again. "What's your name?" she asked, regarding Camilla with intense interest.

"You may call me Miss Smith," Camilla replied after a moment's consideration.

Dorinda nodded, then she jumped off the bed and began wandering around the room, absently touching everything in the way that children do, the silver hairbrush on the dressing table, the crystal vase full of roses, the cushions on the striped sofas. "Perhaps you would like to try on one of Aunt Charlotte's hats," she suggested. "They are quite beautiful, probably even more beautiful than Miss Motterly's. She and Uncle James are visiting, you know. *They're* afraid of Philip too. I could steal one for you and bring it here and you could try it on—a hat, I mean." She skipped back to the bed. "Would you like that?"

"Oh, above all else, but you'd best not. I'm certain stealing is something your brother would not approve of —and as I learned with Miss Motterly, anytime you try to do something you ought not do, chances are you will be immediately found out and put in the most humiliating predicament!"

Dorinda accepted this with a wise nod. "Tell me another story," she promptly begged. "That other one was so very funny. Do you have more?"

"Many more, I'm afraid." Camilla smiled at her, glad of the rosy color that had come into the girl's cheeks when she'd laughed, and noting the sparkle in her gray eyes. "But first there's something you should do and I'll wager you know what it is."

"No . . . I don . . ." Suddenly, Dorinda leaped back, balling her little hands into fists. "Oh no, don't make me go see Philip!" the child pleaded, the hunted look returning to her eyes. "I won't! I won't!"

Camilla held out a hand to her. "Dorinda, I would never make you do anything you didn't want to do. But you know you ought to. He'll be angry if you keep him waiting, and surely you realize they must find you sometime. It's much better if you go on your own and face him. Be very brave. Then come back later and tell me all about it. It will make a wonderful story! And then," she added, "I'll tell you another story—one even better than the first."

"You will? Promise?"

"Solemnly, upon my honor, may a witch turn me into a lizard if I don't."

Dorinda chuckled. "Well, all right." She gave a long sigh. "I suppose I must go. But it isn't easy to be brave— or good."

She trudged to the door, then spun about and sent Camilla a beseeching glance. "But if he wishes to send me away will you speak to him on my behalf?"

"Indeed I shall."

Much relieved, the child sent Camilla a grateful smile, then closed her eyes for an instant, resigning herself to the inevitable fate before her. With dragging steps she went out the door.

"You'd better be here when I come back!"

Camilla heard the softly called words just before the door shut behind her.

Where else would I be? she thought wryly. She leaned back against the pillows, wondering about this household she found herself in. Why was there such difficulty between the Earl and his family? According to Dorinda both of his brothers were also frightened of him. Either they were easily intimidated, or there was another side to the Earl which she hadn't seen. The man she had met last night, for all his height and presence and cool demeanor, had not frightened her. As a matter of fact, beneath that rakish exterior, she had sensed a careworn soul, a man with both laughter and pain hidden away behind that magnetic face. Unless the laudanum she'd been given had dulled her senses, creating false impressions that would not hold up in the light of day.

If only she could meet him again, she could be sure.

When presently a pert-faced maid with hair the color of ripe corn entered the room, bearing a silver tray laden with chocolate and biscuits on china dishes, with a small bowl of marmalade and honey nestled beside a white linen napkin, Camilla nearly laughed in delight. *I must be dreaming,* she thought as the aroma of fresh-baked buttery biscuits tantalized her, making her stomach rumble. *Any moment now Gwynneth is going to drench me with ice-cold water and probably break the pitcher over my head as well.*

"Excuse me, miss." The maid dimpled. "Lucy and Irene will bring water for your bath shortly. Is there anything else I can do for you?"

The maid spoke these words politely enough as she set down the tray, but Camilla saw the curious way in which the girl gaped at her.

"Your name is Kate, isn't it?" Camilla tilted her head to one side as the girl nodded and curtsied again. "Tell me, Kate," she said conspiratorially. "Exactly what is it they are saying about me belowstairs?"

The girl's round brown eyes grew guarded. "I'm not sure I understand, miss . . ."

"Oh, don't tell me, let me guess." Camilla's eyes danced. She took a sip of the chocolate. "I daresay one story has it that I am near death and will never recover—and that I will spend the remainder of my days here with a private nurse and doctor."

Kate's jaw dropped. Camilla chuckled. She went on briskly, "And no doubt another person, possibly Cook, is saying that I received no more than the tiniest scratch and that his lordship will have me shipped out this very afternoon. And I am certain there are many variations of each, plus a few others too absurd even to repeat."

The girl was staring at her in such amazement that Camilla couldn't help but burst into laughter. Working in a tavern and in Miss Motterly's employ had given Camilla a very good idea of how quickly and wildly gossip could spread among servants, and she had already realized that within Westcott Park, stories were flying about the Earl and the girl he had struck down in the road. Rumors, gossip, innuendo. None of it would affect her—how could it? She would be leaving England in a very few days. But his lordship was another matter. He had behaved honorably and very generously after the mishap, and she didn't want any unkind speculations arising about him.

"Perhaps you'd like to know the real story," she suggested, knowing that even though the truth might not be as fascinating as some wild rumor, it would nevertheless provide Kate with a moment of self-importance among the hierarchy of servants below. She related as matter-of-factly as she could how she had been walking down the road in utter darkness, too exhausted even to realize her danger, and how miraculously his lordship's considerable skill with the ribbons had spared her life when he'd come upon her in the blackest hour of night, at high speed. She pointed to her sprained ankle, ventured a guess that she would be in the house no more than four or five days, and mentioned that she was most grateful for his lordship's consideration.

She could plainly see that Kate was longing to ask her just what she was doing on the road in the middle of the night, who she was, and where she was from, but the girl couldn't summon up the courage to question the Earl's guest. Which was just as well, Camilla reflected complacently, because she could not offer a candid answer anyway. Not to his lordship, not to this pleasant little maid, not to anyone.

It was awkward and a bit painful maneuvering in and out of the marble tub, but with Kate and Lucy and Irene's help, Camilla managed it. It felt wonderful to scrub herself clean in the steaming perfumed water, to wash her hair with the rich lathery soap that smelled delightfully of lilacs, and to soothe her bruised body as she luxuriated in the huge marble tub. She patted herself dry with the thick, soft blue bath towels Lucy had fetched, then dressed in the garments Mrs. Wyeth had chosen for her. This included a gray high-necked cambric gown that had belonged, she learned, to little Dorinda's former governess, dismissed by the Earl because she couldn't control the child.

"She was about your size," Kate observed, looking Camilla up and down, "but she had freckles all over her face, and her teeth stuck out. She screeched, that one did. Dorinda hated her. The child put a spider in her bed, and that ninny woke the entire household with her screeching."

Camilla laughed, and Kate joined in. "When the Earl sent her packing, she was so beside herself, carrying on and crying, that she up and left without remembering all of her clothes. This is one of them she forgot. Not a ball gown, exactly, miss, but then, you won't be doing any dancing, will you?"

"Not on this ankle, I'm afraid. Not anytime soon." Camilla perched on her one good foot, and held the back of a gilt chair for balance. In this pose, she studied herself in the looking glass framing the marble dressing table.

Not so very bad, she thought in surprise. Weed. Did she look still like a weed? She was tall, yes, but not as thin as she had supposed. Having no looking glass at the Rose and Swan with which to observe her own appearance, for good or for bad, she knew very little about the way she looked, only what she remembered having been told at the workhouse by those who dubbed her "Weed."

What she saw was startling. Her freshly clean hair

spilled in thick waves past her shoulders, gleaming like molten copper in the sunlight. Velvety green eyes gazed back at her, wide-set, and intelligent, starred by long, curled dark lashes. *Why,* she thought, with a little jump of her heart, *I look . . . pretty.*

The gown fit snugly. With a flush of embarrassment she realized that it accentuated the curves of her figure, soft, shapely curves, she realized, which had always been hidden by the baggy layers of her large, shapeless work dresses and aprons. Camilla, constantly in a hurry either to get down to work or up to bed, had never paused to study the changing shape of her own body when she undressed. Now she was astonished to see that she possessed sweetly rounded breasts, a tiny waist, and hips that curved lushly beneath the cambric gown. She looked, she realized, not like an ugly, gangly weed at all—she looked like a woman.

It was a shocking, but not at all unpleasant, discovery.

Her moment of revelation was interrupted by the sound of a horse's hooves crunching on the paved drive outside her window. Camilla turned her head at once, thinking it might be the Earl returning from a morning ride.

Her room overlooked the front of the house, with its splendid flagged courtyard elegantly flanked by rose gardens and winding maple groves. In the distance through the autumn-plumed trees glimmered the jewel-blue radiance of the lake.

Directly beneath her window, as Camilla slipped onto the window seat and leaned toward the mullioned glass, she saw a man in breeches and a tan riding coat dismounting from a white horse. She knew at once that he was not the Earl of Westcott. This man was tall, yet still several inches shorter than the Earl; he had fair hair and possessed a slimmer build, though he moved with similar athletic grace as he sprang up the steps.

"Lord Kirby," Kate supplied at her elbow.

Suddenly, below, as if he had heard, the man glanced up and saw the two feminine faces pressed against the window. Beneath the meticulously combed fair hair he had light skin, and a long, smooth jaw—he was good-looking in an intelligent, aristocratic way. When he saw the young women peering down at him, his noble brows rose, and for an instant there was the twinkle of pleasant blue eyes. He grinned as both women drew hastily back from their vantage point.

"Lord Kirby is a neighbor, no doubt come to pay a call upon Master James," Kate explained as she helped Camilla onto one of the blue and white striped settees beside the large potted plant. "He and his twin brother practically grew up with his lordship and Master James. Thick as thieves the four of them were, according to Mrs. Wyeth. Mercy me, Dorinda will be glad to see him. She is ever so fond of Lord Kirby, you know." Kate fluffed the bed pillows and dusted the marble nightstand and dressing table with brisk efficiency as she talked. "And he just dotes on the child. He seems to understand her moods and tempers too. It's him who's always after his lordship to take the little girl places, to fairs and outings and the like, but his lordship claims he never has the time."

"Does he? How sad."

Camilla thought of Dorinda's round little face and her dread of seeing her brother and wondered yet again about the true character of the man who had given her shelter. At the same time, she searched uncomfortably for a way to change the subject. Fascinated as she was by all these tidbits about the Westcott Park household, she was nevertheless beginning to feel a trifle bad about engaging in gossip about her host. Kate did like to rattle on, and at first it had been instructive to learn something of the household in which she found herself, but now she began to feel guilty about encouraging intimate details and critical comments about the man who had given her safe harbor.

She feigned weariness, and closed her eyes. "Kate, I'm sorry but I need to rest. I'm afraid the bath tired me more than I could have possibly imagined."

"Well, to be sure it's only natural," the girl said sympathetically as she whisked the dust rag over the last of the knicknacks on the dressing table. "By tomorrow you'll be feeling more the thing. But, miss, you don't want to be healing too quickly," she warned with a grin as she slipped toward the door. "You surely don't want to be sent off before the ball."

Camilla opened her eyes. "What ball?"

"Oh, it's going to be something wonderful to behold." Kate's brown eyes glowed. "There is a ball every December at Westcott Park—the most splendid ball in the county. It's a tradition with the Audleys. And this one, you can be certain, will be the grandest of them all."

"Why is that, Kate?" Camilla couldn't resist asking.

"Because his lordship, according to everything *I've* heard, is in love for the first time in his life. And the young lady, the most sought-after young lady in London, so they say, will be in attendance. It's fair certain his lordship will host the most spectacular ball ever held at Westcott Park—all to impress her, naturally. And," Kate added with a wink, just before she closed the door, "if you're lucky, you'll still be here and might get a glimpse of all the elegant ladies and gentlemen, maybe even of Lady Brittany herself!"

A ball. Alone in the blue and cream room, Camilla

leaned back against the cushions of the settee, and tried to picture it. The chandeliers brilliantly ablaze overhead, the checkered marble floor, flowers everywhere, the music flowing like wine. Among all the dazzlingly attired guests, she could see the Earl quite clearly in her mind's eye. He would be resplendent in his superbly cut evening clothes, his dark hair smoothly brushed away from his face, his wide shoulders set off by the cut of his jacket. His expression would be nonchalant, cool, but his eyes would smolder as he spun about the dance floor with some entrancing young girl in yards of spangled white tulle. And all the women would be like sparkling jewels, Camilla thought, the men as breathtakingly elegant as princes from a faraway land. There would be champagne, lobster patties, and little cakes, and probably hundreds of other wonderful things to eat, things Camilla in her limited experience couldn't even imagine. And music, lovely, lilting music, she thought dreamily, music that filled the soul and made one yearn to dance, to be held in a man's arms and whirled about the floor until you were breathless and light-headed and positively dizzy . . .

Suddenly, she jerked herself out of her reverie. She had been picturing herself dancing, of all the ridiculous things —and the man she had been dancing with was the Earl! Such foolishness! Camilla was mortified by her own daydreams. Shrewd, practical, sensible Weed, the girl who maneuvered her way around a tavern full of drunken seamen and brawling factory workers with deft ease, who had survived the workhouse years by being tougher and more stubborn than Mrs. Toombs, who knew the slums of London far more intimately than she did the gardens and mansions of the ton, this Weed was becoming softheaded and romantic?

No, she wasn't. She didn't know what was happening to her, but she wasn't going to let it continue. Why, only a day ago she had been a nondescript part of the fog-shrouded, grimy London scene: the taverns and alleys, the beggar-strewn streets, the stench of garbage, the yowling cats, the red-eyed rats scurrying in corners. That was her world, that was where she had come from, where she was comfortable. But now she was mentally plopping herself into a world to which she could never belong. She was a dreamer. A fool.

Just because you were born a squire's daughter, you think you're entitled to a grander life than the one that's been handed out to you. Well, Papa's money and estate are all lost, Papa and Mama are gone, and you are a workhouse brat, a servant, no better nor no worse than any other.

Stop dreaming.

She must have hit her head when the carriage knocked her down, she thought scornfully. She must have loosened up some of her brains. She forced herself to try to think of something else, besides Westcott Park, the ball, the Earl. Not the murderer, either, that was too frightening, and she didn't want to be frightened. Instead, she thought about the man from Paris who had made inquiries about her. Why was he looking for the girl with the golden lion charm? And why had Mrs. Toombs lied about it?

Once more, she fingered the chain around her throat. It was a mystery, she admitted, one she wouldn't solve until she reached Paris and asked some questions. But who could that unknown man be, and why was he looking for her?

Camilla had no answers. Weariness overtook her as the sun glided across the calm turquoise sky, and she slept at last upon the settee, not waking until dusk, when Kate brought both her supper and alarming news.

"It's Dorinda, miss." Kate shook her head dolefully. "Poor, poor babe. Only wait till you hear. She's in the most awful trouble."

6

"It is too bad of him to confine you to your room," Camilla exclaimed in ready sympathy, and Dorinda, red-eyed and defiant, sniffled her agreement.

Camilla had persuaded Kate to "borrow" one of the Earl's ivory-handled walking sticks, and by leaning on this Camilla had hobbled her way through the maze of gold-chandeliered corridors until she reached the nursery wing of Westcott Park. There, in a spectacularly beautiful room wallpapered in yellow roses, sitting tearfully upon a four-poster featherbed adorned with gauzy curtains of white satin, she found the miserable prisoner of Westcott Park. But much as she sympathized with Dorinda's unjust fate, she couldn't help admiring the dazzling prettiness of this fairy-tale suite of rooms, with the airy bedroom and playroom twice the size of the Porridge Street Workhouse bedroom where all the children slept together.

The adjoining door led to Gertie's quarters. It was shut and locked. But Dorinda's bedchamber was a frothy vision of bright yellow and white striped curtains, a lovely

mahogany bureau, and a round play table about which
were set two small, sturdy wing chairs upholstered in yellow damask. There were several lace embroidered pillows
plumped on the bed, a row of china dolls gracing the
mantel, all dressed in exquisite gowns and possessing real
hair becomingly curled about their painted faces, and
shelf after shelf of storybooks, whistles, marionettes, and
kaleidoscopes cramming the mahogany bookcase against
the wall. There was also a spinet with a cushioned bench,
and a giant white rocking horse sitting majestically in the
center of the room, complete with gold satin ribbons
braided through its silken mane.

"Philip is the meanest brother in the whole world. I
hate him—I hate him!" Dorinda whispered fiercely, and
promptly burst into tears.

Camilla forgot the beautiful trappings as she sank
down upon the bed and drew the weeping child into her
arms. For all her riches, Dorinda was every bit as lone-
some as Hester. All of the rocking horses and china dolls
in the world did not help her to feel loved.

She let the child weep in her arms for several moments,
until the little shoulders went slack and still, and the
gasping sobs subsided into sniffles. All the while she
stroked the little girl's hair, thinking the situation
through. At last, hearing Dorinda quiet, she said softly,
"Tell me why he punished you, dear. Did you indeed go
down to see him as you promised?"

"Yes, but I never should have gone," Dorinda cried
bitterly. "I should have hid in the Pirate's Cove instead.
He'd never have found me there."

"The Pirate's Cove?"

"In the maze, behind the rose garden, there is a patch
of shrubbery, and if you part the shrubs and go through,
there's a little path that leads to a glade, sheltered by the

trees. No one can find you there, not if you're very quiet.
And there's a wall around it, a high wall. I go there sometimes and pretend that a pirate hid his treasure there, and
I dig with a little stick in the dirt, and imagine all the
lovely gems and pieces of gold. And it's my secret place,
my Pirate's Cove. I should have gone there today!"

Camilla's face softened with a sympathetic smile.
"What did Philip say when you went to see him? Tell me
everything now. You weren't impertinent, were you?"

"What's that?"

"Impolite."

"Oh no." Dorinda heaved a sigh and her silvery eyes
darkened suddenly with malevolence. "But Gertie told
him the horridest lie! She said I misbehaved and wouldn't
learn my lessons, and she told him that I kicked her shins,
which was not true at all, I merely trod on her toe by
accident and fell against her shin and it was all an accident . . . well, mostly. And besides, she deserved it!"

"Oh, Dorinda, you *didn't*." Camilla gazed at her in dismay. But much as she tried to suppress it, a giggle escaped her. "Dear me, what am I to do with you? You're a
naughty child—but then, so was I. How long must you
stay in this awful dreary prison?" she inquired, with a
smiling glance around the charming white and yellow
room.

"Two whole days." Dorinda suddenly threw a pillow
across the bed. It struck a writing tablet on the round
table and sent it sailing to the floor, loose pages scatter-
ing. "And I'm to have no visitors," she added darkly.
"Not James, not Charlotte, not Jared—no one. If Philip
catches you here, he'll probably lock you in *your* room."

"I'll risk it." Camilla tilted the child's chin up with her
finger. "Your brother simply wants you to learn not to
kick people you don't like," she said, feeling the urge to

defend the Earl, for some reason she didn't understand. "And he's right, of course. It's totally unacceptable behavior. Now, if you really want to get revenge on Gertie, I can tell you exactly what you must do. I'm an expert at sneak attacks, you know. Back in the tavern where I work, there's a girl named Gwynneth Dibbs, who is the meanest creature alive. . . ."

"Meaner than Philip?"

"Far meaner than Philip," Camilla assured her. "And when I want to pay her back for something horrid that she has done to me or someone else, I think and think until I come up with a perfect way to take revenge—but of course she must never be able to prove that I was the one . . ."

A knock at the door made her break off, and she and Dorinda stared at each other in alarm.

"Who's there?" the little girl called, jumping up and running to the door, both hands pressed against the panels.

"It's Charlotte," came the soft reply. "Quick, let me in, pet."

Dorinda pretended to be afraid to open the door, lest her brother's wrath descend upon her. While Charlotte in a low tone tried to persuade her, Camilla went into the wardrobe as quietly and quickly as she could. By the time Dorinda admitted her, Camilla and her walking stick were well hidden, surrounded by dainty little gowns of every imaginable hue, velvet-lined cloaks and muffs, and boxes of tiny shoes and boots and bonnets. Through a thin crack in the wardrobe door, she could see Dorinda and her smiling visitor.

How absurd. She wondered what this Charlotte would say to her if she was discovered. Scarcely daring to breathe, Camilla peered out and listened with great curiosity to the conversation going on in the bedroom.

"It is so kind of you to visit . . . oh, what have you brought? It's a kitten!" Dorinda squealed with joy as Charlotte flipped open the lid of the basket she carried, and the child saw the kitten nestled inside.

"She's to keep you company while you're confined to your room," Charlotte explained, helping the child to lift the tiny gray and white creature from its makeshift bed of soft towels, and watching with satisfaction as the little girl cradled the bundle of fur against her cheek. "Jared found her near one of the sheds while he was out riding today," Charlotte continued, setting down the basket and taking a seat upon the sofa. "He searched all about, but couldn't find the mother or any others of the litter, so this one must be the sole survivor. We didn't know for certain if Philip would let you keep a kitten in the house, so James and Jared and I have decided it would be better if you didn't ask him. Then," she added simply, "he can't say no, can he?"

Dorinda stroked the downy fur, snuggling against it. "It's the best present I ever received! But how will I keep Gertie from finding out? She'll be sure to tell Philip!"

"Oh, don't worry, we have a most excellent plan!"

Spying from inside the wardrobe, Camilla decided that she liked Charlotte Audley very much. She looked young and sweet and kind, and she didn't sound at all stuffy the way Miss Motterly had. She wished she could step out of the wardrobe and get a better view of Charlotte's lovely gown of cream-colored dimity. But that was impossible at this point, so she kept quiet and watched as Dorinda stroked the kitten and asked about the plan.

"Jared and James and I decided that we'll take turns keeping the kitten in our rooms. We'll bring her to you when Gertie has her nap or has gone to bed for the night. That way, no one need know she's here."

"You mean we'll sneak about with her," Dorinda cried joyfully, clearly loving the idea.

Charlotte gave a discreet cough. "Let's just say we'll keep this little darling a secret. For a while, at any rate. But really," she said, rising to her feet and giving Dorinda a hug, "I must go now, dearest. I would die of fright if Philip were to catch me breaking his edict, and James is waiting to walk with me in the garden."

"He is? Are you going to kiss him?" the little girl asked impishly, her eyes dancing.

"What an impertinent question." Charlotte laughed. "Of course I shall. But don't tell anyone."

Dorinda set the kitten in the basket and followed her to the door. "Where's Jared? Isn't he going to visit me, too?"

"I'm sure he will. He is most sympathetic to you."

"I knew he would be. I'll bet he said that Philip is an ogre!"

"Now, now," Charlotte murmured in dismay, "he said nothing of the sort, and you mustn't say things like that either. It's most improper."

"Philip says we're an improper family. He says we all lack self-control and dec . . . decorum."

"As if he should talk! He is the worst one of all! At least James only boxes a little now and then and—" She broke off, realizing how thoroughly improper were her own remarks and added hastily, "Of course Philip is a very fine person and . . . and only wants the best for you all. Even James says so, and Jared, too, and my papa insists he is quite the thing. Certainly all of London worships at his feet." She went on as if to herself, "They actually seem to enjoy being sneered at by the Earl of Westcott."

Inside the wardrobe, Camilla felt a distinct tickle in her nose. She held her breath. Oh no, she couldn't. Not yet . . . She squeezed her eyes shut in concentration. If only Charlotte would leave . . .

"Thank you so much for the kitten," Dorinda was saying happily. "She is the loveliest thing I ever saw. Now I must think of a name for her."

Leave, Charlotte, please leave. Camilla screwed up her face in an effort of enormous concentration. The sneeze was coming and it was going to be a loud one. Drat that kitten . . .

"Good night, dearest. Remember to hide that basket should Gertie come."

The door had scarcely clicked shut behind her when Camilla could hold back no longer. "Ahhhh*choooo*."

The sneeze seemed to rock the wardrobe.

The door opened. Dorinda peered inside. "I beg your pardon, I quite forgot about you. Look at this darling little kitten." As Camilla rather dazedly emerged from the darkness, the little girl held the tiny ball of gray and white fur up for her examination. "See? What shall I call her?"

"Ah . . . *chooo!*"

"Are you coming down with the sniffles?"

Camilla's eyes watered. "It's the kitten. I always sneeze around cats. I get this awful tickle in my nose. Dorinda, she's very pretty and sweet and I wish I could hold her, but I'm afraid I'd better leave before I sneeze the house down around our ears. Ah . . . *choo*."

"Tickles!" Dorinda laughed. "I'll call her Tickles."

At that moment another knock sounded at the door.

"For someone who isn't allowed visitors, you seem to have a good many," Camilla whispered in dismay.

"Jared?" The little girl called eagerly, running to the door.

"Philip," came the deep, unnerving reply.

Camilla and Dorinda exchanged shocked glances. For a moment there was horrible silence, then, at a frantic gesture from Camilla, the child found her voice.

"What—what is it?" she gasped.

"I would like a few words with you."

"J-just a moment, if you please."

Camilla found herself huddled in the wardrobe once more, this time clutching both the walking stick and the basket with the sleeping kitten. *How did I get myself into this pickle?* she wondered through the thrumming of her heart. It was too absurd for words. As she stood there, her ankle beginning to ache, her eyes watering, she wondered if she was cursed with ill luck for the rest of her life. A ferocious tickling feathered her nose and seemed to fan into her throat as Dorinda opened the bedroom door and admitted the Earl. Camilla could do nothing but clutch the basket tight in her arms and close her burning eyes.

She heard the Earl's footsteps cross the room and halt. She guessed him to be a few feet short of the bed, and could picture him standing there, tall and dark, with Dorinda gazing nervously up at him.

She fought against the torturous urge to sneeze.

"There is something more I have to say to you, Dorinda." The Earl's deep, cool voice carried quite clearly through the door. "You may sit down, you know." Camilla heard the rueful note enter his voice as he added, "I shan't eat you, my girl. Sit down and stop looking so terrified. Surely you don't think me as evil as all that?"

"I beg your pardon," Dorinda squeaked out. "What was it you wished to say to me?"

Listening inside the wardrobe, Camilla heard the faint weariness beneath his quiet words. "It occurred to me that you might not understand all of my reasons for demanding proper behavior from you. I feel it necessary to explain. All of this—your punishment, the rules I lay out, the decorum demanded by your governess—they are entirely for your own benefit, Dorinda, not mine. I wish I could make you see that." He paused. "What was that sound?"

Camilla's eyes flew open as the kitten mewed. In her arms, the previously sleeping creature was stirring alarmingly within its basket. *Oh no you don't. Stay still!* she silently implored. The kitten was stretching, its eyes opening. As she watched, aghast, it lifted its head to stare up at her with iridescent unblinking eyes. *Don't move. Keep quiet,* she mentally instructed. As a tiny pink tongue wrapped itself around her fingers, she gasped back a sneeze.

"I didn't hear anything," Dorinda said.

After what seemed like an interminable silence, the Earl continued in his cool, calm manner. "Do you want to grow up to be a respectable young lady, to be invited to parties and balls, to picnics and drives in the park?"

"I'd much rather travel to Egypt and ride on a camel. And see the mummies. There's a book in your library with the funniest pictures in it—"

"Dorinda, you won't travel anywhere if you don't learn proper conduct first." He cut her off sharply. "You won't leave the boundaries of Westcott Park until you're as old as Great-aunt Lucretia unless I am assured that you won't be a disgrace to yourself—and to me," he added roughly. "For a start, you'd best listen to your governess and obey her. Pay attention to your lessons. Above all, you must behave with decorum. And then, when you grow up, you will be a very happy and sought-after young lady," he finished.

"Like Marguerite?"

A heavy silence followed the question. "Marguerite," said Philip carefully, "did not follow the rules of society. I do not wish you to follow in her footsteps."

"You're afraid I'll die like her if I—"

"You will not speak of her, if you please."

"Yes, Philip, but—"

"That is all I have to say, Dorinda."

Camilla felt the sneeze coming. She couldn't hold back a moment longer. She wrinkled her nose, she scrunched up her face. No use . . . *Ah* . . .

"I am sure," the Earl was saying smoothly, "that you are sorry for your most improper treatment of Gertie and will write her an appropriate letter of—"

"Choo!"

"I didn't hear anything!" Dorinda squealed.

Philip flung open the wardrobe door.

Staring inside, beyond the rainbowed assortment of frilly gowns and accessories, he found himself facing Miss Smith. But the Miss Smith he saw today looked considerably different from the filthy creature he had encountered last night. Gone was the dirt on her face and the straggly hair, gone too were the shapeless rags covered in mud. The woman who peered out at him now was a tall, copper-haired beauty wearing a modest gray dress and a flushed countenance.

Miss Smith looked guilty as a thief. But she also looked incredibly fetching. Even through the dimness of the wardrobe he could observe the way her neat gown accentuated her comely figure. Her hair, long and dark as bronze, fell in soft, luxuriant waves around a surprisingly lovely, finely sculpted face. If he had encountered her elsewhere he wouldn't have recognized her.

She had a walking stick tucked under one arm, and clutched in her other was a kitten in a basket. The walking stick, he noted wryly, looked remarkably familiar.

"I can explain," she said in a harried tone of voice— and sneezed again.

Philip glowered at her. Stretching out a powerfully muscled arm, he removed the basket from her and handed her his handkerchief in its stead.

"Do come out of the wardrobe, Miss Smith," he drawled.

Gratefully, Camilla obeyed this request.

"Th-thank you, your lordship."

She smiled tentatively at him. He was managing to appear coolly composed and even stern, but she saw that beneath his nonchalant demeanor he was every bit as startled to discover her in his sister's wardrobe as she was to have been discovered. And though he was making every effort to appear angrily forbidding, the kitten had now stretched its tiny paw outside the basket and was pressing it against the Earl's broad chest.

He glanced down at the little bundle of fur and scowled.

Dorinda gave out a broken sob.

"Don't hurt my kitten!" she pleaded.

Camilla crossed the room to her, leaning upon the walking stick. "Now, Dorinda, don't be a ninny. No one is going to hurt your kitten," she soothed.

The Earl's keen gaze fastened on the walking stick. "Pray make use of whichever of my belongings may suit you, Miss Smith," he invited dryly.

Camilla sneezed again. "You're being sarcastic, aren't

you, my lord? Well, I suppose I deserve it, but I only
borrowed your walking stick for a short while—so that I
could visit Dorinda."

A distinct glint entered his gray eyes. His glance
swerved from Camilla's fine-boned face to that of the
little girl staring up at him in terror.

"Ah, yes. Dorinda. Which of you vixens would care to
offer an explanation for this vastly interesting situation?"

"Miss Smith is my friend," Dorinda burst out, unable
to control her agitation a moment longer. "She came to
visit me—that's all! And she's the nicest friend I have!
You have to let me see her! And you have to let me keep
Tickles!" She snatched the kitten from the basket and
clutched it to her heart, a mulish expression tightening
her mouth. "I won't let you take her away, I won't!"

"Dearest, your brother has no intention of taking your
kitten away!" Camilla knelt down beside the child, bal-
ancing rather precariously upon her good foot. She
smiled coaxingly into the defiant little face. "He's delighted you have a little companion to take care of, and
I'm sure he is confident you can teach Tickles very good
manners so that she will be a welcome addition to the
household. Isn't that so, your lordship?"

The Earl glanced from one questioning, hopeful face
to the other, and responded dryly: "If Miss Smith says it,
it must be correct."

"You mean . . . I can keep her?" Dorinda breathed
in disbelief.

"You may keep her, providing you teach her, er, good
manners." He took Camilla's arm and raised her to her
feet, seeing that she was teetering rather precariously.
The kitten, sensing triumph, began to meow as she tried
to climb up Dorinda's shoulder.

"If you wish to teach Tickles good manners, Dorinda,"

Camilla said quickly, aware of the heat of the Earl's strong hand upon her arm, "you must set a good example. A fine way to begin would be by thanking your brother for the favor he has granted you."

Dorinda's face lit with a beatific smile. "Oh yes. *Thank* you, Philip, thank you so very much. I promise Tickles will be a very good cat, the best cat in all of England!"

"I expect nothing less." His eyes rested upon the little girl for a moment, and his expression softened. Then he shifted his glance to Camilla, and the cool look returned to his face. "Now," said Philip, "I shall escort Miss Smith back to her room. I suggest you ring for some cream for your pet, Dorinda. And maybe," he added thoughtfully, "some bread to soak in the cream—and then you may feed it to her in small pieces. I seem to recall James and I doing something similar in ancient times when we were young."

"You did?" Dorinda gaped at him. "You had a kitten?"

"As many as four at once." He grinned suddenly, his face lighting. "Ask James to tell you about the morning we spent five hours getting them down from the apple tree behind Eden Copse."

"Oooh, what happened?"

For a moment he seemed about to launch into the tale, then he stopped suddenly, a shuttered expression coming over his face. "It's better if you don't know," he replied curtly. "It certainly won't serve you as a good example of proper behavior."

Dorinda looked disappointed, and as if she were about to say exactly what she thought of proper behavior. Camilla interjected quickly: "Now, young lady, you have skirted the rules of your punishment enough for one day. Your brother has been exceedingly generous. But I'm a trifle tired, and I must leave you and Tickles to enjoy each other's company."

She flashed Dorinda an encouraging smile, and began to limp toward the door with the aid of the walking stick. The Earl frowned after her.

"You're supposed to be off that foot, Miss Smith," he murmured, and before she realized it he had tossed the walking stick aside and swept her easily into his arms.

Camilla managed to protest that it was hardly necessary, but she couldn't help admit the burst of pleasure that rushed through her as she was held quite helplessly in the Earl's strong arms. Ignoring her protest, and the echo of Dorinda's giggles, he bore her from the room and down the series of corridors that led back to her own quarters. She stole a glance at his face. Unruffled, that was how he looked, she thought, as though it was nothing remarkable to carry a woman in his arms, as if she weighed no more than Dorinda's kitten.

She was struck again by how magnetically handsome he was, by the firm, autocratic line of his nose, the stubborn set of his jaw, the glinting intelligence and cynicism gleaming out of those hard gray eyes. He exuded a kind of cool, hard charm—irresistible, she imagined, in the drawing room . . . and in the bedroom. For he was a creature of the flesh, a man of strong passions—she had no doubt about that.

Camilla had had much opportunity to study men while toiling in the tavern, and she instinctively knew the look of a man who was practiced in the art of love—not boors like some of the drunken oafs who awkwardly fondled and drooled over the serving wenches—but those experienced, confident men who knew how to seduce with a lift of the eyebrow, a slight, knowing smile. The Earl of Westcott had a firm, sensuous mouth, she observed, fascinated. And an aura of virility about him that was as explosive as dynamite. She, who had never received attention from any of the men, who had safely woven her way through the tavern in her armor of drab, ill-fitting clothes and tangled hair, found herself wondering what it would be like to have such a man look at her the way she had seen them look at other women. The way this man, the Earl of Westcott, undoubtedly looked at the woman who was going to be his bride . . .

When he rounded the corridor that led to the main wing of the house, the Earl nearly collided with a tall, slim youth who seemed to be about sixteen years of age, sporting riding clothes and muddy boots.

"Philip! Sorry!" the youth exclaimed, halting his headlong rush in the nick of time. He was a lean-jawed, good-looking boy with the Earl's same dark hair and gray eyes, set upon a youthfully earnest face. His expression contained a mixture of innocence and vulnerability markedly lacking in his elder brother's countenance, but the resemblance was nevertheless strong.

When he saw the girl in his brother's arms his mouth dropped open. "What . . . who . . ."

"Allow me to present Miss Smith," the Earl said with perfect equanimity. "My brother, Jared. He is usually far more articulate."

"I . . . well, you . . . Oh, the wench you struck down in the road!" Jared exclaimed with sudden insight. Then he flushed beet-red. "Beg pardon, miss. But . . . I've heard all about you . . . at least—someone mentioned —I'm terribly sorry about your accident."

"Thank you." Camilla felt the color rushing into her own cheeks. She wished the Earl would set her down. It was mortifying to meet his relations while in this absurd position, being held like a child in his arms.

"My ankle is better now. Kindly set me down and I can walk the rest of the way . . ." she began, but he shook his head at her, looking clearly amused.

"Perhaps you're used to ordering your customers about in that tavern, Miss Smith, but in my house, things go according to my wishes—no one else's."

Camilla resisted the urge to try to struggle free—it would appear even more undignified than her present position, she reflected. In retaliation, she addressed herself to Jared.

"Dorinda is waiting to see you," she told him, and saw his eyes—which had been examining her with great curiosity—brighten.

"Is she, the poor little duck?"

"She's not allowed visitors," the Earl informed him. His arms tightened around Camilla—warningly, she thought, but felt not at all afraid.

"She's counting on you, Jared," she added with an encouraging smile.

She thought she heard the Earl grind his teeth.

Jared threw his brother a wary glance. "Philip, really, Dorrie didn't do anything all that bad. I seem to remember hearing James tell how you kicked *your* tutor once when you were a boy."

Camilla's eyes flew to the Earl's face. *Did you, your lordship? How indecorous of you.* She laughed silently. It struck her, not for the first time, that for a man who claimed such a fervent wish for propriety, the Earl did not appear the ideal role model. He demanded behavior from members of his family that she highly doubted he was capable of attaining himself—no, from her reading of his character he possessed both a quick temper, the knack for taking swift, unexpected action (as evidenced by his carrying her in this absurd way through Westcott

House), and a stubborn streak, all of which he probably shared with the other members of his family. Yet for some reason he seemed determined to stamp out those qualities that made his family—from the little she had seen of it—so interesting.

"This is not about me." The Earl shot Camilla a look that would have terrified a less composed woman. When she calmly gazed back at him, he swung his scowling glance back to his brother.

"Don't feel too sorry for Dorinda," he advised roughly. "No doubt she has had a veritable parade of visitors since her imprisonment began. The child will probably kick her governess again tomorrow simply to ensure for herself the same degree of attention."

At this Jared grinned. The Earl went on silkily, "And that reminds me of something, Jared. A Mr. Wimpnell is coming to call tomorrow. Do you have any idea what it is he wishes to speak to me about?"

The grin faded like a light extinguished from a window. Jared's cheeks emptied of color. "No, sir, none at all," he managed in something of a croak.

Poor Jared. He was a very poor liar. Camilla sensed the Earl recognized the lie as well—Jared obviously knew perfectly well what story would be poured into his elder brother's ears, but was too frightened to admit it. Though unafraid before, she did feel a shiver as she saw the utter coldness enter the Earl's gaze.

"If you should think of anything you'd like to discuss with me before my interview with Mr. Wimpnell, I will be most interested."

Jared swallowed hard. "Discuss with you? No, certainly not. I don't know anything about it. Uh, I'd better look in on Dorinda. A pleasure, Miss . . . uh, Smith."

He hurried away down the hall, disappearing around a

corner where a portrait of some austere ancestor frowned down upon all who passed. The Earl continued in silence until he reached the Blue Room. He set Camilla down upon the settee, that same remote coldness still glinting in his eyes.

No wonder Jared was too afraid to confide in him, though Camilla guessed things would go far better for him if he did. This family certainly needed a bit of patching up.

She tried to stem her interfering instincts. She'd lost numerous positions because she'd felt she knew best how to manage things, though her employers had not seen the matter the same way. The fact that her ideas were superior to theirs hadn't mattered—they had resented her "putting herself forward into things that were none of her concern."

This family, she told herself, was also none of her concern. But she couldn't help feeling that she could help them in some way.

While the Earl had carried her down the corridors, Camilla had been thinking back on all that had occurred today, including the conversations she had overheard in the wardrobe. Several things in particular stuck in her mind. She wanted desperately to ask the Earl about "Marguerite." Who was she—and why didn't the Earl want Dorinda to speak of her? And what mischief was this Mr. Wimpnell going to report about Jared? Curiosity burned within her, but she refrained from voicing her questions. It was none of her business, after all. Still, she thought, as she eased herself back onto the settee cushions, there was something she had to discuss with the Earl that was even more important. Despite her annoyance with his high-handed behavior in the corridor, she had to tell him something and make him truly listen.

"Before you go," she said quickly, reaching out to touch the edge of the Earl's riding coat sleeve, "may I ask something of you?"

Here it comes, Philip thought. *This minx is going to prove now that she is really very common after all—she is going to try to extort money from me with promises not to make a scandal of the accident if I line her pockets. Well, she will have a rude awakening if she thinks me a pigeon to be easily plucked.* He had expected as much from her, despite the innocent glow of her face and the vibrant luminosity of her eyes, and he had been surprised only that she had waited so long before playing her ace.

He was foolish, he realized, to have let her witness any of his dealings with Dorinda or Jared. The gossip might injure them, and that was the last thing he would want. Damn his own impulsiveness in bringing her into the main house. He should have thought this through more carefully before saddling himself with someone who would try to make trouble.

Not that he couldn't easily handle her—but he hated to take time off from the matters requiring his attention to rid himself of an impudent, ungrateful little baggage . . .

"Go ahead." Dangerous quiet rang in his voice, like the sound of steel beneath a velvet scabbard as he waited for the copper-haired girl to speak.

"It's about Dorinda." Camilla, seated upon the settee, plucked artlessly at the skirt of her gown. She looked up into his eyes with earnest straightforwardness, and saw his expression sharpen. "You see, she is really quite frightened."

His brows lifted. "You're impertinent, Miss Smith. Do you really think the child has reason to fear me?"

"Of course not!" She shook her head and went on, "It's not you, your lordship—it's Gertie. That governess of hers has been telling her falsehoods, threatening her that you would send her to a workhouse if she doesn't behave. And—"

"*What* did you say?"

Philip sat down abruptly beside her and grasped her arm.

Camilla nodded. "You heard me correctly, my lord."

"Continue," he ordered, unaware of how tightly his fingers were digging into her flesh.

"It is just as I said. Gertie threatened to have the child sent to a workhouse." Camilla felt a rush of relief as she saw the shock transform his face. She had *known* he cared for Dorinda, far more than he let on. If it was so obvious to her, why couldn't his own family recognize it? "Dorinda has been terrified of her"—she paused—"and of you because of Gertie's claims. I thought you ought to know about it."

He sat silent. He stared at her as if he was weighing every word she said against everything he knew of the governess he'd hired.

"You're absolutely certain of this, Miss Smith?"

Camilla replied simply, "It is not a matter about which I would lie, sir. Dorinda told me herself. I know when someone is telling me a Banbury tale, your lordship, and I can assure you, Dorinda was not. Her fear was real."

Philip rose with a curse and paced across the room. He returned swiftly and stared into the face of the woman whose green eyes were fixed upon him with such unwavering earnestness.

"I am greatly in your debt," he managed to say, keeping control with effort over the fury pounding through him. "I assure you, Miss Smith, that this matter will be dealt with."

"Oh yes. I'm sure it will be. I *knew* you would be appalled," she couldn't resist adding. As his brows drew together in a puzzled way she explained, "I understand perfectly how it could happen—a man in your position . . . you must be so busy and . . . and there are so many demands placed upon your time and energy. It isn't possible for you to know the character and methods of every person in your employ . . ."

He said ruefully, "Miss Smith, your excuses wound me far more than if you were to criticize me. Dorinda is my responsibility, and the hiring of a decent governess is very much my duty. I have been negligent, perhaps in more ways than one. But no more. Truly, ma'am, I am in your debt."

She blushed. "Not at all. I simply felt you had to know."

His gaze lingered on her face a moment, noting the full, soft lips, the feminine curve of her chin, the brilliant dark-lashed eyes, which seemed to glisten in the lamplit room. The maid had drawn the curtains against the dusk and the room was now softly illuminated, casting a burnished sheen to Miss Smith's cascading curls. Weed? Why in hell had anyone ever called her Weed?

Philip underwent an emotion he didn't usually feel. He knew a sudden burst of pity for the girl sitting before him. From the little she had told him, it was apparent that her life had not been easy. She seemed to be a young woman of high intelligence and excellent character. Her lot in life was unfortunate for one so uncommon. Perhaps there was a position for her in the household, he reflected, one she would prefer over slaving as a tavern wench. After all, he was now in need of a new governess for Dorinda . . .

But he didn't want to jump into anything too quickly.

What did he actually know about this girl other than what his own instincts told him? He said slowly, "Your ankle is healing reasonably well? Perhaps you would feel well enough to join us for dinner tonight?"

"Us?"

"My family."

Camilla swallowed hard. "That is not necessary, your lordship," she murmured. "Thank you, but I could hardly . . ."

"We dine at seven. Mrs. Wyeth will see that you have all that you need. Including a walking stick more appropriate for a lady. Until later, Miss Smith."

He actually smiled at her then, a quick, electrifying smile that made her heart flutter like maddened butterflies in her chest.

Without another word he strode from the room with the ease of a man accustomed to making all arrangements and having them unfailingly carried out. Camilla stared after him in dismay—but her feelings of uncertainty warred with a flurried excitement.

How will I know which fork to use, and which spoon? I'll surely spill soup on my lap.

But above all her anxiety she was really wondering, *Why did the Earl invite me? It is the strangest thing I can ever imagine.*

Maybe she should say she was too tired to go, or that her ankle was worse. Maybe she should have a tray brought to her room—and simply imagine them all downstairs . . . what they were doing, saying, eating, wearing?

She mentally upbraided herself. When life offered you a chance, you ought to take it. This might be the first and last time she was ever invited to sit at an Earl's table. But, by heaven, she vowed to herself, pressing her hands to her hot cheeks, she would do it with her head held high and enjoy every moment of it.

Even if she couldn't eat a bite.

It was all highly irregular.

The news that the Earl had invited the mysterious "Miss Smith" to dinner sent shock waves throughout every corner and corridor of Westcott Park, from the servants' quarters to the family's private chambers. Everyone agreed it was odd enough of the Earl to have brought the chit he'd run down into his own home—and then to ensconce her in the Blue Room—without going so far as to include her in a family gathering. "Though, in truth," Mrs. Wyeth remarked to Cook with the superiority of her close and longtime relationship with her master, "taking her in was not so odd when you remember that his lordship was forever dragging in strays when he was a boy." Beneath his reckless ways and his inherent Audley wildness, she told Cook with a fond shake of her head, he had a rare soft heart. But the announcement that Miss Smith would be joining the family for dinner that evening stunned even her.

And Durgess went so far as to predict gloomily that he feared for his lordship's welfare, since surely the young miss was up to no good and would bring down trouble on all of their heads, taking advantage of the Earl's most unwise and excessive kindness.

Privately, neither Jared nor James nor Charlotte could make sense of it either. Making amends for injuries caused by the accident was one thing, but this was quite another. Either the girl was a very clever schemer, or Philip must be up to something. Not a dalliance with the chit, of course, for if it was an illicit affair his lordship sought with her he would scarcely flaunt her before his family.

"I've long ago given up trying to understand Philip," James said as he stood behind his wife's dressing table chair, struggling with his cravat. "But count on it—he has his reasons. Philip always has his reasons."

Charlotte glanced at his scowling face in the mirror, then rose, her turquoise silk skirts rustling. "I don't understand him at all, James. He . . . he frightens me," she confessed. "I know he didn't wish you to marry so young . . . and I know that was only *part* of your troubles with him, but . . ." She raised troubled eyes to his and bit her lip. "I used to think there might be a way to smooth things out between the two of you, but when I'm around Philip I'm too unnerved even to collect my thoughts, so if there is a way, I for one can't think of it. And he despises me for my fear of him," she added quietly. "I know that, too."

"It's not you he despises, love, it's me." James temporarily abandoned the intricacies of his cravat, put his arms around her and sighed. "It's never going to be possible to smooth things out with Philip. I'm trying to accept that. But I confess I miss him . . ." His voice trailed away disconsolately, and Charlotte reached up on tiptoe to kiss his smooth-shaven cheek.

"If he knew about me, he'd hate me even more," she said in a low tone. "Don't try to deny it, James. He'd insist you were indeed foolish to marry me—and oh, James, perhaps he'd be right! Are you sorry you married me? I couldn't blame you if you were!"

"Shh. Don't talk such foolishness." James fervently pressed his lips into the palm of her hand. "You're an angel to put up with me—and with this family. I've never done anything to deserve a woman like you. Charlotte, don't fret. I've told you it . . . it doesn't matter." For a moment his eyes were shadowed with some inner pain that he struggled to suppress. He forced himself to smile at her and hurried on soothingly, "And as for Philip, you have no reason to fear him. Philip would never hurt you. I'm his quarry. Come," he added bracingly, "let's go down to dinner and see what nasty doings my brother has in store."

"Is she really having dinner with you?" Dorinda demanded of Jared when he visited her briefly in her room on his way down to dinner. "Oh, how I wish I could be there! Miss Smith tells the most comical stories!"

"Does she? Well, I warrant she won't tonight. What Philip has in store for her I can't imagine. But it's stranger than strange that he should invite her to dine with us!"

"Why?"

Jared paused in the midst of tossing a ball of yarn for the kitten to catch. "Well, she's not . . . one of the family."

"Neither is Lord Kirby, and he comes to dinner quite often!" Dorinda pointed out.

"That's different!"

"Why?"

"Guests are one thing—serving maids are quite another!"

Dorinda pursed her lips, thinking. Her gray button eyes shone brightly in the cheerful lamplight of the delightful room. "Well, perhaps Philip feels that Miss Smith wouldn't be here in our house if it hadn't been for him running her down. Oh, I heard Mrs. Wyeth telling Gertie all about it," she said knowingly as his mouth dropped open in surprise. Recovering himself, Jared reached out and tousled her dark curls.

Grinning, Dorinda ducked away and smoothed her hair. "Besides," she added in loyal defense of her friend, "Miss Smith's manners are perfectly lovely. There is no reason she cannot be a guest, just like Lord Kirby and Lady Asterley and all those other people who come to dinner. Or"—and here her eyes lit with sudden wild hope—"maybe Philip will fall in love with her and marry her and she can stay here always! I would like that above all else!"

Jared gave a hoot of laughter. "*That* is something that will never come to pass!" he assured her. "It is common knowledge, among everyone but silly little ducklings like you, that Philip is in love with Lady Brittany Deaville. And even if he weren't, he would never, ever marry a serving maid."

Dorinda's face fell. "Who is Lady Brittany Deaville?" she inquired in a tone that hinted strongly of dislike even without knowing a thing about the woman her brother had named.

"She is a very beautiful, very enchanting lady," her brother went on, admiration and appreciation shining in his boyish face. "If I were a few years older, I'd court her myself," he confided with a sheepish grin. "But she can have her pick of men. All of 'em want her."

"Well, if Philip wants her, she'll pick *him,* of course," Dorinda exclaimed, intensely loyal to her brother despite her fear of him. After all, no one was handsomer, stronger, or braver than Philip, Dorinda knew that for a fact—even if he did make her life miserable with his frowns and his rules and his lectures on propriety. "He is so very handsome and smart, you know—and from what I hear he is most sought after by all the mamas in London looking to marry off their daughters! And no doubt he is more agreeable to them than he is to you and me and James."

Jared stared at her, too stunned by this pronouncement to speak for a full minute. When he found his voice again, he managed to demand, "Where on earth did you hear *that,* Dorinda? About all the mamas in London, and that Philip is sought after?"

"Gertie and Mrs. Wyeth," she supplied smugly. "They always think I am not attending and say a great many things I oughtn't hear when they're close by. It is most amusing!"

"Eavesdropping is very bad ton."

"Pooh. Don't scowl at me! You're getting to be as bad as Philip!" she accused him, and bubbled with laughter as he recoiled at the comparison. "I'm beginning to prefer Miss Smith to both of you!" she added, then clasped his hand and squeezed it apologetically. "I'm only funning, you know, Jared. No one is as dear as you. Except Tickles —and Miss Smith. Oh, you will like her so well when you get to know her! Promise you'll come later and tell me all about dinner," she pleaded.

Jared promised, but could not get away before he had suitably petted and admired the kitten. At last he sauntered from the room, his hands stuffed in his pockets.

Good luck, Miss Smith, he thought as he ran lightly

down the stairs and headed for the drawing room, thinking of the impishly pretty young woman he had met earlier that day in the corridor.

"I hope Philip does not intend to eat *you* for dinner instead of the delicacies Cook has prepared."

Downstairs in the drawing room, the Earl was pouring brandy for Lord Kirby, who had also been invited for dinner that evening.

"I'm intrigued—this young lady you struck down in the road sounds like she is quite out of the ordinary. It must have taken courage for her to report the governess's conduct to you." Alistair Kirby studied his longtime friend. "Even most of our acquaintances would quail at the thought of broaching something so unpleasant to the wicked Earl of Westcott."

Philip's eyes lit with amusement. "When you have met her you'll see that it would take far more than the likes of me to make Miss Smith quail. She is quite a self-possessed young woman."

"I caught a glimpse of her at the window when I rode up today." Kirby seated himself upon the gold brocade sofa, stretching out his long legs. "You don't mind that James told me about the accident?"

Philip kicked the embers of the fire, stirring up a hearty blaze. Beyond the emerald velvet draperies of the drawing room the October wind howled as if it were already November, but the salon was cozily warm and inviting. "Not at all," he replied, turning his back to the flames. "Since when have we kept secrets from each other? Our friendship is too longstanding for that. Even though we haven't seen as much of each other recently."

"Except for the masquerade last night. And even that was brief. Lady Brittany, alas, claimed most of my attention," Kirby murmured, and Philip caught the glimpse of mischief in his light blue eyes.

Philip's lips twitched at this subtle reminder that it was Kirby who had won the honor of dancing the boulanger, the quadrille, and the waltz with Brittany—while he himself had been virtually ignored by the lady throughout the evening. Though he was still irritated by the memories of that disastrous party, he couldn't help grinning at his old friend as he dropped into the wing chair opposite him, their familiar positions whenever they used this room. On the wall above Kirby's head gold-framed portraits of each of Philip's parents gazed back encouragingly upon him. His father, stout, gray, and handsome was smiling his genial smile, but the artist had captured the spark of devilment in his eyes, which seemed to mock: "Come on, boy. Never let it be said an Audley let another man get the better of him where a woman is concerned!" His mother, the dark, impetuous, laughing beauty who had had all of London swooning when she made her come-out, seemed to gently tease him as well. And Kirby, well, Kirby would certainly press his advantage with Brittany at every opportunity, and be certain to inform Philip of his progress each step of the way.

Philip fixed him with a steely smile. "Enjoy the lady's company while you may," he rejoined easily, and tossed off the rest of his brandy with careless grace. "I have vowed to win her, my friend—and so I shall. The lady and I will be betrothed by Christmas."

Kirby set his glass down on the small ivory table so forcefully that some of the brandy nearly splashed out. "You have vowed . . . ? Egad, you sound confident. To whom have you made this vow?"

Philip grinned at his friend's confusion. "To March-field," he said coolly. "He challenged me to a wager last

night while we were gaming. He put up ten thousand
pounds while I staked both my matched grays and the
new bays I bought at Newmarket last week."

"You made a . . . a wager over Brittany?" Kirby's
thin mouth drooped open in stunned dismay. Then a hint
of anger entered his blue eyes. "Philip, you know as well
as anyone it's very bad ton to make wagers over a lady. I
find it astonishing that you would bandy Brittany's name
about in a common bet . . ."

"Don't you think I cursed myself—and Marchfield—
when it was done?" Philip shot back. He stood up to his
full height, and took a furious turn about the room.
"Damn it, I'm none too happy about it either. But
Marchfield goaded me beyond endurance, Alistair. And I
was foxed, to boot. I was so angry with Brittany over the
way she evaded me all evening—treating me like a green
schoolboy whose suit she would not even consider—that I
let my temper get the better of me. Anyway, it's done,"
he finished curtly.

"So you mean to marry her only so that you may come
out the victor in this wager?" Kirby demanded, his aristocratic mouth twisting with disapproval.

"Don't be an ass." Philip threw him a scornful glance.
"I've meant to win her all along. Now I simply have more
reason to press my suit. To both defeat Marchfield and
wed the fair Brittany will be a very sweet conclusion to
this entire affair."

Kirby picked up his brandy goblet once more and regarded Philip over the rim. "You assume no other competition but Marchfield, my dear friend. Perhaps neither
of you shall win the lady's hand," he murmured coolly.

Now it was Philip's turn to stare. A hard light entered
his eyes, yet there was shrewd humor in their gray depths
as his gaze met and held that of the tall, fair-haired man

lounging opposite him. "I have never feared a competition with you, my dear friend." He echoed Kirby's salutation with faint mockery. "I acknowledge your charm with the ladies—a great many ladies—but when it comes to the fair Brittany, I am confident of a happy outcome—happy for me," he added with a wicked smile.

There was one tense moment, when the only sound was the ticking of the mantel clock, and then suddenly, Kirby chuckled, shaking his head. "You sound exactly the same as when you predicted you could handle my father's bays unassisted in his curricle at the age of nine!" he exclaimed. "And, by Jove, you did it, right under our parents' noses. I thought your mother would swoon and need smelling salts when they tried to bolt with you, but she merely cheered you on—and kissed you when you brought them back, sedate as a pair of dowagers at tea!"

"Winning Brittany will be far easier than subduing those bays," Philip predicted with a calm grin.

Kirby laughed again. "Well, we shall see, won't we?"

Philip poured them each another brandy while they waited for the rest of the company to assemble. It was good to be with Kirby, to relax with the bantering friend who had been his close companion throughout childhood. He and James had been used to thinking of themselves almost as brothers with the Kirby twins, Alistair and Maxwell. The four boys had ridden and swum and climbed trees together all their young lives, and as they'd grown in years and size, so had their pranks and escapades similarly expanded. Of course the Kirbys couldn't match the Audleys when it came to sheer daring and foolhardy stunts like climbing onto the roof of Westcott House and trying to walk along it without falling—an incident that had resulted in ten-year-old James's breaking several bones in his arm and leg and being bedridden for a month. But what the Kirbys lacked in imaginative physical daring they more than compensated for with their expertise at concocting some of the boys' more mischievous pranks—such as filling the sugar bowl with salt before one of Lady Kirby's afternoon card parties and causing all of the guests to cough, gasp, and choke over their tea. Roundly cuffed and banished to their separate rooms for that escapade, the boys had snuck out of their houses at midnight against all parental knowledge and met in their secret hiding place behind Eden Copse. There in the Pirate's Cove they had pledged their friendship and unity—a four-way boyhood pledge that had endured for many years.

The only thing that had broken it was the untimely death of Alistair's twin, Maxwell, years later—a tragic death caused by the same horrible accident that had claimed the life of Philip and James's fifteen-year-old sister, Marguerite.

Since that night, when the bright, daring spirit that was Marguerite's had been snuffed out so horribly, Philip had tried his damnedest to change his own ways. He felt deep in his soul that it was the cursed Audley recklessness that had killed Marguerite and Maxwell. With an overpowering sense of despair, he had come to believe that unless his family's weakness for rash behavior could be expunged, they were all doomed to tragedy and unhappiness. He held himself, as well as James and Alistair, to blame for the accident. If he had been home, Marguerite would never have been involved in the escapade. She would never have had the chance to set foot outside the house that night, would never have been anywhere near that damned cottage.

Alistair Kirby had been devastated by his twin's death, and for some time after had traveled in Europe. When he returned, there was a noticeable change in his relationship with the Audley brothers, as well as in their own relationship with one another. Philip and James had become estranged, and the days of pranks and boyish adventures were gone forever. Manhood had come to all of them, and they were all soberer individuals for the tragedy that had left them each bereft. But the friendship remained, buried beneath the sorrow. True, it was a more reserved, mature friendship, and they saw each other less often, but the bonds were still there, and the comfortable companionship shared among Alistair, James, and Philip still existed—indeed, Philip guessed, the bonds would always exist. Nevertheless, he still found it difficult to be alone in a room with both James and Alistair—it always seemed as if someone was missing—as someone was: Maxwell, and of course, most hauntingly of all, Marguerite.

This evening would be easier, Philip acknowledged as he took a sip of his brandy and settled his shoulders back in his chair. There would be diversions. Jared would be present, and so would Charlotte—and Miss Smith.

When James and Charlotte entered the drawing room several moments later, he rose to his feet and greeted them perfunctorily, all the while wondering how that green-eyed ragamuffin with the lively face and pert tongue would fare in the evaluation he planned for her tonight. Much as he wished her well, the skeptical side of his nature warned that she would likely prove unfit to serve as Dorinda's governess. She was well spoken and intelligent, true, remarkably so for her station, but if her education and accomplishments were lacking, and if she could not conduct herself with proper etiquette at dinner, he must dismiss the idea and put out an advertisement for Gertie's replacement instead.

He had already dismissed the overbearing governess immediately after his conversation with Miss Smith. The interview had been brief and icy. He had advised the woman to be gone by morning.

Philip planned to tell Dorinda the news himself after dinner—and to release her from her punishment, as well. Philip could imagine how her little face would light up when he told her, and found himself wishing it was possible to raise Dorinda in a disciplined manner without having her hate him, but he had no idea whatsoever how he could accomplish this. If Miss Smith, whom Dorinda liked, could be of help, he would certainly choose to take advantage of it.

And there was always Brittany, he reflected as he watched the drawing room doors in anticipation of Miss Smith's arrival. Brittany was famous for her elegant deportment and her accomplishments. When they were wed, she would set an outstanding example for Dorinda to follow—and inspire the child to follow in her very enchanting footsteps.

Upstairs in her room, Camilla's hands trembled as she tried to clasp her charm necklace about her throat.

"Let me help you, miss," Kate offered, stepping forward with an eager smile. She had taken to the mysterious young woman whom she'd been assigned to wait on, and couldn't help wanting to do her best for her. Kate had cleaned and polished the gold of Camilla's cherished necklace and now as she fastened the clasp about the girl's neck, the dainty charm in the shape of a lion glittered brightly on its delicate chain.

The necklace was Camilla's only adornment.

Yet, as Camilla surveyed her reflection in the dressing

table mirror, she decided it was lovely in its very simplicity and she wished for nothing else.

Pleasure seeped through her as she gazed at her own image. She had never dreamed of seeing herself look as she did now, in this simple high-necked gown of dull yellow crepe, her hair unclasped, brushed smooth, and rippling in a riot of glowing copper curls down her back and shoulders.

I'm not beautiful, she admitted to herself after a candid, piercing appraisal, *but I'm not exactly an ugly old weed either.* She certainly must look a far cry from the ragged waif his lordship had first seen in Edgewood Lane.

"Are you ready, miss?"

Clutching the pearl-handled walking stick Kate had brought to her along with her gown, she turned from the mirror. "Yes, Kate, I hope so." She grinned nervously. "I also hope his lordship hasn't forgotten that he invited me. I'll certainly feel foolish walking in on them all if he has—or if he's changed his mind."

"Don't you worry about that, miss. His lordship never forgets anything. And he rarely changes his mind. He always knows just what he is up to, even if none of the rest of us do." The girl chuckled.

With these words echoing in her ears, Camilla headed toward the door before her courage could desert her. When she opened it, she gave a little half-gasp, for in the corridor outside a husky liveried footman in green velvet hovered at full attention.

"His lordship requested that I assist you downstairs, ma'am."

For a moment she didn't fully understand, then his meaning dawned on her. "You mean . . . carry me?"

At his nod, Camilla shook her head. "Thank you, but no. I am perfectly able to walk."

"But his lordship—"

"—has nothing to say in the matter," she said crisply. She gave him her most haughty, Miss Motterlyish nod of dismissal. "That will be all."

She waited until he had reluctantly turned and marched off before continuing her slow limp toward the stairs. If only this ankle weren't sprained! It galled her to be treated like an invalid, and this carrying-about business had gone on quite enough. Camilla had always thought it would be heavenly to be pampered and waited on, but this coddling was going too far. She was accustomed to being active, to doing things for herself, and the thought of being carried down to his lordship like a sack of coal filled her with distaste. She would descend the stairs under her own power and do it as gracefully as she could, or else she would merely slide down the banister and hop off at the end—landing neatly on her good foot, of course. For one instant at the head of the winding beautifully polished stair she was tempted to do just that, but her better judgment forbade it. The antics she'd perfected at the workhouse had no place at Westcott Park.

As she started down the proper way, however, she heard a howling scream from the direction of the nursery wing. She froze in alarm.

That was Dorinda's scream, she was sure of it.

She hurried toward the sound as quickly as she could, half-running, regardless of the pain shooting through her ankle.

Downstairs, in the meantime, Philip was headed to his library to unearth a book Alistair Kirby had inquired about, when he saw his footman, Claud, passing through the corridor.

"Where's Miss Smith?" Philip demanded. "I requested that you assist her down the stairs."

"Yes, your lordship." Claud's knees knocked together as he stiffened to attention before his master's sharp glance. "I tried, but the lady refused, your lordship."

"Of all the stubborn little fools." On an impulse, Philip turned on his heel and sprinted past the lackey and up the staircase. Perhaps Miss Smith was too headstrong and willful to make a suitable governess, after all, he thought, exasperated. She couldn't even discern what was best for herself, so how could she be expected to teach such matters to Dorinda?

It irked him that she had crossed him. No one in this house did that—except Dorinda upon occasion and he always made sure his little sister knew how fruitless and ill-advised that was. Perhaps Miss Smith, while she was under his roof, needed to learn the same lesson.

Camilla was out of breath by the time she reached the nursery wing. She heard gasps, the pounding of feet, furious screams, and high-pitched shouts as she reached the head of the corridor. Rounding it, she froze for a moment in shock. What she saw made her grit her teeth and tighten her spine, and she started forward at once.

"Miss Smith—help!" Dorinda cried as she clung to Gertie's billowing black skirts. The governess was working her way furiously along the corridor, trying with every step to swat the little girl away by swinging her carpetbag at the child.

"She . . . has Tickles. She's taking her away! Help me, Miss Smith, help me!"

Red-faced and huffing, Gertie threw a wild-eyed glance at the advancing Camilla. One arm was hidden beneath her bulky cloak, while with the other she batted again at Dorinda, who ducked, but held fast.

"Stop that at once, Gertie," Camilla commanded. "You don't want to hurt the child."

The desperate, cornered expression worn by a captured animal had come over the governess's flabby countenance. In the duskily lit corridor, she faced Camilla with something like a snarl.

"The brat is making up tales again," she declared, and bending over with difficulty tried to swing the carpetbag at Dorinda once more. She straightened defensively as Camilla came abreast of her and grasped her firmly by the arm. "Ah, take your hand off me, and stand away," Gertie screeched. "This don't concern the likes of you. I won't tolerate any more nonsense. I haven't seen her dratted kitten—what would I want with a disgusting animal? His lordship dismissed me and I'm leaving, that's all. But I'll kick this brat if she won't let go . . ."

"You'll do no such thing." Camilla heard a faint mewing sound from beneath the folds of the cloak and instantly she yanked it off the older woman to find Tickles squashed into a basket over her arm.

"I'll take that," she said, and snatched the basket before Gertie could stop her. Quickly, she handed it down to Dorinda and said with an urgent note in her voice, "Run along with Tickles now, Dorinda. Everything is all right. I'll see Gertie on her way . . ."

"Oh no, you won't! I'll go when I'm ready! This brat has cost me too much as is, without me giving her a bit back!"

Camilla had already realized that Gertie's dismissal had driven the governess far past the edge of reason, and that she had lost whatever sense of scruples she once possessed. Now, in horror, she saw the woman suddenly grab up a brass candlestick from the little claw-footed table set in the corridor and raise it over her head, and she knew she had to protect Dorinda at any cost. Gertie, huffing like a teakettle too long over the fire, advanced upon the child with clear intent to do her harm.

"Dorinda, run!" Camilla flung herself in front of the child, barring Gertie's path.

"Put that down at once!" she ordered, holding the walking stick up as a shield.

The governess shrieked, "Get out of my way and leave the child to me!" Her face shone with sweat, and her voice thickened. "Well, I warned you . . ."

Camilla ducked as Gertie swung the candlestick and the heavy brass whistled past her head. Off balance, Gertie stumbled and Camilla used the opportunity to shove the woman backward. Then everything seemed to happen at once. Gertie sprawled to the floor, and Dorinda screamed. At the same time Camilla heard, incredibly, the Earl's voice command:

"Get back, Miss Smith. I'll handle this."

She glanced up to find him towering beside her, staring down at the cowering Gertie.

Camillia was never so glad to see anyone in her life— until she saw the expression on his face.

8

Fear choked her. For a moment she feared the Earl was going to commit murder.

"Your lordship, no one was hurt . . ." Camilla cried, putting a restraining hand on his arm, but he paid no attention to her.

Taut with fury, he wrenched the candlestick from Gertie and held it between long, white-knuckled fingers. An instant later he hurled it down the hall. As it crashed into the paneled wall, the noise reverberated through every corner of the corridor.

"Get up, you," the Earl bit off in a tone so like a growl that Camilla flinched.

Too frightened to move, Gertie cowered on the floor looking up at him, her pudgy face the color of ashes. "I said *get up*!"

Then there was even more commotion as the corridor suddenly filled with people: Jared, James, Charlotte, and Lord Kirby, as well as Mrs. Wyeth trembling like a leaf.

"Philip, what's happened?" James ran forward as Philip yanked the sniveling governess to her feet.

Camilla turned in time to see Charlotte kneel down and enfold the tearful Dorinda in her arms.

"One of the maids heard screams from the nursery wing and reported to Durgess," James rushed on. "I happened to overhear. My God, what is all this?"

The Earl had a firm grip on Gertie's arm as she began to protest that she hadn't done anything, that it was all a mistake, and she had never any intention of taking the kitten. For all of his fury, he seemed to have himself well in hand now. Only the muscle throbbing in his jaw indicated the extreme emotion pounding through him. He ignored Gertie's pleas and turned to Jared, firing off his words like bullets.

"Take Miss Fitzsimmons to the stables. I want her off this property at once. Tell Peters to drive her into the village and stay with her there until the public coach comes through. He is to put her on it and remind her that if she ever sets foot within a hundred miles of Westcott Park again, I will personally turn her over to the constable and let him lock her up for the rest of her days, as she deserves."

He turned back to Gertie, his expression glacial. "And as I doubt you will find a position requiring the care of children in the future—since you will have no recommendation to show to any respectable family—I suggest you go back to your home in Yorkshire and spend the remainder of your days there. I will make inquiries from time to time, and if ever I hear that you have left your family in Yorkshire or that you have gone to work for another household where children are present, you will live to regret it. That is my personal vow to you," he added. "Do you understand?"

She stopped sniveling long enough to nod at him and whispered thickly, her eyes bleary with tears, "Yes, your lordship. You're very good, your lordship. I never meant any harm, your lordship . . ."

"Jared, get her out of my sight."

Hastily, Jared led the governess away.

It was Philip who took charge of everything then, and ordered everyone, including Dorinda, downstairs to the dining room.

"You may join us for supper," he told her, "and explain exactly what has happened. I only saw the last part of it."

"It was Miss Smith who saved me—and Tickles." Her tears forgotten already at the mention of supper with her family, downstairs as if she were a real young lady, Dorinda sprang up from the haven of Charlotte's arms and bounded toward her brother. "If it hadn't been for Miss Smith, Gertie would have stolen Tickles. She was so brave!"

"I know," said Philip. "I saw her."

His gaze sought Camilla's in the corridor and rested upon her face. Camilla felt her heart lift as she saw the warmth and admiration in his eyes.

"I didn't really do anything." Suddenly she felt shy. "Fortunately you came when you did and all was well."

He took her hands in his. His were warm, strong, hearty with life. The intensity he emanated washed over her anew. "We are in your debt. Words cannot express . . . But come, I want to perform proper introductions and this is hardly the place. If you'll allow me, Miss Smith . . ." And without waiting for permission, he once more lifted her in his arms and carried her past the others, who watched in openmouthed bafflement.

Just as they reached the end of the hall, the kitten's fur achieved its inevitable effect upon her, and she sneezed.

"Bless you," the Earl said, and Camilla had the strongest impression that he meant it.

*   *   *

It was a far different dinner from the formal one Camilla had anticipated earlier. Everyone sat around the huge carved mahogany table in the one-hundred-foot-long paneled dining room talking at once. The table was bedecked with china and crystal and flowers, and so much ornate gold flatware that Camilla would have been utterly confused as to which implement to use except that Lady Charlotte, seeing her panic, discreetly set an example for her at the beginning of each course. And how many courses there were—tempting dishes of meat and fish and roasted capons, steaming soups and delectable jellies, kidney pies and sweetmeats, cheeses, fruit and tarts, a feast as magnificent as any Camilla could ever have imagined, delicious and satisfying, and all beautifully presented beneath fluted silver covers.

What was the most remarkable thing about that dinner, though, was not the array of dishes or the number of courses or even the excellence of the food—it was the boisterous mood of the diners. Everyone wanted to know what had occurred in the hallway with Gertie, why she had been dismissed, and then, upon hearing of the threats she had been using to control Dorinda, everyone wanted to congratulate Camilla for having rescued little Dorinda from the clutches of such a monster.

Jared, returning from his mission, banged his fist on the table and said that if he had known the whole, he would have thrown the woman into the lake instead of foisting her off on old Peters. James told Camilla in low tones how grateful he was for her protection of Dorinda, Charlotte smiled at her with a warmth that lit the room, and Lord Kirby after listening quietly to her attempts to minimize her own part in the matter, advised her to accept her accolades without protest, for the Audleys, once united upon a subject, were not likely to be swayed by anyone or anything.

"You are a heroine, pure and simple," he said, smiling. He was even more attractive face-to-face, Camilla realized, for having peered down at him from the window she had not received the full effect of his lanky height, his charmingly cordial manner, his elegant yet kind-featured countenance. His deep-set eyes and his smile were both surprisingly gentle. "On Dorinda's behalf, we all salute you."

She went scarlet as they drank a toast to her health, and then her gaze traveled, as it so often had during the meal, to the Earl. Sitting at the head of the table, he had for once seemed on easy terms with the rest of his family, and Dorinda, placed on his right, had even won a grin from him when she had embarked on a long tale about the grim destiny she hoped would befall Gertie Fitzsimmons, beginning with the public coach losing a wheel and careening off a cliff (of course all of the passengers except Gertie managed to escape), and going on to relate how Gertie would be shot at by highwaymen and pecked at by birds, then rained upon in a ferocious storm, and lost in a boggy, haunted forest.

"And don't forget the honeybees," Camilla added, folding her napkin as she finished the last tiny bite of a delectable boysenberry tart. "While she's in the forest, she will stumble into a hive of honeybees and be stung by hundreds of them for hours as she is chased through the darkened wood."

"And then," James added in a dramatically lowered tone, getting into the spirit of the tale, "she will tumble into a deep, black pit full of snakes that will wind themselves around her neck."

Dorinda turned to Jared, eyes lighting expectantly. "Your turn," she prodded.

"And spiders will crawl into the pit and spin a web around her while she struggles with the snakes," he said gleefully.

She clapped her hands. "Lord Kirby?"

Kirby finished the last of his wine and his eyes twinkled first at Camilla, then at the child. "Naturally," he said, "the Queen of the Spiders will crawl into the pit and bite off her fat, ugly toes, one by one."

Charlotte took up the story. "And when the spiders are finished with her," she said with a theatrical flourish in her soft, pretty voice, "horrid, red-eyed bats will fly down and entwine themselves in her hair."

"And," finished Philip as his little sister turned eagerly toward him, and he saw that with all of these gruesome stories the nightmare of what had passed with Gertie in the hallway was fast fading into an unpleasant but no longer threatening memory, "she will be carried off by the bats to the cave of an evil wizard, who will keep her prisoner for all of her days in a cage filled with rats and lizards and wolves, and each evening at the stroke of midnight all the forest creatures for miles around will hear her pitiful screams."

"Good." Dorinda beamed. Her gray eyes were sparkling nearly as brightly as the candles in the gold chandelier overhead. "And I hope it all comes true."

"Bloodthirsty little ghoul, aren't you?" Camilla gasped, laughing.

The Earl grinned. He had, Camilla noted, a most disarming grin. "We Audleys have a policy of always avenging ourselves threefold for whatever our enemies hand out to us. It all began when Great-great-grandfather Edwin, the fourth Earl of Westcott, hacked off the fingers of the man who tried to steal his lands." Camilla's eyes widened, but he went on matter-of-factly, "And then there was the time Great-grandfather Fergus ran his sword through the highwayman who tried to steal his emerald stickpin and his ruby signet ring. Oh, and my own mother once poured a glass of champagne down the neck of a duchess who dared to say that Mama's wild set of sons must be a sore trial to her."

James and Jared both nodded and chuckled in corroboration of this story, and Camilla found herself laughing appreciatively. Beneath her amusement, she was glad to know that they were a family who stood up for themselves and who, above all, stood together. Sitting here, watching them all at dinner, she had seen the strong resemblance among them, the dark good looks, the quick intelligence and strength behind the charm, the direct manner. Since she was a direct and quick-thinking individual herself she found herself surprisingly in harmony with them, and that had made the time spent over the meal seem to fly by.

Now she felt more intrigued by the Audleys than ever, more curious about why, with so much love obviously among them, with so much family pride and spirit, there was this gulf separating Philip from his younger siblings, this tension, which for a little while, at least, had seemed to lessen.

"We know how to take care of our own," Philip concluded, rising from the table and offering Camilla his arm. "In fact," he said, a gleam in his eyes, as he looked down at her, "Gertie Fitzsimmons is fortunate we live in a so-called civilized day or we might have let Dorinda have a go at her with a sword. You'd have liked that, wouldn't you, Dorry?"

"Ever so much."

"Maybe we should fetch her back," James suggested wickedly, as the others followed Philip and Camilla toward the richly paneled double mahogany doors.

"No, no, this is quite enough," Charlotte exclaimed, tucking her arm through her husband's with a rueful shake of her head. "Let's have no more grisly talk, I beg of you. Miss Smith is surely shocked. Such sentiments, even in jest—and before Dorinda . . . it is . . ."

"Scandalous?" Jared chuckled. "That's us, Charlotte, you should know that by now. To be born an Audley is to be born with a wild streak—there's nothing we can do about it."

At this, Philip turned back from the door and his gaze touched his younger brother's lean, youthful countenance for a moment. His brows were drawn together, his mouth unsmiling. His glance shifted to little Dorinda beside him.

"I hope to God you are wrong about that, Jared."

The convivial mood was broken.

While the others hurried ahead into the gold salon adjoining the library, Camilla found herself suddenly alone in the hall with the Earl and Dorinda.

"You're angry again?" Dorinda asked, shrinking against Camilla's side as her brother's gaze, cold once more, lingered on her.

"Not with you, Dorinda." His voice was surprisingly gentle, holding a resigned, almost sad note. Philip motioned to Kate, waiting at the foot of the stairs to take the little girl up to bed. "Run along now. You need your rest and I wish to speak alone to Miss Smith."

"Oh, please," Dorinda dared to plead, clutching at Camilla's hand. "Can't Miss Smith tuck me in bed and tell me a story? She tells the best stories! I want to hear more about Miss Motterley and that horrid woman in the work-

house. Did you know, Philip, that Miss Smith actually
lived in a workhouse?"

"Yes, Dorinda," the Earl acknowledged. "I did know
that. Do *you* know that my patience with you is running
thin? Stop playing for time and go. Before I lose my temper and then even the redoubtable Miss Smith will be
unable to save you."

But there was a flicker of humor in his eyes as he spoke
the words, and Dorinda grinned shyly up at him before
trotting off with Kate to fetch her kitten, which had been
sleeping by the kitchen fire all through dinner.

"You're quite good with her, your lordship." Camilla
smiled, her hand resting lightly on the walking stick.
"She's a sweet child, and it's plain she adores you."

"She hates me, you mean," he corrected. "Don't try to
bamboozle me, Miss Smith. I know how Dorinda feels."

"She adores you," Camilla repeated firmly. "But she is
petrified of you. At least, she was until today. Now that
Gertie is gone . . ."

"That is what I want to discuss with you." To her surprise, instead of continuing into the gold salon, he took
her arm and guided her into the library instead. He
closed the door, and they were suddenly alone.

When she found herself seated beside him on a sofa of
deep crimson Camilla felt a little breathless. The Earl was
looking at her with interest, even warmth in his eyes. In
his close-fitting coat of blue superfine that accentuated
his wide shoulders and broad chest, with his snow-white
stock impeccably arranged and his smooth raven-black
hair brushed back from his brow, he looked incredibly
handsome. She had no idea what he was going to say to
her, but she had a sudden memory of her dream lover in
her last escapade—when he had come to her on a black
steed and swept her away with him into the starry, wind-

swept night. Only now she saw the Earl of Westcott clearly in her dream—*his* was the face of her magnificent lover whose identity had always been hidden by the shadows. She fought the mad impulse to reach out to the Earl, to throw her arms around him and lift her lips for his kiss . . .

Madness! This wasn't a dream. This was real, and she brought herself out of the clouds and back to the library with a vigorous shake of her head.

"Why are you shaking your head?" The Earl stared at her, brows raised. "Is something wrong?"

"No. Oh no. I beg your pardon." She felt the hot blush stealing up into her cheeks and nervously fingered the charm around her neck.

What she couldn't know was that the warm glow that had lit her eyes when she'd been lost in her dream was still there. The Earl found himself studying the pert, eager face before him in fascination. It was difficult to believe that this slender, radiant-eyed young woman with the heavy mass of lovely copper hair framing a face delicate as a seashell was the same wretched creature he had run down in Edgewood Lane last night. One observation he had made last evening still held true, though—there was nothing common about Miss Smith.

Or about Weed—or whatever her true name was. Still, if she was going to be governess to Dorinda she would have to be more forthcoming. She must allow him to investigate her background, and she would therefore have to answer his questions. He was certain that when the girl realized the position he was offering her she would cooperate. Philip's instinct told him that Miss Smith would be very good for Dorinda—she was lively, kind, and levelheaded, and she was also obviously well bred. Despite her unfamiliarity with some of the intricacies of fine dining, such as which implement was to be used for stirring her coffee and which for eating fruit, she had managed well enough at table following Charlotte's lead. Most striking of all, her overall manner at dinner had been gracious, winsome, almost elegant. Natural elegance, that was what she possessed, Philip mused, and it was this quality that made him so curious about her. Something told him that Miss Smith's life had been as varied and unusual as she was. For some reason he felt himself drawn to her, feeling oddly protective. Though why he should feel that way he couldn't fathom, for his obligation to her would come to an end after her ankle was healed.

She was watching him now with an expression of mingled apprehension, curiosity, and hopefulness on her face, which made her look touchingly vulnerable. He reached up and without thinking ran his thumb along her delicate cheek.

"Don't worry, Miss Smith, I'm not going to bite you," he said softly. "Although," he added, "I'm considering the possibility of removing all the candlesticks from the house. In the past two days, they have twice been used as weapons against members of this household."

"Did you have to remind me of that, your lordship?" The gentle touch of his hand burned Camilla's skin. It was all she could do to sit still and endure the delicious scorch of it. She murmured: "I'm so sorry for hitting you last night. I told you that. At least it seems the bump has nearly gone away," she offered hopefully.

"Ah, but not the memory. It's a miracle I didn't have nightmares when I went to bed after such a frightening experience."

"Now you are making sport of me," she accused, and lifted her chin. "I believe it would take a great deal more than a tap on the head to give an Audley nightmares."

He laughed. Leaning forward, he grasped her hands in both of his. "You're very acute, aren't you, Miss Smith? And very intrepid. I admire both of those qualities." His face took on a thoughtful expression, his eyes searching deep into hers. "As a matter of fact, you seem to be a very admirable young woman. That is why I want to make you a proposition."

Philip saw her eyes widen, felt her hands stiffen in his before she jerked them away. "I do not wish to hear it, sir," she cried, and rose abruptly from the sofa.

"You misunderstand," Philip said quickly, coming to his feet, but when he tried to grasp her she wrenched herself away and started for the door. *Women,* he thought in exasperation. *They all think men want only one thing.* "Miss Smith, I don't intend to seduce you," Philip said, torn between irritation and amusement. He overtook her easily as she limped toward the door and seized her arm. Before she could try to break away, he turned her to face him and pulled her close. "Miss Smith . . ."

"Let me go! I know of only one kind of proposition that a man like you would make to a girl of my station and I beg you will not insult me further by actually speaking it!"

He held her fast, mentally cursing himself for his poor choice of words. He had never meant to set her off like this, or to wound her with a degrading insult. That she found the prospect so humiliating was to her credit. But Philip knew he had to straighten out the misunderstanding quickly or they would both be even more embarrassed than they already were. He backed her up against the wall and held her fast, one arm hooked around her waist. Gazing down into her outraged face, feeling the blazing heat of those fiery green eyes, he suddenly grinned.

"Miss Smith," he enunciated in a careful tone, as if

speaking to a very slow-witted child, "I am *not* interested
in seducing you. I am planning soon to become betrothed
to a very lovely woman—Lady Brittany Deaville—and my
intentions toward her—and toward you, are completely
different—but entirely honorable."

Camilla's wrath died away as his words sunk in. She
searched his face and saw sincerity in it. For a moment
she had been so blinded by the insult she thought he
intended that she had reacted on instinct, but now reason
came trickling back. At least partly. It was difficult to be
reasonable and to think clearly when the Earl was holding her like this, when he was so close that she could feel
the strong beat of his heart against her breast, feel the
strength of his arms, the magnetic heat of his body. He
looked annoyed with her, but also determined to keep
her here like this until he had finished what he had to say.
But Camilla found her senses swimming, and knew she
couldn't concentrate or think properly unless there was
some distance between them. She tried to jerk away once
more and his grip tightened until she gave up and stood
still, looking up at him in helpless despair.

"Stop being melodramatic," he told her, as if she were
no older than Dorinda. "For God's sake, I don't mean
you any harm and certainly no dishonor."

"Then let me go," Camilla said, trying to sound coolly
insistent, and instead appalled by the betraying tremor in
her voice.

"Not until you've heard me out."

His jaw, she noted suddenly, had a distinctly stubborn
set to it. He wouldn't let her go until he was good and
ready. It was a dizzying, heady sensation to be held so,
and she had to fight against the pleasure of it with all of
the good sense and willpower she could muster.

"Well, then?" she managed to say with only a faint quiver. "Go ahead—say what you must say."

She struggled to keep her mind upon what he was going to say next.

"I want to know more about you, Miss Smith. Not for my own lascivious purposes," he added hastily, seeing her look. "I simply want to interview you for the position of Dorinda's governess."

Dorinda's governess? Camilla was too stunned for a moment even to respond. And then she never had the chance to do so.

Suddenly, the library door swung open and Jared burst in, saying: "Lady Brittany and Lord Marchfield wish to know if—"

Jared broke off, halting in astonishment. Beside him, an incredibly lovely blond girl and a tall man with mocking eyes stared at the Earl of Westcott in undisguised amazement. It wasn't difficult to understand their shock. The Earl's powerful arms were clasped around the very slender waist of a fetching young woman completely unknown to them. They both immediately drew the same unmistakable conclusion: Philip Audley looked for all the world like an ardent lover caught in the midst of stealing a kiss.

"I see we've come at an inopportune time," the tall man drawled mockingly, his tawny eyebrows shooting up in wicked amusement.

The blond girl had gone deathly pale. "Forgive our intrusion," she murmured in a tight, breathless voice. For one lightning moment her glorious violet eyes sought Philip's searchingly, their vivid depths betraying an intense pain; then a shuttered expression came over her exquisitely lovely face and she blasted him with a frigid smile. All the while her small gloved hands tightly squeezed the painted chicken-skin fan clutched between her fingers.

Philip let go of Camilla at once. He was cursing inwardly. Of all the damned unlucky pieces of timing. His brain raced for some way out of this pickle, some way that would rescue Miss Smith's dignity—and his own— and that could somehow turn threatened scandal into advantage.

He strolled forward toward the newcomers, his expression coolly nonchalant, though inside his thoughts were churning.

In that one instant when she'd first seen him with Miss Smith, jealousy had blazed clearly in Brittany's face. He realized that he'd been right all along—her feelings for him were far stronger than she'd been letting on. He knew an immediate sense of triumph, and with it the beginnings of an idea—a wild, daring, tactically brilliant idea that would win Brittany for him and save poor Miss Smith's reputation.

He'd promised not to dishonor the girl, and yet he'd put her in a position that compromised her reputation every bit as much as if they'd been caught beneath the bedsheets together. Explaining what had just gone on between them was impossible. And to introduce her as Dorinda's new governess or potential new governess would cast her in a highly unflattering light—she would appear to be nothing but a servant selling herself to secure a position—and he would appear to be the kind of man he detested, the kind that forced housemaids and governesses to sleep with the master of the house in order to keep their employment. There was only one way to save Miss Smith's reputation and in a way, his own—whatever was left of it—a way that would also serve his own purposes. For if making Brittany jealous was the key to winning her, he could now accomplish two things at once.

"Your presence, Brittany, is never an intrusion," he said with an easy grin. "I'm delighted to see you. And you, Marchfield, are as welcome as always." A glint entered his dark gray eyes as he met and held the other man's suddenly wary glance.

"Allow me to introduce Miss Smith. She is . . ." He hesitated only an instant before continuing smoothly, "She is Charlotte's cousin, visiting us from Hampshire. And," he went on blithely, as Miss Smith, who had sunk into a wing chair the moment he'd let her go, blinked at him and stared as if he had gone mad, "she has just made me the happiest fellow in all of England. She has done me the honor of agreeing to become my wife."

 No one was more thunderstruck by Philip's announcement than Camilla. Her eyes wide with shock, she simply stared at him, too numb to speak or move.

Deafening silence reverberated through the library. Lady Brittany's mouth had actually dropped open in a most unelegant gape, and Lord Marchfield eyed the suave Earl with a mixture of suspicion and incredulity that did not flatter Camilla as she observed it. Only Jared showed remarkable aplomb. After a brief flash of shock, clearly illumined on his young face, he grinned broadly and hurried forward with outstretched hands.

"My compliments to you, Philip. You don't deserve her by far."

He kissed Camilla's hand with surprising grace for one so young and gave her a wink.

To Camilla the entire episode was unreal, and totally absurd. One moment the Earl had asked her to become Dorinda's governess. An instant later, he publicly announced that she was going to become his bride—and he had said this to Lady Brittany, the woman he planned to marry.

It was impossible to ask questions, equally impossible to comprehend what was happening. Either the Earl had gone stark raving mad or he was playing some monstrous game that she couldn't begin to fathom. Well, she knew he wasn't mad. That darkly handsome face was too shrewd, the face of a man always alert and in control. His eyes gleamed ironically. He was clearly enjoying himself. And he was up to something—but what?

It would serve him right, she thought dazedly, as suddenly her ankle began to throb, *if I exposed his story for the lie that it is*. But Camilla knew she would never do that. She refused to explain it even to herself, refused to explore what was in her heart, but she knew she would never do anything that would cause him pain.

He strolled toward her, holding out his hand. With his back to the others, his face now wore an expression of concern. It looked genuine. "Your ankle pains you?" he asked in a quick, low tone.

Then, to the others, "Miss Smith suffered an injury recently in a carriage accident . . . do come in and allow me to make proper introductions."

To Camilla he spoke softly as Jared ushered Brittany and Marchfield into the library, and called to James, Charlotte, and Kirby to join them. "Quick, Miss Smith. Your given name."

"Camilla," she whispered back.

"Good girl." He patted her on the shoulder and turned with his flashing smile to the others. As Lord Kirby, James, and Charlotte followed the little party into the library, Philip squeezed her shoulder and whispered, "Simply follow my lead. It will be all right. I won't let any of this hurt you."

Then he was smoothly introducing her to the most beautiful woman she had ever met. Despite Philip's protest, Camilla forced herself to rise so that she could gaze at eye level into the indescribable face of Lady Brittany Deaville. In her gown of pale blue satin, which snugly draped her lush figure, Brittany was a shining vision, a portrait of golden, vivacious beauty. With a little uncontrollable stab of dismay Camilla noted the other woman's classically perfect, fine-sculptured features and her enormous eyes, which looked a smoky shade of purple in the bright light of the library. Lady Brittany's elegant nose had a distinctly patrician tilt to it, and her graceful neck would evoke envy from a swan. With her delicate complexion and richly golden hair arranged in the latest fashion, she stood before Camilla as some breathtaking model of perfection. Even the alabaster paleness that had come over her at Philip's announcement only enhanced her enchanting demeanor, making her appear as delicate and regal as a royal princess.

"Lady Brittany Deaville, may I present Miss Camilla Smith." The Earl's tone subtly took on a harder edge as his gaze shifted to the tall brown-haired man beside Brittany. "And Lord Marchfield—an old acquaintance."

"How lovely to make your acquaintance," Brittany murmured through clenched teeth. Lord Marchfield, however, had no difficulty in speaking or in studying the girl before him with razor-edged scrutiny.

He stared deep into Camilla's eyes and then lifted her hand to his lips in a slow gesture. "Your servant, Miss, er, Smith," he drawled. A quick, cold grin touched his sardonically handsome features. "Allow me to felicitate you on your coming nuptials. Though I must say I am shocked at Westcott for keeping you a secret from us all. Or is this, mayhap, a whirlwind affair born only precious hours ago?"

There was no mistaking the mocking undercurrent in his voice, despite his carefully bland expression. Camilla felt a chill run through her at his touch and the stab of his piercing blue eyes made her want to step back a pace. But she held her ground with the staunch dignity that had gotten her through all the difficult circumstances of her life. Beside her Phillip spoke coolly, but she sensed his intense dislike of the man before her.

"Miss Smith and I have been acquainted for some time. We've only recently renewed our friendship, however, and the rest," he said, drawing her closer with an easy smile, "can only be explained by those who understand the passions of the human heart. Isn't that true, Camilla?"

For one confused moment, hearing him say her name with such tenderness and pride, almost as if he truly loved her, Camilla felt herself growing dizzy with a spiraling hope. Then her good sense and the tension she felt in his arm as it rested lightly about her shoulders, reminded her that this was all a ridiculous farce, a charade.

"Ye . . . es, your lordsh—Philip. It all happened too suddenly to explain." She managed to smile at him, though her knees were shaking beneath her gown. She caught sight of the expressions worn by James, Charlotte, and Lord Kirby as they overheard the substance of the conversation, and had to choke back a hysterical laugh. Their faces all mirrored the shock she herself was feeling.

Only Philip and Jared seemed to be enjoying themselves.

"Have you set a date for the grand occasion, Philip?" Jared asked boldly as everyone found seats in the large, high-ceilinged room lined with books, and comfortably appointed with Aubusson rugs, brass chandeliers, numerous writing desks, and several groupings of comfortable chairs.

"Not yet." Philip, seated beside Camilla on a tan sofa, stretched out his long legs. He looked completely at ease. However, beneath the placid surface he showed to his guests, he was thinking quickly. He had started down a daring path. Now every word spoken had to be weighed and calculated if he was to pull this stunt off. He only hoped the girl beside him would not ruin everything with some chance remark. So far, Miss Smith was handling the situation with remarkable poise. But he knew he had to get her away from Marchfield and from Brittany as soon as possible until he could begin to prepare her for the challenges ahead.

Glancing at her face, he saw how pale and still she appeared. Her green eyes glowed with more brilliance than ever within that delicate white face. Poor Miss Smith. He was sure she'd never expected anything so bizarre to occur when she'd come down to dinner tonight. As a matter of fact, Philip observed wryly, she and Brittany both looked as white as parchment. James and Charlotte were equally pasty, he noted, glancing calmly around the room. Kirby, at least, seemed to have caught on to the game underfoot, and though he didn't understand it, it obviously appealed to his sense of the ridiculous. As Philip met his gaze, Kirby sent him a quizzical glance, his mouth quirking upward, and his eyes alight with mischief in much the same way he had looked when as boys they had plotted some wild scheme. Philip's answering smile sent a silent message of appreciation for his cooperation in the present farce. Immediately, Kirby turned to Brittany, complimented her on her gown, exclaimed how delighted he was that she had come up to the country, and asked how long she would be staying. Damn him, Phillip thought abruptly, his good-natured feelings toward his longtime friend suddenly blotted out by sharp jealousy. Leave it to Alistair to take advantage of this situation to press his own suit with Brittany.

But it won't do him any good.

When Brittany replied to Kirby's questions, she still sounded rather dazed, but Philip learned that she and Marchfield had come up to Marrowing Hall as part of a large house party. Their decision to call upon the occupants of Westcott Park after dinner had not been purely an impulse. They had come specifically to issue an invitation for a dinner party, with cards and dancing, to be held at Marrowing Hall on Thursday evening.

"Camilla and I will be delighted to attend." Philip accepted the invitation card Brittany handed him from Lady Marrowing with equanimity. He turned toward his brother. "James?"

"Oh yes." James found his voice at last. "We will be delighted." He nudged Charlotte, who was still speechless over the announcement of Philip's betrothal. "Won't we enjoy such an evening, Charlotte?" he prodded. "Though of course, I know how busy you shall be—helping your cousin with all of the wedding arrangements. But surely you wouldn't care to miss dinner at Marrowing Hall?"

"Oh no. I mean, oh yes. It sounds lovely." Charlotte's face flushed a rosy pink. She seemed so flustered that James, taking pity on her after putting her in such an awkward position, added: "She's so overjoyed about the marriage, you see. It's something she's always hoped for."

"Indeed?" Lord Marchfield's clever gaze swung back to examine Camilla again, seeming to take in her modest gown, simply dressed hair, and her obvious lack of jewels, as well as her peculiar silence. "How is it, Westcott, that you've managed to keep this charming prize hidden from us for so long? Why, even last night, at the Hampton masquerade, you gave no clue that your heart was spoken for—at least, not by the most delightful Miss Smith."

"It is actually quite simple, Marchfield." Philip squeezed Camilla's hand encouragingly as he spoke, but his palpable dislike for the other man came out unconsciously in the hard pressure with which he gripped her fingers. Without realizing it he was hurting her. Suddenly, she gave a little gasp, unable to endure it any longer. Instantly, he let her go, all the while speaking in a nonchalant way to his enemy.

"Out of respect for Camilla, I have remained silent. You see, she had not felt herself ready for any commitment of a serious nature and for that reason I have kept my feelings private. She hasn't yet had her come-out, you see, due to the fact that she has been in mourning. She is now ready to have her season in London. I haven't wished to press her, naturally, since she has had such little experience in society and it is only right that she have the opportunity to decide her true feelings after she has tasted something of London life. But tonight she has done me the honor of agreeing to accept my proposal— though no announcement will be made until the end of the season."

"So it is not all settled between you?" Lady Brittany said quickly, her gaze flying to his face.

"On my part, yes." Philip's gray eyes touched her coolly. "My heart was smitten some time ago, and I have been only trying to forget Camilla in despair of winning her. But now . . . now I have much more than hope to sustain me. After one season, a season in which I shall endeavor to secure her affections in every way that I can," he said with a tender smile at the girl beside him, "I hope with all my heart that this lovely lady will cast off all her doubts and formally announce our engagement."

James made a little choking sound. Camilla felt hot color rush into her cheeks. What a wicked, shameless liar! But why? What was the purpose behind all this?

Suddenly, with blinding clarity, she understood. She saw the flash of hope flare in Brittany's eyes, felt the quivering look she shot at Philip, and knew in that instant the reason for this deception. She felt ill. Enough. She couldn't take another minute of this without having time to think. Shakily, she came to her feet.

"My love, what is it?" Philip instantly stood beside her, steadying her.

"I'm afraid my ankle is a trifle worse. I—I have been up and about too long this evening . . . Forgive me for cutting short the evening, but I must go to my room and rest . . ."

"I never should have let you tax yourself like this." Philip sent Brittany and Marchfield a dismissive glance. "Kindly excuse us. Camilla must have her rest. Charlotte, perhaps you would care to accompany us upstairs and help see Camilla comfortably settled."

"Why, yes, surely—with pleasure." Charlotte jumped up, all too glad to escape the library.

As Camilla hastily bid the visitors good evening and started for the door, Philip suddenly gripped her arm. "No, my love, you have spent too much time on that poor foot already tonight."

He took the walking stick from her with firm gentleness, handed it to Charlotte, and then, before Camilla could protest, he swept her up into his arms.

"Not again!" Camilla burst out without thinking, and Philip laughed.

"Yes, again. But," he added, with a wicked smile

meant, Camilla realized sinkingly, to torment Brittany, "this will only serve as practice for the night I can finally, as your bridegroom, carry you officially over our bedroom threshold."

And with these parting words, he strode from the room clasping her tenderly in his arms. Brittany's rigid posture and frozen smile as she watched them depart did not escape him.

Upstairs in the Blue Room Philip set Camilla upon the bed. "Charlotte, kindly leave us a moment."

"Your lordship . . . I—I do not know if I should . . . this is all so improper . . ." Charlotte's voice trembled. Her eyes filled with tears. "What are your intentions here? You are making me a party to something abhorrent . . . my mama warned me what would be if I married into this family . . ."

"Spare me your hysterics."

"But, my lord, this entire situation is scandalous, it's . . . despicable . . . all those lies you told—I shall not . . . oh, what are you doing?"

"Take your sniffling to James—perhaps he tolerates it, but I won't." Philip grasped her by the arm and quite ruthlessly put her from the room. As he slammed the door, Camilla bleakly noted the harsh expression on his face.

"You were rude to her," she chided in a low tone, trying to be calm, trying not to let him see how shaken she was. He was obviously not a man to tolerate weakness, tears, or missish demonstrations of distress. "She is a gently bred girl and she spoke from true concern."

"I am concerned too—about you, Miss Smith." He dismissed Charlotte's worries with a wave of his hand and came toward Camilla, pausing beside the bed to stare down at her. "You were superb down there. I'm sorry to have put you in that spot, but," he added with the flicker of a smile, "you conducted yourself admirably."

"I did what was necessary to get through the situation. But I don't understand why you said all those ridiculous things to those people."

"I know you don't. I'll try to explain. But first—your ankle. Is it very painful?"

"No," she lied. "It only hurts a little."

He gave her a long, keen look. "You can't bamboozle me, my girl."

"Bamboozle?" Camilla stared at him, her eyes widening with indignation. "*You,* who made up that outrageous story downstairs, dare to speak to *me* about bamboozling? You are the master of it, my lord!"

He gave a short, rueful laugh. "Be that as it may, I'll send Mrs. Wyeth in with some laudanum for you after we've done. Any fool can see you're in pain. You've had a far too adventuresome evening, and spent far too much time on your feet. I accept the blame for all of that—and for more. It seems I am guilty of considerably complicating your life, Miss Smith."

"It was already quite complicated before I met you," Camilla murmured, thinking of the murdered man, the note now hidden inside the bureau drawer, and the mystery of the charm around her neck.

He flashed her a quick, scrutinizing glance. Slowly, he paced to the window and stared out at the gleaming crescent of the October moon. It sailed softly through a sea of stars against the backdrop of velvet darkness.

Camilla thought he looked lost in thought, his face taut with concentration. She fought the urge to go to him, to cradle his face between her hands and kiss away the frown from his brow. If she didn't get control of these odd bursts of feelings, she would certainly make a fool of herself—and break her own heart. She quelled her anxiety and waited, slipping off her shoes and shifting her foot more comfortably on the silken covers, wondering what he would say next.

At last he turned from the window and dropped into one of the chairs near the fire, looking far too large and sturdy for the delicate seat. He spoke in an even, coolly direct tone that went to the core of her anxiety and immediately helped to allay it.

"I'm going to speak bluntly because I believe you are a sensible young woman who would prefer honesty and frankness to a lot of pretty phrases. Am I correct?"

"Your reading of my character is as skillful as your ability to invent imaginative tales."

He leaned forward, and his long fingers worked to unknot his cravat. As he removed it, his gray silk evening shirt fell open, revealing a patch of crisp dark hair upon his broad chest. He seemed unconscious of his own actions, so caught up was he in the discussion about to enfold, but Camilla watched him in fascination, her skin growing warm. "I found it necessary to make up that Banbury tale for those people, as you call them," Philip said, "in order to save both of our reputations. It wouldn't have done for me to introduce you as Dorinda's potential governess." He scowled, and raked a hand through his coal-black hair. "Unfortunately, the situation in which we were discovered was compromising, and though we both know that nothing the least bit romantic or passionate took place between us, no one coming into that room—particularly not those two people—would have believed that for one moment."

"You were trying to spare my reputation? I don't see why." Camilla fidgeted with the folds of her gown. "I am only a servant girl, your lordship," she said quietly.

"Those people don't know me, and I don't know them. What possible difference could it make if they thought I was the kind of girl who would . . . that I was . . ."

He stood up and strode toward her. He halted beside the bed and gazed down into her pale oval face. "You know perfectly well that it makes a difference. Whatever your background, Miss Smith, you are *not* a common serving girl. You don't deserve to be mired in a mess of my making, nor tainted by it. I may enjoy the reputation of a rake," he said, a shade of bitter mockery in his voice, "but even I draw the line at entangling innocent young women in a scandal of my own doing."

She took a deep breath. She didn't know what to say. No one had ever shown this sort of consideration for her feelings, much less her reputation. He was a mystifying man. "I appreciate your gallantry, sir," she murmured at last. "Thank you."

"Don't!" he bit off, his eyes darkening. He turned violently on his heel and paced the length of the room. "I don't deserve thanks. I've embroiled you in something that must be damned uncomfortable for you, but I promise I won't let it harm you and I will make it worth your while."

Camilla watched him stalk back and forth, unable to keep from noting the strapping perfection of his physique, the lithe, powerful way he moved, the sheer masculinity he exuded.

I should leave this house, she thought, fearful of the betraying emotions in her own heart. It was dangerous to stay here, perhaps even as dangerous, in its own way, as it would be to face the pursuit of the murderer once she left Westcott Park. The Earl, this man whom she had met only yesterday, had the power to singe her cool flesh with his lightest touch. His gray eyes mesmerized her, his voice did strange things to the blood in her veins. He made her think of things, want things that could never be. He filled her thoughts, her heart, and she scarcely knew him. But she knew enough. She knew that beneath the cold, harsh exterior of the tyrannical head of the house, beneath the nonchalance of the careless, charming but heartless rake, beneath the dark, suave sophistication and ironic sense of humor that masked the Earl's true nature like an impenetrable suit of armor, lurked a hot-tempered boy with a kind soul and a noble heart, a sad, honorable man whose private pain was buried deep beneath the flinty, polished surface.

He turned to her, his gray eyes smoky in the lamplight. "Do you want to hear what I have to propose?"

"It isn't marriage, is it, your lordship?" She managed a small, shaky laugh. "I'm afraid I could not accept."

He smiled. "No, of course it isn't marriage. But, if you will pretend for a little while—until after our traditional Westcott Park ball—that you are Miss Camilla Smith, cousin to poor insipid Charlotte, and recipient of my deepest affections, I will pay you a thousand pounds and see you established in whatever position in life you choose."

"I don't want your money!" She started to jump up from the bed, agitated past the point of lying immobile, but he reached her in two quick strides and pushed her back.

"Let me explain it all. I think you'll agree that we will both come out the better for this little charade—if you play your part well, and if I don't misread the character of the woman I adore."

She froze at this, and fell back. Philip's hands dropped away. He smiled down at her.

"It's really quite simple. For the next month or so, pretend to be Charlotte's cousin and my intended. Accompany me to London. I guarantee you'll have a wonderful time. I'll escort you to balls, parties, the theater and the opera. You shall have the most fashionable gowns, cloaks, hats, jewels—everything to show you off as a young lady of fashion and high style. I want no shabby-genteel miss —you must be of the first stare of fashion—it's essential. And when it is time for our ball here at Westcott Park," he added with an offhand grin, "you will be the guest of honor."

"What you're proposing is a . . . a hoax! One that will be played upon all of society, upon all of your friends!"

"Yes." He raised his brows at her. "So?"

"How can you contemplate something like that?"

"I began something tonight with that little lie of mine and now I must finish it," he said grimly. "And besides, it will help me in my goal. There is one thing you must understand before we go any further."

"Yes?" Camilla sensed what was coming and braced herself.

"I mean to marry that beautiful little vixen downstairs, the incomparable Lady Brittany. I've made up my mind to it, and I've also committed myself to a little wager on the matter."

Wager? Camilla stared at him blankly.

To her surprise, he flushed. It was the first time she'd seen him lose his composure since this whole fiasco of an evening had begun. "Lord Marchfield also wishes to wed Brittany," he explained tightly. "So does Kirby, for that matter, and half the men in London. But Marchfield is a particular enemy of mine—the reasons are not important now. He challenged me, and I bet him that I would be betrothed to Brittany by Christmas or else give over to him two matched pairs of my finest horses."

"You wagered your horses over Lady Brittany's hand in marriage?" she croaked. Horrified, Camilla didn't know whether to gasp or burst out laughing. Philip suddenly sighed, and sat down beside her. Gently, he cupped her chin between his thumb and forefinger.

"Shocking, isn't it?" His grin was rueful. "It's the Audley curse. We're a scandalous family—can't resist a dare or a wager. I'm trying to do better, Miss Smith, believe me, I'm trying, but Marchfield goaded me beyond endurance. The point is: now that the bet has been made, it must be won."

"But do you *wish* to marry Lady Brittany?"

She was holding her breath, waiting for his answer. When it came, her spirits sank like a leaden anchor.

"With all my heart," he said vehemently, and an arrow of pain shot through her at the determination glinting in his eyes. So he loved Brittany, after all, and wanted her, not only to win his stupid bet but for herself. *Well, why not?* she thought, thinking of the beauty down below. Brittany was stunning and elegant, and every inch his equal in society. And she—Camilla? A pawn, a tool, to help him achieve his end.

"Brittany has been playing a game with me," the Earl continued, his tone taking on a note of silken amusement. "Last night at the Hampton masquerade she behaved as if I didn't exist. She evaded me the entire evening, and danced the night away with Kirby and Seaton and Marchfield, knowing all the while she was driving me into a fury. The little minx." He chuckled softly. "Now, Miss Smith, it is Brittany's turn to suffer the torment of jealousy. Let her think there is an understanding between you and me, let her think that my affections lie elsewhere—that she has lost me. If I know my darling Brittany, it will drive her mad with desire. Human beings always want what they believe they cannot have, don't they?"

"Yes," she whispered bleakly.

"Don't look so distressed." He released her chin, and brushed a wayward lock of copper hair from her brow, twirling it for a moment between his fingers. In the silence that fell between them, Camilla heard the song of a nightingale outside her window, haunting, lovely, and infinitely sad.

"You'll enjoy yourself in London, Camilla. And no one need ever know the truth. When we have driven Brittany quite wild with jealousy and she can resist baring her heart to me no longer, we will say that you have decided against marrying me, and are returning to your childhood sweetheart in Hampshire, Lord Somebody-or-other, and then I will pay your packet to Paris, and provide you with a handsome sum that will allow you to settle there in style —if that is still your intention?"

"It is." Camilla had been thinking hard all the while he talked. Now she said, taking a deep breath, "Your plan won't work, your lordship. I can't help you."

"Why not?"

"I can't go to London. There are reasons why I must leave for Paris as soon as may be."

"What reasons?"

She shook her head. "I'm sorry—my reasons are my own. I can't share them with you—but it is impossible for me to go to London."

Studying her face, his eyes narrowed. "You're afraid of something. Or someone."

Startled, she met his piercing gaze. Something of the truth must have shown in her eyes, for he immediately grasped her hand and said, "If you're in trouble, Miss

Smith, I will certainly help you. But you must explain . . ."

"No, no, I'm in no trouble," she cried, suddenly afraid he would get too near the truth. She didn't want to involve him or his family in her plight—the only solution was to go on her way as soon as possible. "I cannot do as you ask, that's all I have to say, and I would be very grateful if you would let the matter go at that."

"You don't know me very well yet," he said softly. "One of my faults, which my family is fond of reminding me, is that I always insist on getting my way. Barring any good reason, I will insist that you go along with my plan. Unless I am far mistaken, Paris will still stand in a month when this is over, and you can go there then. You'll fare much better there, whatever your business, with a purse full of money. Be sensible, Miss Smith. It is certainly to your advantage to cooperate with my plan," he said firmly. "Unless you have a dislike of lovely clothes and possessions?"

"Of course not, but . . ."

"Unless you dislike parties and elegant balls?"

"No, no, but . . ."

"Unless you so dislike being in my company that you would break out in hives at the very notion?"

"No . . ."

"Then it's settled. I won't accept no for an answer, Miss Smith." He pressed a quick kiss to her fingertips, and rose. "I'll send Charlotte in now. No doubt she is bursting with questions for you—and it is good that you two get to know each other, since you're going to pretend to be cousins. And by the way, Charlotte will instruct you in all the absurd niceties of getting on in society. She may be a timid mouse but she knows her way in the highest circles and will give you some valuable guidance."

"This isn't settled," Camilla protested, her tone resolute. "I haven't agreed to anything, your lordship!"

"You'd better start calling me Philip. It will seem odd otherwise." He sauntered toward the door.

"Mrs. Wyeth will bring you some laudanum shortly. Then you'd better get some sleep. Tomorrow and the next day will be quite busy. You'll have a great deal to do and learn before the Marrowing party. Good night, Miss Smith—er, Camilla."

With only a brief maddening grin he was gone. A moment later, before Camilla had time to draw breath, Charlotte literally dashed into the room.

"Oh, that odious man. What did he say? Miss Smith, what madness is this?" Charlotte paced back and forth with frantic distress.

Camilla was too confused and overwhelmed at first to do more than shoot the girl a stunned look.

"Moonstruck madness," she managed to respond at last in a low tone. "That's the only explanation. Lady Charlotte, tell me the truth." She swallowed. Her next words came out in a dazed whisper. "Has anyone *ever* succeeded in saying 'no' to that man? How did they manage it?"

Charlotte looked blank, and merely threw up her hands in despair. Camilla, sinking back against the pillows, decided that she would gladly trade everything she possessed in the world if only she could learn that answer.

When the sun streamed into her room the following morning, Camilla awoke, sat up, and remembered that it was time to face up to the hard thinking that lay before her. Last night she had been too exhausted and distracted by her throbbing ankle to wrestle with her dilemma, but with the dawning of the fresh, crisp new day, with the lush, splendid beauty of Westcott Park beckoning beyond her window, and the knowledge that the Earl was expecting her to begin this charade in earnest at a formal diner party at Marrowing Hall only two days hence, she felt impelled to confront the issues before her.

She wanted to do it. She wanted to stay on—even for a little longer—at Westcott Park. There was no denying it. And it wasn't only because the prospect of entering into an entirely different life from the one she had always known held an enticing allure that drew her like a fairy spell toward the enchanted forest. And it wasn't only because she would, for a short time, have pretty clothes and the opportunity to ride in luxurious carriages and to see

wonderful plays and meet all the exciting, fashionable
lords and ladies of the ton. There was a whole other reason why the Earl's proposition tempted her, she acknowledged, stretching her arms above her head and then shov-
ing the tumble of coppery curls from her eyes.

The Earl himself.

The prospect of spending hours with him, of talking to
him, riding with him, dining with him on countless occa-
sions made her heart leap with eagerness.

Of course she knew she was being totally foolish, even
idiotic. The Earl would never notice her as a woman, and
would never think of her as anything but a serving maid
who was helping him in his scheme to win Lady Brittany.
But it would be enough, she reasoned, hugging her arms
around herself in the big satin-sheeted bed. It would be
enough merely to be in his company awhile—and to help
him achieve his heart's desire.

Camilla was certain that once he was happily married
to Brittany, he would become more lenient and understanding with Dorinda, and would probably soften toward
James as well. A happy home life could change a person
in remarkable ways, and once the Earl was wed to the
woman he loved, he and his family would be bound to
find themselves drawing closer together. They would, she
told herself, find again the contentment that apparently
they hadn't known in quite some time.

Moreover, she reasoned, twirling a strand of hair between her fingers, the Earl had given her no reason to
believe he'd accept no for an answer. What choice did she
have, really, but to go along and do her best to get
through this strange muddle?

As she swung her legs over the side of the bed, however, another thought struck her. She felt a sudden pinch
of fear.

The murderer. She guessed he was probably a member
of the ton, perhaps someone who had even attended the
Hampton masquerade with Philip and all of his friends.
What if she was to encounter him in London? She
wouldn't know him, couldn't possibly recognize him. But
he could recognize her—or could he?

She limped to the mirror. Her ankle, after throbbing
intensely last night, seemed much better today, and only
hurt slightly as she walked. Still, she gripped the back of
the dressing chair as she paused and regarded her reflection in the oval looking glass. Would that madman recognize her? she wondered.

The girl he had seen that night at the White Horse Inn
had been wretched and ragged, her hair hanging limply in
her face, her thin frame laden with layers of baggy, ill-
fitting servant's clothes. The light had been dim, her face
had been dirty, and there had been very little time.
Wasn't it possible—probable even—that a man consumed
with hate and fury and the madness she had clearly seen
in his eyes wouldn't be able to recognize the same creature when she was transformed by gowns and jewels and
crimped hair, and when she was in the company of one of
the most noted members of the ton?

Surely he would never expect the bedraggled servant
girl who had fled from him in terror to show up on the
arm of the Earl of Westcott, looking every inch a fashionable young lady?

She stared at herself. It was still difficult to believe how
different she looked from the way she thought of herself.
Even this morning, with the sheer white nightrail Kate
had lent her flowing over her slenderly curved figure, with
her coppery hair loose and wavy around her shoulders,
and her skin glowing in the glorious morning light, she
looked and felt so different from that girl who had

scrubbed and mopped and served at the Rose and Swan beneath Gwynneth Dibbs's watchful eye.

Camilla Smith, she whispered to herself. Lady Charlotte's cousin. Fiancée of the Earl of Westcott.

Madness, this was sheer madness. And yet, she must be mad too, for she knew exactly what she wanted to do, and she couldn't deny the wild impulse driving her. She wanted with all of her heart to play this role and to enjoy for one month this most enchanting adventure—but for one month only, she told herself severely. Until the ball at Westcott Park. Not a day longer.

Then, she reasoned, meeting her own eyes in the mirror with firm intentness, she would leave London, leave the role of Miss Smith, and above all, leave the Earl of Westcott behind forever.

She went to the bureau and dug out the note for Mr. Anders. She held it up between her fingers, staring pensively at the scrawled words. While she was in London, she would find a way to send this note anonymously to the authorities, with a letter explaining how it related to the murder at the White Horse Inn. Perhaps the information she could provide would somehow lead the authorities to the murderer. That would eliminate both her own danger and her sense of responsibility in the matter.

Her heart lightened a bit at the thought. Then another idea playing in the back of her mind surfaced, reinforcing her decision to go along with the Earl's scheme. The Earl had promised her a handsome stipend in exchange for her help with his plan, hadn't he? Well, when she reached London she would ask him for a partial payment in advance, and use some of the money to buy warm winter clothes for Hester, and food for all the workhouse children. It was the chance of a lifetime, an opportunity to earn more money than she could ever hope to accumu-

late at the Rose and Swan, or even as a shop girl, and to
use it to help the children in the workhouse.

Maybe she could even manage it so that she could see
Hester again, she thought hopefully—perhaps spend
some time with the child, and explain why she must go
away.

It all added up to one thing. She was going to play the
part the Earl suggested. It would benefit him, and Hester,
and the London authorities searching for the murderer—
and she decided, with a heartfelt little sigh—it would give
her a brief, precious peek at the grand and gracious way
of life she had never dreamed of seeing.

She joined Charlotte for breakfast in the dining room a
short while later and found her nervously sipping a cup of
coffee.

"Miss Smith!" Charlotte exclaimed, looking askance
when Camilla entered. "Is your ankle better? Er, do have
a roll. There are eggs and ham and potatoes on the sideboard, as well." A tiny, tension-filled pause, then she
burst out with: "Have you decided about the Earl's proposition?"

"I suppose I have. I'm going to *try* to play the part his
lordship wishes me to play," Camilla replied, slipping into
one of the handsome wine-colored upholstered chairs
that flanked the enormous table. The chair was delightfully comfortable, the glowingly polished, handsome
room a pleasure to behold. But in the morning light spilling in from the garden, Charlotte looked wan and tired,
as if she hadn't slept well. And she didn't appear precisely
pleased by Camilla's response. In fact, an expression of
dismay flitted briefly over her heart-shaped face, then was
quickly replaced by one of rigid politeness.

"Are you truly opposed to the idea?" Camilla asked a
bit anxiously, for though Charlotte's attitude was cordial,

the girl seemed even more uneasy and nervous than she had before. "I won't pretend to be your cousin if you truly are against it," she said firmly, "however much his lordship tries to insist."

Charlotte shook her head. "You don't know Philip if you think it possible to resist his decrees," she said bitterly. "In this house, his word is law. And even James, who usually is most vehement and decided in his own opinion and ways—bullheaded, one might even say, like all the Audleys—even James, when it comes to Philip, gives way before his brother's will. I think it is because he feels guilty."

"Guilty about what?"

Charlotte, spreading jam on one of the fragrant, buttery little rolls Cook had baked early that morning, froze as she realized what she had said, and a deep flush traveled up her neck. She sent Camilla a stricken look.

"I mustn't say any more. Please, I beg you will forget I said such a thing."

Despite the curiosity gnawing at her, Camilla could do nothing but nod. "Don't give it another thought," she said lightly. But she was wondering: *What does James have to feel guilty about? And perhaps if I knew that, I would understand the source of all this trouble between him and the Earl.* Aloud, she went on in her calm way, "Charlotte, I hope you will speak plainly to me about this unusual charade his lordship has proposed." She clasped her hands in her lap. "Do you wish me to refuse?"

"I . . . you . . ." Charlotte floundered a moment, then bit her lip. "James and I disagree," she said at last, looking miserable, and Camilla immediately concluded that what had occurred in the library last evening had resulted in an argument between them during the night. "James doesn't see anything so dreadful about Philip's plan. I vow he's as reckless as Philip! But you can't simply go about flouting the rules of society!" She passed a weary hand across her eyes. "I was raised always to observe a certain decorum, to accept the rules and restrictions set down by polite society, and not to do anything that would cause a scandal. If this deception were to be discovered, Miss Smith, we would all be in the most awful predicament!"

"Then," said the Earl from the doorway, "I recommend that it not be discovered."

Camilla gave a little start, and turned her head to watch him stride into the room. He looked splendid in a buff riding coat and tight-fitting tan breeches, his Hessians polished to a high gleam. In contrast to Charlotte's drawn appearance, the Earl this morning looked rested and fit, the picture of health and virility. There was a relaxed set to his lean jaw, and his pewter-gray eyes held the cool, calmly determined expression Camilla was beginning to know.

Charlotte tensed and studied the gold-rimmed china cup before her as the Earl heaped a hearty portion of the repast arrayed on the sideboard onto his plate and settled himself beside Camilla.

"I trust you're ready to begin your lessons." It was more of an order than a question.

A martial light entered her eyes. "You're assuming that I'm going to do as you wish, your lordship. Now, I may not know much about the highest circles of society, but I do know that it is never wise to assume anything."

"I don't assume, Camilla—I insist," he said silkily. "Don't tell me you're having second thoughts. I was under the impression it was all settled."

He poured himself a cup of steaming coffee, then slanted her a cool glance. "Don't slouch at table, my girl," he advised. "Shoulders back. That's right. And set your knife just so when you're finished. Not that way, like this. And I think that color is not as becoming as some others upon you," he added, with a critical eye at her dark gray gown. "Pale pink or rose would suit you better—and green, any shade. Blue would do nicely, as well. The dressmaker should consult with me before you make your final selections. I'll make myself available to her this afternoon."

Her cheeks burned beneath his offhanded criticisms. "I thought Lady Charlotte was to be my teacher, not you, your lordship," Camilla replied with asperity, her chin lifting. She turned toward Charlotte. "Wasn't that your understanding?"

Charlotte nodded, twisting the folds of her napkin in her lap. The Earl took a leisurely sip of his coffee and set down the cup, regarding Camilla steadily.

"If you're going to be ready to hold your own with Brittany Deaville, Lord Marchfield, and that damned group making up the house party at Marrowing Hall, Miss Smith, you're going to need all the help you can get. Not that you don't speak beautifully, and your manners are perfectly charming, but there are many things you have yet to learn. The intricacies of our rather frivolous society may seem unimportant to you, but believe me, others will think it distinctly odd if you don't recognize the names of the patronesses of Almack's, don't flirt with your fan in the precisely accepted manner, don't hold your fork in just such a way, and don't appear fashionable, elegant, and impeccably attired in the most becoming toilette possible at every occasion."

Camilla glanced over at Charlotte. The girl nodded in agreement.

Camilla swallowed. Suddenly, the food on the plate before her did not appear quite as appealing. "You make it sound as if everyone sits in constant judgment upon everyone else—looking to find fault."

"They do."

"Everyone?"

"Most everyone. Personally, I don't give a damn what anyone thinks—that's the Audley creed, by the way," he added sardonically, and drained his coffee cup. "But for you, it will be different. My plan will never succeed if you don't pass inspection with flying colors."

She tried to stay calm through the quivering in her stomach. "It sounds horrid."

"It is—but only if you let it bother you." Suddenly, his eyes softened and he gave her one of his rare, warm smiles. "Once you've mastered a few of the more mundane idiocies, you'll be able to relax and enjoy yourself, I promise. But you'll have to work hard at first—and it's time for your first lessons to begin. First, however, you'd better outline for both Charlotte and me a list of your accomplishments, if any."

Her accomplishments.

"I can carry two trays full of ale tankards at once through a crowded taproom and not spill a drop."

He fought back a smile. "Impressive," he drawled nonchalantly. "Is that all?"

"I have an excellent memory, your lordship. Do you think that my reciting all the lyrics to sailors' most popular drinking songs would endear me to your friends?"

"Doubtful. You'd have to sing them."

Charlotte made a sound like a choked moan.

"My lord," Camilla said with a tight little smile, "perhaps this is not such a good idea, after all. You see, I have no accomplishments."

"Can you draw?"

"No."

"Do needlepoint?"

"No."

"Play the pianoforte?"

"Not a note."

The Earl regarded her dispassionately. So she had none of the so-called accomplishments valued in a young woman by society. Neither did he, but no one cared if a man could sketch a bowl of peaches, or embroider handkerchiefs or other such nonsense. It didn't matter, he told himself. She could get by for a few weeks without such superfluous skills. Still, studying her in the clear morning light, he considered abandoning this entire plan. Last night, heady with the triumph of Brittany's jealousy, it had seemed a fine idea, rather unconventional to be sure, but not impossible to pull off, and certainly not as scandalous as many of the stunts that went on undetected in the hightest circles. This morning, however, Miss Smith's own hesitation communicated itself to him. Her admitted lack of accomplishments could be overcome, but her lack of confidence, if it wasn't only momentary jitters, could be disastrous. Where was the self-possessed, intrepid creature he had first encountered?

"Charlotte, leave us a moment."

"Your lordship, if you're going to bully Miss Smith . . ." Charlotte choked out bravely, but she paused when he turned his icy glance upon her. "I—I cannot in good conscience allow it . . ." she whispered.

For a moment Philip studied her as if seeing his brother's wife for the first time. "So you have some pluck, after all, do you?" His gray eyes lit up. "Not only have you spoken directly to me without James to support you but you have challenged me." Suddenly he grinned. "Perhaps you're not as timid as you pretend," he murmured approvingly. "But you may go with a clear conscience, Charlotte. There's no need to fear for Miss Smith at my hands. She is the vanquisher of Gertie, remember? And more than able to stand up to me. I still have a lump on my head to prove it, don't I, Miss Smith?"

Camilla clamped her lips together at this and refused to be drawn into an answer. Charlotte, baffled, glanced from one to the other of them, then rose somewhat hesitantly from the table. "Miss Smith?" she asked at last.

"I am not in the least bit afraid of speaking privately with his lordship."

"Well, then . . ."

Charlotte's skirts rustled as she left the table. When the huge double doors were closed behind her, the Earl rose and paced the length of the room. "Do you think me a fool?" he asked after a moment.

"You? Of course not."

"Then you trust my judgment?"

She thought she saw where this was leading, and answered a bit more cautiously. "I suppose so—in most matters."

He came to stand beside her and put a hand lightly on her shoulder. "Miss Smith—no, Camilla, for we must get accustomed to being familiar with one another—do you trust me when I say that I have the utmost confidence in your ability to pass yourself off as Charlotte's cousin?"

She pushed her chair back and stood to face him, lifting her head so that she could look directly up into his face. He was studying her with an intent expression that almost made her forget what she planned to say. Almost, but not quite. "It is myself I don't trust, your lordship," she answered quietly and with complete honesty. "I don't think I can fool all those people."

"I think you can."

"Why?"

He smiled then, the corners of his sensuous mouth curving upward, a glint of humor entering his eyes. Camilla felt her heart turn over as he lightly touched her cheek. "Because you somehow possess an intrinsic elegance, my girl, which cannot be assumed or learned or taught. That alone will get you by. The rest is just . . . frosting. However, our society devours frosting, so you must have it in abundance. Therefore: lessons. But first, tell me something. I'm not trying to pry, but I must know a little of your background. Surely you did not learn to speak and move the way you do in a workhouse. What is your story, Camilla?"

She hesitated. "It is not particularly interesting."

"I will endeavor to stay awake until the end."

She laughed at this, as she guessed he intended. "Come out onto the terrace," he invited, taking her arm. "We'll talk there."

The terrace was an enchanting spot nestled beside the south gardens. Flanked by gorgeous flower beds and shrubs it was dappled with sunlight, and partially shaded by a beautiful oak. A miniature rose garden hummed with the drone of bees. There was a stone bench against the wall; nearby a stand of beeches spread their branches upward toward the brilliant turquoise sky, and a rambling stone walk bordered by neat shrubs led away from the garden and down toward the maze and the verdant copse beyond.

They sat upon comfortable rattan chairs in the sunshine. Several feet away a small fountain gurgled beside a marble statue of a child with one hand gracefully outstretched, holding in his palm a single perfect rose.

"Lovely," Camilla breathed, gazing around her with pleasure.

"My sister used to love this terrace," the Earl said almost to himself. He looked about him, and seemed to notice the exquisite site as if seeing it through someone else's eyes. "She'd come here every morning for her lessons. Her governess, Miss Pym, didn't seem to mind. She used to tell my mother that Marguerite did better when she studied outside. She came alive in the sunshine, with the birds singing in the trees and the roses blooming at her elbow."

A shadow crossed his face. He seemed to give himself a shake. "That's all in the past." His voice was harsh. "My sister died three years ago. We're talking about the present now."

Yet he shifted his shoulders so that he was half-turned away from her, and continued to gaze sightlessly at the charming statue bearing the single rose.

He looked so bleak, his powerful shoulders slumped forward, his eyes gone suddenly dull. A chill touched her, even as the warmth of the sun washed over the flagged stones beneath her slippered feet. What had happened to Marguerite? How had she died, and why did it haunt him so?

She wanted to ask, but didn't dare. The subject seemed painful enough without delving further.

"I'm sorry," Camilla said simply. Silence fell over the terrace, save for the peaceful drone of the bees, the sudden blissful chirping of an unseen bird amid the autumn plumage of the trees.

The Earl shook off his reverie and turned to her again. "The subject is you, Miss Smith. I think it best we stick to that. Tell me your story."

As much to divert the conversation from the unhappy tone it had taken as to answer his question, she told him, explaining as simply and matter-of-factly as she could.

After all, if she was to embark upon this mad scheme, he had a right to know something about her, and it wasn't as if she had anything to be ashamed of. She told him that her true name was Camilla Brent, she told him of her early years at Brentwood Manor, of her parents' death in a carriage accident, and at last, of the discovery of her father's debts and her placement at the workhouse. "I am not clear on the details," she said, "but there was nothing left to provide for me after the accident." She shrugged her shoulders in a delicate gesture. "None of the villagers felt comfortable taking in the squire's daughter to their homes, thinking their cottages too humble, I suppose—so I was sent away to London." A short pause. "That is all."

Something twisted deep and hard within him as Philip heard those quietly spoken words. That is all. Her calm acceptance of the difficult fate served up to her was to her credit, but it rattled something inside of him. He turned his head quickly to look at her yet again. This girl, Camilla Brent, was a squire's daughter, she had been gently brought up, and in her early years had known luxury and comfort; she'd been educated, pampered, no doubt, and carefully taught, only to lose the parents who had cherished her. Worse, she'd next been cast off, destitute and alone while still a child, into one of those wretched workhouses. Now she worked in a tavern, of all places. Yet, she had not once since he'd met her complained of her lot, bemoaned her lost place in society, or asked anything of him or anyone else, even sympathy. She sat beside him at this very moment with a quiet dignity that put his own moments of self-pity to shame. Perhaps tragedy had touched him, perhaps James was lost to him, and perhaps the responsibilities of running the estates, coupled with the real and intense fear for his siblings, weighed heavily on him at times, but he had no cause to sigh, not when this slender girl with the delicate cameo face and burning green eyes accepted her own misfortunes without a tear.

He came to his feet and paced across the terrace and back, stopping before her. "You don't belong in the Rose and Swan," he said abruptly. "You won't go back there. When this is all over, we'll think what you're to do. But I won't allow you to go back to being a tavern maid."

He meant to be kind, Camilla knew, but his words stung her pride. His pity cut through her like a blade. Whatever her circumstances, however dreary her fate, it was still *her* fate. She wasn't about to let anyone—even the Earl of Westcott—take charge of her life. She was her own mistress, had always been so, and Mrs. Toombs and Mr. Dibbs would certainly testify to that, as would Miss Victoria Motterly and all of the other employers with whom she had been so briefly and disastrously acquainted. She rose to face him, tilting her head up to meet his eyes. Her own sparkled with defiance.

"I may not have position, your lordship, or a great many worldly possessions, but I have sense and wit enough to make my own decisions, thank you. Kind as you have been to me since the accident, you cannot 'allow' me to do anything. As the matter stands, I have no intention of returning to the Rose and Swan. But that is my affair, not yours. I told you that I am going to Paris, if you recall, when this is over. That decision hasn't changed."

"Why Paris?"

She clenched her dainty jaw in a way that both amused and exasperated him. "That is my business."

"Is there a young man waiting for you there?" he demanded.

She stared at him in astonishment, feeling a hot blush

steal into her cheeks. "No!" she cried, starting to spin away from him. "There is not."

He caught her arms. "You're certain? Then why are you blushing?"

For a moment she didn't know what to say, for she couldn't explain it herself. She gasped, opened her mouth, closed it again, and blushed brighter. "Oh, you're insufferable!" she burst out, trying to wrench free, but unable to break from that iron grip. Studying her embarrassment, he chuckled suddenly.

"I beg your pardon. I didn't mean to insult you—or to pry into your personal affairs." Amused, he pulled her closer, his eyes warm with humor. Camilla tensed, trying desperately not to respond to his nearness, to the easy strength emanating from him, or to the mesmerizing spell of his eyes, which now searched her face with such disconcerting keenness.

"It's only that you seemed so determined, Camilla," the Earl went on. "I thought perhaps there was a young man, someone you had arranged to meet. I know how headstrong young girls in love can be."

"Do you, my lord? Why doesn't that surprise me?"

He grinned at her jibe. He gave her a light shake. "Minx! But we are talking about you. So you are not in love with some oily Frenchman?"

She took a deep breath. "I have never been in love," she assured him crisply. "I do not have a romantic nature."

She pushed away the memory of the powerful dreams that haunted her sleep. Those didn't count. When she was awake, in the daytime, she was practical, sensible, and far too realistic to be influenced by the yearnings that came in the soul of night.

She added quickly, "I think I have told you all you

need to know about me. Except, perhaps, that I did work as a lady's maid for a time in the household of a viscount, and I learned something there of the speech and mannerisms of a genteel young woman—I suppose that background might come in handy in this scheme—but if you're not satisfied," she rushed on, "then we'll forget this entire matter and I'll simply leave. My ankle is already much better, and I could go today. Perhaps that would be best after all."

"Miss Smith." He pulled her closer, the corners of his mouth lifting. "Be quiet. You'll not escape that easily. I need your help, and I am perfectly satisfied with what you've told me. So . . ."

"Yes?" Breathless, she waited, staring up at him while her heart suddenly began to hammer in her chest, beating faster and faster as his gaze studied her, lingering first upon her eyes, then drifting down to fasten upon her mouth, then returning slowly to meet her gaze again.

It occurred to Philip suddenly that she would no doubt find a host of suitors once she made her appearance in London. She was quite fetching, even in that dark gray gown. Its somberness could not dim the brilliance of her expressive eyes, nor mar the animated charm of her face, radiantly aglow in the sunshine dappling the terrace. Her blush, though, revealed to him just how innocent this disarming ragamuffin actually was. He added gently, brushing a stray lock of burnished copper hair back from her cheek:

"You will have to play the part of a woman in love if my plan is to succeed. It is essential. Do you think, Camilla," he said slowly, "you could manage to behave as if you were in love with me?"

Her throat felt dry. Her hands were clammy. She

moistened her lips with her tongue in a nervous little gesture that was unconsciously feminine and appealing.

"I—I suppose I could. I'll certainly try, your lordship."

"Philip." As he spoke the word, and stared down into those wide, river-green eyes an urge came over him, as tender and reckless an urge as any he had ever known. He followed it without thinking. He leaned down suddenly toward that breathless, entrancing face, and kissed Miss Camilla Brent lightly, gently on the mouth.

It was a tender kiss, surprisingly delicious. She tasted like flower petals dipped in honey, he thought, his arms tightening around her. Her mouth was rosebud soft, inviting, even parting in instinctive surprise at the light pressure of his mouth, and her lushly curved body melted against his with a sweet natural warmth.

He kissed her again, more deeply, hungrily, acting on instinct, not by any design. Nice. Very nice, indeed. When he lifted his head and smiled at her, he caught the dazed, dreamy look in her eyes. Then she blinked, focused in on him, and suddenly seemed to snap out of a stunned dream.

"Oh!" Her whole body went tense. With a little outraged gasp, she jerked away.

Taken aback by his own brash actions, Philip let her go. "Miss Smith . . ."

"How dare you!" she breathed, her hands flying to her throat as she took two steps backward, nearly stumbling over a chair.

His arms shot out and steadied her, then dropped to his sides. Damn it, he felt like a schoolboy, floundering in his own mind for some explanation of his actions. "Instruction, Camilla—that's all," he said hastily, coming up with a logical explanation that almost sounded convincing even to himself. "If we're going to play the part of lovers, it seems a bit of instruction is in order."

"Kissing lessons? Is that the kind of lessons you had in mind for me?" she gasped, her face now flaming to the color of the roses growing alongside the terrace.

"No, not initially." Philip felt sweat breaking out on his brow. Damn, what was wrong with him? He was saying and doing all the wrong things. This was about winning Brittany, after all. Why the hell had he kissed Camilla Brent?

"It won't happen again," he said firmly. *It damn well better not,* he thought irritably. He didn't need any more complications in his life. "I give you my word."

She was trembling. Her reaction to the kiss terrified her. She had enjoyed it far too much for her own good. *Enjoyed it?* she thought in helpless alarm. She had loved it, loved the feel of his arms around her, loved the heat and warmth of his mouth pressed against hers. Elation flooded through her, mingling quickly with dismay.

She was headed for disaster. This would never work. She ought to run away now, flee, before she ventured any closer to the abyss that was quickly opening before her.

"If I'm to stay at Westcott Park and play this role you wish me to play there must be only a business arrangement between us," she heard herself lecturing. Shakily, she drew herself up tall and spoke with as much steadiness as she could muster. "I won't be used—or ill-used. If you have hidden purposes, my lord . . ."

"I don't." Philip felt shaken too, and he didn't understand it. Damn! He also didn't understand what had impelled him to kiss the girl. Audley rakishness, he guessed. Nothing more. Yet . . . a strange feeling of tenderness had surged through him when he'd held her close like that. He couldn't understand it. Yes, she had looked

sweetly delectable—even irresistible—standing there with
the sunlight gilding her hair, her eyes soft and wondering,
her lips seeming to beckon him, but damn it, if he was
going to pull off this escapade and win Brittany—which
after all, was what he wanted, wasn't it?—he had better
stick to business. He was aware of the new wariness in
Miss Smith's green eyes, of the anger in her face. He
didn't want to do anything to hurt or frighten the girl. She
was doing him a valued service, after all, and she deserved the same respect as anyone else in his employ. The
fact that there was something insistently appealing about
her shouldn't complicate the matter.

He couldn't afford any personal involvement. And
there would be no future in it for her—hell, for either
one of them. He had her reputation and her feelings to
contend with—and her innocence.

For once in his life, he couldn't afford to play the rake
—not in any form, not to any degree.

Besides, Philip reminded himself yet again, he was
about to marry Brittany.

"Miss Smith—Camilla." He spoke formally. "I apologize. Between us there shall be a business arrangement,
nothing more. You'll be well rewarded if you help me,
and you'll have my gratitude as well. And," he added,
"throughout the course of our arrangement you'll have
my respect. I give you my word as a gentleman on that."

"Ah, but are you a gentleman?" she asked shakily.

The sun passed behind a cloud and the October day
went suddenly still and cool. A grim smile touched
Philip's eyes. Suddenly his face looked harsh in the sunlight. "Some might debate the point, but you have nothing to fear from me."

Yes, yes I do, Camilla thought, the blood pounding in

her ears. Or was it herself she feared? But she made no comment.

"We have an agreement then? A strictly business agreement?"

"Yes." She looked down at her hands. "I think I should consult with Lady Charlotte now."

"An excellent idea," he agreed briskly.

But as she turned to go, Dorinda slipped through the French doors onto the terrace, with Tickles cradled in her arms.

"*There* you are, Miss Smith." She ran up to them excitedly. "Will you tell me a story, please?"

To her brother she said defensively, "I have no governess now, so there aren't any lessons to learn, are there?"

"Not for today, but I will find you a new governess, Dorry, and quickly—you can count on that."

"Why can't Miss Smith be my governess?" the little girl exclaimed, her eyes lighting with inspiration. She turned rapturous, hopeful eyes to her brother. "Oh, Philip, it would please me above all things!"

"I'm afraid that is impossible," he replied with a rueful smile in Camilla's direction. Suddenly, he pulled out his gold watch and glanced at it, frowning. "Miss Smith has another duty in this household for the time being. And you are not to annoy her while she is engaged in work she is doing for me," he said distractedly, and Camilla saw that his mood had changed.

His face had tautened, he looked colder, grimmer. He was suddenly the aloof Earl with more on his mind than a serving maid and a young child full of questions.

"I have an urgent appointment," he said to Camilla. He patted Dorinda absently on the head. "I must go. We can discuss your progress tonight at dinner."

And he was gone, striding through the doors with his

long-limbed rugged grace, leaving Camilla and Dorinda alone on the terrace, staring at each other in silence.

What have I got myself into? Camilla wondered in dismay.

A business arrangement, that's what. She stared down at the little girl beside her as Dorinda tugged at her skirt.

"What kind of work are you doing for Philip?" she insisted on knowing. The kitten meowed, as if echoing her question.

Camilla did not even hear. She was lost in thought. She was remembering that kiss, when Philip had clasped her in his arms and caused the world to ebb away. All of the tension drained out of her. Dreamily she contemplated one lovely month of living in such a blissful fantasy, and then with a start, she returned to her senses. She stared at Dorinda, and at Tickles, then turned to where the Earl had disappeared through the French doors.

For a moment, she felt keenly the perils of the fantasy life she was about to enter. She knew that if she were wise, she would shun the dangers it posed.

But she knew she could not.

She had to remain at Westcott Park. She had to go to London. It was all necessary, in order to help Philip and ultimately, his entire family. It would help Hester, too, she reminded herself, and the other workhouse children —as well as the authorities.

It was the right thing to do.

But all the time she knew she was telling herself a lie.

She was staying because she wanted to stay, for herself and no one else. It wouldn't last forever, but for a short while, she could pretend that all those midnight dreams of hers had come true. She could pretend that Philip Audley really did love her. And when it was time, she would leave and never look back.

"What kind of work are you doing for Philip?" Dorinda asked again, more insistently.

Camilla gave her a faint, slow smile as a bird fluttered down to perch atop the fountain, then quickly flew away. "We're playing a kind of game, Dorinda—for a short while."

"A game?"

Camilla nodded and reached out to stroke the kitten. "This is a game that grown-ups like to play sometimes, as well as children." She sighed. "It's called make-believe."

During the next two days Camilla was kept busier than she could ever have anticipated. Her waking hours were crammed with intense instruction from Charlotte on everything from proper deportment to acceptable conversational topics, from the strict rules regulating the famous ballroom at Almack's to the listing of the best and most fashionable shops on Bond Street. There was all manner of information to learn and memorize, including the names of places and people whom it was fashionable to casually mention during the course of conversation, and most important of all, there was the long list of customs and terminology used among the ton, all of which she must be familiar with.

"Never speak across the table to anyone at dinner, as we did last night." Charlotte warned, pouring tea late in the afternoon and handing Camilla a cup. "That's all right for an informal family gathering—in most households, at least—but never in company. You must take care to speak only to the persons beside you. And," she added urgently, "never wear a morning dress to dinner. Which reminds me, we must go to Madame Fanchon's the moment we get to London and purchase some more gowns for you. Only the most elegant, most dazzling will do once we reach the city—and it will serve Philip right if the cost is frightfully excessive!"

"Oh no, we mustn't," Camilla protested, certain that the Earl had no such major investment in mind.

"Oh yes, he told me himself to spare no expense in outfitting you. No one will believe that he has fallen madly in love with you if you are not of the first stare of fashion. Nothing could be worse than for you to appear to be shabby-genteel! Philip is known for his excellent taste. Why, Weston makes all his suits and he is regarded as quite the best of tailors. No one in London would expect anything other than the most stylish of toilettes to be worn by Philip's fiancée. Didn't you see that gown Brittany was wearing? Well, you must match—even sur-pass—her elegance."

Camilla could see that now she had started, Charlotte was beginning to enjoy her role in the charade, though she still had qualms about all the pitfalls awaiting Camilla in society.

"And you must remember the difference between a barouche and a landaulet, which is the dowdiest of things," Charlotte rattled on, speaking of everything her active mind touched upon that might relate to Camilla's imposturing. "A barouche, though, is highly fashionable. When we get to London, I'll take you driving in one. We'll go to Bond Street and there you will do your real shopping, for there are so many fashionable shops, and I know of the most delightful millinery which will have just the kind of hats and bonnets to best suit you. Wonderful confections—you will adore them."

"They sound horribly expensive," Camilla said, taken aback.

"Indeed. But that is Philip's problem, not ours," Charlotte finished, and James, coming in the door just then, chuckled, and kissed her.

"I'm glad to see you're entering into the spirit of the game, Charlotte." He seated himself on the sofa beside her and accepted the cup of tea she poured for him. "We'll make a real Audley out of you yet. Now, Miss Smith, you seem to have no difficulty in playing along with Philip's wild schemes. You did magnificently in the library, under what must have been most awkward circumstances." He grinned.

"All I did was follow his lordship's lead. There seemed nothing else to do." Camilla smiled back at him. James Audley was relaxed and open when his brother wasn't present. When he was with Charlotte, especially, the vague air of weariness seemed to fall away from him, and his diamond-blue eyes shone with pleasure. Camilla sensed that they adored each other; she also sensed, though, that at times there was some unspoken strain between them. Occasionally she had noticed an expression of sadness flit over Charlotte's delicate face—then James would glance at her, his eyes worried. He would then say something meant to make her smile, or else he would simply come to her and squeeze her hand. Camilla wondered what problem beset them, but she also marveled at the warmth and ease that most often characterized their relationship. This was due largely to the easygoing, fun-loving nature she sensed in James Audley —a nature much like that she observed in Jared and Dorinda.

She wondered if Philip, beneath his sardonic exterior, also shared this good-humored approach to life—when he wasn't being stern and frowning at everyone. It was telling, she thought, that Philip Audley was both proud of his family's reputation for recklessness and unconventionality, and that he despised it. Within himself, she suspected, there was a constant struggle to come to terms with his own nature, to blot out all of the impulsive, mischievous temperament that characterized his siblings, and to maintain the strict decorum he felt necessary for the master of the house. Yet despite all the value he placed on self-discipline and good sense, he had not been able to resist making a scandalous wager on the outcome of his suit with Lady Brittany—or resist entering into this wild plot with Camilla. The reckless side of his nature, she decided, was still obviously very much alive.

"Is there any word on when his lordship will be back?" she asked, trying to keep the eagerness from her voice. The Earl had left Westcott Park for unexpected business in London on the same day they had spoken on the terrace. She hadn't seen him since.

"Without fail he'll return in time for dinner at Marrowing Hall," James assured her. "Aside from that, who knows? Philip doesn't exactly confide in me about any of his dealings."

Dorinda and Jared burst into the parlor at that moment, both talking at once. Dorinda wanted to know if someone would tell Cook she had permission to sample the fresh blackberry pie, and Jared inquired in a low tone of his brother whether a Mr. Wimpnell had recently come to call.

"I've no idea. Why—who is he?" James narrowed his gaze. "Out with it, you rapscallion. What mess have you landed in now?"

Jared flushed the color of cherries, tripped on the rug, and caught himself just before crashing into the tea tray.

"Dash it, James, that's doing it up too brown!" he protested. "And in front of the ladies—and Dorinda. You ought to be ashamed."

"I've a feeling you're the one who's ashamed," his brother retorted.

"He's been gambling again, that's what I think," Dorinda piped in matter-of-factly. Everyone stared at her. She shrugged.

"I overheard Mrs. Wyeth talking to Durgess."

"Speculating, you mean!" Jared exploded. "They've no cause to think any such thing!"

Poor Tickles was so startled by his loud voice and angry tone that she leaped from Dorinda's arms and streaked out the door. "Now see what you've done," Dorinda cried. She wasted no more time on the adults in the parlor, but raced toward the hall in pursuit of her pet. "She'll probably hide in the cellar and eat some dreadful rats . . . oh, how could you, Jared . . ."

Her voice trailed away as she ran past the staircase and disappeared in the long corridor that branched off into two separate wings.

Jared sank into a chair, looking so mortified that Camilla decided it would be best to leave him alone to confide in James. She leaned toward Charlotte.

"Perhaps you would accompany me upstairs? There is something I should like to discuss with you . . ."

"Oh, don't run off on Jared's account," James said heartlessly. "He's been in the soup ever since he was sent down from Eton."

"It seems this family won't be happy unless the whole world knows my troubles," Jared muttered bitterly.

Camilla looked from James's blithe countenance to Charlotte's sympathetic one, and then she could bear it no longer. "Well, perhaps if you tell us your troubles, we might be able to help." She offered Jared a reassuring smile. "Nothing you can say will shock me, you know. I have worked in a tavern for years now and have heard some tales there that would no doubt peel your ears off."

"For goodness sake, Camilla, don't ever say any such thing to anyone you should meet in London!" begged Charlotte.

"Of course not!" Camilla shot her an indignant glance. "I may not possess town polish yet, but I'm not lacking in brains!" She turned back to Jared. "Yes?" she urged.

But he merely shook his head and would say no more. Camilla sensed his despair, but there was nothing else she could do. For the next half hour, he tried to appear in his usual bantering spirits, and then he excused himself to go riding before supper.

Later, though, when she came downstairs early for dinner and found herself alone, she happened to pass the little salon near the pantry stairs and saw Jared staring morosely out the window. Pausing on the threshold, she noted that his wide young shoulders sagged, and his hands were shoved deep inside the pockets of his waistcoat. Her heart went out to him. In the light from the oil lamp, she saw that his young face was filled with misery.

"Whatever it is, Jared, surely it cannot be as bad as all that," she said quietly, stepping into the room and closing the door.

He spun about and immediately tried to fix a smile upon his face, but it was no use. Camilla saw the despair in his gray eyes, so like his brother's, and she read in them a pitiful hopelessness. "Don't try to gammon me," she said firmly, and coming forward, took his hand. "Tell me all about it. You won't shock me, and I have found that there is always a solution to every problem if only a person has the courage to follow it through."

"You don't understand . . . you just don't know—I'm in the worst fix!"

"Please let me help you."

He stared at her a moment, holding back his emotions with an effort. But he instinctively sensed the calm, self-assured competence of the young woman waiting so patiently before him. He gave way before her kind smile and the pressure of her hand squeezing his. He blurted out: "All right, I'll tell you but first you must promise not to say a word to Philip!"

"Certainly not—not a single word."

He paced to the divan and threw himself down upon it, tearing his fingers through his glossily curled hair. "It's these damned debts," he ground out between clenched teeth.

"Gambling debts?" Her heart sank. "So Dorinda was right?"

"Yes. You see," he went on, sinking down beside her and throwing himself back against the cushions, "I became friendly with this group of fellows at Eton—splendid fellows, actually! We got into the habit of kicking up larks together . . . nothing really awful, of course, but . . . well, all that's not important. Before I was sent down from school for . . . well, it doesn't signify—we went to London. Playing hookey, you see, and well, one of the fellows, it doesn't matter *which,* managed to get us into some gaming clubs and . . . well, the upshot of it all is I lost five hundred pounds."

"Five hundred pounds?" Camilla couldn't keep the horror from her voice. The sum was staggering. For several moments she could only gape at him. "But that's a fortune," she gasped. "How on earth could you ever hope to . . . Oh, Jared!"

"I told you it was hopeless." He groaned, and buried

his face in his hands. "Mr. Wimpnell, the proprietor of Paxton House, the club where I lost the bulk of it, had been dunning me at school, but I'd managed to put him off. Only now he has discovered that Philip is my guardian until I'm of age and last week I had a letter . . . well, you remember that Philip said he was expecting a visit from the cursed fellow."

"And you claimed to know nothing about it."

Jared hung his head. "Cowardly, wasn't it? You must think me despicable."

"No. Oh no!" She clutched his hand and held it tightly, thinking hard. "Jared, you made a mistake. A costly mistake, but not a . . . an evil one. You certainly didn't murder anyone—or even cheat on your exams—or pick a pocket, for heaven's sake. I've heard far worse confessions than yours," she assured him warmly, trying to make up for the shock she had displayed. *Think, Camilla, think,* she admonished herself silently, closing her eyes a moment in concentration.

She opened them presently and gazed at Jared, hope dawning in her eyes. She said slowly, "This Mr. Wimpnell —he didn't have the opportunity to call on Philip, did he? I mean, Philip left for London and never mentioned another word to you about the matter."

"That's true, but he didn't leave until noon that day. Mr. Wimpnell could have come in the morning."

"But your brother never summoned you, and never mentioned anything. Don't you think he would have?"

"He'd have bitten off my head," Jared snorted.

Camilla wasn't sure about that, but she said nothing. "Would Philip be able to loan you the money to pay off the debt?"

"Well, of course. For him such a sum would be trifling. But I don't want him to be involved in this—it's my debt and I intend to repay it on my own—only it might take me months to do so and Mr. Wimpnell doesn't seem inclined to wait."

"Then he must be persuaded." She stood up briskly and took a turn about the small room. Outside the tall windows, the late afternoon sun glinted in a lavender sky, casting long, zigzagging shadows on the rose gardens and hedges of Westcott Park. "Do you have any money at all to give him toward paying off the debt?"

"Fifty pounds," he muttered glumly. "A mere drop in the bucket."

"Then here is what you must do," she said, whirling back toward him with an air of decision. "You must arrange to send him the fifty pounds somehow . . ."

"Bob, one of the grooms, will do it for me."

"Good." She came forward and grasped his hands. "It will all work out then, you'll see. Send a note with the money explaining that you'll be in London shortly and will discharge the rest of your debt immediately upon arriving. Then, we must contrive to get Philip to let you come up to London with us . . ."

"But where am I to get the money?"

"I will lend it to you."

"You . . . will . . . lend . . . Good God, no!"

"Oh, I know you think I don't have it and I don't . . . yet. But you see, your brother promised to pay me a thousand pounds for being an impostor, and I will ask him for half of it when we get to London. If I give you four hundred and fifty of it . . ."

Camilla did some rapid figuring. She could give Jared the bulk of her advance payment, and still have fifty pounds to spend right away on Hester and the children. When the month was up, and she received the rest of the money, she could send most of that to the workhouse, as well. Oh, the food and warm clothes it would buy! She herself was accustomed to getting by on very little—the most she would need was fifty pounds for her journey to Paris and that would be more than enough—it would even leave her a goodly sum for several days' stay at a pleasant inn or rooming house until she could get settled and begin her search. It wouldn't matter if Jared was never able to repay the money—she knew she was being vastly overpaid anyway. To think that she would be earning a vast sum of money for the chore of wearing beautiful clothes and attending lovely parties—and dancing with the Earl of Westcott! It was ridiculously, incredibly absurd—and the sensible girl who had grown up in the Porridge Street Workhouse knew that there were far better ways to spend that money. But before she could begin to explain her reasoning to Jared, he surged to his feet, flushed and trembling. He addressed her in a thunderous tone startlingly reminiscent of his eldest brother.

"No! No, no, and no!"

"But you haven't heard . . ."

He gripped her shoulders. "I can't take your money, Miss Smith. Good Lord, what do you take me for? I could never accept a loan from a lady and . . ."

"You're very kind, Jared," Camilla pointed out, "but I am not precisely a lady, as you well know. I am in truth only a serving maid and so you need have no scruples . . ."

"You are every inch a lady and I'll plant anyone a facer who says otherwise!" he countered furiously, growing even more agitated.

Camilla was touched, but she couldn't help shaking her head. "Listen to me, you dear sweet Sir Galahad. Your noble sentiments are appreciated—deeply appreciated," she added with a somewhat misty smile. "But they're impractical. If I am in possession of an extra four hundred and fifty pounds which I don't need, and you are in desperate want of that sum, and we are friends"—and here she gave him a winsome smile—"as I hope we are, then," she continued as he nodded, "it makes perfectly good sense for me to lend you the money, and when the time comes that you can repay it, I will gladly accept."

"It's wrong," he said flatly. "Not that I don't appreciate . . ."

"Oh, fustian!" Camilla threw up her hands. "Jared, do stop playing the gallant and be sensible. It will save your neck!"

"But it's highly unconventional to take money from a woman . . ."

"Since when have the Audleys been bound by convention?" she challenged. Jared met her laughing gaze and gave out a short chuckle.

"You ought to be in Parliament," he muttered. Yet there was respect in the appreciative gaze he flashed at her. "All right, Miss Smith, you win. I'll—I'll do it. Thank you! But if Philip ever finds out about this he'll wring both of our necks."

"He won't. Why should he?" Camilla smiled. The sound of voices in the hall recalled her to the dinner awaiting them. "Goodness, how long have we been here? We mustn't keep the others waiting. I must have my lessons, you know—if I do something awful at the Marrowing party, we'll both be ruined, since the entire plan will be finished before it's barely started."

"Somehow, I don't think you're the kind of girl to fail at anything," Jared said slowly. He took her arm, looking suddenly happier than he had all day. "Shall we?"

"By all means."

Dinner went well, but Camilla curled up in her bed that night with the disquieting knowledge that her life was becoming every day more complicated, rather than less so. She lay in the darkness for quite a while listening for some sound outside her window to indicate that the Earl might be returning, and she imagined him, in that silvery space of time between wakefulness and sleep, charging up to Westcott Park on a black steed, the magnificent animal of her dream. She then pictured him climbing up to her window, slipping one leg over the side, and coming to her in her bed . . . but here the daydream ended, and sleep overtook her—a blank, dreamless sleep, alas, from which she awoke rested and refreshed.

There was no sign of the Earl all of the next day, and even when she went upstairs to dress for the Marrowing party, he had not returned. Lord Kirby had come to call and amused her by teaching her how to play whist in the parlor, but there had been no word from the Earl all through the afternoon, through tea, through the hour when Kate came to dress her hair and help her on with the ice-blue taffeta gown she would wear to dinner. Only as she sat before the dressing table mirror and clasped on the opal earrings that Charlotte had loaned her did she hear the horses' hooves clatter onto the drive below.

"That must be his lordship, now!" Kate exclaimed, flying to the window to peer out. "Oh yes, 'tis! Miss, only wait until he sees you! He'll be that surprised. You look like a princess!"

Camilla resisted the overwhelming urge to jump up, run to the window, and peer out for herself. She sat frozen on the gilt chair, suddenly feeling every nerve ending in her body vibrate, and an anchor seemed to plummet inside her stomach.

"Kate, I'm not sure I can do this!" She lifted wide eyes to the flushed, excited little maid. "I don't know if I can go to dinner at Marrowing Hall!"

The girl gaped at her. "Why, to be sure you can. You must—his lordship is expecting you, isn't he?"

"Ye . . . es."

Charlotte knocked on the door just then. "Camilla . . . oh! Oh, you look lovely," she breathed.

"I do?" Camilla couldn't believe the quaver in her voice. If she spoke like this all night she would be doomed.

Charlotte, pink-cheeked and ravishing in a gown of tea-rose silk, came forward with a smile lighting her face. As Kate slipped out of the room with a quick curtsy, Charlotte put an admiring hand to the gleaming curls arranged about Camilla's glowing face. "Up until this moment I wasn't sure any of this would work, but now that I see you—Camilla, you not only look as though you could be my cousin from Hampshire, you look as if you could be the new toast of London. In fact, I shouldn't be at all surprised if you don't steal a good portion of Brittany Deaville's thunder."

All I'd really like would be to steal the Earl's attention, she thought woefully, and then pushed the dangerous thought from her mind. She knew only too well how unthinkable it was that there could ever be an alliance between herself and the Earl of Westcott. Such a thing, even if he were ever to feel the slightest *tendre* for her, would be disastrous for his family and his social standing. It would disgrace him in the eyes of all his peers. No, she knew the strict limits of her role in the charade about to go forward.

Besides, he loved Lady Brittany Deaville. And, she had

to admit to herself, they would suit admirably. No doubt about it.

"Philip has only just arrived," she told Charlotte, trying to sound calm, though her heart was racing.

"Oh, how could he be so late? Well, never mind," the other girl added hastily, reading the nervousness in her protégée. "He won't keep us waiting long. No doubt he'll be changed and ready to leave before we've had a glass of ratafia in the drawing room. Come along now."

Camilla wanted to stay rooted to her chair. She *wanted* to crawl under the bed and hide from the world as Dorinda had done when Gertie had pursued her. Just the thought of facing Brittany Deaville and Lord Marchfield again, not to mention the other guests who would be present tonight, made her throat close up and her knees tremble.

But Charlotte was holding open the door, smiling encouragingly, and there was nothing to do but go downstairs and face whatever lay ahead.

At least her ankle was better. It scarcely hurt a bit as she swept into the hall after Charlotte, the taffeta and lace train of her gown rustling behind her.

But she wasn't entirely free from pain. As she descended the curving staircase, the thought of how she was helping to ensure Philip's marriage to Brittany brought forth an ache deep in her heart.

Well, she had agreed to this knowing full well the consequences. And now that she had promised the money to Jared, it was definitely too late to back out.

She straightened her shoulders and stiffened her spine as she sailed into the elegant, fire-lit parlor where James waited for them both. *It's for a good cause, and it's going to be fun, if you don't let yourself get carried away,* she scolded herself. But she had an unnerving feeling that she might have waded into water that was a bit too deep for her, and that before she was finished, she might very well drown.

12

"Would you care to play something for us, Miss Smith?" Lady Marrowing inquired as the assembled party seated themselves in the long drawing room of Marrowing Hall. Lady Marrowing, a tall, florid-faced woman with regal carriage, was by no means beautiful, but she possessed a warmth and straightforwardness that lent her a certain handsomeness, and it had made Camilla feel comfortable from the start. In addition, Lord Marrowing, a short, stout man who suffered from gout, had greeted her as affectionately as if they were old friends, then had winked at Philip and congratulated him on picking such a beauty. Reassured by the promising start, Camilla felt that dinner had gone well, but now, with the grand piano looming before her like a sleek, gleaming monster, she found herself at a standstill.

"Well, actually, I do not play," she began somewhat hesitantly. Immediately she observed the horror on Charlotte's face, and added swiftly: ". . . well enough to entertain company."

"Perhaps Brittany would care to play for us," Lord Kirby quickly suggested. He acknowledged Camilla's grateful look with a smile, then turned to Brittany, breathtaking in mint-green silk beside him. He gazed beseechingly into the blond girl's violet eyes. "For me?" he implored in a tender tone.

The dazzle of Brittany's smile lit the room. She rose gracefully and seated herself at the piano.

As she began to play, Camilla became more than ever aware of her own shortcomings. Not only was Brittany an unsurpassed beauty, she was also most properly accomplished. Camilla couldn't help but admire the skill with which she played, her fingers dancing over the keys with just the right degree of restrained enthusiasm—in short, with perfect elegance.

Camilla stole a glance at Philip as the music filled the room. He stood by the fireplace, a little apart from the rest of the group, which included James, Charlotte, Lord and Lady Marrowing, Marchfield, and Miss and Mr. Fitzroy, an animated brother and sister from Berkshire, as well as a rather mousy young woman introduced as Lady Jane Drewe, who stammered whenever anyone spoke to her. Philip, who always appeared totally at his ease, seemed to miss nothing that went on about him, and Camilla was certain that Lord Kirby's open flirtation with Brittany would not have escaped his notice. Marchfield and Mr. Fitzroy had also shown Brittany a great deal of attention throughout the evening, but to her amazement, the Earl had exhibited no outward sign of jealousy or even annoyance. He had appeared as always, nonchalant, mockingly amused by all that went on about him, conducting himself with the cool, easy grace that characterized him.

In fact, he had amused everyone at dinner with his

sardonic replies to Miss Fitzroy's raptures over Lord By-
ron's poems, he had eaten and drunk with all apparent
pleasure, and he had shown Camilla such dazzling attention that for a few moments—if she hadn't known better
—she might have believed he really was in love with her.
His eyes had smiled into hers as they chatted, exerting a
dizzying effect, which she fervently hoped he could not
guess at.

Now, though, as Brittany played the piano, Camilla observed the admiration on his face, and a vise tightened
painfully around her heart. Her face felt stiff from the
forced smile on her lips, and it took an effort to keep her
thoughts on the music.

Everyone applauded heartily when Brittany had finished. Mr. Fitzroy begged for more, but she rose with a
laugh.

"Oh, it is Lady Jane's turn, I do believe."

At this poor Lady Jane turned pale as death. "No . . .
no, I c-couldn't . . . p-please, someone else!" She
looked so dismayed that Camilla heard herself speaking
to cover the girl's embarrassment.

"Charlotte plays charmingly! I would so love to hear
her have a turn!"

The words were out before she realized it—all she had
been thinking was to save Lady Jane from what was obviously a painful predicament. It never occurred to her until she had spoken that perhaps Charlotte could not play
well at all. Fortunately, however, this wasn't the case, for
James quickly seconded her recommendation, and Philip
in his sardonic way added his entreaty, so that Charlotte
smiled, and quite willingly took her place at the piano
bench.

The moment she began to play Camilla realized the
vast difference between Charlotte's abilities and those of

Lady Brittany. Brittany played well, but Charlotte played brilliantly. Every note was thrilling, heart-wrenching, her fingers flew nimbly, spiritedly over the keys, and she threw her entire self into the music. Camilla, whose experience with music had been limited to hearing faint strains of poorly rendered Beethoven wafting into the upstairs hall of the Motterly town house when she had been employed there, immediately recognized the true passion and artistry that Charlotte displayed. One glance at the Earl's face showed her that he, too, was surprised. Why, Charlotte must never have played in his presence before! Everyone in the drawing room listened, enraptured, and when Charlotte finished, they begged her to play more. With a pleased nod, Charlotte obliged.

Only Brittany appeared a trifle put out as the beautiful music filled the room once more. She didn't like it when her own star was dimmed by another's brilliance, Camilla realized, and suddenly hoped any envy over Charlotte's talent would not put a strain on their relationship once they became sisters-in-law.

When Charlotte had finished her third piece, Brittany leaned forward to smile at Camilla.

"Miss Smith, if you do not care to play, perhaps you will entertain us with a song? Surely you and your cousin have performed together at family gatherings. Do share with us one of your favorites."

Camilla froze. She became aware that young Mr. Fitzroy and his sister had joined in urging her as well, and Lady Marrowing was smiling encouragingly, even coming forward to lead her to the piano. Lord Kirby was biting his lip, and James appeared stunned to silence, while Brittany eyed her with strong curiosity, a slight smile curving her lips as she observed the other young woman's hesitation.

Camilla swallowed, wondering frantically what to do. Suddenly, Brittany whispered something to Lord Marchfield. He glanced sharply at Camilla and then nodded, an unpleasant smile curling his lips.

Seeing his look, something hardened inside her.

"Why, yes, I'd be honored to sing," she said smoothly, and rose in one fluid motion from her seat.

As she approached the piano she noticed James staring at her with trepidation, but he looked bewildered as to how to help her. She glanced toward the Earl, wondering if she would find apprehension in his gaze as well.

But the Earl looked cool as ice. He strode forward, bowing to Lady Marrowing. "Allow me to escort Camilla, ma'am. I wish to make a request, a song I particularly enjoy."

And then he was gripping her elbow, leading her to the piano, where Charlotte waited, eyes wide.

"Faint," Philip said quietly in Camilla's ear.

"What?"

"If you can't sing, you must pretend to faint. I'll simply tell them you're not feeling up to snuff after your late carriage accident, and we'll go home. Do it quickly," he urged as they reached the piano.

So, like Lady Brittany and Lord Marchfield, he thought her such a poor creature that she could not even sing a proper song? Maybe, she mused, he thought she'd sing one of the sailors' ditties she'd teased him about the other day. A mischievous gremlin took possession of her, and the impression she had, from the corner of her eye, of Brittany's smug anticipation of her failure sealed the matter in her mind. She shot him a smile of great sweetness. "But I *wish* to sing, your lordship," she murmured.

And with that she bent toward Charlotte and whispered something he couldn't hear.

A moment later, Philip found himself sinking into a wing chair not far from the fire. The seat afforded him a clear view of Miss Smith's enchanting face, though at the moment all he could think about was his desire to wring her dainty neck.

He had no idea what would happen next. Didn't she realize on what thin ice she was treading? Well, the girl had courage, that was certain. More courage than he possessed at this moment, he thought wryly. In the next few moments, this whole wild scheme could very well fall apart—disastrously—in plain view of everyone.

Then Camilla clasped her hands before her, smiled directly into his eyes, and began to sing.

She sang a simple country ballad. It was a song with which all were familiar, yet never had any of the company heard it sung so beautifully. Her voice was sweet and pure, each note she sang was exquisite. No one in the drawing room moved as the melodic sound of her voice filled the air. They all sat, transfixed.

Watching her, Philip felt the stirrings of unexpected pleasure. Brittany's excellence on the pianoforte paled before the mesmerizing beauty with which Miss Smith sang her little ballad. Her singing, he realized, was as unaffected and charming as she was herself.

His thoughts shifted to the memory of how surprised he had been by her appearance this evening. When he'd joined her and James and Charlotte in the drawing room before coming here, he'd come to a dead standstill at sight of her. Miss Smith, in her ice-blue gown, had stunned him. She'd been radiant, with her hair the color of molten bronze, and her figure enticing in the low-cut silk. He'd been unable to recognize a single trace of the ragged and filthy waif he'd run down on Edgewood Lane in the pert, lovely woman who'd greeted him with a soft

smile in his own drawing room, and who, as she sat beside
him in the carriage tonight, had smelled so deliciously of
a light and flowery French perfume.

*Whatever happens with Brittany, Camilla Brent must not
go back to that tavern,* he thought. *She is above that, far
above that.* Perhaps only a few days ago the fate of a
serving girl called Weed would have been no concern of
his, but now there was no turning back. He would see her
settled in some respectable position where she wouldn't
have to be a drudge for drunken sailors—or wait upon
spoiled, demanding young women. It was the least he
could do. Then the song was finished, and everyone was
applauding and complimenting Camilla, urging her to
sing again.

Philip noticed with satisfaction that Brittany seemed
the least pleased by Camilla's success.

So it was working, after all. He forced himself to tear
his gaze away from Brittany's rigid countenance, beautiful even with that adorable little frown between her
brows, and focused deliberately on Camilla. It wouldn't
do for Brittany to see him staring at her. But every time
she saw him watching Miss Smith with deep affection, he
would score another point. So Philip smiled at Camilla,
and nodded his approval. He couldn't help being impressed once more by the natural grace with which she
accepted the compliments the company showered upon
her.

Camilla, blushing, was trying to refuse their pleas for
another song, but her audience was persistent. Mr. Fitzroy in particular begged her to sing another. "For you
have the most enchanting voice," he cried, gazing at her
with a rapt expression Philip found annoying.

"Yes, do sing again." Philip gave her his lazy smile as

he added his entreaty to the others. "Your accomplishments never fail to surprise me—or to give me pleasure."

There was nothing to do but comply, so she sang again, then rose with resolution from her chair.

"Miss Fitzroy, it is your turn to entertain us. Won't you honor us with a song?"

But Miss Fitzroy played the harp, not the piano, and though she was a lively girl, her musical abilities did not equal those of her predecessors. She was kindly praised, and thanked, and then the party broke up into small groups, some playing whist, others chatting by the fire.

Camilla found herself near the long, draperied windows with Philip. "You enjoyed frightening me, didn't you, you little minx?" he said in an undervoice, while he lifted her hand to his lips and kissed it, the picture of gentlemanly deportment. "I ought to box your ears!"

"You wouldn't dare! I'd box yours right back," she warned, and he threw back his head and laughed.

"Damned if you wouldn't," he growled softly.

"You are beginning to understand me, my lord," she smiled saucily up at him. "Good. After all, it was your idea to play this hoax on everyone, and you said I might enjoy myself."

"I didn't mean at my expense, brat!"

"Is that any way to address a lady? No wonder Lady Brittany will not have you."

She realized immediately that this quip went beyond the mark. She cursed her own propensity for saying exactly the wrong thing. "I'm sorry," she said quickly, in her direct way, but it was too late. His eyes had narrowed with anger. He stood before her, tall, lean, menacing, looking as though he really would box her ears—or worse.

"Don't be angry," she breathed.

The hard look on his face chilled her. "Allow me to point out that you overstep your bounds, Miss Smith."

"I have a habit of doing that," she admitted, and bit her lip. "Why do you think I have been discharged from every position I've tried to maintain? I always manage to say the wrong thing, to offend someone by thinking I know the best way to handle this or that . . ." Her voice trailed off.

Philip, seeing her very real chagrin, felt his anger dissipating. It was melted away completely by her next words.

"Of *course* Lady Brittany will have you," she asserted. "What I said was only a jest. Surely you are not unaware of your own appeal, sir, to the opposite sex."

A gleam entered his smoky eyes. "Such a suspicion has occurred to me upon one or another occasion. However, the lady in question seems to be made of sterner stuff."

"Pooh! It is clear to anyone with eyes in their head that she is in love with you."

"Is she?" Fascinated, he regarded her with appreciation. He leaned closer. "Aren't you doing it up a trifle too brown, my girl? You flatter me, but even one as confident as I am wouldn't go so far as to call Brittany's behavior toward me loverlike. Still," he murmured, "I don't believe my suit was ever disagreeable to her. And now that she thinks she can't have me . . ."

"Exactly. She wants you more than ever, your lordship. And I am convinced she is in love with you. I'd lay you a monkey she'd scratch my eyes out if given half the chance."

"Would she?" His gray eyes gleamed and the firelight touching his face gave him a devilish, sardonic aspect. "Well, we'd best not give her the chance. After all, they are such very pretty eyes."

Camilla caught her breath, surprised by the unexpected compliment. No one had ever said anything remotely like that to her before, certainly no one as dashingly handsome as the Earl. "Thank you, your lordship." She dimpled up at him, absurdly warmed by the compliment, and unaware of how completely charming she looked, with the mass of copper ringlets framing her expressive face, and her soft lips parted in an unaffected smile.

"Philip," he muttered in exasperation, and gave her arm a shake. "Don't forget."

"I'll try," she promised, coloring guiltily.

At that moment Lord Kirby and Mr. Fitzroy came up to commend her on her singing and by the time she had thanked them both, and engaged in a short discussion with them about a proposed picnic outing the next afternoon, she found that the Earl had moved off. Still smiling at Mr. Fitzroy's flirtations, she managed from the corner of her eye to watch the Earl approach Brittany near the fireplace. As he spoke, that faint, handsome smile upon his face, the beauty turned swiftly from Lord Marrowing to gaze at him. Camilla couldn't help admire the way she slanted a dazzling smile up at the Earl. Her luminescence glowed through the room. Even from twenty paces away Camilla saw the smile's warmth touch and envelop Philip, felt the spark that flew immediately between the two of them.

Good, it is working, she thought to herself, pushing away the tiny pain in her heart. *After all, the sooner this is all over, the sooner I can be on my way to Paris.*

She turned away, but couldn't help stealing glances occasionally at the Earl, locked in intent conversation with Brittany. He left her presently, and came back to Camilla, showing her all the attention and consideration expected of one who is about to become officially engaged. He was

very good at this game, Camilla thought rather bleakly.
For the rest of the evening, though she smiled and made
pleasant conversation with all of the assembled guests, a
strange flat feeling enveloped her. Even the pronounced
attentions of Mr. Fitzroy, who was clearly captivated with
the very refreshing Miss Smith, as Lord Kirby whispered
in her ear, could not banish the sour feeling in her stomach. *I must have eaten too many sweetmeats,* she told herself, trying to shake off the sensation. She laughed at Mr.
Fitzroy's jokes and played whist with Lord Kirby, trying
not to let on that her spirits had drooped.

At length when Philip's carriage bore them home and
drew up at Westcott Park, she felt weary beyond measure.
James and Charlotte had both complimented her whole-
heartedly on her success this evening, but she replied au-
tomatically, and had to force a frozen smile onto her lips,
receiving only small pleasure from their praise.

Her knees sagged a bit as Philip handed her down from
the carriage. "Is your ankle troubling you?" he asked with
concern.

"No."

"You seem tired."

"I am—a little."

He looked at her sharply as they went into the house
but said nothing more until after he had helped her out
of the blue silk pelisse the dressmaker had rushed to her
that very day. "You did admirably tonight, Camilla.
Thank you for your help."

"There's no need to thank me." She spoke crisply. "We
have a business agreement, do we not? I'm simply doing
my best to keep up my end of the bargain."

"And you're doing wonderfully," Charlotte put in,
placing a light hand on her arm. "Why, I nearly fell off
the piano bench when you sang so beautifully."

"Brittany didn't like it above half, though," James chuckled.

"Serves her right." Philip set his hat and gloves on the hall table. He was obviously not a bit tired and in a fine humor. "Tomorrow, we're to go riding and then have a picnic at Silver Lake. The day after," he added, "we'll depart for London."

"With Jared and Dorinda?" Camilla quickly asked, remembering her plan to help Jared.

"Jared may come," Philip said, "but not Dorinda."

James frowned. Charlotte squeezed his arm.

"Dorinda will be disappointed, Philip." James steadfastly refused to drop his gaze despite his brother's cool stare. "Why must she be left behind? It doesn't seem fair. The child doesn't even have a governess anymore . . . what is she to do all day . . . "

"I have already made some inquiries about a governess when I was in London," he returned shortly. "As a matter of fact, I plan to settle the matter once we return there. But Dorinda will do well here. She likes the outdoors, and one of the maids can look after her. Mrs. Wyeth will see that she is occupied and happy. Besides," he added curtly, "I seem to remember that I am in charge of our sister's well-being, not you."

"That doesn't mean you're making the right decisions concerning her!" James retorted.

"You can be sure no harm will come to Dorinda while she is in my charge. Do you doubt it?"

James glared at him a moment, tight-lipped. Then his glance dropped.

"How could I?" he asked, his mouth twisting with bitterness.

"Just so."

Tension vibrated through the hallway.

For a while, earlier, it had seemed as though the brothers might declare a truce, but now all the old hostility and resentment had risen to the surface again. James looked angry and miserable. A muscle twitched in his jaw, and poor Charlotte's usually sweet countenance was taut with suppressed anger. Philip, Camilla realized wearily, had donned his icy armor. In the light cast by the huge branch of flickering candles on the wall sconce, his eyes gleamed as cold as winter frost.

Wanting to ease the tension, Camilla spoke up.

"If you let Dorinda come to London, I'll look after her," she offered. "She would so enjoy the journey. She loves to be with the family and I . . . I know she would be desolate if we left her behind."

She lifted imploring eyes to Philip, but he turned away.

"You'll have plenty to occupy you while we're in London. Dorinda would be a distraction, and I want you to concentrate on what lies ahead of you. Charming a houseful of guests at Marrowing Hall is child's play compared to what awaits you in London."

A note of brusque command entered his voice. "Go upstairs now and get some rest," he told her. "There are certain things I want us to accomplish tomorrow regarding Brittany."

Charlotte looked alarmed and glanced quickly at Camilla.

"What kind of things?" Camilla asked.

But his good mood had vanished. "You'll find out tomorrow," he said with more than a hint of impatience. "Good night." And with these curt words of dismissal, he stalked into his study and closed the door.

James grimaced. "Don't mind Philip," he told Camilla as he gazed at the thickly paneled study door as if trying to peer through to the man locked inside. "He's not angry with you. It's just . . . he's a tyrant when it comes to ordering Dorinda's life. Jared's, too, for that matter. But he means it for the best. I've escaped, more or less, by marrying. I think that's partly what infuriates him, he can't control me anymore."

"Why? Why does he need to control any of you?" she burst out.

James loosened his cravat and sighed. "Because of Marguerite," he said in a low, unhappy tone.

"Your sister . . . the one who died?"

James nodded. He and Charlotte exchanged forlorn glances. "James, don't," Charlotte whispered.

But he looked straight at Camilla. "I caused her death, you see. It's a long story, but that's what it comes down to in the end. Marguerite died because of me, and Philip holds me accountable. But what's worse, he holds himself accountable as well."

"I don't understand."

James spoke quickly. "Philip was away when Marguerite died. He was fighting a duel with André Dubois—a protégé of Marchfield. I was left at home in charge . . ." His voice trailed off. He bit his lip as Charlotte put a hand on his arm as if to comfort him.

"Don't think about it, James," she begged.

"It doesn't do any good to relive that night," he said slowly. "But none of us has ever been the same since. And though sometimes I hate Philip, I know deep down that he's only afraid for Jared and Dorinda, afraid of not taking good enough care of them, afraid that he'll fail in his responsibility to them. So," he finished, and took Charlotte's arm as they started toward the stairs, "you must forgive him if he seems cold, even dictatorial sometimes about Dorinda. He wants what's best for her, though it isn't always easy to see that."

"I know he does." Camilla was thinking hard. There were still so many unanswered questions, but she couldn't ask James any more. The subject was obviously painful for him. But what he had told her shed light on Philip's behavior. She thought she understood now some of the haunted sadness she'd seen in his eyes. It also explained much of the tension between him and James. But how had James caused Marguerite's death? And what exactly had happened to her?

They reached the landing and turned into the wide corridor that led to the private bedchambers. She bid James and Charlotte a somber good night.

It felt wonderful to slip out of her gown and her satin-bowed slippers and into a dainty nightrail of cream silk edged in lace. Camilla perched in the window seat and rested her cheek against the cool glass, pondering the night sky. Wistfulness filled her. She had as many questions as there were stars. But one thing was certain. The Earl of Westcott cared for his family—he cared deeply.

But he's going about protecting them in a most tyrannical way, she observed with a wry little shake of her head.

Perhaps I can convince him to try a gentler approach, she thought hopefully, and then caught herself up in the thought. *Here I go again, trying to manage everyone, even an earl.* But Philip Audley and his family were more than mere titled strangers to her now—she cared about them. Especially Dorinda. The little girl needed love and affection more than rules and lessons. Somehow or other, Philip ought to be made to realize that.

But as Camilla readied herself for bed and blew out the candles, it was no longer Dorinda who lingered in her mind. It was Philip himself, so tall, so splendidly handsome and rakishly sophisticated, yet, she thought, her eyes softening in the darkness—so bleakly alone.

Brittany, for all her elegance and beauty, didn't seem to know how to vanquish that empty sadness inside him. Or maybe she simply hadn't had a chance yet to try. *I could manage it,* Camilla thought, smiling to herself as she pulled the covers up to her chin. *If he ever looked at me the way he looks at Brittany, I'd make him happy even if I had to bottle sunshine and serve it up for breakfast.*

But more likely Philip Audley would be a creature of the moon and the night, she thought, curling one hand beneath her cheek as she turned on the pillow. He'd be a man at ease in the mystery and sensuous power of the darkness, a man as worldly in the bedroom as he was in the drawing room. Her heart beat faster as she imagined for one breathless moment what it would be like to be alone with him in a room glinting with moonlight, to be taken into his bed, to be held in his arms and kissed . . .

Don't think such thoughts, she scolded herself, sitting up abruptly and pressing her hands to her hot cheeks. An earl and a serving girl? It was too impossible for words. *He is going to wed Lady Brittany and you're pledged to help him. Better think about tomorrow, when Brittany won't be the only one to receive some surprises.*

Philip was in store for one himself, she reflected uneasily.

Thinking of what she had to tell him about the proposed picnic outing, Camilla had a strong feeling she would encounter that famous Audley temper once again. Only one possibility provided her with a gleam of hope.

Maybe it would rain.

13

"You can't *what*?" Philip demanded as Camilla faced him over the breakfast table.

They were alone. Dazzling October sunshine spilled across the gleaming mahogany table invitingly set with pristine white linen and flowered china. There was not a cloud in the flawless blue sky, Camilla observed with misgiving. Charlotte and James had not yet come down, and Durgess had reported that Master Jared had gone out riding early. Dorinda had the sniffles and was taking tea and toast in her bed.

"I'm sorry," she repeated, meeting Philip's stare with lifted chin. "But I've never ridden a horse in my life. Well, maybe a pony when I was very little," she amended. "I don't precisely remember. But we didn't have any horses for pleasure riding at the workhouse."

He scowled. Of course they hadn't. He should have thought of that before making these plans. "Well, we can't afford to let such a small matter get in the way," he decided ruthlessly.

"Couldn't we go driving in the carriage instead?" she began, but he silenced her with a frown.

"It will look bloody peculiar if we start changing the arrangments now. Besides, Brittany is a first-rate rider and she'll want to show off. Don't worry—I'll give you a gentle mount and you'll manage. Finish your breakfast quickly and we'll have time for a few instructions."

Camilla dropped her spoon. "Now?" she said, and nearly choked on her biscuit.

"Now."

A short time later she found herself practically running beside him to keep up with his long strides as he headed toward the stables. "Do you have a very small horse?" she asked breathlessly.

"We have one pony—he belongs to Dorinda. But she's nearly outgrown him." He threw her a mocking grin. "You'd look ridiculous riding him."

"Perhaps not. Maybe we should just see . . ."

"Trust me, Camilla, I have a horse you can handle." He paused a moment, letting her catch up to him, and they faced each other on the graveled path. His critical eye surveyed the flushed, worried young woman whose face was turned uneasily up toward his.

In the rich claret riding habit, Camilla Brent looked every bit as aristocratic as Brittany Deaville herself. Tall and willowy, the tight habit clung to her figure, revealing every curve, and the color brought out the vibrant glow in her eyes and skin. Her thick hair was tied back with a black ribbon and she wore a pert feathered little riding cap over her captured curls. She looked charming, yet elegant, as though she had been to the manor born. Which, he reminded himself, she had been—literally. Born to the manor of Squire Brent, a daughter if not of nobility, of landed gentry at the very least.

But she might be a princess, he thought, so lovely and delicate is her face, so graceful her figure. Weed. How could anyone ever have called this comely creature Weed?

"You're afraid of horses, aren't you?" he asked directly, reading the anxiety in her expression.

She shook her head. "Only of falling off one."

"If you pay attention to my instructions, you won't fall off—or be thrown off, which is much worse."

He said good morning to the groom sweeping out the stable yard—Jerome—calling him by name, then threw open the stable door and led her inside. "Here she is. This is Marmalade."

He had paused at a stall where a broad-backed chestnut horse with large, velvety eyes nuzzled at a feedbag. "She's the mare Marguerite rode when she first graduated from a pony," Philip explained, regarding the horse fondly. "She's fairly old and completely gentle. So gentle that my hellion of a sister didn't ride her for long. One week, maybe two, then Marguerite was on to the friskiest colt in the stable."

Camilla stared up and up as he led Marmalade from the stall.

"Marmalade," she said softly, almost like a prayer. Then, suddenly, she burst out: "Is this . . . *really* necessary?"

She looked so nervous Philip had to choke back a laugh. He had a sudden urge to smooth that troubled look from her face by stroking her cheek. Instead he cupped her chin firmly in his hand. "Where's all that pluck and courage?" he teased, but his eyes were cool. "Isn't this the same girl who knocked me on the head with a candlestick a few nights ago? Who sang like a nightingale before a room full of strangers only last eve-

ning? Come now, buck up and pay attention. We only
have a short time to make you look like a halfway compe-
tent horsewoman."

"If you think it's possible . . ."

"I know it's possible."

He was surprisingly patient, Camilla found, as he
showed her how to mount the mare, how to sit with her
feet resting in the stirrups, how to hold the reins between
her gloved hands and guide the horse with boot and crop.
At first she felt uneasy and insecure from the great height
of Marmalade's back, but after a short time following the
Earl's suggestions she began to lose her fear and to feel a
bit of confidence coming back to her. She was not by
nature a timid or fearful girl and it was only her inexperi-
ence that had made her so reluctant at first to try. It had
seemed an impossible task to accomplish in a short time,
and she hadn't wanted either to fall or to make a fool of
herself before the rest of the company, but after an hour
of Philip's expert instruction, she felt much more comfortable, and his next suggestion made her feel even more
confident that she could carry the day off successfully.

"You and I won't wait for the others to arrive at Westcott Park at noon—we'll start out early and meet them
near the lake." Philip was watching her walk Marmalade
around the stable yard. Her carriage and seat were good,
he noted approvingly, and she no longer looked as
though she was about to screech in terror. "That way," he
pointed out, "you'll only have to ride *home* in the company of the others, and you'll have had the practice of
riding there under your belt."

"Excellent strategy!" Camilla smiled thankfully at him.
"I shan't have to *trot* or gallop or anything, shall I?"

"I'll make certain you don't," he promised grimly. "If
the others gallop off, we'll linger behind and pretend that

we want some time alone together. It wouldn't be considered at all unusual for a couple in love to let the crowd move ahead of them. In fact, that will explain our riding out ahead of the others at the start, as well. They'll think we've been trying to manage a few moments alone together in the park—which will rankle with Brittany, unless I miss my guess."

The prospect appeared to afford him great delight. Camilla nodded, and patted Marmalade's neck. *Why shouldn't it?* she asked herself crossly. After all, that was what this entire charade was about. She tried to concentrate on the role she was going to play, reminding herself that if all went well today, tomorrow they would go to London. She could receive the advance portion of her stipend, and begin to help Jared and Hester. And she would also have to begin thinking of a way to smuggle an anonymous message to the authorities, along with that note for Mr. Anders.

There was much to do, and she couldn't afford to let her mind dwell on unimportant matters, such as Philip's love for Brittany, which must be very great indeed for him to go to all this trouble and expense to win her. As Jerome appeared with Philip's great, black stallion—a spirited devil by the name of Satan, Philip informed her—she planted Hester's face inside her mind and thought of all the good this was going to bring to her.

If she noted the lithe grace with which the Earl of Westcott mounted the half-wild stallion or the easy authority with which he controlled the beast, or how wide his shoulders were beneath his tan riding coat, she gave no sign of it. With her mouth resolutely set, and her eyes dark with concentration, she walked Marmalade alongside Satan in the direction of the lake.

It was a beautiful day, and Philip made light conversation as they rode, pointing out various points of interest along the way. The gardens, the orchards, the maze, and the meticulously manicured emerald lawns of Westcott Park could not help but captivate her—it was like living in the midst of a beautiful park and a lovely wood all at the same time.

I could stay here happily for the rest of my days, she thought, gazing at the birds that sang from the birches, at the domed sky spread across the peaceful countryside like a sapphire canopy.

When they reached the appointed picnic site her pleasure grew. "Oh, how delightful," she exclaimed, real joy on her face. Several hundred yards away, the lake glittered in the sun. A pair of swans floated serenely on the silver-blue surface. The clearing itself was thick with smooth grass, and shaded here and there by clumps of gnarled oaks. Squirrels darted, chattering, among the low shrubs and rocks, and birdsong filled the sky. She knew that Charlotte was to bring the picnic hamper laden with cold chicken, bread, cheese, and tarts, and her enthusiasm for the outing grew. Especially now that she felt so comfortable on Marmalade.

"What lies beyond that fence?" she asked, pointing toward a low brick wall just south of the lake.

"Pastureland. The meadow slopes downward here, though, so it gets a big boggy beyond that point. You don't want to ride there unless you fancy sloshing through mud."

She watched him dismount with ease from the saddle and ventured, "How do I get down?"

"With my assistance." He grinned, and reaching up, drew her gently to the ground. His arms were strong and tight around her waist as he set her upon the soft grass.

"How's the ankle?" he inquired, and she noticed that he hadn't removed his hands from around her waist yet.

"Much better. I rarely even feel a twinge now."

"Good."

Still he hadn't taken his hands from her waist. In fact, his grip tightened and he was drawing her closer, dangerously close, she felt, as her senses took in the powerful nearness of his body. The clean, spicy scent of him drew her; instinctively she yielded against the pressure of his arms. Staring up into the dark, compelling face and the eyes gazing so intensely into hers, Camilla fought to think clearly.

"My lord . . ." she began in a voice not quite as firm as she had hoped, but he only shook his head and pulled her closer.

"*Philip.* Say it, Camilla."

"Philip—what is this about? I don't think . . ."

"Good, don't think. I've thought it all through very carefully. The others will be here shortly. I've decided that it would be excellent strategy, as you put it before, for Brittany to find us trysting."

Her heart was racing. "Is that what you call it?" she breathed.

He laughed, a deep, husky sound that sent the blood shooting hot as fire through her veins. "I think," he continued softly, "that she should catch us in the midst of a kiss. Now this is all simply part of our arrangement, I swear to you. But it will be a very effective device if properly managed. Do I have your permission?"

No. She ought to say no. It was improper, foolish, dangerous, even. To kiss a man like this as part of a ploy? She must be mad even to consider it. Yet, gazing into those gleaming eyes, gray as the dawn, something wanton burst into flower within her. Her heart pounded with wild anticipation, and she found her gaze lingering on his sensuous mouth. She remembered that kiss on the terrace and, heaven help her, she wanted more.

"You're certain this is necessary."

"Completely certain."

Suddenly, hoofbeats sounded, and glancing over, they saw a group of riders cantering toward them across the park.

"Perfect timing, Brittany, my love," he muttered with a short laugh.

Then he drew Camilla closer still, sliding his hands to the small of her back, pressing her against him. He lowered his head and kissed her with every evidence of wild, enflamed passion.

Was he pretending to kiss Brittany? she wondered fleetingly as his mouth moved insistently over hers and his powerful arms held her close. Then she forgot to wonder anything as the delicious wildness of his lips captured hers again, her own mouth parting beneath the insistence of his tongue, and she felt the solid world slipping away.

His hands clutched her tighter, closer, moving up and down her shoulders, her spine, burning her flesh. Instinctively, her arms went around his neck, pulling him closer. Hungrily, she kissed him back. A million years or maybe one moment passed before she heard Brittany's light, cool voice across a short space of grass.

"Marchfield, we seem to have an unlucky knack for intruding. *Do* forgive us, Philip."

He released Camilla and slowly glanced up. Camilla felt dizzy, and had to resist the urge to cling to him. Still stunned by the impact of those hot, ardent kisses, she noted with admiration the expression of surprise he managed quite credibly, appearing to have had no inkling anyone else in the world existed during the span of time he was kissing Camilla. He showed not the slightest hint of embarrassment as he greeted the group of young people dismounting nearby.

"Forgive *us,* Brittany. We were forgetting ourselves." Holding Camilla by the hand, urbane and cool as always, he led her toward the new arrivals.

"James—Charlotte, you have our picnic lunch? Camilla and I have worked up quite an appetite riding."

"Mrs. Wyeth outdid herself. We've enough food in here to last a fortnight," his brother chuckled.

While Philip spoke to Mr. and Miss Fitzroy and Miss Drewe, Brittany, who was ravishing in a peach-colored riding habit and plumed hat regarded Camilla with her catlike smile. "Your mount is wandering away," she pointed out, and Camilla saw that Marmalade, never tethered, had drifted near the pasture wall. "But," she laughed, exchanging a glance with Marchfield, who stood as always at her elbow, "she looks far too meek to run off. Poor Miss Smith! Couldn't Philip find you a more worthy mount in his stable?"

"Of course he could, but I chose Marmalade for myself." Camilla cast wildly in her mind for a plausible reason. She noticed with a little grimace that Brittany herself had been riding a spirited gray mare, one that looked every bit as restive as Satan. "She reminded me of my own dear sweet Gwynneth, the horse I first learned to ride upon," she explained, finding secret amusement in having named a horse after her old tormentor. "I'm afraid it was a sentimental choice, but I don't regret it. She has the sweetest nature imaginable."

"I'm sure she does, but surely that isn't all you look for in a mount."

"No, indeed."

"It's a trifle disappointing," Brittany confided, her violet eyes fixed closely on Camilla's calm face. "But I had hoped we might have a race this afternoon."

Marchfield lifted his brows in a sardonic manner. "Poor Miss Smith," he said, echoing Brittany's words in a way Camilla found gratingly annoying. "You won't stand much of a chance on that beast, I'm afraid."

Lord Kirby overheard this remark and joined the group. He winked at Camilla. "If it's a race you're planning, save yourself and the rest of us the trouble, Marchfield. Philip would win—he always does."

"He's never raced against Marchfield—or against me," Brittany pointed out.

Kirby, more attractive than ever in a buff coat and brown breeches, his fair hair glinting in the sunlight, threw back his head and laughed. "Delightful girl, he has raced against *me,* and if I can't beat him, no one else in this select little gathering can, I assure you."

"Do you concede his superiority over you as easily as that?" Brittany teased, but there was a slight edge to her tone. "How poor-spirited of you. I would have thought you had a better opinion of your own abilities."

"Fair beauty, you wound me." Kirby shook his head, eyes dancing. "But the truth, however painful, must come out. When it comes to horses or pistols or fisticuffs, Philip is a nonpareil. None can beat him, and that includes you, Marchfield. Even James, with his fancy for boxing, could not plant his brother a facer if he chose. But when it comes to swords, my lady," he added, with a cool bow in Brittany's direction, and a grin at Camilla, "I am the master. Philip as a boy was skillful, but he could never best me at swordplay."

"It's true." Philip, coming up to the party with the others, chuckled. "You have a knack for that unexpected deadly thrust that quite undoes every opponent. Try as I could, I could never match your skill. But let us not forget to give James his due. He was always the uncontested winner of another contest."

"Really?" Charlotte asked eagerly. "What?"

"Pie eating."

Everyone burst out laughing, and Camilla joined in, relieved that Brittany had been steered away from the topic of Marmalade, and in particular feeling grateful for Lord Kirby's quick rescue. Having guessed at the Earl's game, and still being his rival for Brittany's affection, he nevertheless had twice now tried to help Camilla in dealing with an awkward situation, and she felt herself warming to him more than ever. It was a beautiful afternoon, and she suddenly felt happier than ever that she was here, embarked on this strange adventure with all these unlikely new friends.

The group trooped across the clearing to the level spot where a gaily flowered picnic blanket had been spread across the carpet of grass.

"Yes, James could eat more pies in a quarter of an hour than any of us—Philip, Maxwell, me—or any of the village boys who thought themselves so hearty," Kirby continued. He clapped the grinning James on the back. "I remember one time he consumed fifteen peach pies to our three apiece—and lived to tell the tale."

"Don't remind me," James groaned. "I was sick for a day after!"

Kirby's face softened. "You turned so green Max thought you would die. He made you promise never to do anything so idiotic again. And Marguerite said—"

Here he broke off, and bit his lip. He threw Philip a tense look, as if concerned for his reaction, but Philip was gazing fixedly at his boots, his expression unfathomable. Kirby continued in a note of forced cheeriness.

"Well, let's see what Mrs. Wyeth has packed for us today. No peach pies, I trust."

The moment was passed over quickly, but Camilla had seen the tension that whipped through Philip at the mere mention of Marguerite's name, and she also noticed that familiar bleak look enter James's eyes. Lord Kirby, too, seemed quieter than usual for a while, but as the picnic hamper was unpacked and the contents exclaimed over in pleasure, the painful memories were pushed aside, and the jovial banter resumed.

The day was lovely, the company in the mood for entertainment. Despite Kirby's blunt prediction of the winner, a race was indeed proposed and accepted. Philip obligingly entered into a race against Brittany, Lord Kirby, Mr. Fitzroy, and James.

Charlotte invited Camilla to join her and the other young women, who also declined to race, on a mission to gather flowers, but before she could accept, Lord Marchfield, who was lounging against a nearby tree, called out to her.

"Do not desert me, Miss Smith. I have no desire to hurtle across the park on horseback, nor to hunt flowers. Save me from boredom by gracing me with your company."

There seemed no way out of this invitation. Camilla cast an uneasy glance at Charlotte, who appeared equally at a loss. "I believe you must accept or appear rude," she whispered, before Miss Fitzroy tugged at her hand and led her away.

While the riders mounted, Lord Marchfield joined Camilla. "Come, Miss Smith, I know the perfect spot from which to view this race. There," and he indicated a long, level rock jutting up near the edge of the lake. Marchfield spread his riding jacket upon it with a gallant gesture.

"The finish line is to be at that tree. You can determine the winner firsthand. But of course you're certain it will be your beloved Philip."

"I hope it will be."

"Your attachment to one another appears to be firm. Forgive my saying so, but that is odd considering the fact that only a short few days ago, Philip was vying ardently for the attentions of another."

She stiffened. The man either suspected something ha-vey-cavey, or he was merely trying to stir up trouble. Well, she had no intention of aiding him in any way.

"The tone of this conversation is improper, sir." Camilla gave him the same direct stare she had often fixed upon drunken coachmen, merchants, or sailors in the Rose and Swan when their attentions grew abusive. Not many men could stand without flinching before that fiery gaze. "What has passed between the Earl of Westcott and myself is our concern, not yours. If I do not question what is in his heart, why should you?"

"A mortal blow," he mocked, clutching at his chest in a sarcastic manner.

Camilla gathered her skirts and prepared to move away.

"Your manner is insulting, my lord," she said in a low tone.

"Wait. I beg pardon." He grasped her sleeve, and a placating tone entered his voice. "I don't have the Earl of Westcott's polished address—I speak too frankly some-times, but I assure you, my dear, Miss Smith, I mean no harm."

Liar, Camilla thought, but she paused, regarding him coolly. She wondered exactly what had caused the palpa-ble enmity between him and Philip. Something more than this bet regarding Lady Brittany. Hadn't James said something about a duel the night Marguerite died, a duel fought with Marchfield's protégé?

"You and Philip are acquaintances, but not friends, I think," she said slowly, watching his smooth face. He looked startled at her blunt comment for just a moment, then the mask of suaveness settled back into place, and he laughed.

"You are perceptive, as well as lovely, Miss Smith. I commend my acquaintance, Philip, upon his excellent taste. He had best be careful when he brings you to London, though. Some other suitor might steal you away."

"That is no more possible, your lordship, than that you could win this race on foot. Look, they're off."

Satisfaction rose within her as Satan immediately sprang out ahead of the others. Camilla couldn't help observing the easy command with which Philip rode the stallion across the open land. A strange feeling of pride came over her as she watched his expert horsemanship, admiring the obvious skill that even she, a novice, couldn't help but recognize. At one point as the pack thundered across the open meadow, James's gelding drew near to the magnificent black stallion, then fell back. Brittany and James were neck and neck. Suddenly, Brittany's horse, spurred hard, jumped forward and caught Satan as the two horses swept beneath the overhanging branches of a tree. Together they rounded the curve for the final stretch.

"Lady Brittany rides splendidly, don't you agree? If Philip isn't careful, she'll catch him," Marchfield murmured in Camilla's ear.

Camilla made no reply. Her gaze was glued to the pair riding hellbent across the emerald field, their horses' manes flying, hooves flashing like lightning bolts across the grass.

"Go, Philip. Go, Satan," she breathed, and beside her, she heard Marchfield chuckle.

"No use, Miss Smith—Brittany's ahead!" he crowed, but scarcely had the words escaped him when Satan plunged forward like a fireball, streaking across the finish line a length ahead of the mare.

Before she even realized it, Camilla jumped up, clapping her hands in excitement. The next moment though she gave a scream. Brittany, in reining in her horse, had a sudden mishap. She neglected to detect a slight rise in the land, and the mare, still galloping hard, stumbled badly. Brittany tumbled from the saddle.

Instantly Camilla and Lord Marchfield started toward her, but Philip, wheeling Satan at her cry, reached her first.

"Brittany, little love, are you all right? Dear God, are you hurt?"

Philip leaped from Satan's back, and cradled Brittany in his arms. She gazed up at him, whispered something, and her arms crept round his neck. A smile of relief lit his face as he pressed a fervent kiss to her brow.

Camilla froze. She felt like someone had slammed a fist into her midsection. The fear and tender concern with which Philip cradled the blond girl in his arms was unmistakably loverlike. And his passionately uttered words had been clearly heard by Marchfield, as well as by her.

Beside her, Marchfield had gone very still. Then he threw her a taunting glance.

"As you can see, Miss Smith, our sweet Brittany appears to be much more to the Earl than a mere acquaintance, even if I am not."

She was still studying Philip's anxious face. Somehow, she managed to compose herself enough to answer Marchfield's jibe.

"Philip's concern for a lady who is a friend as well as his guest does him credit. Lady Brittany is certainly far more than an acquaintance to him—and I hope she will be to me, as well, when Philip and I are married. If you'll excuse me, I must try to help her."

She hurried forward and knelt beside the injured girl. Brittany, a little pale but looking mostly winded, looked up at her with an oddly triumphant smile. "It's nothing, the merest scratch. How foolish of me! I haven't fallen off a horse since I was five! Philip, I do believe I can stand. Oh!" Her knees buckled and she put a slim hand to her temple. "Perhaps not—the world is spinning dreadfully." Her smile widened enchantingly as he swept her into his arms.

By now the others had joined them. "Do you think you can ride?" Kirby asked, taking her hand.

"Oh yes, indeed."

"We'd better not risk it." Philip shook his head. "You'll ride with me on Satan, and I can hold you up. One nasty spill an afternoon is quite enough."

"Please," Brittany protested, "I'm sure that isn't necessary. How silly of me to cause such a stir. My poor mare . . . Marchfield, Kirby . . . someone tell me . . . is she all right?"

The mare was not hurt, but the outing had clearly come to an end. The picnic hamper was hastily repacked, the horses gathered, and in a short time everyone prepared to ride back to the house. Brittany rode side-saddle before Philip. Now that Philip's plan for the two of them to linger behind would no longer be feasible, Camilla knew she would simply have to do her best to keep up with the others. Fortunately, she guessed that the group would return at a sedate walk out of consideration for Brittany's dizziness.

I can manage this, she told herself. *Just go slow and steady, as Philip instructed.*

But she felt extremely uncomfortable—everyone seemed to be watching her, and it didn't take long to figure out why. Philip's obvious tenderness toward Brittany had not escaped anyone's notice—and she realized that Miss Fitzroy and her brother, as well as Miss Drewe and Lord Marchfield, were regarding her in various degrees of pity and amusement.

She was in their eyes a woman scorned.

James brought Marmalade to her. Even he seemed nonplused by the situation. "Philip is acting like a damned fool," he muttered. "Now that chit thinks she's got him in her pocket all over again."

"I believe it will not be necessary for me to go to London after all," Camilla said faintly. "It seems clear he has achieved his purpose. They both look perfectly content together . . ."

But even as she spoke her words trailed away, for Brittany, long used to being the center of attention of a dozen beaux, could not refrain from basking in her own glory under these dramatic circumstances. While held protectively in Philip's arms, she continued to smile enchantingly at Lord Marchfield, to speak fondly to Lord Kirby, to beg Mr. Fitzroy not to think her a poor creature for what had occurred. And a frown now darkened Philip's eyes as he realized his own error in letting the beauty see his hand.

He was glancing toward Camilla, his gaze resting on her momentarily before he spoke.

"My love, will you ride beside us? Your company will help to soothe Brittany's spirits."

She marveled at the cool, even calm of his voice, which

betrayed none of the chagrin she knew he must be feeling.

Nodding her agreement, she let James assist her in mounting Marmalade. But something went wrong.

The moment Camilla was in the saddle, the gentle-tempered mare rose up on her hind legs and whinnied furiously. Camilla had all she could do not to fall off. Clinging desperately to Marmalade's mane, she screamed. James made a grab for the bridle, but Marmalade, panicking, plunged forward, the bit clenched between her teeth.

Camilla shrieked again as the horse, bucking frantically now, raced straight toward the pasture wall.

Camilla tugged at the reins in desperation as she tried to slow the mad charge. Marmalade seemed possessed; it was all Camilla could do to simply stay in the saddle and not tumble beneath her flying hooves. A branch scraped Camilla's face, the wall loomed before her. She gritted her teeth and braced herself for the worst.

Surely old Marmalade could not attempt to jump so high! she prayed. Yet the horse gave no indication of slowing as the wall rose up straight before her. With her heart in her throat, Camilla braced herself for disaster, but at the last moment, Marmalade slid to a petrified halt, and the girl on her back went sailing straight over the mare's head—and nose first over the wall.

The rest of the party shouted in alarm. Philip, despite having to pull Brittany down from the saddle along with him and thrust her into Miss Drewe's thin arms, reached the wall the same moment as James, with the rest of the pack hard on his heels.

He got a foothold and boosted himself up enough to see over. He stared in disbelief.

Camilla sprawled facedown in mud, covered from head

to toe. As he watched, she lifted her head. Her face and hair dripped with black, boggy slime.

"Are you hurt? Can you move?" Philip jumped over the fence and sloshed to her side, heedless of the mud splattering over his own clothes.

Camilla coughed, gasped, and wiped mud from her lips with her sleeve, then saw that her sleeve was equally filthy. What was the use? To her dismay, a horrible shaking had taken possession of her, her shoulders twitched and trembled.

Philip gathered her, mud and all, into his arms. "Are you hurt?" he asked again, his voice tense with urgency.

Was she? Dazed, she shook her head.

"Only my pride," she whispered. Then as she looked into his handsome, anxious face, at his fine coat streaming with slime, and her own lovely habit, ruined beyond repair, the absurdity of her situation got the better of her. Suddenly, crazily, she began to laugh.

Philip stared at her a moment, this slender, filthy girl, covered in mud, looking much as she had the first time he met her, and something quivered inside him at the sight of her glowing eyes and mirthful gasps. Just as suddenly, he joined in.

"She's unhurt," he called to James and Lord Kirby, who had also scaled the fence and were preparing to jump down. His arms shook so with laughter that he nearly dropped her back into the mud. This made them both laugh harder.

"They've both gone stark raving mad," James exclaimed to Kirby, but Kirby, his blue eyes gleaming in the afternoon sunshine, only grinned.

"I haven't seen Philip laugh like that since . . . well, for a long time," he said thoughtfully. "That girl is good for him, James."

Looking at his brother collapsed in the mud alongside Camilla, the two of them chortling and clasping each other like children, James could only shake his head. But he wondered for one strange moment if Kirby could be right.

14 The Earl of Westcott created quite a stir when he arrived in Berkeley Square the following day with an entourage worthy of a king. His guests included his fiancée, his two brothers and young sister, and his brother's wife. A score of liveried and uniformed servants accompanied them. Seven carriages heaped with baggage were necessary for the journey, and it took the Earl's quick-moving footmen the better part of an hour simply to unload all of the family's belongings.

No one strolling or driving down the street at that time had an opportunity to glimpse the Earl's betrothed, however, for she was whisked inside the house quite swiftly. No one saw more than a flash of her elegant blue pelisse and matching bonnet, but rumors were already spreading in the drawing rooms of London society.

"She is an Incomparable," said one young dandy sporting a yellow coat and puce pantaloons, speaking with authority.

"She is a plain dab of a thing," Florence Persimmons, Lady Brittany's friend, proclaimed.

"Well, if she is cousin to Charlotte Audley she is no doubt a boring, straight-laced chit. Lady Charlotte's people are certainly good ton, but as prim and conventional as a pack of bishops," Lady Asterley concluded.

Her friend Lady Jersey, patroness of Almack's, held a different opinion. "Westcott would never offer for a straight-laced, conventional chit. If he is truly betrothed to her and this isn't simply another one of those ridiculous rumors circulated about him, I predict she will be every bit as unusual and fascinating as he is."

Inside the mansion at Berkeley Square, Camilla settled in quickly. She was delighted that Philip had changed his mind at the last moment and decided to let Dorinda accompany them to London, after all. He engaged a new governess for her, a plump, bright-eyed young woman named Miss Brigham, who came highly recommended, and who instantly showed a partiality for dark-eyed little girls, and for cats, dogs, and assorted other pets. The moment she'd seen Tickles she'd burst forth with an account of the time her papa had brought home a monkey for her and her brothers, and all the mischievous tricks it had engaged in, and Dorinda had been instantly captivated.

The house in Berkeley Square was all anyone could wish for, furnished in excellent taste, containing countless elegant salons and drawing rooms, and staffed by an army of attentive servants. Camilla found the spacious rose and cream bedchamber assigned to her every bit as enchanting as the Blue Room she'd grown so fond of in the country, and her only source of turmoil was nervousness over the upcoming tests she faced, and a strange feeling at being back in London, no longer as a serving maid but as a young lady of fashion and consequence.

The first few days in London as Miss Camilla Smith

were a blur to Camilla, a hazy confusion of dressmakers, mantua-makers, jewelers, and visitors calling to pay their respects to the Earl and his guests. She greeted everyone she met with her usual friendliness and warm manner and had no idea what sort of impression she was making. But since all she had to do was sip tea, munch cake, and make simple conversation, it wasn't much of a challenge. She was aware though that those who came to call studied her —her face, her figure, her gowns, the way she held her teacup, the answers she gave—but constant drilling with Charlotte had given Camilla confidence at such encounters, and she felt fully comfortable with her own performance. Her days were full and stimulating, what with the visitors, shopping in Bond Street with Charlotte until she thought her feet would fall off, and trying on more clothes than she had ever imagined in existence.

"Is this really necessary?" she had demanded of Charlotte when they trudged up the elegant street to the fourth milliner in one day.

"Oh yes, absolutely necessary," Charlotte assured her, glancing about delightedly as they entered the plushly appointed shop. "Madame Modane is all the rage. If you are to impress everyone in London, you simply must have one—perhaps two—of her famous hats."

This is certainly better than a day spent scouring glasses and mopping the floor at the Rose and Swan, Camilla acknowledged as she tied beneath her chin the satin ribbons of a cunning confection of pink satin roses and beads and lace. She tilted her head to one side, suddenly startled at her own grand reflection. How elegant she looked, in her apple-green walking dress and matching gloves. No one, even Mrs. Toombs or Gwynneth, would recognize the stringy-haired Weed in her shapeless work rags in this charmingly outfitted young lady with the crimped hair and flushed cheeks, accompanied by a pretty girl in turquoise ruching who was obviously of the first stare of fashion.

"She'll take it," she heard Charlotte telling Madame Madone, despite the fact that it was frightfully expensive. Camilla bit back an instinctive protest. Charlotte and Philip had been drumming it into her that she must spend lavishly if she wanted to create the right impression— every penny spent, Philip had assured her, that familiar determined glint in his eyes, would be worth it when their goal was achieved.

So she accepted the hat tucked away in its bright bandbox and at last she and Charlotte, with all their purchases, left the shop and started toward Philip's waiting town carriage. But as they neared it, a beggar boy of about twelve roused himself from the curb and held out a filthy hand.

"A shilling for my supper, miss," he pleaded.

Camilla stopped short. She stared into that grimy, hopeless face, and at the thin body draped in rags, and a heavy vise tightened around her heart. All of this time shopping, laughing with Charlotte, pretending to be someone she wasn't, and there were still orphans going hungry, still children in the slums without shoes or stockings or a roof over their heads. And Hester still locked away in the workhouse, without a proper blanket, and all alone.

She reached into her bag and pulled out a sovereign. She placed it in the boy's palm.

"Thank 'ee, miss!" he breathed, joy and wonder lighting his face.

Beside her, Charlotte waited, uncomfortably aware of the odd looks they were receiving from passersby. "Have you no family?" Camilla asked the boy, oblivious of the stares.

"No, miss."

"Where do you live?"

He shifted uncomfortably from one foot to the other. "In the alley down by the glass factory with some other fellows. Tain't too bad, miss, 'cept when the north wind blows at night."

"There is a workhouse on Porridge Street. Do you know it? If you go there, you'll find shelter." It wasn't exactly a home, but far better than an alley or a curbside. "They'll keep you there and feed you and you can learn your letters until they can apprentice you out. Here, this will smooth the way with the woman who runs the place." She took another sovereign from her reticule. "If I give it to you, will you go there now—instead of back to the alley?"

He hesitated, staring longingly at the shiny coin she held. He licked dry, sore lips. "Aye, miss," he said without conviction.

"What is your name?"

"Simon."

She grasped his arm gently and peered directly into his round peat-colored eyes. "Simon, I trust you to go to the workhouse. It's a decent place—far better than what you have now. You won't have to beg for food anymore. And there are other boys and girls there with whom you can make friends. You'd like that, wouldn't you? Now, you'll go to the workhouse and give the coin to Mrs. Toombs? You'll try it there? Truth, now!"

"Aye, miss." He bobbed his head. "Swear to it, I do!"

She gave him the coin and watched him run off in the direction of Porridge Street.

"You don't really think he'll go there, do you?" Charlotte asked as Simon disappeared around the corner.

"I'm not sure. I hope so. I had to try."

"I don't know how he came to be here," Charlotte murmured, looking around her in distress at the pretty shops and flower-bordered street. "This part of town doesn't see much of that—begging, I mean. Thank goodness."

Camilla threw her a sharp look. "Yes," she said evenly, "it is upsetting to see people hungry and cold when one is spending a fortune on finery. It's much better to pretend such people don't exist."

Charlotte gasped, but said nothing. They ascended the steps of the carriage in silence and settled back against the velvet-lined upholstery. Charlotte took a deep breath as the driver started back toward Berkeley Square.

"I didn't mean it that way," she said quietly. "I know that there are unfortunate people in London. James and I support our church charities, and Philip of course is most generous to a great many causes. But . . . seeing someone like that . . . face-to-face . . . I never have . . . I didn't imagine . . ."

"No," Camilla said gently, forgiving Charlotte as she saw the real dismay in her face. "You couldn't imagine, not if you haven't been exposed to it. But there is a great deal of misery in this very city—a whole ugly world as far removed from Berkeley Square and Westcott Park as can be."

They rode in silence for a while. The sun was slanting behind clouds, the air outside the coach windows growing chill. Camilla thought of Hester and vowed that tomorrow she would find a way to send a donation to the workhouse through a reliable messenger—and somehow get her hands upon a new woolen blanket and warm coat for Hester.

When they reached the mansion, Charlotte informed her that they had an hour to rest before they must dress for Camilla's first public appearance in the city.

"Philip is taking us to the opera," she announced.

Camilla's mind hurtled with dizzying speed from her secret plans back to the mission before her, the mission that was making her aid to Hester possible. "Tonight?" She blinked, startled. "I thought we weren't going out until next week."

"He wanted it to be a surprise. He felt that if he told you earlier, you'd be nervous all day."

"How astute of him! But—what am I to wear?" For a moment, panic set in and her brain whirled with visions of the dozens of elaborate gowns of all fabrics, styles, and ornamentation purchased in the past few days. Never having been to the opera, she had no idea what would be appropriate.

"The rose blush satin with the demi-train," Charlotte responded instantly. "Don't be a goose, your abigail will help you. And so will I. It will be *fun.*"

Fun. The way that picnic outing by the lake had been fun? Ever since that disaster, Camilla had been uneasy about her debut into London society. Even though Philip had assured her later that same afternoon, after she'd bathed the mud from her body and lathered it out of her hair, that she'd done beautifully, she couldn't shake off the feelings of unease. Why, she'd made a perfect spectacle of herself, sailing straight into the mud. Every time she thought of it she blushed with humiliation.

But Philip, later that afternoon, had taken her hands in his and insisted otherwise.

"I was the one who made a fool of myself, getting carried away when Brittany was hurt. I almost ruined everything. As soon as she suspected I still had feelings for her, she started flirting like a lightskirts with every man in sight. No, your falling into the mud saved me from making matters even worse. Otherwise, I would have ridden home with her tucked on the saddle beside me, and she'd have felt like she'd won. She was mad as fire when Marchfield insisted she ride with him and you and I walked home side by side, laughing like a pair of lunatics."

He had grinned down at her. "I won't make such a mistake again. From this point on, I will be devoted only to you—my darling Miss Smith."

"I'm flattered, certainly," Camilla had responded, laughing. Then she had grown serious. "But won't it be a little difficult explaining—afterward—what went wrong between us? I mean, if we tell everyone we are actually engaged . . ."

"We say only what we said in the library at Westcott Park—that we are intending to wed, but everything is not perfectly settled between us. It's done all the time. That will give us enough room to maneuver when we put it out that you have cried off and gone home to marry your childhood love."

"I see. And you and Brittany will be free to be happy together."

He smiled with satisfaction. "Exactly."

One other thing had disturbed her about the picnic—Marmalade's sudden unpredictable change in disposition. Philip had an answer for that, also. "I found a burr under her saddle," he informed Camilla grimly. "That's why she tried to buck you off."

"But how would she get a burr?" Her gaze flew to his

face as she reached the inevitable conclusion. "Someone must have put it there!"

"Marchfield." Philip's eyes had burned with anger. "That scoundrel has hated me for a long time, though I never thought he'd stoop to such a dangerous trick."

"But why would he want to harm *me*?"

"He didn't—not really. If you'd been any kind of a horsewoman, you'd have gotten the mare under control without taking a serious fall. That's no doubt what he expected. But he probably thought it would cause enough of a ruckus that I'd be obligated to see to you, and he'd have the benefit of dancing attendance on Brittany."

"A dangerous ruse, don't you think?" She found it shocking that anyone could risk another person's safety merely to achieve his own ends, but then, remembering the cold, mocking set of Marchfield's face and his gloating eyes after her accident, she could readily believe him capable of it.

"He's a dangerous man." Seeing her worried look, he had gripped her hands. "You have nothing to fear, Camilla. Nothing like this will happen again. I would never let anyone hurt you. It's me he hates, remember, and believe me, I intend to remind him why. Marchfield will pay dearly for that trick of his."

Gazing up at him, she shivered. The ominous smoke-gray glint of his eyes almost made her feel sorry for Lord Marchfield. "What do you intend to do?"

"Something that will knock his nose out of joint and teach him not to meddle with me—and mine."

That was all he would tell her on the matter. But now, as she dressed for the opera, she couldn't help thinking about Marchfield. The man seemed so cold, almost inhuman. Those icy blue eyes. . . .

Suddenly, a chill shot through her. No, she tried to tell

herself. It couldn't be. But she sank down on the bed and pressed her hands to her face, thinking: Could it be Marchfield?

The murderer had had blue eyes. He had probably been a member of the nobility, and he had probably attended Lady Hampton's masquerade. She knew that Lord Marchfield met all three of those qualifications. It was at the masquerade that he had made the bet with Philip.

Was it possible that he had left the ball afterward and killed Anders at the White Horse Inn?

She sat down upon the dressing chair and shut her eyes, trying to picture Marchfield behind that hideous mask.

It could have been him, but it was impossible to say for certain.

She realized she was crushing the delicate fabric of her gown. She unclenched her hands and went abruptly to the bureau where her gloves and hankerchiefs were folded. Digging underneath she found the crumpled note she'd brought with her to London. Somehow or other in the next day or so, she must find a way to get this, with an anonymous letter of explanation, to the authorities.

A knock at the door made her shove the note back beneath the folded handkerchiefs.

"Come in," she called, dismayed by the slight quaver in her voice.

It was her abigail, Mary, a stout, ruddy-complexioned woman of middle years and crisp good sense, who possessed, Camilla had discovered, an artistic eye and excellent taste. "Lovely, miss—just lovely." Mary beamed, and held out to her a white velvet box. "This is for you, miss, from his lordship. With his most sincere compliments, he said."

Inside the velvet box nestled on a bed of pure white satin reposed a glowing pearl necklace centered by a large brilliant pink amethyst that exactly matched the rose-blush shade of her gown.

"It's . . . exquisite," Camilla breathed, lifting the necklace up in awe. Forgetting Mary's presence for a moment, she whispered, "Oh, I can't accept this. It's too expensive . . . I can't . . ."

"Of course you can, miss, and so you shall," Mary declared. "And don't overlook the matching ear bobs. See? These long dangly pieces are a bit daring for a young girl just coming out, but they're gorgeous, and you can get away with them. Your looks are special, you know, not only pretty, but . . . unusual, striking. Oh, they'll be right smart on you, that you can be sure. His lordship was absolutely right when he picked them out for you."

Camilla couldn't think what to say. She remained lost in thought as Mary fastened the pearl and amethyst necklace around her throat and began to dress her hair. She was thinking of all the expense Philip was going to merely to win Brittany Deaville. And Brittany didn't need that much persuading, from what Camilla had been able to see. Why, the girl clearly wanted him right down to her fingertips, but she was letting pride and a swelled head get in her way.

She wondered if Brittany would be at the opera tonight. Maybe that was why Philip had decided to attend. And why he wanted Camilla to appear at her best. She gazed at her reflection in the pier glass, the low-cut rose-blush gown hugging her figure, the necklace winking in the candleglow. Her eyes seemed to shimmer like jewels themselves, and her cheeks glowed almost as pink as the gem at her throat.

She was suddenly eager to see Philip's reaction to all her primping.

When she swept downstairs, with the glittering ear bobs set off by her upswept copper curls, the demi-train drifting behind her in a cloud of rosy gauze, and her satin slippers whispering on the steps, she felt as though she were floating. Philip came out of the library, looked up at her, and stopped dead in his tracks. He stared, a thunder-struck expression on his face.

"You're ravishing," he said at length, taking her hand as she reached the bottom of the staircase. "Camilla—you look utterly captivating."

For the first time in her life, Camilla felt shy. "Thank you for the necklace," she managed to say. "It's beautiful . . . but so frightfully expensive. Of course, after I leave, you will sell it . . . or give it to . . ."

"Shhh." He put a finger to her lips. His eyes, dark as mist, scanned her from head to toe. There was a look of pleased, almost wolfish appreciation upon his lean face.

"The necklace doesn't begin to compare to your loveli-ness. By God, I never imagined—" He broke off, and gave his head a shake. "Who would ever have expected you'd turn out like this?" he mused in wonder.

Camilla glowed at his words and the warm expression in his eyes. He was stunningly handsome in his black eve-ning clothes, looking taller, stronger, and more like a dark, reckless pirate than ever. An emerald stickpin in his cravat was his only adornment other than the lace foam-ing at his sleeves and the gold signet ring gleaming on his finger. Warm pleasure rushed through her as he slowly lifted her hand to his lips and pressed his mouth against her slender fingers.

"You look very splendid, too," she assured him in her earnest way, and Philip threw back his head and laughed.

Just then, Charlotte and James emerged from the drawing room and stared at her in amazement. Camilla felt as if she were in a dream. This was not her—not Weed—so splendidly dressed, wearing beautiful jewels, going to the opera with the Earl of Westcott and his family. This was a girl existing inside a lovely dream from which she would soon awaken and find herself back in her attic at the Rose and Swan, with Gwynneth dumping a basin of water over her head because she'd slept past dawn.

The entire evening was one she felt she would never forget. The opera enthralled her with its lush costumes and grand scenery, with the passionate music washing over her with a vibrancy that made her tingle from head to toe. From the Earl's box seats she could see and be seen by all the distinguished and glittering members of the audience, most of whom appeared to derive far more satisfaction from studying the other occupants of the boxes than in watching the opera performed.

During the intermission Philip left the box briefly. While he was gone, Lord Kirby came to pay his respects, as did Mr. Fitzroy, accompanied by another young buck, Lord Winthrop. Mr. Fitzroy, clearly enamored of the lovely young woman with the dark copper curls and brilliant green eyes, paid almost reverent respects to her, and seemed oddly reluctant to introduce his friend, and the reason for this soon became clear. Lord Winthrop immediately dropped down on one knee, clutched at Miss Smith's rose-gloved hand, and said:

"My aunt has told me about you. Freddy here has told me about you—and still, still I was not prepared."

Camilla heard this dramatic speech in stunned amazement. "Prepared, pray tell, for what?" she inquired, won-

dering who on earth his aunt was, and what both she and
Freddy had told him.

"For your beauty—your exquisiteness. My aunt—she is
Lady Asterley, you know, who visited you yesterday—she
said you were a devilish handsome young woman, with
very pretty manners. And Freddy, he told me you were an
Incomparable—and that you sing like an angel. But, Miss
Smith, my dear Miss Smith, I never thought . . . never
dreamed . . . never imagined . . . Forgive me. I prattle
on like a fool, but all I really wish to say is that I am your
devoted servant!"

Camilla burst out laughing. Then she recovered herself, spread her fan in the way Charlotte had taught her,
and responded, dimpling, "How very gratifying. Do you
know my cousin, Lady Charlotte? And her husband . . . "

"Oh yes, yes, charmed to see you again . . . But, Miss
Smith, allow me to say that I hope you will attend my
aunt's dress ball Tuesday evening? She is sending you an
invitation on the morrow."

"How kind of her. I should be delighted," she exclaimed. She remembered Lady Asterley as a beak-nosed
matron in a puce gown and turban who had stared at her
very hard all through tea and left without giving any indication whether she approved or not. Apparently she had.

Mr. Fitzroy impatiently began vying with Lord Winthrop for her attention. "Would you care to go for a drive
in the park tomorrow, Miss Smith?" he managed to say
before Winthrop could continue.

Lord Winthrop turned on him with an irritated scowl.
"I was about to invite Miss Smith for a drive, myself," he
said through gritted teeth. "Dash it, Freddy, you interrupted me . . ."

"That's because if you had your way you'd keep her all

to yourself and never give anyone else a chance to speak a word," Mr. Fitzroy rejoined smugly. "Miss Smith?" he inquired, with a disarming smile as he turned back to Camilla once again.

"Miss Smith is already engaged to drive in the park— with me," came a voice from the door of the box.

The Earl of Westcott smiled silkily at the two startled young men. "Isn't that correct, Camilla?"

"Yes, indeed," she agreed at once, stifling a laugh at the frustrated expressions of her would-be suitors. "But I would be delighted if you would both come to tea the following day instead—and you, too, Lord Kirby," she added, including the latter in her invitation, as he finished a low-voiced conversation with James and Charlotte.

"Pleasure." Kirby grinned at her as Lord Winthrop and Mr. Fitzroy echoed his acceptance.

All three left the box as the curtain went up once more, and Philip, slipping into his seat beside Camilla said softly, "Impertinent upstarts. Don't they know we are be-trothed? It's bad enough they've been throwing them-selves at Brittany for weeks—now they've got to make cakes of themselves over you."

Her eyes were sparkling as she turned to him. "Oh, but they're so sweet! It is wonderful to be courted and com-plimented. I have never in my life had such an experi-ence, and I daresay it is tiring for someone like Brittany who is incessantly hounded by suitors, but for me—well, it is most enjoyable!"

"Don't enjoy it too much," he said in her ear, just as the music began to build. "Remember you are supposed to be my fiancée. It won't do at all if it looks to Brittany as though I can't hang on to your affections."

"Are we truly going driving in the park tomorrow?" she whispered.

"I said so, didn't I? Now be quiet and watch or people will begin to hiss at us."

But there was a light note in his voice as he chided her, and she leaned back in her seat, oddly satisfied. She didn't care if people did hiss at her—the prospect of spending an hour alone with him on the morrow filled her with an inexplicable elation. She stole a glance at his ruggedly chiseled profile and smiled to herself. Even if he was only spending time with her to make Brittany jealous, she didn't care. She would be with him. She could pretend . . .

But pretending could be dangerous. When this charade came to an end, she would probably never see him again. He would marry Brittany, have children with her, and she would go off to Paris to begin a new life, alone. An icy emptiness seized her at the thought. It had all been so easy these past days to accustom herself to the grand life at Westcott Park, to the Earl's family—even to think of them as her own. But they weren't family. She was an outsider, masquerading as one of them. She didn't belong, never had, never would.

She couldn't think about that now. For tonight, she was here in a London that was more dazzling, more magnificent and exciting than anything she had ever imagined. For tonight, she was beside the most fascinating and seductive man in town, she was the woman in whose ear he was whispering, whose arm he held as they walked, the one he looked at with admiration, even if it was only pretend admiration . . .

Pretend. Make-believe.

With all of her heart as the curtain at last went down on the opera, and Philip placed her gold-spangled shawl about her shoulders, she wished it could be real.

15

"Jared, here it is—four hundred and fifty pounds. Don't lose it, whatever happens! Do you think it will satisfy Mr. Wimpnell until you can get the rest?"

"It will have to satisfy him." Jared stared down at the pouch full of money Camilla handed him. They had just met in the hall and ducked into the library, where full sunlight streamed into the lofty oak-paneled room.

Jared shook his head. "Miss Smith, how can I ever thank you?"

"There are two things you can do for me, Jared. One is to promise me you won't gamble anymore."

"That's easy!" he answered promptly. He grimaced. "I never want to see the inside of a gaming hall again—at least not until I've learned how to play better . . ."

"Jared!"

"I'm jesting! I promise. What else can I do for you?"

"When you've finished seeing Mr. Wimpnell, I would be ever so grateful if you could make several purchases for me. If it isn't putting you to too much trouble . . ."

"Of course—what sort of purchases?"

She handed him a list, which he read aloud.

"A half dozen woolen blankets, wool cloth, buttons, bread, cheese, a ham hock . . . what is all this, Camilla?"

She took the list from him, folded it in half, and stuck it inside the upper pocket of his coat. "I wish to send some provisions to the workhouse where I grew up—and in particular to one special little friend there—Hester. With the wool cloth and buttons I can make her a good heavy winter coat."

Jared blinked at her. "Do you ever think of yourself? That money Philip gave you for helping him—it's supposed to be for *you*. Instead, you're using it to help every one *but* yourself."

She smiled ruefully and twirled before him in her gown of cream-colored muslin with the scalloped neck and tight-fitting sleeves edged in Brussels lace. "Do I look as if I'm wanting anything, Jared? On the other hand, you need the money to save yourself from serious trouble— and Hester and the other children are wanting for so many things . . ."

"Of course I'll help you," he interrupted promptly, seeing the somber shadow cloud her face. "It's just that you're the most generous person I've ever met, Miss Smith. I admire you—more than anyone I've ever known."

"Thank you, Jared," she said softly. The cloud lifted and her cheeks glowed warmly with the compliment. "I must get my bonnet," she told him, moving with a smile toward the door. "Philip is taking me driving this morning and I wouldn't want to keep him waiting."

"And I've kept Mr. Wimpnell waiting long enough," Jared said with disgust. "Damn the man. But at least

Philip didn't find out anything about it. Thank God. That would have been the end of me."

"As it might be yet."

Philip's voice came clearly from behind one of the high-backed burgundy leather chairs set beside the window. A moment later he rose, staring coolly at the horrified pair near the door.

"Eavesdroppers never hear good of themselves!" Camilla cried indignantly, admonishing him with the first thing that sprang to her mind. Jared had turned white as marble and seemed to be searching without much success for words.

Philip sauntered toward them, all lazy grace and elegance. But his eyes burned with fury, Camilla saw, and her heart sank. She braced herself for his wrath, but he spoke with icy calm—and that was far worse, she decided, than if he'd shouted.

"You disappoint me, Jared." He bit off the words with rapier sharpness. "Not only did you lack the courage to face me with Wimpnell's threats but you stooped to taking money from a lady. I suggest you return that pouch to Miss Smith at once, while you still possess a shred of dignity."

Jared, very white around the mouth, handed the pouch back without meeting his brother's eyes.

"It may interest you to know," Philip said coldly, "that your debt to Mr. Wimpnell was discharged some time ago."

There was only the ticking of the walnut clock in the library. Both Jared and Camilla stared at him in amazement. Philip seemed to be keeping his temper in check with supreme effort. "He came to see me at Westcott Park—I warned you in advance, remember? I rather foolishly hoped you would come to me first and confess your difficulties."

"I wanted to, Philip, but I thought you'd bite my head off."

"I might have. Or I might have understood. *You* might have given me the benefit of the doubt. Instead, you stayed away."

"I didn't want to disappoint you."

"Didn't you? Or were you merely a coward?"

Jared flushed crimson and his eyes shone with outrage as he endured his brother's scorn. Before he could speak out in his own defense, Philip went on in his grim, scathing way.

"I satisfied your obligations, Jared. But, I swear by the devil himself, you will repay every penny of the money to me. Severe deductions will be taken from your quarterly allowance and you will consult with me about your daily whereabouts and amusements for an indefinite period of time."

"Gladly." Jared expelled a sigh of relief. "Anything to have Wimpnell off my back. All this time, it's been weighing on me—if I'd only known . . ."

"You would have known if you'd come to me like a man," Philip retorted. "But we'll discuss this further at a later time. I've a few more things to say to you that are not fit for a lady's ears."

Camilla's slim brows lifted. "There are few words in the English language which I have not already encountered many times over," she assured him tartly. "Be that as it may, there is something I must say in Jared's defense. The arrangement between us was my idea, not his, and he should not bear the brunt of your anger for *that*. His conduct toward me has been unexceptionable. And in addition, he is a very fine young man, whom you ought to be proud of . . ."

"My dear Miss Smith," Philip said in a dangerously icy tone, which made Camilla's courage waver, "as I recall, I am paying you to pretend a tendre for me which you do not feel. I am not paying you—nor am I interested in—your opinions about the character of my brother. Kindly keep them to yourself."

She stiffened. Jared started to protest against his brother's harsh words, but Camilla spoke first, her eyes flashing fire.

"I see it is impossible to talk reason to you, my lord. You think only your own opinions matter—and not anyone else's. Well, here is a portion of my wages, sir," she cried, reaching into the money pouch and withdrawing a coin. She tossed it at him. "You are not paying me for today. I am taking the rest of the day to do as I wish—so you will not be burdened either with me or my opinions."

He caught her arm as she started to sweep past him.

"Oh no you don't."

"Philip," Jared said miserably, "Don't take this out on Miss Smith. It's me you're angry with. This was all my fault—"

"Leave us," Philip interrupted wrathfully, his eyes never moving from Camilla's furious face. "I want a few words alone with Miss Smith. You and I will speak later. What are you waiting for? Do you seriously think I'm going to beat the girl? Not that she doesn't deserve it, but I believe you know me better than that."

"You may not beat her, but you're going to shout at her, and blame her for this mess, which is all my fault, and . . . and I won't have it." Jared grabbed his brother's arm and tried to free Camilla, but she spoke up quickly, suddenly alarmed that he and Philip would come to blows over her.

"Jared, please go. I'm not afraid of him," she added scornfully. "In fact, there are a few things I would like to say to your brother that are not suitable for *your* ears."

"But—"

"Go!" She and Philip both shouted at him simultaneously.

Jared, shocked, stared from one to the other of them, and then a slow smile spread across his face. "You're evenly matched, I suppose," he drawled, backing toward the door. "But, Philip, if I were forced to lay odds, my money would be on the lady."

"You don't have any money," Philip flung at him between clenched teeth, just before the solid oak library doors thumped shut.

Philip stared down at the girl whose sizzling glance was scorching him with its intensity. *Keep your mind on the matter at hand,* he commanded himself, though part of him was wondering why in hell she had to look so beautiful when she was angry. Her extraordinary eyes seemed to burn right through him, her full lips were set in an adorable pout, and one naughty strand of her hair had come loose from its chignon and was dangling enchantingly over her nose. She flipped it back impatiently, and wrenched her arm from his grasp. She looked both mad as fire and determined as hell. It was a combustible combination.

"We're going to have a talk," he informed her, trying to remember why he was angry.

"Can I stop you?"

"Don't even try. Why do you find it necessary to interfere in my family's affairs? Jared's debts are for me to

handle, not you. If you can't see the impropriety of what
you tried to do—"

"Oh, it's propriety, we're talking, are we, my lord?
Well, since when are you one to speak of propriety with
such reverence? Aren't you the same man who is paying a
serving wench to pretend to be your fiancée so that the
lady you love will come running to heel like a dog? Just
where is the propriety in that, my lord?"

"Stop calling me 'my lord.' "

"Why should I? You don't treat me as though I were
your equal. You don't treat anyone as though they were
your equal—even your own family. They're all afraid of
you. How can you expect Jared to come to you of his own
accord when he has every reason to believe you will be
odious to him and . . . and punish him? And the way
you look at James sometimes would be enough to
frighten anyone—but you don't frighten him—you simply
make him unhappy. And Dorinda craves your attention,
but—"

"Enough!"

His face had gone white. Deep agony was etched in his
face. His eyes mirrored an unspeakable pain.

Camilla gasped, her hands fluttering to her throat.
What had she said? How could she have hurt him like
this?

For hurt him she had. He turned on his heel and
walked to the window. For one long moment, she stared
after him in stricken dismay.

"Forgive me," she choked, and ran to him, grasping his
arm. "Oh, Philip, please forgive me. It isn't true, not really, your family does love you—they love you terribly.
You mustn't mind me, I'm always saying the wrong thing
—anyone would tell you so . . . ."

"You told the truth. Never apologize for the truth, Camilla." His voice was level and unbelievably calm. But there was tension in his muscular arm as she gripped it feebly.

"It's only partly true. The part about them loving you is true, also. Everything is not always just what it seems on the surface. Families are complicated. Emotions aren't always clear. Love, hate, fear, respect, tenderness. They can all run very close together. Philip, I know how much you love all of them, and despite everything else, they know it, too."

She found she was crying. Not for herself, but for him. She, who never could bear to hurt anyone or anything, had caused him immeasurable pain. And this to the man who had been better to her than anyone in her life since her parents' death. The man who had treated her always like a lady, who had taken her in and confided in her, and made her, for a time, part of his family. The cruelty of her outburst was more than she could bear.

He turned suddenly and stared hard into her face. "Why are you crying?" His voice was harsh now.

"I . . . hurt you."

"Camilla, don't cry. Not for me. I deserved everything you said."

"No, you didn't deserve it," she whispered. She reached up impulsively and touched his face, that lean, strong, handsome face, hoping to somehow lessen the bitterness in his eyes. "I lost my temper—I exaggerated everything . . ."

"One of the things I like best about you is that you always tell the truth. Don't hand me fustian now, my girl. I've made a fine mess out of this family, and well I know it."

He meant to pinch her cheek, to try to lighten his words. He swore that's what he meant to do. Instead, he ran his finger along it caressingly. Instantly he sensed the tremor that ran through her.

Something inside of him responded, tightened with a yearning that was familiar, and yet not familiar. He stared into her face, saw a myriad emotions reflected there: wonder, softness, eagerness, concern. And pulled her suddenly, unthinkingly into his arms.

Before he knew it, he was holding her close, gathering strength from the feminine softness of her body, comfort from the touch and smell of her rose-scented hair nestled against his cheek. "Camilla, Camilla." He wondered why it healed him just saying her name.

"It's all right, Philip." She clung to him, her eyes misty with the need to reassure him, to undo her painful words. "Jared, Dorinda, James—*they're* all right."

"I've tried to do the best for them—tried to squelch this cursed Audley wild streak right out of them all—but there's no getting rid of it." Why was he telling her all this? Stranger still, he couldn't stop. "And all I've done is made them hate me." He groaned, closing his eyes for one moment against the painful truth of his own failures.

"They don't hate you." She leaned back within the circle of his arms and smiled at him, that earnest, entrancing smile that came right from the bottom of her soul. "Whatever you've done, I know you've had your reasons. I . . . I shouldn't have interfered."

She looked so sweet, so worried and caring and forlorn, he suddenly felt an overwhelming urge to kiss her. Talk about the Audley wild streak! He fought against the tantalizing impulse with all his strength, knowing it was wrong, improper, and completely against their agreement. But he could feel her breasts pressed innocently against his chest, and the touching sincerity of her glance seemed to burn right through him. He realized almost dazedly that the act of holding her in his arms was not helping matters. Deliberately, he let her go and stepped back, drawing a deep, steadying breath.

"I promised you a drive in the park, Camilla. Fetch your bonnet, and we'll go."

She gazed at him a moment, a long, searching gaze, and a fierce tension seemed to vibrate through the air between them. Then, without another word, she nodded —and for once obeyed him without question.

When she was gone from the library, he raked his fingers through his hair in frustration and stared unseeingly at the massive shelves of books lining the paneled walls. His library consisted of thousands of volumes of history, novels, poetry, and philosophical essays, all containing centuries of insight and wisdom. Yet, standing before them, he groped in vain for insight into his own strange behavior. Something about Camilla Brent cut through all of his plans, all of his defenses. With her, he couldn't stay angry. With her, he found himself wanting to talk about and think about things he'd never discussed with anyone —all the painful events of recent years that he'd bottled inside, trying so hard to be strong for his family, trying to save them from the truth only he was privy to, from their own rash natures.

Maybe it was because she was an outsider that he could talk to her, open up to her. It would never have occurred to him to confide any kind of weakness or despair to Brittany. He realized suddenly that he had never even had a serious conversation with Brittany. Certainly she had never shown any kind of an interest in his family. He wondered for a moment how she would have reacted to Jared's problems.

She would have come to me at once and told me the whole so that I could take care of it before a whiff of scan-

dal could arise, he decided. But then, Jared wouldn't have confided in Brittany. He'd have been too intimidated by her.

There was nothing intimidating about Camilla, however. She was honest and sweet and far too caring to evoke anything but trust. Outspoken, yes. A bit unorthodox, yes. He grinned at the memory of her hidden away inside Dorinda's wardrobe, sneezing with the kitten in her arms. And the sight of her covered with mud after Marmalade had tossed her over the fence. And singing so angelically at Marrowing Hall. She was outrageous and delightful and thoroughly sensible, all at the same time. But maybe that was why everyone around here—even Charlotte, who'd shown a surprising flair for deception—felt so damned comfortable with her.

Philip realized at that moment that Camilla had become more to him, more to them all, than merely a paid employee performing a temporary service. She had become a friend.

He was waiting in the hall when she descended the stairs several moments later. He saw a fetching vision in delicate muslin floating toward him, with a plumed ostrich feather hat perched adorably atop her crimped curls and her pelisse over one arm.

"My lady, your carriage awaits," he said gravely, but his eyes gleamed with pleasure as he helped her on with her pelisse and escorted her out into the sunlight.

"Will you drive very fast?" Camilla asked eagerly. "I've always wondered what it would be like. When I heard about your ride to Newmarket in under four hours I tried and tried to imagine how it must feel to thunder along so swiftly that everything is a blur. It must be very exciting."

He cast her an odd look as he dismissed the groom

holding the horses and handed her up into the curricle. "Who told you about Newmarket? It was months ago."

"Oh!" Camilla blushed, then laughed aloud. "I heard about it in the tavern. Everyone knew you had won your famous wager—all of London was talking. And you see, one of the other serving girls has a cousin who is one of your footmen. So we knew all about the bet and the exact time of your run and how amazed all of society was with your victory."

"I see. And the name of this very talkative footman?" he inquired dryly.

"I don't believe Fredericka mentioned it—oh, Andrews, maybe, or was it Walters?"

He grinned. "Your memory is as exceptional as your riding skills, I see. I don't recall anyone by either of those names in my employ. We had a Sanders once, and a groom named Anders, but that was a long time ago . . ."

"Anders?" Camilla gave a start on the seat beside him. Despite the blustery October air, her skin went ashen beneath her rosy cheeks. "Not . . . not Henry Anders?" she asked quickly.

"Yes, but that couldn't be this girl's cousin. Henry Anders left my employ some three years ago and went to work for Marchfield and I haven't heard from him since."

His tone was grim. Glancing at his profile as he guided the pair of prancing grays through the London streets, she saw that the harsh, forbidding expression had descended over his features once again.

"No, Anders wasn't Fredericka's cousin . . . it's just—the name is familiar. I—I met a friend of his once in the Rose and Swan who . . . mentioned him. You sound as though you didn't care much for the man."

"He was discharged under unfortunate circumstances," Philip replied curtly.

"Oh. Did he . . . steal something or . . ."

"He was derelict in his duty." For several moments
there was silence between them. Camilla was trying hard
to figure out a way to ask more questions about Anders
without seeming rude or awakening suspicions. Philip
seemed loath to talk about him, but she had to know
more.

"You sound very bitter about it. You disliked him
then?"

Beside her, Philip steered the grays past a street
sweeper and a cavalcade of carts, all the while thinking back three years, three years to the time when
Marguerite had still been alive. "Henry Anders allowed
my sister to ride out alone the night she died. Hoyden
that she was, she was following James and the Kirbys on
some wild escapade of theirs. If Anders had stopped her,
if he'd alerted someone—her governess or Mrs. Wyeth,
someone—maybe she and Maxwell Kirby would still be
alive today."

"I didn't know. I'm sorry." Camilla tucked her chin
into the fur collar of her pelisse. A quivering bolt of
shock ran through her. She wondered if it was mere coin-
cidence that the man who had been murdered in the
White Horse Inn had worked for Philip—and then for
Marchfield. Something bothered her about the entire
matter, but she couldn't quite sort it out. But how interesting that there was a connection between Lord Marchfield and the murdered man. Could it be that Anders had
been blackmailing Lord Marchfield all these years—perhaps first forcing Marchfield to hire him and then making
him pay exorbitant sums of money?

But why? What was the blackmail about?

She shivered, and Philip glanced at her sharply. As the

horses passed between the gates of Hyde Park, he turned them onto the carriage road and slowed them to a walk.

"You're cold. Here, try this." He reached under the seat for a red wool blanket, which Camilla gratefully tucked around her lap. But she couldn't explain to him that it was not the brisk autumn air that was making her cold. It was the frightening thoughts churning in her mind. She tried to focus on something else. This wasn't the time to sort through this confusing new information. Later, tonight, when she was alone and could reread that letter from Silas. If she continued to ponder the situation now, Philip would notice her anxiety and question her, and she had no intention of telling him or anyone about the murder. It would be wrong to involve anyone who didn't have to be involved. This was her problem—and she had always prided herself on not relying on anyone else to solve her own difficulties.

"You're very quiet," Philip remarked after exchanging a greeting with an acquaintance on horseback who cantered ahead up a parallel path.

"I was thinking about Jared." Beneath the blanket, Camilla crossed her fingers to excuse the lie. To her relief, it turned both of their attention to a different subject, one she was far more eager to discuss.

"I owe you an apology about Jared," he said shortly, throwing her a swift glance. "You were trying to help him today—and you were most generous. I shouldn't have lost my temper with you. I should rather have thanked you for caring about him."

"How could I not?" she said warmly. "He was so despondent when he confided in me."

"I think," he said quietly, "that is what rubs the hardest. That he would confide something so serious to you—and not to me."

"He is in awe of you, Philip." She turned on the seat and gazed intently at his rugged profile. "He wants your approval so badly, and dreads your disapproval. He's young, and for all his brashness and humor and charm, he's uncertain of how to go on in the world. Deep down, he knows he needs your guidance."

"I haven't done a very good job of helping him to seek it out, though, have I? I swear to you, all I've wanted is to protect him, to somehow protect all of them."

"You can't protect them from themselves," she said softly. "They are who they are. And they're wonderful. Surely you see that?"

"I see that they're Audleys through and through. Just as I am."

"That's a fine thing. And don't try to bamboozle me into thinking you disagree!"

Despite his bleak mood, he couldn't help a crooked grin. "It's good in some ways, not in others. But . . . well, I suppose the only way you'll understand is if I explain something to you which only a select few know." He pulled the horses to a halt beside one of the deserted footpaths where late-blooming roses quivered in the breeze. He stared straight ahead.

After a moment he went on. "When my father died, and I inherited the title from him, I also inherited something else. No one knows this, Camilla, except his solicitor and the bailiff, but . . . my father had allowed his estates to become endangered. Westcott Park was mortgaged to the hilt, and the other seats were nearly squandered. I inherited a staggering debt. He had let his love of gaming get the better of him, and he had been losing heavily for some time, more than a year. He kept borrowing, trying to recoup, and getting in deeper. No one—of course—knew anything about this. When I took over after his death I discovered the mess his finances were in—they were a shambles."

Shock poured through her. She could imagine how devastated he must have been when he'd heard the news, and could picture him facing the solicitor while still in mourning for his father. How he must have reeled, knowing that the responsibility for rescuing his family from debt and scandal fell now on his shoulders.

"How terrible for you," she whispered, a catch in her throat.

She sought for words of comfort, though his composed expression didn't seem to merit them. Still, she knew that beneath his calm strength, he must have felt terrible pain, the pain of shock and deep despair, as well as an inevitable sense of betrayal. "It must have been a horrible period for you. I can understand a little of it, I think. My own father succumbed to the same temptations," she said gently, "and with the same results."

He turned to her then, remembering what she'd told him of her story.

"When my parents died," she continued quietly, "my father's debts were discovered. They were ruinous."

Yes, she understood, Philip realized, his chest tightening. And how much worse it had been for her, a child, helpless to correct a situation already beyond all hope, with nothing left even to provide for her care. At least he had enjoyed the time and means and power enough—as an adult and a member of the nobility—to act.

"Go on," Camilla urged, her hands clasped before her. "Tell me the rest."

"The details of it all aren't important," he continued curtly. "I managed, through measures of strict economy, and several rather daring investments, to hold off our creditors. And fortunately, my unorthodox shipping in-

vestments paid off handsomely. There was money to re-
duce the debts, and to reinvest. It seems I have a knack
for business—not a good recommendation in the ton, but
very useful in life." A wry smile lit his face for a moment,
warming the harsh planes. "At any rate, I was able to buy
back the mortgage on Westcott Park and start to manage
the lands at a profit—with none of my brothers or sisters
even being aware of how dangerously close they had
come to losing their home, and their standing. But I
knew. And for the first time I began to worry about how
this cursed Audley wild streak which had destroyed my
father's soul would show itself in each of us. But it wasn't
until after Marguerite's death that I grew truly afraid."

She wanted to ask, and didn't want to ask. But she
had to know. Camilla moistened her lips. "How did
Marguerite die?" It was a whisper, soft as the breeze.

He leaned back in the curricle, letting the reins fall
slack in his hands. The grays pawed the ground restively.

"I'll tell you," he said heavily. "I haven't discussed it
with anyone since the night it happened, but . . . I'll tell
you, Camilla. Then you'll understand what's gone wrong
between James and me. I'll tell you exactly how my beautiful little sister—with so much life ahead of her—died a
horrible death. I'll tell you exactly what happened to
Marguerite."

 "One night while I was away in London, James and Alistair and Maxwell Kirby decided to ride to the neighboring village, disguise themselves as common farm boys, and spend the evening drinking and carousing with the locals in the tavern. Apparently there was a serving wench who had, ah, caught James's eye. It was a stupid schoolboy's prank," Philip went on grimly, "and it went very wrong. Marguerite, all of fifteen, and full of mischief, had overheard their plans, and begged them to let her accompany them—also disguised as a boy. They refused, sent her off, and let themselves think that was the end of it. But James should have known that would not stop Marguerite. A more head-strong, mischievous girl never existed, and I'm sure all she could think of was that James would be out enjoying an adventure while she was ordered to spend the evening alone, sewing or reading with her governess."

Camilla could picture the spirited young girl setting her own adventurous plans. "So she sneaked out after them."

"Yes. She told Miss Pym that she had the headache,

and pretended to go to bed. In truth, she crept to the stables, took that half-wild horse of hers, Midnight, and rode off alone down the highway. The next thing James knew, she showed up at the tavern dressed like a boy, in clothing stolen from one of our young grooms. She ordered a tankard of ale, cool as you please. James was furious—he started to drag her out of there and take her directly home, but Alistair and Maxwell, who were both feeling the effects of the liquor they'd drunk in a short time, offered to take her in his stead. They were both feeling sick, and had had enough of the game. James, however, with his iron stomach, still felt in fine fettle, and he confessed to me later that the serving girl in the tavern had shown an interest in him. So he let Marguerite go with the Kirbys and . . ."

He paused, his hands clenching and unclenching on the reins. "What happened afterward wasn't their fault. It was bad luck, pure and simple, brought on by Marguerite's foolish impulses in venturing out alone, and James's carelessness in not seeing to it that she returned safely."

A sudden gust of wind rattled the branches of the trees overhead and a flurry of red and golden leaves swirled down around the curricle. Camilla brushed a leaf from her lap and plucked one gently from his shoulder as Philip stared ahead at the elegant banks of trees arranged around Hyde Park.

"It was misty that night, wet and dark, with no moon or stars to guide them. Alistair told me afterward that Marguerite—not having indulged in enough foolishness for one night—challenged them to a race home. Half-drunk, they agreed. They set off, and soon Alistair, who stopped to be sick along the road, had fallen far behind. He rode on and on with no sign of them ahead. It began to rain, a hard, driving rain. Alistair was near the border of his family's property, and he knew of an abandoned care-taker's cottage at the edge of it. He sought shelter there. But as he rode toward it, he saw flames shooting through the tops of the trees. He became sober quickly, he told me later. He rode pell mell toward the flames and then saw it was the cottage burning. Marguerite's and Max's horses were tethered outside, mad with fright. They'd taken shelter there before Alistair caught up to them and . . . we don't know exactly what happened, but we pieced together that in trying to build a fire, Max, more drunk than sober, accidentally overturned an oil lamp and set fire to the place. It went up in a flash—just like *that.*" Philip snapped his fingers.

"Neither of them made it out the door. By the time Alistair got there and tried to rescue them, it was too late." He closed his eyes. Slowly, he buried his head in his hands. "They were both dead," he muttered, as if to this day he could scarcely believe it.

Camilla's shoulders slumped. She felt a lump rising in her throat and tried to swallow past it. It was so horrible, these two terrible needless deaths. Marguerite, only fifteen, with so much life ahead of her, and Maxwell Kirby, the carefree, fun-loving young man who had perished with her. Her heart ached for all of the young men involved in that ill-fated escapade. No wonder neither James nor Alistair Kirby nor Philip could bear to speak of Marguerite. But there was something she had to say to Philip, even though he wouldn't like it.

"Thank you for telling me. I . . . it's a tragic story. I'm so very sorry. But, Philip, the fire wasn't James's fault. How can you blame him for Marguerite's death? You don't blame Alistair, surely. And James had no way of knowing such a disastrous chain of events would occur."

"He never should have gone out that night on such a

mad adventure! And he should have personally seen his own sister home safely to her door—James was sober, Alistair and Max were not. If James hadn't been so busy toying with that serving girl, if he had dragged himself away in order to ensure his sister's welfare, he might have been the one taking charge of building a fire in that cottage, and he would have been sober enough to do it properly. If James had been with her, there would have been no fire. Marguerite would be alive today. If I had been at Westcott Park, instead of dueling with André Dubois, the same thing might be true. Marguerite would have lived." He stared at her, layer after layer of pain buried deep within those fathomless gray eyes. "I blame myself," he whispered, "as much as James."

"*If.* If, if, if." Camilla reached up tenderly and cradled his face in her hands. Her voice broke. "You can't punish James and yourself forever! Philip, James is *alive.* So are Jared and Dorinda. You can't bring back Marguerite, but you still have a family that needs your love, that desperately wants your love. Love them, Philip, cherish them. Let your anger and your pain fade into the past—bury it like a dead thing in the earth! It is only destroying you and everyone you care about."

"I can't."

"Yes, you can. I've seen you with Dorinda, with all of them when you forget for two minutes that you're supposed to be looking out for them, squashing any signs of the Audley nature. But you can't wipe out who they are, what they are. You have to love them for it and accept it and try to teach them to be wise. You've learned, haven't you?"

"To some extent. I had no choice."

"Well, maybe you should tell them the truth, about your father, about the need to channel this wild Audley recklessness that concerns you so—which I happen to find quite appealing! I don't mean you should tell Dorinda, of course, she's too young, but James and Jared, surely, ought to know."

He stared at her thoughtfully. She fought the impulse to brush back the stray lock of hair that had fallen over his brow. *Oh, stop being so foolish,* she chided herself firmly. *Isn't it obvious he has more important matters to worry about than that you are in love with him? It would ruin everything if he were to guess.*

There was friendship between them now. She sensed it and was intensely grateful for it. It was more than she had dared to hope for, and it was the most that could ever be between them. But it was precious and important and real, and she would do everything she could to live up to the demands of friendship. If that meant giving practical advice, and listening to his troubles, and trying even harder to help him win Brittany's hand, she would do it. It also meant sparing him from discovering the depth of her true feelings. That must never happen. He couldn't know how she felt. She would simply have to be very careful and circumspect in everything she said or did, in order to hide the truth.

"I suppose I could tell them," Philip said slowly. "Maybe it would help Jared to realize how dangerous gambling can be. It might help him to control himself in the future, in case he hasn't already learned his lesson."

He picked up the reins and turned the horses toward a return path as the wind began to whistle around them.

"The weather's turning," he muttered abruptly. "I'd best get you back before you freeze. Hardly the way to repay you for listening to my troubles."

"There's no need to repay me," she murmured, her thoughts having moved on to James and Charlotte. "One more thing I don't understand, Philip," she said. "James has changed, from all that I have seen. He is a responsible young man now married to a very respectable young woman. Why is it that you can't accept him and Charlotte?"

"He met her only a year after Marguerite's death. I thought he was far too young to marry or to know what he wanted in life. It seemed another form of recklessness to tie himself down at his age, especially with a girl he'd only known for two months. They had a whirlwind courtship and insisted on marrying quickly. I tried to stop them —I wanted them to test their feelings over a period of time—but James insisted. He was as determined as he's ever been to wed the chit within that same year. I had no choice but to relent, even though I was certain he was making a mistake."

"But it wasn't a mistake," she pointed out gently. "He and Charlotte are very much in love. Surely you can see that."

"Yes, even I can see that," he conceded with a short laugh. "It's plain as pie they're happy together. But having voiced my objections so strongly, there's an awkwardness among us all now that we can't get over. Charlotte has always appeared terrified of me, which I confess, makes me want to box her ears. Instead, some devil inside me makes me enact the role of cruel tyrant that she seems to expect."

She put her hands over her mouth and tried to stifle a laugh. "You do it on purpose? Shameless!"

"I wish I could stop, but . . . you know, it's easier when you're around." He grinned. "I've noticed, Camilla, that I don't feel quite so devilishly malicious whenever you are in the room. Why do you think that is?"

"Perhaps because you're so busy trying to eliminate my

errors and shortcomings before I make a fool of myself in society that you don't have time to torment poor Charlotte."

He chuckled. "Your errors and shortcomings are rapidly disappearing before even my critical eyes. You amaze me. If I didn't know better, I'd think you'd been raised as carefully as a duke's daughter or a marquess's, and you know, they are very high in the instep."

"Brittany is a marquess's daughter—are you saying *she* is high in the instep?" Camilla teased.

The grays turned through the gates of the park and into the traffic on the street. He answered her in a thoughtful tone. "In a way. Brittany is gentility itself—a lady through and through. She is the particular kind of lady who is the soul of propriety, as is her mother. They worship protocol and detest all that is unconventional. They would both be shocked by some of our Audley ways. I've tried to be on my best behavior during this courtship so as to not frighten her off, but it isn't always easy." Rueful laughter shook him. "If Brittany even had an inkling about this bet of mine with Marchfield, for example, she'd send us both to the devil. And it *is* bad ton. She'd be absolutely correct to be thoroughly disgusted with us."

"Oh no. I think it would be terribly romantic to have two men vying for my affections—ready to tear each other's throat out for the sake of my love."

"You do?" He stared at her incredulously, amused by the rapt glow in her eyes. "And you claim not to be the least bit romantic?"

She drew in a sharp breath. *Little fool, he's going to see through you like a windowpane if you're not careful,* she admonished herself, mortified by her slip. She'd been thinking how lovely it would be to have Philip so desperately pursuing her, making a wager with another man,

fighting for her, doing everything in his power to make
her love him.

"I'm not romantic, but . . . I expect any girl, even
sensible ones, would be a little romantic if they loved
someone," she prevaricated. "Oh, look, there is Brittany
and Florence Persimmons now—riding with Lord Marchfield." Relieved at the distraction, she waved eagerly and
Philip nodded a greeting as they passed the riders.

"Marchfield isn't wasting a moment," he said crossly,
and set his mouth in a hard line.

"No, but I don't think it will do him much good. Did
you see the way Brittany looked at me? She was shooting
daggers at me. Surely that indicates that she is very jealous."

"Perhaps." He frowned and lapsed into silence, obviously preoccupied with his own thoughts.

Camilla sensed his frustration and guessed he was
thinking about his deep longing for Brittany. What he
really yearned for was to have her here in his curricle
beside him, to be kissing her, holding her in his arms,
making plans for their wedding. How tiresome it must be
for him to be stuck in this charade, dancing attendance
upon a woman in whom he had no personal interest. Her
spirits sank down to her kneecaps. For a time, she had
deceived herself into thinking he actually enjoyed spending time with her. Idiotic dreamer! Her happiness of a
short time ago, when she'd felt a bond between them,
dissipated. She cursed herself for her own stupid dreams
and turned her head away so that Philip would not see
the tears sparkling on her eyelashes.

Philip drove the horses toward Berkeley Square at a
fast clip, eager to leave the memory of Brittany and
Marchfield behind him. A feeling of dissatisfaction
nagged at him, yet he couldn't place the cause for it. He

had been perfectly content—more than content, he had been close to feeling happy—before their appearance. But seeing them, especially together, served as a reminder of the task before him.

Task! He wondered at his own strange choice of words. What was he thinking of? Winning Brittany's hand wasn't a task, some dreary chore to be completed and put aside. It was his greatest desire, his coveted goal. Marriage with Brittany would set him on the proper course, ensure an end to his rake's tendencies, and help establish a stable home for Dorinda, and Jared too. Her elegant gentility would help discourage those wayward Audley tendencies, and her passionate beauty and laughter . . . those would warm his soul and his bed, making their life together complete. Brittany. Soon she would be his, he promised himself. He glanced at the silent girl in the curricle beside him. With Camilla's help, he couldn't fail.

When they entered the house, Durgess announced that Lord Kirby, Miss Drewe, and Mr. Fitzroy had arrived separately to each pay a call upon Miss Smith. They had left their regrets at having missed her, he relayed, his sour face as impassive as ever. Camilla replied absently to this as she set her bonnet upon the gold-inlaid hall table and began to unbutton her pelisse. She couldn't help feeling downcast at the unsatisfying tone the latter part of the drive had taken and at the reflection that Philip was unhappy and impatient with the charade. She had been enjoying it all so much that she had sometimes forgotten how temporary it was, but now she realized that all too soon this enchanting game would come to an end. She would leave England after the Westcott Park ball and never see Philip, nor any of the Audleys again.

Fingers trembling, she had difficulty with the topmost

button of her pelisse and fumbled with it as Durgess waited to take the garment from her.

"Allow me," Philip reached out to help her, but she jerked away. No. She couldn't bear to have him touch her —not until she had her emotions in check.

She mumbled, "It's nothing, I can manage," and tugged harder than she intended, not realizing that her necklace had become entangled in the button's thread. The button and chain snapped off at once, clattering upon the marble floor. While Durgess pursued the button that had gone spinning beneath an airy fern beside the table, Philip stooped and retrieved the charm and broken chain. He held them up between his fingers, their molten gleam catching the late afternoon glow streaming through the fanlight.

"Oh no!" Despite herself, tears of dismay burned her eyelids at the sight of the broken necklace.

"I'm sorry." He read the distress obvious in her face. "This has special meaning to you, doesn't it?"

"My parents gave it to me. It's all I have left of them." She bit her lip and reached out for the tiny lion charm.

But he was staring at it, with its graceful lines and curlicues. An odd expression entered his eyes. He gave her the broken chain but made no move to give the charm back. "It's very interesting. Does it have any particular significance?"

"None that I know of." She suddenly remembered the Frenchman who'd come to the workhouse in search of the orphan with the lion charm. "Except . . . well, it doesn't matter."

He sensed her hesitation in speaking before Durgess, and took her arm. "Come into the petit salon."

She allowed him to lead her into the petit salon, a small yellow and green–papered room charmingly furnished with yellow velvet settees, high-backed damask chairs, and bright flowers in vases set upon the sofa table and mantelpiece.

"You were about to tell me the significance of this charm."

"No, I already told you, there is none." Camilla shook her head. "It's only that the last time I visited my little friend Hester at the workhouse she told me a strange story. It doesn't make any sense to me, and I would have thought she was making up a Banbury tale, except that Hester insisted it was true, and she isn't the kind of child to lie."

She paced to the mantelpiece where a small fire burned in the grate, and stretched out her hands toward it, grateful for its warmth. Behind her, Philip watched every move.

"What did the child say?"

"She said that a Frenchman had come that afternoon looking for an orphan—a specific orphan, one who owned a charm in the shape of a golden lion. But Mrs. Toombs, who runs the workhouse, insisted that she knew of no such orphan and had never even seen such a charm."

She turned away from the fire and gazed directly at Philip, tall and silent near the door. "Mrs. Toombs was lying. She knew this charm well—when I first came to the workhouse she tried to take it away from me. It was a battle of wills."

"I don't need to ask who won," he remarked, and the laughter in his eyes leaped across the room and infused her with sudden warmth. Despite her low mood, Camilla couldn't help but smile.

"Yes, I triumphed. When she finally let me out of the

cellar the next morning, she told me I could keep the bloody necklace and take it with me to the devil."

The laughter faded from his eyes. He suddenly saw her, a frightened, grieving child, having to do battle for the one memento left of her family. He pictured her helpless, at the mercy of a bullying harridan and something sliced through him.

"I keep forgetting what a difficult life you've had. I suppose I can't even begin to imagine the things you have gone through . . ."

"I didn't tell you that to gain your sympathy," she said quickly, embarrassed. "You asked me about the charm—and that's all I know. That a Frenchman was interested in it, and in the orphan who possessed it."

"And," he said slowly, watching her expressive green eyes where he knew he would find the truth, "that is why you were headed to Paris. To find out more."

Caught. She could do nothing but nod. An impish grin curved her lips as she gazed up at him. "Now you know my secret. You know that I wasn't going to France because of being in love with some man. I *told* you."

"Yes, you certainly did." Suddenly, he strode toward her and grasped her hands in his large, strong ones. "You're very sweet, Camilla Brent, do you know that?" he asked softly. "Sweet and innocent." He shook his head. "Whatever you do, you can't go to Paris alone. It's no place for a beautiful girl without a protector. Now, wait," he ordered as she started to protest.

"I'm not trying to hinder your search—I want to help you. Let me see what I can find out about this matter. I am not without some connections." He squeezed her hands gently. "Perhaps I can discover some information for you before the ball at Westcott Park. Do I have your permission to try?"

"And if I say no? You'll give up the idea?" she countered, knowing full well the answer.

"Certainly not—but for the sake of propriety, I thought I'd ask." He grinned down at her. "Minx," he said fondly.

Her heart turned over. She felt her hands tingling at his touch, felt her body growing warm at his nearness. "Since you're going to do whatever you wish anyway," she said as crisply as she could, forcing herself to pull her hands from his, "I not only give my permission but I thank you. It's very kind of you."

Suddenly, she had the strongest urge to reach up on tiptoe and kiss him. The Audleys are not the only ones to have wild, reckless impulses, she warned herself in horror. For a moment, gazing into his darkly handsome face, with those piercing gray eyes fixed so intently upon her, she feared she would give in to the madness. To refrain from acting on it, she stepped back, putting a good two feet between her and Philip's tall, lean form. She dug her fingernails into the palms of her hands.

"I promised Dorinda I'd play dominoes with her before supper." She forced a bright smile and did a sidestep around him. "Thank you for the drive. And for your help with the charm. Will I see you tonight?"

"I'm afraid not, I'm going to my club."

She fought not to show her disappointment and left him with a cheerful wish that he enjoy his evening. Upstairs in her room, she faced the looking glass, hands clenched into fists, and regarded her own flushed, tense countenance in dismay.

"I am not in love with Philip Audley," she told herself angrily. "I am too practical to fall in love with him." She stamped her foot at herself, her voice rising. "I am *not* in love with anyone."

A mocking voice whispered inside her head.

Liar. Wretched, foolish liar.

She would have been better off if she'd never left the Rose and Swan, never felt the caress of silk gowns upon her skin, never slept in a featherbed, with a fire in her bedroom hearth, never tasted the delicacies of a noble's table, or enjoyed the pleasant conversation of people whose breath didn't reek of ale. She would have been better off if she had never felt the powerful strength of the Earl of Westcott's arms around her, never tasted his kiss, never gazed into those mesmerizing eyes. Better off if she'd never seen his smile, heard his voice, or seen him stride into a room, all sleek black elegance and sardonic humor. He was part knight, part pirate, part lonely little boy. And he was now and forever, part of her.

Camilla kicked off her cream-colored kid slippers, threw herself down upon the four-poster bed, and let the hopeless tears flow.

He wiped the tears from his cheek as a knock sounded upon his study door. He was too proud a man to display his grief to the world, even to old Jean, his most trusted servant. But at times the hopelessness threatened to swallow him.

Jean entered. He was small, thin, and elderly. He bowed low, his dark eyes glittering with excitement in the dim candlelight. "Monsieur le Duc, she will speak! That cursed woman at last wishes to tell you what she knows."

The Duke started in his chair, then gazed almost dazedly at the servant, hope dawning in his bleary eyes. "Bring her to me at once," he commanded in a level tone kept steady by the most supreme effort.

When Jean hurried away, the Duke began an inward struggle to maintain his composure and to keep his hopes from being raised beyond what was reasonable.

How long had he forced that woman to stay here in the château—locked in a comfortable bedchamber, of course, served the most excellent food, kept unharmed—save that she could not leave? She had been warned that she would be a prisoner until she told him all that she knew about his daughter, but she had been obstinate—until now.

Would she truly reveal to him something that would be of use in finding the girl? Or was this merely a ploy to try to gain her freedom?

We shall soon know, he thought grimly.

He rose and paced across the study, staring out at the hills and fields cloaked in nightfall. Somewhere in this world, his daughter lived and breathed. But where? Where would he find her, his only living child? And how could he ever explain to her the twisted chain of events that had brought them to this circumstance?

The Duke thought back nineteen years, to the foolishly debonair young man he had been, wed by arrangement of his family to a high-born beauty he scarcely knew, while amusing himself in a discreet liaison with Paris's most desirable courtesan. Genevieve had bewitched him for a time—oh, how she had bewitched him. He had been bedazzled by her sensuous beauty, her hypnotic allure, and her astonishing sexual expertise. And then he had learned that his freshly charming young wife was expecting a child—and somehow, things had changed. He changed. Over the months they had been together, he had actually fallen in love with his sweet, lovely Antoinette, and he had determined to end his arrangement with his mistress.

When Genevieve had informed him that she, too, was carrying his child, he had been stunned. He'd assured her that he would provide for her and the child, but he had firmly put an end to their relationship, confiding—to his

later regret—that he loved Antoinette and would from
that day forward be true to her.

He'd never realized how his announcement had af-
fected Genevieve, how deeply, obsessively, she had cared
for him. He'd never had a clue of the monstrous deed she
had perpetrated, of the mad desire for revenge that had
driven her to do the unthinkable—he'd had not the
faintest suspicion until that doctor's daughter had come
to him recently and told him the horrible truth she had
learned in her dead father's diary . . .

As fate would have it, both babies were born upon the
same day—both of them female. Antoinette's child was
healthy, lusty, but the Duke was informed by messenger
that Genevieve's baby had been stillborn. Though mourning the loss in his heart, the Duke had been relieved.
Without a child between them, there was now no tie to
Genevieve; that chapter in his life could now come to a
definite close.

He never saw Genevieve Saverne again. Instead, he
immersed himself in his life with Antoinette and their
child, Lisette. He had been blessed with four joyful, mem-
orable years, until tragedy had robbed him of everything
he cherished. Antoinette and little Lisette had voyaged to
Lisbon, where he was to join them shortly—but the Duke
never had the opportunity. Their ship had been lost in a
storm at sea. Antoinette and Lisette had perished along
with all the other passengers and crew. The irrevocable
news had come to him at the château that his wife and his
only child were dead.

He'd been devastated.

The Duke had never married again. He'd spent his
days lonely, mourning, unable to forget his beautiful wife,
his enchanting little daughter. Somehow, the drab, empty

years had passed, one by one, and slowly he had grown old, tired, and weary of living.

And then, not long ago, the doctor's daughter had come to him—distressed beyond imagining. And the tale she had unfolded to him had seemed incredible, except that she had the diary in her hands, with the doctor's own words scrawled upon it, to prove everything . . .

Genevieve's baby had not died. Genevieve's baby had been born very much alive. In a diabolical plot borne of obsessive love and a sick thirst for the most secret of revenges, Genevieve had paid Antoinette's doctor and the midwife accompanying him to do a deed so heinous it was nearly beyond comprehension. She had bribed them to substitute her baby for Antoinette's, to steal the Duke's legitimately born daughter from her cradle, and put in her place the child born to his mistress—a child that would be raised as a noblewoman from that day on. No doubt Genevieve had derived a gloating satisfaction to picture *her* child ensconced in the Duke's home, showered with every luxury available, coveted and cherished and raised like a duchess, while the Duke's legitimate child had been given away like an abandoned kitten to a childless couple touring France, an English couple with whom the doctor was acquainted, according to the diary. The squire and his wife who had taken her to England to be raised as their own had not known that she had been stolen from her rightful home; they thought she was an orphan, a gift from God bestowed on them in answer to their own prayers . . .

The Duke whirled from the window. He lifted his lined, careworn, still-handsome face to the portrait of Antoinette above his desk. "I am trying to find her, my love," he whispered thickly. "I am trying to find the child we never knew—our child, our little one—"

He broke off as the door opened and Jean ushered in
Suzette.

"What have you to say? Where is my daughter?" he
demanded with as much restraint as he could given the
heavy chains dragging at his heart.

"You know all that I know, Monsieur le Duc," she spat
at him. "Did not that cursed doctor's daughter tell you
the name of the couple to whom he gave over the child?"

"You know that she did. You know as well, you evil old
woman, that the man I sent to find this couple learned
that they died in an accident, and the child was sent away
to a workhouse or an orphanage somewhere in England."
The Duke stalked toward her, his blue-veined hands
clenched at his sides.

"And you know that my men searched the country for
word of her. But we have reached a dead end, Suzette.
Not one of the workhouses or orphanages acknowledged
having received a child by the name of Camilla Brent into
their care. Not one had any knowledge of the golden
charm in the shape of a lion which the doctor tucked into
the baby's blanket before he gave her over to the squire
and his wife. We are at a standstill. You must know more!
You must be able to aid me! Have you no shame, no
remorse for this terrible deed of your mistress, a deed
you helped to perpetrate?"

"I have no regret for my service to Madame!" Suzette
cried scornfully, glaring at him through those merciless
ferret eyes. "But Madame is dead and I wish to leave this
place now, so I will tell you the one thing that I know,
which perhaps will help you. If I do," she said, straightening her stooped, round shoulders and meeting his furious
eyes with defiance. "If I do, will you give me your solemn
pledge that I may go from this place and be left in
peace?"

"You may go, and may I never set eyes upon your evil countenance again—but as to peace, that will depend upon your conscience and upon God," the Duke said, fighting to keep from striking her.

Suzette smiled, a cold, triumphant smile. "Very well then, Monsieur le Duc," she went on mockingly. "Several years ago, Madame decided to find out for herself what had become of the child she stole from you. She learned then of the death of this English couple, and she initiated her own search for the girl. She found her, at a particular workhouse in London."

"London! But we inquired at each one . . ."

"Ah, but you underestimated Madame once more," Suzette crowed. "At the time, Madame paid the people in charge a most handsome sum—in return for their silence. She ensured that if anyone else were ever to inquire about this Camilla Brent, they would be met with blank denial of her presence at that particular workhouse. She ensured that any search you might ever begin would lead to a dead end and be very much in vain."

The Duke went perfectly still. The scope of Genevieve's malevolent brilliance continued to stun him. He said in a careful tone, making very certain he understood: "So one of the administrators we questioned lied —one of them knew something of Camilla Brent or the lion charm—and deliberately denied the truth."

"Yes. And this pair was well rewarded in advance for their silence!"

"Tell me now, old woman, the name of these people— of this place—or by all that is holy you shall not leave this château alive!"

Suzette met his livid gaze, unafraid. "Toombs," she flung at him, very like a butcher tossing a dog a bone. "Mr. and Mrs. Toombs—of the Porridge Street Workhouse in London. *They* may be able to help you find your precious child—for a price!"

And she turned and shuffled toward the door. Jean and two footmen outside barred her way, but the Duke spoke in a bitter tone.

"Her presence taints this house. Let her go—and may the devil take her!"

Jean closed the study door, leaving him alone. He stared up at the portrait of Antoinette, and his face shone with the faintest sheen of hope as he lifted his weary eyes to that ever-glowing countenance. "Perhaps, *chérie,* perhaps we will find her after all," he whispered, his words as soft and fervent as a prayer.

"Our little daughter is there—*somewhere*!"

But where?

17 Dusk had fallen over Westcott Park that night when Charlotte came to Camilla with the news that Dorinda was suffering from a case of the sniffles and was confined to her bed. When she added that Miss Brigham had confided the lively young miss was not only feeling poorly but was also down in the dumps, fretting over having to lie still, Camilla immediately offered to keep her company for the evening. Charlotte came up with another plan: together the young women ordered a special supper be sent up to the nursery wing and made a little party for the child. Before long, James and Jared, unenthusiastic about dining downstairs alone, sought them out. They sauntered into Dorinda's room, demanding permission to join the nursery party and were delightedly welcomed.

Dorinda, red-nosed and bleary-eyed, with Tickles asleep at her feet, seemed more than satisfied to be treated like an invalid if she could be the center of so much attention.

It was a pleasant evening for everyone. They entertained Dorinda by playing dominoes and lottery tickets, and then Charlotte and Camilla answered all of her questions about the parties and operas they had been attending, including a schedule of the upcoming soirees in store for them.

"I wish I was old enough to be 'out.' " Dorinda sighed, stroking a finger between the kitten's ears. Tickles had awakened long enough to stretch, yawn, and settle herself comfortably against the little girl's side as she sat propped up on pink silk pillows in the bed. "Grown-ups are allowed to have all the fun—children aren't permitted to do anything."

Jared grinned at her. "You wouldn't like most of these parties, anyhow, silly. You have to be polite and quiet. No running or skipping allowed."

"I know that." Dorinda glared at him, and sniffled, then reached for the bowl of soup Camilla had left beside her bed. "But even if you can't run or skip, you can dance. And that would be ever so much fun—especially in a very full skirt, with a train, and someone very handsome—like you, Jared—for a partner."

"Dancing!" Camilla dropped the ball of yarn she'd been rolling up after Tickles had left it strewn about the floor. A dreadful suspicion overtook her. "I just thought of something, Charlotte—will there be dancing at Lady Asterley's party tomorrow?"

"Of course. Don't tell me you can't dance?" Charlotte gasped in horror.

"Of course I can dance—at least, I *think* I can—if only I am taught the steps," Camilla explained, trying not to alarm her.

"James, why didn't we ever think of that?" Charlotte wailed, turning a distraught glance upon her husband.

"Philip should have been the one to think of it, Char.

Now, don't go getting yourself in a quake. We can teach Camilla what she needs to know tonight. Right now, as a matter of fact."

"I'll help," Jared offered eagerly, jumping up from where he was sprawled on the floor beside the rocking horse.

"I'll watch!" Dorinda said with satisfaction, her eyes sparkling at the thought of the entertainment in store for her.

Before long, Camilla found herself breathlessly spinning about the room with first James and then Jared while Charlotte played the spinet and called out instructions for her.

The country dances were easy to learn, and the quadrille did not pose much of a problem, but for some reason the waltz proved to be a challenge for her, and she found herself stepping on Jared's foot repeatedly.

"Try again," Charlotte insisted when Camilla would have given up. Determinedly, Charlotte began to play once more. Jared, laughingly assuring her that she had not hurt him, that she was light as a feather, and quite graceful really, placed his arms around her waist. One, two, three, four, one, two, three, four—breathlessly she went sailing round and round, until dizzily the pair of them crashed into the Earl of Westcott, who had just stepped through the doorway.

"Ohh!" Camilla cried out as she came up hard against Philip's muscular chest. Immediately, the Earl's arms went around her, steadying her. Jared, who had nearly lost his balance during the collision, had released her inadvertently as he stumbled into the door.

"Philip!" Jared muttered darkly. "Didn't see you!"

"No, how could you? You were too busy gazing into Camilla's eyes—and very lovely eyes they are, too," Philip responded evenly. Despite his polite tone and offhand manner, Camilla saw that his thoughts were elsewhere. There was something troubled lurking in his face. She wondered what was wrong. He had gone to his club tonight, and Charlotte had already informed her that whenever a man went to his club he did not return until very late. It was not yet nine o'clock.

Maybe it is only the strain between him and Jared, she thought doubtfully. Jared had confided in her that they had not spoken to each other since the eruption that morning, so it could be due to that. But instinct told her there was something more.

"Jared and James and Charlotte have been teaching me to dance," she said, searching his face for a clue as to what was disturbing him. "You see, Dorinda has the sniffles so we came up here to keep her company."

"The sniffles?" Philip's attention sharpened, and he glanced over at the small figure peeping out at him from the silken covers on the bed.

"It's a mild case of the sniffles—Miss Brigham said so —and I don't need to rest, so please, oh, *please,* don't make everyone leave," Dorinda burst out in a desperate plea, which sounded on the verge of tears.

Philip went to her and touched her cool brow. "I won't make anyone leave, Dorry," he said in a soothing way. "But I'm sorry you're not feeling well." His lazy smile suddenly lit his face. "I'm sure the sight of your brothers dancing must be most amusing to you, though. May I stay and watch, too?"

"Oh yes! Tickles wants you to stay, as well!" she added gleefully as the kitten suddenly roused herself and began to meow.

He scooped the animal into his arms and settled down with her on the nearest chair. James remarked that he must have found it deadly dull at White's to return so early. Philip shrugged.

"The cards held no fascination for me tonight—nor did the company there." His restless gaze moved to Camilla again.

"Don't let me interrupt. Go on with your lesson."

"I'm afraid I've stepped on Jared's toe once too often," Camilla said ruefully. "I wouldn't blame him if he didn't want to dance with me again."

"Oh, but I do." Jared grasped her hand and swung her toward the center of the floor. "You've got the hang of it now, Camilla, admit it! It's actually starting to be fun!"

"Well . . ." Camilla wasn't sure she wanted to do this before Philip's watchful eyes, but Charlotte began suddenly to play, Jared's arm tightened round her waist, and then they were whirling again, round and round the room, and James was calling out encouragement.

"That's it! Well done!"

Dorinda cried excitedly, "Watch out for his toe! Try to get through the whole thing without . . . oops!" And the little girl fell to hysterical giggling as Camilla trod on Jared's foot yet again.

"I'm going to disgrace myself and cripple my partners at Lady Asterley's ball!" she wailed as Jared continued to spin her round the room, and Philip couldn't help grinning.

Being here in this room with his family was relaxing him. Strange, he didn't usually see them this way—Charlotte so gay and comfortable, James at ease, Jared trying to act sophisticated and gallant while he was still as gawky as a long-legged young colt, Dorinda sweet and exuberant. They were all enjoying themselves, he realized, and much of that was due to Camilla. She put them at ease, naturally, effortlessly. There was something so refreshing

and simple and warm about her that everyone in the
room felt the glow of her kind spirit, and it made all the
colors seem brighter, all the smiles wider, the very air
tingle with happiness and excitement. Suddenly, he stood
up and set the kitten onto Dorinda's lap.

"May I steal your partner for a dance?" he addressed
Jared with quiet formality.

Taken by surprise to find his brother treating him with
respectful cordially instead of angry sarcasm, Jared swung
Camilla to a halt before him. He glanced at her for guidance. "If the lady wishes."

Philip turned questioning eyes to Camilla.

Her pulse had begun to race. She felt warm color
flooding her cheeks. *Calmly now,* she told herself, and
unconsciously smoothed a hand over her lemon-yellow
muslin skirt. *He is only being polite. Don't make a fool of
yourself in front of them all.* "I'd be delighted," she said in
a decorous tone worthy of royalty and inclined her head
in the elegant way Charlotte had taught her.

Philip grinned and pulled her into his arms so suddenly
and so tightly that she gave a slight gasp. As Charlotte
began to play once more, she found herself waltzing with
a partner vastly, excitingly different from the two who
had given her instruction. James's dancing had been
smoothly polished, his manner encouraging. Jared had
been more eager and boisterous than proficient—waltzing with him had been wild, carefree fun.

Philip waltzed with masterful elegance. He held her
close against his tall, muscular frame, guided her with
ease and assurance, smiled down at her with sophisticated amusement.

"Don't look so worried," he advised her. "This is supposed to be enjoyable."

"I'm so afraid I will step on your toe . . ."

"You won't."

"How do you know?" She tried to concentrate on the rhythm of the music as he whirled her expertly around the room.

"Because if you step on my toe, I'll hit you over the head with a candlestick," he whispered warningly so that only she could hear.

Laughter bubbled from her lips. "And what if you step on mine?" she asked him, her green eyes glowing into his. She forgot to concentrate, lost in the dark handsomeness of his face.

"You then have my permission to inform all of the ton that the Earl of Westcott is a clumsy oaf unsuited to dancing with ladies of quality."

"Surely, then, no well-bred lady would ever wish to dance with you again," she teased.

"Except you?"

"Well, yes, I suppose . . ."

"Then I should be perfectly content," he told her, his arm clasping her even tighter, and Camilla stared up at him in amazement.

He sounded serious. His eyes gleamed into hers with a dark solemnity that baffled her. Her heart turned over, then flipped back again. What was going on?

The dance was over. She realized suddenly that the music had stopped, that James and Jared and Charlotte were crowding round, offering praise and congratulations.

"You two looked splendid together," James exclaimed. "Camilla, you bring out the best in my brother. You actually made him look as if he knew what he was doing."

Philip gave him a playful punch in the arm. "When it comes to charming beautiful women, I knew what I was doing when you were still hanging on to Nurse's skirts," he retorted.

"I'm the one who taught Camilla how to waltz," Jared put in, and suddenly began lurching round the room with an exaggerated limp. Dorinda clapped her hands in delight as everyone burst into laughter. But the smile vanished from Camilla's face when she glanced over at the little girl and saw how flushed she appeared, and the overbright stare of her eyes.

"Dorinda, you're feverish!"

She rushed to the bedside and touched a light hand to the child's brow, as Philip had done earlier. The hot skin confirmed her suspicion.

"This has been enough excitement for one evening," she said firmly, and with gentle hands helped the little girl to lie down upon her bed, draping the satin sheet across her tiny figure.

Charlotte hurried to inform Miss Brigham, and Philip suggested that his sister needed sleep.

But Dorinda clung to Camilla's hand. "Tell me a story," she begged. "I don't want to sleep."

"Dearest," Charlotte put in, returning to stand beside Camilla and smiling soothingly down at the child. "I'll be happy to stay and tell you a story if you wish. And Miss Brigham will be here in a moment. She'll sit with you until you feel comfortable enough to fall asleep."

"I want Miss Smith to stay. I want to hear a story. Miss Smith, you tell the best stories! Oh, please, don't go away." Dorinda's voice was tremulous. Her little face peered up at Camilla so pitifully that Camilla's heart went out to her.

"Silly, of course I'll stay. One story, though. Your brother is right, you need your rest. Afterward, you must curl up like a little kitten yourself and fall fast asleep. Is it a promise, Dorry?"

"Promise."

Camilla sat down beside her on the bed. To her surprise, instead of leaving, Philip turned down the lamp and lingered near the spinet, watching her. Jared and Charlotte, blowing out all but two of the candles in the wall sconces, each settled into comfortable chairs.

"Well, now, let's see. Oh, I know." Camilla's voice took on a pleasantly dramatic tone in the shadowy dimness. She clasped Dorinda's hand in hers as she spoke. "This is a story my own mother used to tell me when I was a very little girl. It was my favorite and I don't believe I've ever told it to you before."

"Is it the one about the mermaid and the evil troll?" Dorinda murmured, stifling a yawn.

"No." Camilla shook her head as the adjoining door opened and Miss Brigham tiptoed in. At a signal from Philip, she waited silently near the door.

"Is it . . . the one about the princess trapped in the tower?" Dorinda persisted.

"No. Do you want to guess all night, silly nilly, or do you want to hear the story?"

"The story." Dorinda smiled, gave a little cough, and looked expectantly up at Camilla.

"Very well, then. This is the story of a poor farmer and his wife. The farmer and his wife were very kind, and they lived in a lovely little white cottage, and had three pigs, five cows, and a henhouse full of chickens, but they were not happy. They had no child. All they talked about and thought about was the day when they would have a little child of their own to hold and to hug and to love, but they didn't know that an evil sorcerer had put a spell on them, and decreed that they would have no child of their own.

One day, when the farmer and his wife were traveling through a neighboring village, they met an old gypsy crone who offered to sell them their heart's desire.

" 'You don't know our heart's desire, and even if you did, you could not sell it to us,' they replied sadly, and started to walk away. But the gypsy woman used magic to freeze them where they stood. And she spoke to them while they could not get away.

" 'Your heart's desire is a child. A little child to hold and hug and love,' she said, and the farmer and his wife gasped because she had guessed the truth. She waved her arm, and they could move again, but they did not run away.

"The farmer moved closer to the gypsy crone and asked, 'Can you truly help us?'

"She told him to return to the rosebush at the edge of the village at midnight, and she would bring him his heart's desire.

"That night, when the moon was bright, and the sky as dark as coal, the gypsy came to the rosebush, and it was midnight. True to her word, in her arms, she held a tiny baby girl wrapped in a blanket.

"The gypsy handed over the child without speaking. The farmer paid her in gold coin and returned to the inn where his wife waited. They were overjoyed. They decided to call the little girl *Rose* because the gypsy crone had given the child to them beside the rosebush.

"The farmer and his wife loved little Rose more than they had ever loved anything else. She was a beautiful child, as graceful as a flower, as warm and bright as the sun. Everyone was happy—until the sorcerer discovered that the farmer and his wife had a child, that they had found a way around his spell—and then he became very angry. He came to the farm and tried to envelop Rose in a puff of smoke so that he could spirit her away, but do you know what happened?"

Wide-eyed, Dorinda shook her head. There was utter silence in the darkened room, no one moved or breathed, and Camilla was aware only of the shadows around her. This was her own favorite part of the story.

"Before the sorcerer could mutter his spell, before he could do more than raise his evil wand, little Rose snapped her fingers at him and ordered: 'Begone!'

"And then there *was* a puff of smoke, and it enveloped the evil sorcerer. When it vanished, he was gone!

" 'He is gone forever!' Rose told her parents, and the farmer and his wife rejoiced, but they also wondered at this lovely, graceful child with her magic powers.

"The truth of it was"—and here Camilla leaned closer to Dorinda and gazed deeply into her eyes—"Rose was really the daughter of the Elvish king and queen. The gypsy crone had stolen her from the Elvish Forest, and sold her to the farmer for his gold. So Rose was actually an Elvish princess."

She stopped. Dorinda sat up. "Go on, go on," she begged.

"But that's the end of the story."

"But . . . what about the Elvish king and queen—and what about Rose? Does she ever find her real parents? Does she stay with the farmer and his wife? There must be more to the story!"

"Of course." Camilla smiled at her, and kissed her brow. "But that part is *another* story. I promised you one story for tonight, Dorinda, and I'm afraid it is over."

Dorinda started to protest, but Philip stepped forward and said quietly, "Dorry, a promise is a promise. The Audley honor is at stake, you know."

She clutched Camilla's hand. "Oh, very well, but . . . you'll tell me more tomorrow?"

"Oh yes, I promise." Camilla stroked the child's flushed cheek. "Sleep now," she urged. Suddenly she sneezed. "Here we go again, just as I feared. I'm afraid I've been too long with Tickles again. So if I'm not to sneeze the house down around our ears, I'd best leave. Good night, dearest," she told Dorinda tenderly.

As everyone bid their quiet good nights to the little girl and moved into the hall, Camilla saw that Charlotte's eyes were red. She'd been crying. A quick glance at James showed her that he looked somewhat drawn as well. She wondered what had happened to upset them.

But before she could try to speak to Charlotte, she and James murmured hasty good nights and hurried off toward their room.

"I'd like to speak with you and James tomorrow morning in the study," Philip was saying to Jared. With relief, Camilla noted that he did not sound angry in the least. He sounded calm, almost cordial. Jared looked wary, however, until Philip burst into laughter.

"I'm not going to turn you into a frog, or make you vanish in a puff of smoke, like Camilla's evil sorcerer," Philip promised. "I simply want to talk to you—both of you."

"I'll be there," Jared agreed, and disappeared in the direction of his room.

Philip fell into step beside Camilla as she started down the corridor. "That was quite a fascinating story."

"I think that was the first story my mother ever told me. It was her favorite, too. I used to beg her to tell it to me over and over when I was a child. I never tired of it."

"Do you remember your mother well?"

"Oh yes. Certain things in particular. The way she used to brush my hair at night, the smile she wore when we all sat down to breakfast in the morning. I remember she smelled like lemon verbena. And she had rosy cheeks, and big, dark eyes."

"Your father had green eyes, then, like you?"

She paused as they reached her door. She wrinkled her nose thoughtfully. "I don't remember."

He said lightly, "It isn't important. Camilla . . ."

"Yes?"

For a moment he stared at her, as if trying to make up his mind whether to say something or not. At last he shook his head. "Thank you for being so kind to Dorinda. Good night."

He strode away quickly, disappearing around the corner. Camilla went into her room and closed the door, leaning against it for a moment.

If only things were different, she thought bleakly. If only she really *did* belong here, if only Philip really loved her and not Brittany. . . . If, if, if.

Weariness washed over her, but as she went forward into the lamplit room, she remembered something she had planned to do tonight. She had to reread the letter from Silas, to try to make some sense of it in light of what she'd learned about Henry Anders today.

She pulled open the bureau drawer and rifled through the pile of handkerchiefs. The letter wasn't there. She moved several pairs of gloves, and completely lifted out the bundle of neatly folded handkerchiefs, setting them on the bureau. No letter.

A knot of foreboding twisted inside her. Fighting panic,

she emptied the drawer, searched it, and then emptied every drawer in the bureau. Nothing.

Camilla clasped shaking hands to her throat. The letter from Silas to Henry Anders was gone, and someone in this house must have taken it.

18 Camilla conducted a rapid survey of the room. Had anything else been moved or touched? Mary had probably been in to straighten up, but aside from that, she had to determine if someone had been searching through her belongings. It didn't take long to discover several things out of place: the dressing table drawer had been left slightly ajar, the invitation cards and notepaper on the writing table were no longer in separate stacks, the pocket of her pelisse inside the wardrobe was turned inside out . . .

Had the murderer himself been here, touched her things, searched her room? Tentacles of fear wound around her heart and clamped tight. Or, she wondered, trying desperately to stay calm, had it been some hireling, someone perhaps who worked in this very household, who had done the dirty work for him?

She paced the room, fighting panic. She could be in danger, everyone here could be in danger. Dorinda . . .

She pressed her hands to her temples and tried to think calmly. There was only one thing to do. She had to discover more about the murder, more about Silas. Perhaps that information would give her some clue as to who had stolen the note, and exactly whom she had to fear.

She had to find out now, tonight.

There was only one way. She ran to the wardrobe and took out the box hidden away in the corner.

A quarter of an hour later, a tattered figure in thread-bare work clothes slipped out of the kitchen entrance of the Earl of Westcott's splendid town house and made her way through the misty evening darkness. The girl's hair was tucked inside a worn and graying mobcap, her slender form hidden by the baggy layers of her much-mended skirts and apron. She carried a basket over one arm. She flagged down a passing hackney and ordered the driver to take her across the city to the factory district, giving him the direction of the Rose and Swan tavern.

Camilla never saw the tall, dark man who followed behind her in the shadows as she hurried up the street and hailed the hackney-coach. Her mind was churning at the prospect of returning to the sordid confines of the Rose and Swan.

In front of this teeming establishment the driver drew up, and Camilla descended the rickety steps. As the hackney clattered off into the mist, she stood a moment on the curb, as if gathering strength, and then went resolutely into the glaring light, stench, and din of the Rose and Swan.

Camilla blinked and wrinkled her nose in distaste as she entered the overflowing taproom. Everything was exactly as she remembered it: squalid tables and benches, the long, sticky bar covered with glasses and bottles, the low-beamed room noisy with bawdy talk and booming laughter and thick with the press of bodies and the reek of smoke. Clara bustled past, not seeing her, the girl's arms laden with a filled tray. Across the room, Will Dibbs tended bar, and Gwynneth poured ale. At the exact moment that Camilla's glance fell upon her, Gwynneth looked up and spied her in the doorway.

The tankard of ale slipped from the red-haired girl's fingers, shattering with a crash on the bar. Will Dibbs screamed a curse at her, but broke off as she lifted one thick arm and pointed at the tattered figure across the room.

His jaw dropped.

"Get out!" he bellowed at Camilla, his face growing purple with rage. "You run off without so much as a by-your-leave—then don't show your face again for weeks, and 'spect to be taken back? Out, out, out with ye!"

The roar of his words was all but drowned by the clamor in the tavern. No one paid any heed to one more raised voice. Camilla didn't either. She moved forward, pushing past the factory workers, seamen, coachmen, and grooms, stepping over a drunk sprawled on the floor.

"Don't be angry, Will," she said hastily, as he opened his mouth to shout at her again. "I don't want my job back. I want to buy a drink."

"You? Don't try to gammon me, Weed, you never touch a drop." He was so flabbergasted by her statement that he forgot to be enraged.

"It's for you." She bestowed a brilliant smile on him. "And one for Gwynneth." She took a gold piece from her pocket and tossed it onto the bar.

Gwynneth Dibbs's mouth dropped open. Before her uncle could touch the coin she scooped it up. "Where'd the likes of you be getting this?" she demanded. A sneer curled her lips as she gazed at the girl she'd always hated.

"Have you taken up a new line of work? Nah—who'd pay good money for someone ugly and scrawny as you?

What's in your basket, Weed?" As she reached to lift back the cloth that covered the large basket, Camilla smacked her hand away.

"You always did have the manners of a troll, Gwynneth."

"Who're you calling a troll?"

Will grabbed his niece's arm when she drew back as if to deliver a punishing right hook. "No brawling, or you'll pay for the damages!" he bawled. "Gwynneth, get ahold of yourself, girl." He wrested the gold piece from her clenched hand. "And you!" He jabbed a finger at Camilla. "What're you doin' here, buyin' drinks?"

"I need you to tell me something, both of you." Camilla spoke quickly now, glancing uneasily about the taproom. "The night I left, or afterward, did anyone come in here looking for me?"

"Sure, the Prince Regent himself came askin' for your hand in marriage!" Gwynneth cried scornfully. "And so did the Duke of Wellington, and the Earl of Westcott . . ."

Camilla's fingers curled around the edge of the bar. She didn't know whether to laugh or to cry. "Will?" she demanded tautly, regarding him with a searching gaze.

He shrugged his ample shoulders. "Naw, not that I recall . . . well, maybe. Come to think on it, there was a fellow asking about a serving maid in a gray apron. Said she'd dropped something on the street and he wanted to return it to her."

Her fingers whitened as they gripped the bar. "What did he look like?"

Will scratched his ear. "How in blazes am I to remember that? 'Twas weeks ago!"

"Surely you must remember something!" she said desperately. "Please, it's . . . it's very important."

"Tall, he was." The tavern owner frowned in concentration. "Wore what looked like a coachman's cape. Blue eyes, I seem to recall. He was here that same night, now you mention it. I was mad as fire because you'd run out that way, so I told him I didn't know or care what had become of that particular serving maid, since she'd gone out without so much as a by-your-leave, and hadn't bothered comin' back." He glared at Camilla and lifted a huge paw in dismissal. "And that's the truth of it. I gave you yer chance and you were the best worker I ever had—and then you deserted me jest like that." He dropped the gold piece into the pocket of his bulging purple waistcoat. "Now, get on with ye and don't be wastin' any more of my time," he grumbled, and disappeared into the kitchen.

"Nor mine!" Gwynneth leaned across the bar, grasping Camilla's frayed gray collar before Camilla could draw back. "I always knew you were no good. What've you been up to? Bet you stole that gold piece, didn't you? Or sold yourself, eh?" Her eyes narrowed. "Course, like I said, who'd buy? Tell me that, if you will."

"Let me go, Gwynneth. My business with you is done."

"But not mine with you. Tell me what you've been up to, Weed, so's that you can come in here all high and mighty, tossin' gold around like it was dirt." Gwynneth yanked the collar tighter, cutting off Camilla's air. Lifted nearly off her feet, choking for breath, Camilla did the only thing she could.

As a dizzying blackness swirled before her eyes, she grabbed up a pitcher of ale from the bar and dumped the contents straight in Gwynneth's face. With an outraged gasp, Gwynneth jumped back, releasing her. Ale dripped down her nose, and from her stubby eyelashes, and soaked the greasy strands of her carrot-red hair. "You . . . you . . . dirty little scumbag! I'll kill you for this!"

she screeched, but as she started to dive across the bar, her uncle returned from the kitchen. He yanked her backward and boxed her ears.

"Get to work and leave Weed be," he scolded. "I've got enough trouble with the customers breaking up the place, I don't need the serving wenches brawling like sailors! Weed, you get out and don't come back. I don't want to see yer face in here agin!"

"You won't, and it'll be my pleasure!" Camilla retorted as she sent Gwynneth one cool final glance. She turned toward the door and began to pick her way through the crowd when she saw Clara beckoning to her from the rear of the tavern.

"Weed, where've you been? I kept thinkin' and thinkin' about you. Oh, I swear I thought you was dead!" Clara hugged her, hidden from Will Dibbs's view by a trio of burly dockworkers making their way to a table.

"It's a long story, Clara. I couldn't help it, I had to go away. Are you all right?" she asked anxiously.

Close up, she noted in dismay the black eye the other serving maid wore.

"Some drunk popped me right in the eye becuz I didn't fetch his gin fast enough," the girl muttered. "No different than usual. But what about you? Weed, the baker's boy, Pete Colpers, was here near every day askin' 'bout you, till Gwynneth grabbed him by the hair and threw him out the door. All the girls have been wonderin', too." She threw Camilla a shrewd look. "Specially since that tall fellow turned up dead."

"Tall fellow?" She clutched Clara's arm. "Who, Clara?"

Clara's whisper dropped even lower. She placed her lips against Camilla's ear. "That tall fellow who was here that night you left. Clever-looking, he was, too clever by half—with eyes that gave me the shivers. Several of us saw him give you a paper and some coins." She stared hard at Camilla as if waiting for confirmation, but when the latter said nothing, she shrugged and went on. "Well, next morning he turned up dead in the alley. All bloody like a stuck pig. We all thought you might be dead, too, Weed."

"I'm not so easy to be rid of, Clara." Despite her light tone, Camilla was trembling. So Silas and Anders, both of the blackmailers, were dead. The murderer had indeed been busy that night. Camilla knew she had to get away from this tumult and smoke. She had to think.

She pressed Clara's hand. "Thank you. I'd better leave before Dibbs or Gwynneth spots us talking—you don't need any more trouble."

"Take care of yourself, Weed," Clara urged, starting to move off with her empty tray. On an impulse, Camilla suddenly reached into her pocket and pulled out a fistful of coins.

"Here, take these." She pressed them into the serving girl's free hand. "Good-bye, Clara, and . . . good luck."

Slipping outside once more onto the darkened street, Camilla hugged the basket close and started toward Porridge Street. She had to see Hester, even if it was only for one last time. She would sneak in, leave the basket of presents with her, and be gone before Mrs. Toombs or anyone else could discover her.

But as she passed a narrow, garbage-strewn alley, a pair of seedy-looking men suddenly emerged from the shadows. Their unshaven faces and gleaming, animallike eyes matched the disreputable stench and grime of their clothes. The taller, broader of the two held a wicked-looking knife, which he slashed in a little warning arc before him as he and his companion, seeing her at the

same instant she spied them, advanced upon her with
alacrity.

Cutthroats. She froze, glancing frantically over her
shoulder. If she tried to run back the way she'd come,
how far would she get?

"Whoa, what have we here?" The broader man darted
forward before Camilla could run and grabbed her arm.
His companion seized the basket.

"Give that back!" With her gaze fixed on the glittering
knife, Camilla tried to sound firm, though her voice
quavered. "There's nothing there to interest you. They're
trinkets for a child . . ."

"Hah, lookee here, Alfie," the man chortled, tossing
the cover back and lifting out the hunk of cheese she had
wrapped in a napkin. "And there's a loaf of bread and
roasted chestnuts and tarts . . ."

"No! It's not for you!" Camilla cried furiously, and
shoved her captor backward, heedless of his knife. Taken
by surprise, he stumbled into a heap of trash and fell,
while the other man reached out for Camilla angrily.

"That wasn't nice of you, missy," he growled, but before he could touch her, a tall figure lunged out of the
darkness and knocked him backward with a bruising right
hook.

"I suggest you keep your filthy hands off the lady,"
commanded an icy, hard voice Camilla immediately recognized as belonging to the Earl of Westcott.

Her astonishment mounted as she stared at him,
brawnily resplendent in a many-caped greatcoat of dark
olive, a beaver hat set rakishly upon his black curls, and a
heavy gold-inlaid walking stick brandished in his most capable hands.

The two cutthroats inched slowly to their feet. They
recognized a member of the quality when they saw one,

and they were certainly seeing one now. The man before
them bore himself with the arrogant assurance of the very
wealthy and very powerful, and they knew well that if
they were apprehended after doing an injury to such as
he, it would go badly for them. More than that, this particular member of the quality was tall, wide-shouldered,
and strong, and gave every evidence of being far more
ruthless and dangerous than they themselves. The shabbily dressed chit walking alone past the alley was one
thing—easy prey—but a fierce and powerful nobleman
with a weapon in his hand and deadly purpose in his eye
was something quite different.

"We don't want no trouble, yer lordship . . ." the man
with the knife wheedled.

"There's no need for any ruckus." The other man
pushed the basket along the ground toward them with the
worn toe of his boot. "We was only trying to be of help to
the lady . . ."

"Remove yourselves from my sight before I call the
constable," Philip growled contemptuously, "or worse for
you, change my mind and inflict my own punishment."

The deadly note in his voice made both the ruffians
quail.

They began edging warily backward out of the reach of
the walking stick.

"Now!" he ordered warningly, taking one menacing
step forward.

That startled them into a run. They disappeared
quickly around the corner of a crumbling building, leaving only the sound of their pounding footsteps echoing in
the night.

Swiftly Philip moved to Camilla's side. "Are you all
right?" he demanded. He grasped her arm, staring down
into her ashen face with concern.

"Yes. Thank you." Relief rushed over her so dizzyingly that she nearly sank to her knees. She was shaking, her breath catching in her throat. She was safe now, she told herself, she was with Philip. She tried to breathe normally. *Safe.*

"How did you . . . find me . . . oh, the basket," she suddenly cried in dismay. "Hester . . ."

He released her and stooped to retrieve the basket of food. Philip regarded it in silence, then fixed her with a keen look. If this basketful of food was a gift for the orphan child she had told him about earlier, why on earth had she chosen to deliver it alone and at night—and why had she gone back into that squalid tavern where she'd once worked? He didn't understand, hadn't understood any of it since he'd started following her when she left the house, but he promised himself that by the end of this evening, he would.

"My carriage is waiting around the corner. Come, we can talk when we're safely inside. I believe we've encountered enough danger for one night, Camilla, don't you?"

"I'm sorry to have caused you so much trouble," she mumbled as they hurried along the street toward the gold-crested coach.

"Thank God I followed you or who knows what might've happened," he muttered as he helped her inside the plush carriage.

"How did you happen to be here?" she asked, settling back against the cushioned squabs with a weary sigh. It was unbelievable to see him here in this seedy section of town, yet for all his elegance, he didn't appear the least bit ruffled or out of place.

"I saw you leave the house and followed you to the Rose and Swan," he explained. He watched her face as he spoke and studied the ragged garments she had donned for her outing. "Not wanting to draw attention to myself, I waited outside, and watched through the window." His eyes narrowed in the darkness of the coach.

"Quite a charming friend you have back there," he drawled grimly.

Gwynneth. She flushed, hoping he couldn't see her in the darkness. "Oh yes, a true paragon," she answered lightly. "Her uncle owns the tavern, you see, and she's always tried to lord it over all of the other serving girls."

"Did she hurt you?"

"Not much."

"I've never struck a woman," he said in a meditative tone, "but I was about to come in and throttle that damned Amazon within an inch of her life. Your solution, however, was almost as satisfying—or should we say, soul-quenching?"

"Gwynneth deserves to be quenched all right," Camilla replied quietly. Her mind was still churning with all that had happened. She kept picturing Silas, in his puce coat, dead in the alley. And Mr. Anders lying in a pool of blood at the White Horse Inn . . . and the murderer in his horrible mask . . . A wave of nausea washed over her.

"You're shivering. Are you cold?" He moved across the carriage to sit beside her, setting the basket onto the floor. His arms went round her shaking body and drew her close against him. The heavy coat smelled nicely of leather and of spice. She sighed as he pulled a fur rug from beneath the seat and draped it around her.

"Better?"

"Yes," she whispered. "Lovely."

The carriage clattered over the slick cobblestones, but

the jolting was softened by the Earl's excellently crafted springs. A watchman on a corner shouted the hour.

"What were you doing at that forsaken place tonight? Wearing these clothes? Why did you leave the house?" Philip gazed down at the slight figure in his arms. She looked almost as she had that first night he'd met her—she wore the exact same tattered clothes, though she was not dirty and muddy and wet as she had been then. But she was frightened. Something was frightening Camilla, frightening her badly, and it was more than the encounter with those cutthroats in the alley.

She'll tell me what is going on before this night is over, he vowed. *All of these secrets of hers are getting a bit too dangerous. She's a far sight too stubborn for her own good.*

"Well?" he persisted, a thread of impatience creeping into his voice.

For another moment she didn't answer. She was making up her mind.

The uncontrollable urge to tell him accosted her. He had trusted her with his secrets. Couldn't she now, with two men dead, trust him with hers? An ache of loneliness throbbed deep inside her. The need to reach out and confide in him crashed over her like a raging waterfall.

She spoke in a soft, tremulous voice he almost couldn't hear.

"I saw a murder."

"What?"

She gripped his arm. "The night you ran me down in the road. I saw a man murdered." Suddenly, she began to shake so badly that she could no longer speak. All of the shock, fear, and reaction she had suppressed since that fateful night spilled out of her. Silent sobs shook her shoulders, her legs went weak. As the carriage drew up in Berkeley Square, Philip lifted her weeping form in his arms. She clung to him, overcome with emotions too powerful to be contained any longer.

He waited only for his coachman to let down the steps, then, without another word, he gathered her close against his chest and carried her into the house.

The lower rooms of the town house were dark and cold, all of the hearth fires extinguished for the night. Philip carried Camilla up to his own bedroom apartment and set her down gently upon the huge bed of sturdy mahogany. He brought her a snifter of brandy and sat beside her on the bed.

"Drink this," he ordered, much as he had the first night she'd spent under his roof.

This time she didn't hesitate. She was shaking all over and she gulped the fiery liquor so eagerly he snatched it away after a moment. "Slowly, my girl, unless you want to be sick. And I won't have you passing out before you've answered my questions."

She took one final warming sip before giving the crystal snifter back to him. Unthinking, scarcely aware of where she was, she threw herself backward onto the plump, luxurious pillows of his bed and closed her eyes, letting the brandy flame through her, letting it soothe away the uncharacteristic hysteria that had gripped her in the carriage.

She heard his beautifully cool voice speaking her name. "Camilla."

She opened her eyes. He was sitting beside her, the hard lines of his face eerily illuminated by the crackling flames from the fireplace. His voice, though, was unexpectedly gentle as he wrapped a coverlet of thick crimson satin around her. "Tell me everything now. And I mean everything. If this is a matter of murder, you cannot dodge the truth a moment longer."

He was right, she knew that. And God knew, it would be a relief to share the knowledge she possessed, to share her terror and her suspicions with someone she could trust. And that meant Philip. Gazing wearily up into those steady gray eyes, glinting so keenly in the firelight, she knew with perfect certainty that no matter what happened, he would help her.

It was the first time in her life—since the day she'd gone to the workhouse—that she had felt she could rely upon another human being.

She sat up, reassured by the knowledge that she was safe within that huge, richly paneled room, with the tapestried wall hangings, the heavy crimson draperies festooned with gold silk tassels to blot out the night, the substantial fire blazing in the hearth, and Philip beside her, strong and wise and ready to help her.

The story poured out—all of it—from the moment Silas had sent her from the Rose and Swan upon her ill-fated errand, through her discovery of Mr. Anders's murder, and the murderer's dogged pursuit of her. She left nothing out, ending with her suspicion that the killer was a member of the ton, someone who had had access to her own room in this very house.

"Because tonight I discovered the note was missing from my bureau drawer. My room had been searched,

quickly and stealthily, from what I could tell." She tried
to keep the tremors from her voice as she contemplated
how close the killer really might be to them all.

Raising her tense face to his, she added, "I keep thinking about what you said today—of the connection between Henry Anders and Lord Marchfield. Did Anders
merely go to work for Marchfield after leaving your employ—or was there more to it, something that would hold
the key to this murder?"

Looking thoughtful, Philip rose and paced across the
room to the fire.

"Tell me everything you can remember of what the
note said."

She knew it nearly by heart. When she told him it was
signed with the name Silas, he started. "Could it be Silas
Tregaron?" he muttered, frowning.

"Who is that?"

"A caretaker of some of the Kirby property. He and
my groom Anders were thick as thieves. What did he look
like?"

She hugged her arms around herself and tried to remember. "Tall. Sharp, unpleasant features. He had
strange eyes."

"That's Tregaron."

"What happened to him?"

"I've no idea." Philip frowned. "Seems to me he hasn't
been in Alistair's employ for some time, but I've no notion exactly when he left. It would be interesting if it
turned out to be near the same time that Anders de-
parted Westcott Park."

"This means that you were acquainted with both of the
blackmailers. Could it be that you also know the man
they were blackmailing?" she asked slowly. "The man
who stole the note from my room?"

Silence. Camilla had never seen him look so grim.

"Are you thinking what I am thinking?" she asked softly.

He prodded the logs with his boot, sending sparks flying as the blaze intensified. Blazing warmth and light flickered out into every corner of the massive, handsomely appointed room. He strode back to the bed.

"Marchfield is a scoundrel," Philip said, almost to himself. "Still, it's difficult to imagine him a murderer." But his tone was thoughtful, worried. "He's amoral, cunning, and ruthless, and I wouldn't trust him with my back turned any more than I'd trust those blackguards we chanced across tonight, but . . . cold-blooded murder." His mouth tightened. "Damn, who knows? If he was being blackmailed, anything is possible. But what did they have to hold over his head—that's what I'd very much like to know."

"He seems to me a very cold man," Camilla ventured. "And there is obviously bad blood between the two of you . . ." She leaned forward and at last broached the subject she'd been wondering about for quite some time. "I heard something about a duel between you and his protégé. Philip, is that the reason he hates you so, or is it simply because you both have feelings for Lady Brittany?"

"The enmity between Marchfield and me can be traced back long before either of us set eyes on Brittany. You're right, Camilla, I killed his protégé, André Dubois, in a duel. I shot him between the eyes." The harshness with which he spoke sent a stabbing chill through her. "And I'd do it all again in a moment without one single regret."

She shuddered. The deadly set of his face frightened her suddenly. "Why?" she asked, wanting to touch him, to see his face soften and relax, yet too intimidated to reach out to him while that cold gleam shone in his eyes. "What did you have against the man?"

He riveted his cold gaze upon her, his voice raw with fury. "André Dubois raped a woman."

Her breath caught in her throat. "Who?" she whispered.

Philip's eyes took on a distant, faraway expression. "She was a young woman named Maura Pike." He let out a weary sigh, and sinking down beside her, crushed the satin bedcovers between his fingers. "I'll tell you the story, Camilla. It's not very pretty. Back in those days I was considered a notable rake. Believe me, I did what I could to live up to my reputation. But I never deceived any woman, or treated one with less respect than her due. There was a young opera singer whom I'd been seeing. To be perfectly frank, Camilla, she was my mistress."

Camilla nodded, saying nothing, waiting for him to continue.

Philip flicked a speck of dust from the sleeve of his jacket. "Maura was a beauty—young, gay, high-spirited. Every young buck in town had their eye on her. But we had a most exclusive arrangement at the time, and she was loyal to me. She caught Dubois's eye one night at one of her performances, and he tried to interest her in a flirtation. She rejected him, as she had all the others. But he couldn't accept that. Dubois was green, arrogant, and full of himself—the kind of man who is particularly obnoxious. He became furious at Maura's rejection. He called her a whore. He insisted that if she was my whore she was his as well, and, like a savage animal, forced himself upon her."

Camilla was very still, watching his face.

"Afterward she threw herself before an oncoming carriage and died almost instantly."

"No, oh no!"

Philip went on as if she hadn't spoken, as if he hadn't seen the quick horror spring to her eyes. "She had left a note in her lodgings for me. It explained exactly what that animal Dubois had done to her, all the things he had said, the humiliation he had forced her to endure. It was delivered to me the next day at Westcott Park, along with the news of her death. I left Westcott Park and tracked Dubois to White's—he was there, cool as you please, with Marchfield playing hazard alongside him."

"Go on."

"I was not subtle," he told her in a flat, chilling tone. "I chose to deal with him without benefit of the usual niceties. I struck the bastard in the face, knocked him clear across the room. Then while he lay bleeding on the floor, I called him out. With such violent provocation, he could hardly refuse to meet me."

"And you killed him."

"I killed him." He dropped his head into his hands. "It was at dawn, only hours after Marguerite died in the fire. If only I'd known. But it was because of Dubois and that duel that I was in London that evening and not at Westcott Park."

"Philip, you lost two people very close to you at almost the same time," she gasped, reaching out with gentle fingers to clutch his arm.

"It was the darkest period of my life." He passed a hand over his eyes, and focused upon her, his face shadowed now with bitterness. "Marchfield accused me of murdering Dubois because I was jealous that Maura had defected to him. He didn't say it to my face, of course, just behind my back. Kirby nearly called him out for it, but calmer heads prevailed upon him. Marchfield never quite got over his resentment, however. Dubois was his nephew, and he had a soft spot for the boy. Boy! Dubois was a cur—and Marchfield is probably no better. But did he commit murder . . . twice? We'll see," he vowed.

"I never wanted to bring the danger here," Camilla muttered. "I'm afraid for all of you now, especially Dorinda. But if the killer *is* Marchfield, and he recognized me, as seems likely, anything might happen."

"It won't." He met her worried gaze with a long, even stare. Poor Camilla, she looked so distraught and touchingly vulnerable, her gleaming curls loosened from their cap tumbling forward over her shoulders as she huddled on the bed, her eyes large and luminous in the firelight. But there was spirit in her, too, as well as fragility. Her mouth was firmly set, her delicate fists clenched, and when he thought back on how she had lived with this terrifying secret and the accompanying memories all this time, he wanted to enfold her in his arms and hold her close until her fear was gone. Sitting on the bed beside her, he covered her hand with his. "I know how to take care of my own," he said deliberately. "Don't be afraid, Camilla."

She was clinging to his hands without realizing it. "What are we going to do? Should I go away?"

"You should not—must not. It is more imperative than ever that I keep Brittany from Marchfield now. Our plan must go forward until it is successful. But I'm going to send Jared, Dorinda, and Miss Brigham back to Westcott Park. They'll be safe there for now, since, if there is any danger, it will be centered here, in London."

"Where I am."

He met her gaze directly. "Where you are," he agreed smoothly. "But you will be quite safe, my girl. I'm going to guard you myself." A ghost of a smile trailed across his face. "After all, we are a betrothed couple, are we not?

What should be more natural than that we should spend every moment together?"

"Do you really think the murderer will try to . . . to kill me?" she asked with a shudder.

"No." Philip shook his head. "He must realize by this time that you cannot identify him, or you would have done so long before this. And now that he has the note from Silas, you have no real evidence against him. You're not a threat to him any longer. If it is Marchfield, or some other member of the ton as we suspect, then he is clever enough to see that."

She turned her head away, gazing into the brilliant orange flames of the fire. A great weariness came over her. "And what if he is mad?" she asked in a low tone. "What if he doesn't care that I can't expose him?"

"He won't get to you. He'll have to get through me first."

She believed him. Comfort fell over her like a warm, downy blanket. There was silence until Camilla remembered the basket she'd intended to bring to Hester. When she asked about it, Philip gave her a long look.

"I'll take it to the workhouse myself tomorrow, if you'd like. And anything else you care to send to the children. But I think you should stay away from that part of town."

"It's where I belong," she reminded him. Her fingers brushed the rough fabric of her much-mended skirt. She hurried on before he could argue with her, "I've been planning to make a donation with some of the money I've been earning." She stifled a yawn, suddenly feeling much more at peace now that she had shared her burden with someone, now that she knew Hester would receive the food after all. "Would you take some money as well and give it to Mrs. Toombs for me? She must be given exact instructions for its use—I want her to buy blankets and

coats and shoes for the children, as well as extra food."
Her eyes wavered closed. "Did Charlotte tell you about
the boy we saw on Bond Street? I hope he went to the
workhouse, I'd hate to think of him sleeping in the alley
on a cold night like this . . ."

Her voice, which had faded to an exhausted mumble,
trailed off completely. She was asleep.

Philip gazed down at her lovely face, peaceful in re-
pose. She looked so young, so vulnerable. Her eyelashes
curled like lace along her cheek, her breath came evenly,
soft as velvet. He reached out and tucked the coverlet
around her shoulders, noting the ragged garments she
still wore, garments that seemed so out of place in this
room of crimson silk, leather, and mahogany. He
smoothed a wisp of hair from her brow, such a delicate,
tender brow.

A soft rain pattered at the window. Philip poured himself a brandy and thought over what he had learned tonight. As the rain intensified, he paced to the overstuffed
easy chair near the fire and folded his long-limbed form
into it. He stretched out his legs and for a long time
studied the girl fast asleep in his bed.

He was chasing her down a pitch-black corridor. There
was no light. She ran blindly, frantic with her fear. She
had eluded him, lost him in the darkness, and she gasped
aloud with relief. She rounded a corner, plunging forward
toward the distant light that beaconed safety. Suddenly,
like a malevolent phantom, he sprang at her from the
shadows. He was covered with blood.

His demonically masked face dripped with the warm,
red liquid.

"Camilla, it's time for you to die!" he screamed at her,
laughing grotesquely, and lifted the knife.

Her feet were glued to the floor. A scream froze in her throat. *She knew she was going to die.*

The knife sliced toward her face as his shriek of joy filled her ears . . .

"Camilla! Wake up. It's all right, you're safe. Do you hear me, you're safe!"

Her eyes flew open, wide with terror, the scream dying on her lips.

"Philip," she choked thankfully as he clasped her to his broad, solid chest, holding her until the trembling of her body eased.

"I dreamed that the murderer was chasing me . . . he was going to kill me . . ."

"Don't think about it." He stroked her hair, his fingers sliding through the soft curls. "It was only a dream, and it's all over now. No one is going to hurt you."

She clung to him, finding strength in the rippling muscles of his back, in the powerful hardness of his shoulders. With strong, soothing hands he cradled her against him, and his calm voice sent her terrors racing back into the dark corners of her mind.

Camilla gave herself up to a long, shuddering sigh. She was safe, she was in Philip's own bedchamber, in Berkeley Square.

His bedchamber? Suddenly, the impropriety of the situation struck her. She really shouldn't be here . . .

"How long have we been back?"

"Awhile. It'll be dawn in a few hours."

Dawn. She glanced around. The fire had died down to a mere flicker. A gray chill permeated the dark-shadowed room.

"It's cold in here. I'll stir the logs . . ."

"No." Panic tore through her as he started to move

away. She gripped the front of his jacket so hard he stared down at her in surprise. "Don't leave, just hold me a moment," she begged, and his arms instantly tightened around her once more.

"Whatever you wish," he said in a lightly teasing tone.

She rested her head against his shoulder. The fear slid away. She felt her body relaxing, reassured by his presence, his strength. Philip, Philip, she thought, her heart crying out with need. Her body and soul yearned in that moment for something other than friendship and concern. She was intensely aware of him, of his clean, male scent, the hard bulge of his muscular arms, the rough bristle of his unshaven chin against her skin. As sensation after sensation compounded, she felt an electrifying tingle burst through her.

Then he felt it, too. A vibrant current flashed between them, something hot, mesmerizing, irresistible. They both jumped back at the same moment, and stared at one another, jolted to the core.

"You should leave," he said hoarsely. "I'll take you back to your . . ."

"No!" Her fingertip brushed his lips, rested there, while her eyes locked desperately on his.

"I want to stay." Dear God, what was she saying?

The truth.

"Camilla." Staring at her, lovely and fragile and pale, her supple body warm and tantalizing against his, pressed against him on his very own bed yet, he tried to be calm, to be noble. But it was damned near impossible. He was only human, and Camilla Brent looked bewitchingly appealing by firelight, a slim pixie goddess with hair spilling forward like molten copper, eyes mesmerizingly aglow with desire. Desire? The girl was terrified, he told himself. That was all. He couldn't pretend it was more than that, or take advantage of her apprehensions . . . he couldn't . . .

"You must go back to your room," he insisted, forcing himself to sound firm, while his eyes were devouring the sweet, sensuous curve of her lips. "I was wrong to bring you up here. But there was no fire kindled in the downstairs rooms, and you were so upset I wanted to get some brandy into you and see that you were warm . . ."

"I want to stay with you."

There. She'd said it again. Her cheeks burned bright red and for one tiny moment she was afraid he'd look at her with contempt or disgust, but instead he gripped her arms so tightly she gasped, and his gray eyes flared like hot coals into hers.

"Do you know what you're saying? What you're doing? Camilla, you're not thinking . . ."

"Yes, I am. Thinking and feeling. Philip, please, don't send me away." She pressed against him, her fingers curling through his thick black hair, her other hand cradling his jaw. "I won't ask anything of you," she heard herself saying in a whisper. "But I want . . . I want . . ."

She couldn't speak it aloud. It was too embarrassing. But she wanted him with a fierce, overwhelming need that blotted out rules, and strictures, and all of society's conventions. Her feelings were deep and beautiful, so why would it be wrong to express them?

Just one night, she told herself. I can live without him the rest of my life if I must, if only I can know one night in his arms, in his bed.

Philip was very still, very tense.

She reached up to him urgently, her whole body quivering, her heart commanding, and she molded her aching lips to his.

"Don't send me away," she pleaded against his mouth.

Philip caught her up hard against him, his arms like steel bars around her. He was on fire. Her kiss had ignited a searing heat that spread through his taut frame like an inferno. Send her away? He wanted more than anything to push her down on the bed and make love to her for hours, exploring every delectable inch of her, tasting all the sweetness of her.

But he couldn't . . .

She clung to him like a delicate vine of ivy to a brick wall. Her luscious mouth was soft and pliant, yet enflamingly demanding against his.

"Oh, God, Camilla, are you sure?" he demanded harshly. He grasped her by the shoulders as he spoke, lowered her to the bed, and leaned over her, the length of him poised above her slender form. Every muscle tensed, coiled with desire held in check, straining to wait until he knew for certain what she wanted . . .

"I've never been more sure of anything . . ." Her eyes glowed yearningly into his, she pulled him eagerly toward her. "Please . . ."

Philip kissed her with dizzying force. She strained upward, trying to lock herself instinctively against him.

He gave up, gave in to the explosive forces drawing them together like a moth and a flame. She was innocent, he could tell, an innocent on fire. She moaned with delighted surprise each time he touched her, and he knew she had never done this before.

That made him want her all the more. A heady combination of fierce protectiveness and purely male desire surged through him. When he cupped her breast, she cried out with delight. He began to massage it with a tantalizing motion that drew a moan of pleasure from her lips.

Philip single-mindedly stripped away her clothes, one

by one, peeling off the ugly layers of worn, mended rags she'd donned to go to the tavern.

"You're beautiful even in these," he whispered against her lips. "But more beautiful without them."

He was the first man ever to tell her she was beautiful. Camilla's eyes, luminous as jade, shone up at him, radiantly mirroring the love that quivered like a perfectly shot arrow through her. Love heated her, pulsing through her in every beat of her heart. It heated her need and her desire.

She took his hand and kissed it. The simple gesture brought an oddly gentle softening to his face.

Thrusting herself upward, she faced him sitting on the bed and her fingers plucked hesitantly at his garments. "Be my guest," he invited, his grin teasing her in a way that made her heart skip a beat. Between kisses, touches, and laughter, she stripped him naked beside her. *How strong and marvelous he is,* she thought, noting the bulge of sinewy muscles, the bronze sheen of his skin, the crisp black hair matting his wide chest. She couldn't help being stunned by the superb magnificence of his body. Stunned, and for just a moment as her gaze slid downward, she felt afraid . . .

"I'll try not to hurt you, Camilla," he promised. He touched her hair. "Don't be afraid."

Afraid? She was too desperately in love for that. "I'm not afraid—I want to . . . Philip, I truly want to . . . Do you really think I'm beautiful?" she couldn't help asking.

The question, so sweet and artless and hopeful, slammed into the wall of his emotions like a pummeling rock. *She's so young, so inexperienced and full of hope. It would be so easy for a man to hurt her,* he thought almost angrily, *so easy for someone to take advantage of her.* For a moment, Philip hesitated, caught between his drives and his conscience, weighing Camilla's own professions of desire against the shreds of his own tattered honor. Then he read the eagerness shining from her eyes, and something snapped inside him.

With a muttered curse, he gripped her shoulders hard, and kissed her, a kiss that was hungry, hot, and devouring, a kiss meant to leave her breathless—and which did.

He was taut with emotion. Not merely passion, Philip realized dazedly, but emotion—real, true, confusing, and unnamed emotion.

His gaze swept the length of Camilla's body, studying, taking, ravishing, without lifting a finger. She was lovely. And willing. His eyes smoldered over her. *Why not?* he thought fiercely. *It's what we both want.* His thoughts raced ahead to the intoxicating pleasures to come.

And at the same time, he gave himself a warning. Go slow, be careful. She deserves an experience that is joyful, unforgettable, and filled with tenderness.

But his gaze fastened keenly on the lushness of her body, and he knew it would demand all of his willpower to hold back.

Camilla, seeing the intensity of his gaze, blushed from the soles of her feet up to the sweep of her delicate brow. When Philip noticed the glowing color, he grinned, and she blushed more, a deeper shade of pink, one that set her creamy skin alight with the hue of rose petals. Some of his tension eased, and he chuckled delightedly, leaning over to kiss her mouth with great gentleness and a masterful thoroughness that left her weak and wanting.

It's like my dream, Camilla thought wondrously as the kiss deepened, and then deepened again. Only far, far better. Philip was no longer only her dream lover, enticing, entrancing, and seducing her through the shadows, he was real, beautifully real—solid and strong, and utterly masculine. He licked his tongue over her parted lips, tracing their soft outline, and Camilla moaned, closing her eyes in pure ecstasy, as feelings she had never imagined before continued to flood through her. When he slipped his tongue inside her mouth in search of hers, she rapturously breathed in the musky man-taste and scent of him. *Wild,* she thought gloriously, he made her feel like something wild and exotic as the night.

A tremor shook her. Camilla's tongue fluttered wildly against his, a dainty sword swinging madly to battle. Even in her most delicious, most astonishing dreams, she'd never imagined . . . never experienced anything close to the sensations rocking her here in Philip's arms, in his bed . . .

Philip tasted her, drank in the delicious, sweet nectar of her, nectar as warm and intoxicating as a simmering pot of honey. He longed to take her then, quickly, to gather her close and plunge inside her, experiencing all of her, laying claim to her, but he forced himself to hold back, to go slowly, carefully, without hurting or frightening the lovely girl who gave herself so eagerly and trustingly into his care.

He knelt over her on the bed, powerful in size and strength, magnetic in the depth and passion of his character, and swore to himself he wouldn't hurt her any more than was humanly necessary. As he tenderly stroked her cheek with his finger, he studied the comely length of her. He fought back a groan. Lord, she was beautiful. Porcelain skin, flesh as soft and warm as satin, eyes brighter and more bewitching than any jewels. Not only did her lush curves invite his touch, but her delicate frame was so alluringly feminine it made him yearn to stroke her and kiss her from top to bottom, to nibble every inch of her.

His eyes hungrily tried to memorize every curve and hollow, the sweep of her eyelashes, the rhythm of her quickened breaths. He would remember every detail until the day he died. She possessed a completely female grace, a body made for thorough loving.

Philip thought of how she'd looked riding Marmalade that first time, her bottom shifting appealingly with every step of the horse. He thought of how she'd danced tonight, gracefully, for all her worries, light and charming despite her mishaps. He remembered how frantically she'd clutched at him a short time ago when the nightmare had besieged her, how small and strong and sure those gripping hands had been. Tenderness welled up within him, joining forcefully with passion, filling him with a need and a want and a fierce, searing urge for this brave, giving woman that would find release in only one way and one way alone.

Camilla. She was a study in contrasts, an innocent girl, a dazzling woman, a waif without means or power, and at the same time, a tower of strength and common sense far wiser and more deeply rooted than he. He studied her hungrily, admiringly, while the fire whispered and flickered and began to die, and the need for her grew, making his breath come in long, raspy beats that matched the pumping rhythm of his heart.

Shyly, eagerly, Camilla watched his face, deriving soft pleasure from the appreciation she read in his intently scanning gaze.

His gray eyes went dark and smoky as they lingered upon her breasts with their twin rosebud nipples taut and sharp as spires. He kissed each one in turn, his tongue licking and caressing in a slow, circular motion that made her writhe with breathless sensations.

When she thought she would burst with pleasure, he

leisurely drew back, eyes gleaming, and let his gaze sweep lower. It skimmed over the firm, rounded whiteness of her belly, past the sensuous curve of her hips, to the dark patch of hair nestled between her thighs.

His finger touched, traced, teased. Camilla gasped. Glistening dampness met his probing finger and he slipped it further into the mysterious tunnel of warmth.

"Philip," she gasped, and he paused, his smile deep and reassuring and secretive, full of pleasures yet to bestow.

"It's only the beginning, my love. Shall I go on?"

"Forever," she breathed, and the laughter rumbled deep in his chest.

He stroked and touched her until she thought she would go mad. With his mouth nipping, nuzzling at her breasts, tormenting her sensitive nipples, then burning a trail of kisses downward to that aching area between her thighs, he awakened her to pleasure beyond anything she had previously comprehended. His mouth and his hands drove her to the farthest edges of passion, and then farther still.

She felt no fear, no hesitation, not a nip of it, only a gripping warmth and need that built inside her to a desperate level she could no longer bear. Camilla clutched him closer with blind need, not fully understanding the urges that drove her to wrap her legs around him, pulling him close and tight against her naked body. She felt his muscles tense and tauten, heard the sharp intake of his breath.

"Not yet, Camilla," Philip whispered hoarsely. His own need was growing ever more desperate, ever more urgent. He was a strong man, but even Hercules would not be able to withstand much longer. Lovingly, he stroked the burnished silk of her hair as it lay spread upon the pillow. He grasped a handful of it in his fist. "Soon, my sweet, innocent, little love, very, very soon."

His mouth trailed kisses up her arm, across her shoulder, her dainty jaw, and into the hollow of her throat. At last he moved atop her, spreading her legs with his muscled thighs, burying his face in her hair.

He breathed a warm kiss into her mouth as he slid inside her. He entered her easily, for she was warm and moist and she gave out only one small, shocked gasp that melted into a low-pitched moan. Philip's tongue flicked around the curve of her ear as her hips rose up to meet his fevered body.

"That's right, Camilla." His eyes glinted now with passion that would no longer be denied. "Meet me, love me, join me," he urged, gathering her close, filling himself with the smell and feel and essence of her.

He breathed in her flowery woman-scent, thrusting into her with ever more powerful movements. As the rhythm of his movements quickened, and the thrusts of his body deepened and grew stronger, harder, increasingly desperate, Camilla responded to him like white-hot summer lightning to thunder.

Her hips swiveled beneath his, her back arched, her arms snaked around him, drawing him close, closer, deep inside of her so that they could truly be one . . .

The world spun like a top. The colors of the room blurred, the smells of the burning logs and fine old leather mingling dizzily with the intoxicating spice of him, and her senses reeled. So this was lovemaking, Camilla thought fleetingly, wildly, before she could think no more. Her fingers tore at him, digging, kneading. He kissed her face, her throat, her hair, he showered kisses upon her mouth, and he gathered her into the storm of his passion with an all-encompassing heat that sent her streaking toward delirium with blue-hot joy.

Then there was only the roaring splendor of him filling her, the thrusts and gasps that tore through them both and melded them in a frenzied burst of ecstasy.

Shuddering, crying with happiness, she gave herself to him, not once, but again and again as the night burned on toward morning.

"You're quite good at this," Philip panted once, hours after they'd begun. "You know, from now on, you must list a talent for lovemaking among your many accomplishments."

"So should you, your lordship," Camilla murmured, dancing kisses across his sweat-filmed chest. She still ached with the need for him, the need to prolong this magical night. "Love me again, Philip," she urged, her eyes glowing in the darkness. She pulled his head down to her mouth, and licked the rugged line of his jaw, where a dark stubble was forming. Her small teeth nipped the lobe of his ear, then pressed a fervent kiss to his lips.

Philip needed no further invitation.

His mouth blazed hot against hers. He tossed aside the coverlet to reveal her glistening body once more, and with a playful growl, threw himself over her.

And they began again.

At last, when dawn's pearly peach light had fully banished both the darkness and the rain they lay tangled peacefully together in the massive bed—both of them spent, sated, and joyously replenished, curled naked and gleaming in each other's arms as the new morning drew near.

20

Camilla awakened slowly, sleepily in the big bed. Pale morning light peeked in around the edges of the heavy draperies. She closed her eyes against it, wanting to cling to the sweet remnants of a blissful sleep. She was in Philip's room, she acknowledged dreamily, and he was here beside her, guarding her, loving her.

She reached out for him, her body sweetly aching for his touch. *Philip . . .*

He wasn't there. She opened her eyes and bolted upright in the bed. Cold hard reality poured over her like ice water. One swift glance around the room told her that she was absolutely alone.

She sank back against the pillows, baffled, uneasy. She touched her bruised, reddened lips as she remembered all that had happened last night and into the dawn.

Perhaps she ought to feel ashamed, but she didn't. She felt deliciously, gloriously alive. Last night Philip had made love to her with unbelievable passion. He had awakened sensations and emotions deep within that she hadn't even imagined before—he had made her feel wanted, needed, wildly wanton, vulnerable, and desirable all at the same time. The sweet as fire memory of her dream lover returned to her. Philip was that same fierce and gentle lover, she knew that in her heart. The feelings and sensations of her dream had all been intensified last night, their lovemaking had been far more joyous and beautiful and intense than in any of her dreams.

And Philip, she thought, her eyes shining at the memory, Philip had been magnificent. How could a man who was so strong possibly be so tender? she wondered, her body growing warm at the memories. She only knew that she wished he were back here right now so that they could make love again. She needed to feel his arms around her, his lips on hers, wanted to know once more the beauty they could create between them.

But where was he?

Lying here alone, the very quietness seemed to mock her. A horrible thought intruded upon her happiness. Could it be that Philip regretted making love to her—that in the light of day he didn't even want to see her? She felt a cruel twisting pain inside her. Maybe he wanted nothing more to do with her. Maybe he planned to end her role in the plan and find some other way to win Brittany. Maybe today he would tell her to leave his house and never come back . . .

Just as her frightened mind was turning over every negative possibility, and tormenting her with their likelihood, the door to the bedchamber opened and Philip himself entered. He looked impossibly handsome, impossibly aristocratic in the pale morning light. Clean-shaven and impeccably dressed in a dark blue coat of superfine, with a white and gold patterned silk waistcoat, and dark, tight-fitting breeches, he radiated strength and assurance and the careless authority of the high-born. His dark hair was glossily brushed, his linen snowy and starched against his swarthy skin. He locked the door and with an enigmatic glance at her, strode into the room.

Camilla's heart hammered in her chest as she instinctively draped the bedsheets up over her nakedness. It was impossible to tell from the expression on his face what mood he was in. A businesslike one, she guessed. Crisp and cool and . . . formal.

He halted at the side of the bed and gazed down at her.

She was opening her mouth to say "Good morning," which seemed a neutral enough comment under the circumstances, but he sat down suddenly on the edge of the bed and spoke first.

"I'm sorry, Camilla."

Her heart plummeted. "For what?" she managed to ask in a reasonably steady tone. This wasn't the way she had expected to start the day—she had hoped to begin the morning in his arms, with sweet kisses and soft words. Anything but this cool formality overhung with an air of regret. She wanted to hold out her arms to him, to kiss the serious expression from his face, but she stayed perfectly still and waited.

He met her gaze unflinchingly. "I made a mistake last night. What happened was all my fault. It never should have—" He broke off, and she saw the muscle working in his jaw. "It never should have happened," he said deliberately. "It won't happen again. Blame it on the Audley recklessness, Camilla, blame it on my own personal lack of self-control. Damn it, it doesn't matter. I accept full responsibility."

Just as he had accepted full responsibility for running her down on Edgewood Lane? He thought of their night together as some sort of accident, a near-tragic disaster that should have been averted? She couldn't move. All she could read in his face was grim regret.

So it was true, she thought numbly, as every drop of happiness drained from her. He hadn't felt at all what she'd felt. He *had* only been using her, enjoying her body as he would that of any woman who made herself available to him. The fact that it was her—Camilla—had had nothing to do with it. Any feelings he had for her, even friendship or the tiniest bit of caring, had had nothing to do with it. It had all been lust, she realized. She felt ill. It had all been merely a raw physical need that once satisfied, could only be regretted as the indulgence of a reckless impulse.

"Don't . . . don't give it another thought." She was proud that she sounded so casual. How could she sound like that when her heart was shattering into a thousand jagged pieces? "I wanted you to . . . I wanted to stay here. You certainly didn't force me." A high, shrill laugh tore from her lips, sounding brittle and false even to her own ears. "My clothes. Give them to me, if you please."

Philip complied. Feeling more awkward and miserable than he ever remembered feeling in his life, he stooped to gather up the tattered garments lying atumble on the floor. As he handed them to her, a moment of doubt assailed him. Her eyes, those clear brilliantly green pools, looked so lost, so empty. He wanted to wrap her in his arms, to hold her tight, to smooth her luxuriant hair back from her face. But that was impossible. There must be no more physical contact between them. He was going to marry Brittany Deaville. Camilla knew that, he reminded himself desperately, she had known that all along.

Damn, this was all his fault. Fury at his own weakness surged through him.

Against all of his better judgment he had allowed Camilla Brent's savory combination of sweetness and spunk to get the better of his good sense. Last night she had been terrified of a murderer, and she'd tumbled into his arms. He'd taken advantage of her fear and her desperation.

If only she weren't such a fascinating woman, with her piquant face and luscious body, her warmth and gaiety and inner courage. But he'd had no right to give in to the temptations she posed to exploit her vulnerability.

Philip hated himself for having lost control. He ought to have thought with his head last night and not his . . . never mind. It was over now. It could never happen again. He would try to make it up to Camilla, he would continue the investigation he'd begun yesterday after she'd told him about that charm. And he'd help resolve this business with the murderer.

It was the least he could do.

He only hoped she wouldn't start hating him as much as he hated himself.

Camilla clenched the garments he handed her tightly in one hand. With the other she held up the bedsheet that covered her. "I must go back to my room," she said quickly, in a chattering tone quite unlike her usual way. "The servants will be talking if—"

"Damn the servants, Camilla. I'm concerned about you." He gripped her shoulders so suddenly that the sheet slipped from her fingers, exposing her full, creamy breasts to his view.

Immediately, he released her and stepped back, and she snatched up the sheet once more. "Kindly leave so that I may dress in privacy," she cried sharply, hating the crimson color she felt flooding into her cheeks. Her humiliation was now complete. "I promise I will be out of your bedchamber posthaste, so why don't you . . . go call on Lady Brittany or . . . or ride in Hyde Park or take snuff—do something you members of the ton are so precious good at doing, and leave me in peace."

He had ruined the friendship between them. Killed it. Well, he thought with bitter self-contempt, what had he expected?

His expression took on granite hardness. "Do you want to leave?"

"Wh . . . at?"

"Do you want to leave London? Cancel our arrangement and go to Paris immediately?"

"Before the ball—before you've won your bet?"

"I won't hold you to our agreement. I can scarcely blame you if you want to go away." He took a deep breath. "You must hate me."

She didn't know whether to laugh or weep. Hate him? She wanted to kiss him—and she wanted to hit him over the skull with a candlestick until his head hurt him as much as her heart pained her.

Hate him?

Sputtering for words, pride came to her rescue. In the same tone she had often used when dealing with Dibbs she heard herself saying: "My personal feelings have nothing to do with this. We have a business arrangement, and I am perfectly willing to see it through to the end. If *you* would like to cancel our arrangement however, I will understand."

"I wish to continue."

"Then there is no problem."

Right, he thought to himself, studying her daintily uplifted chin, the unquenchably defiant sparkle in her eyes. No problem.

"Will you leave now, please? The day isn't getting any younger."

Haughty as a duchess she was, Philip noted, caught between amusement and dismay. He turned on his heel and stalked to the door.

But he couldn't stop thinking about the way she'd looked when that sheet fell away. He didn't want her to leave his bed, much less his house. He glanced back at her huddled form, with the sheet draped protectively across her shoulders. If she only knew how badly he wanted to tear that sheet away again and sweep her naked body into his arms. Damn, if she only had an idea how sensuously appealing she looked, with her hair cascading over her bare shoulders, her smooth porcelain flesh just waiting for his touch.

Better to leave now, he told himself, tightening his jaw. Leave before he made things even worse. Camilla Brent was too damn fetching for her own good—and for his.

The door slammed behind him. Camilla threw a pillow at it. Her fingers clawed the coverlet in frustration, and she whispered, "Good riddance!" A moment later she burst into tears.

Philip didn't love her. *Of course he didn't,* a mocking voice whispered inside her head, a voice that sounded exactly like the hateful voice of Gwynneth Dibbs. *You're nothing, nobody. What makes you think he could ever love you?*

He loved Brittany. That was the truth. She covered her face with her hands and squeezed her eyes shut against the pain. Last night she had tried to deceive herself for a little while, she had been happy to take whatever he had to give, on whatever terms he offered. And she had disgraced herself and made him despise her.

She gasped as the full force of her humiliation ripped through her. She didn't know how she would face Philip or anyone else ever again. She couldn't bear his pity or his scorn. She couldn't endure his polite regret.

Loneliness spiraled through her. How could one regret a night of magic?

She made it back to her room undetected, bathed, dressed, and paced and paced around her room, her mind spinning with the memories. He didn't love her, not even one tiny bit, that much was obvious. But she'd known that all along, she reminded herself bitterly. It had only been her own foolishness that had made her believe the impossible could come true. But couldn't she pretend it didn't matter to her either? She stopped in the middle of the Aubusson carpet and pressed her fingers to her throbbing temples. Couldn't they remain friends, at least until after the ball at Westcott Park, when she would have to leave him?

She didn't have much pride, she reflected ruefully. And they didn't have much time together. She realized that soon he would be betrothed to Brittany, and she would be out of his life forever. Her memories of last night and of the coming days were all she would ever have of him. She had to make the most of them. A strange kind of determination tightened into a hard little ball inside her.

She had to pretend that what had happened between them meant as little to her as it did to him, that it was the result of an impulse, of circumstances that had thrown them together and allowed things to go beyond their control. She had to make him believe that she cared no more than he, that they could go on as they had before, as if nothing of importance had happened to change things between them. But could she?

Her determination mounted. Philip Audley, the Earl of Westcott, was the kindest man she'd ever met. For all of his wealth and breeding, for all of his cool, reckless manner and quick temper, he had never treated her as if she was less than a lady, had never made her feel as if she was anything less than a full and respected partner in this wild plan of his. Her lips curved softly upward as she thought back on how he had taught her to ride Marmalade, on the way he had swept her into his arms whenever he feared her ankle was hurting her, on the way he had teased her about that candlestick. He had defended her against the cutthroats in the alley, and danced the waltz with her in Dorinda's sickroom, doing all of those things with smooth aplomb and effortless mastery. Then she remembered the tender way he had kissed her on the terrace at Westcott Park, and again last night in his bed, kissed her so fiercely and hungrily, his powerful body demanding with a hot need what she had been only too eager to satisfy.

Philip Audley dominated her thoughts even as a seaful of problems dominated her life. Even through her worries about the murderer, and her questions about her golden charm, even through the uncertainty of her own future, which now seemed as dark and hazy as a storm cloud, she couldn't stop thinking about the tall black-haired rake who wanted to marry Brittany Deaville and settle his family down to a normal life. She couldn't stop thinking that *she* could make him happy—if only she were eligible to try.

But that was out of the question. And besides, she reminded herself with brutal honesty, he loved Brittany. Not her—Brittany.

She would help him win Brittany then, as she'd promised. And in the meantime, until this charade was over, she'd hide the secrets in her heart and cherish every moment she could spend with him.

Sometime before noon, having remembered that Dorinda was ill, she forced herself to leave the safe confines of her room, and presented herself in the nursery suite, where Miss Brigham smilingly informed her that the patient was showing rapid improvement.

It was true. Dorinda was sitting up in bed, her dark hair brushed and caught up in a yellow ribbon, a sketch pad on her knee. Peering down, Camilla saw that she was sketching Tickles who was asleep at the foot of her bed.

"I didn't know you were such a talented artist," Camilla exclaimed. Dorinda beamed, and Camilla was glad to see that her color was back to normal, and her eyes had lost their glassy, feverish look. Miss Brigham assured her that the fever was gone, and from observing Dorinda, it was obvious that the sniffles had subsided.

"I'm going home today," Dorinda informed her quite happily.

"Oh?"

"Philip came in early this morning and told me. Jared is accompanying me and Miss Brigham back to Westcott Park. And you're coming tomorrow."

"How nice. It is so lovely at Westcott Park. I know Miss Brigham will enjoy it, too."

"We'll have fun there," Dorinda agreed, obviously looking on the bright side of her situation. "We can go riding together, and take walks now that your ankle is all better."

"Yes, we'll have a splendid time," Camilla murmured, thinking with a sharp pain how much she was going to miss Dorinda—indeed, all of them—when the time came for her to leave.

She took herself off downstairs a short time later, though she wasn't hungry at all. Still, she had to behave normally, and that meant forcing herself to at least pretend an interest in breakfast.

She had no sooner slipped into the deserted dining room, however, than Durgess appeared and handed her a note on a silver tray. At that moment, Charlotte and James joined her, arm in arm.

"Is that message from Philip, by any chance? He asked us to stand in for him today," James said as she picked up the notepaper, observing it was the Earl of Westcott's thick cream stationery, with his title and crest embossed in dramatic black across the top of the page.

"Stand in for him?" she repeated, staring sightlessly at the note.

"Yes, something about bringing a donation to the workhouse on Porridge Street," Charlotte said. "He explained it all to James."

Camilla heard the strain in her voice and glanced up from the Earl's letter, noting with concern that Charlotte's eyes looked puffy and there was a wan cast to her usually bright face. James, too, she observed, appeared somewhat drawn, and he was behaving with an attitude of forced cheerfulness, which hinted to her that something was wrong between them.

But neither appeared to welcome any inquiries, so she bit back the questions on her lips and instead replied, quite truthfully, that she had forgotten all about it.

"Philip said it was important to you, and he had to leave on some business," James went on. "Read his letter, I'm sure that will clarify things for you."

To her mortification, the paper shook in her hands, so she propped it on the table to read it.

Dear Camilla,

Durgess has in his keeping the basket of food and a letter detailing a sizable donation to the workhouse. James and Charlotte will take both to Porridge Street personally and speak to Mrs. Toombs, if you agree. I'm sorry I couldn't handle it personally for you but I have some other important business to attend to today, and it cannot wait.

When I met with James and Jared earlier this morning I followed your advice and told them about our father's handling of his affairs. They were stunned, and angry at first that I never told them before now, but in the end I believe we reached a tolerable understanding—perhaps more of an understanding between us than we have known in some time. They were not only concerned that we almost came to such a pass, they seemed to grasp better than I'd hoped how dangerous our rash, impulsive Audley nature can be if left unchecked. I also informed Jared that he and Dorinda must return to Westcott Park at once. He didn't even argue with me—I believe he took it as a punishment for the trouble with Wimpnell. It's just as well for now. I've decided it would be best for all of us to return to Westcott Park tomorrow. There are fewer comings and goings there, and that means increased safety from outsiders. I'm sure you understand. Our excuse will be that we must get everything in readiness for the ball.

I am sorry for all of my mistakes, from the first moment I met you. I never meant to harm you, and hope we can still save a vestige of our friendship. It has meant a great deal to me—you are the first woman I have ever been able to talk to freely about my problems, my life, my concerns for my family. I would hate to lose that comfortable feeling we've established between us, though I realize I deserve to do just that.

Camilla, there is a great deal at stake, more than we both bargained for at the start of this misadventure. Until it is resolved, we must work together. I'll try not to make that any more difficult for you than it must be. But for your own safety, you must stay in Berkeley Square today, until I return this evening to take you to the Asterley ball. Do not go out with anyone, except James or Kirby.

Until this evening, be very careful . . .
Philip

He couldn't have sounded more businesslike if she were his bailiff, she reflected bleakly. But what had she expected?

She folded the paper neatly in half and looked up to find James and Charlotte watching her.

"It's admirable of you to try to help those people at the workhouse," James commented as he set his coffee cup in the saucer. "Particularly the little girl, Hester. Dorinda confided to me this morning that she wishes she could meet her, especially after all the stories you have told about her. She sounds like an incredibly bright, sweet-natured girl."

Thoughts of Hester distracted her from her own tormented emotions. "Yes, I wish I could see her myself." A yearning filled her. She pictured the little girl's joy at the gifts she would receive. She wondered if she would ever see Hester again. "But if Mrs. Toombs suspects my involvement with the donations to the workhouse she'll ask a hundred questions and kick up such a fuss wondering how it all came about that it will take all afternoon merely to satisfy her."

"We'll take care of everything, Camilla," Charlotte assured her. Charlotte had made no move to touch the food on her plate. She was picking at it absently with her fork, but not a morsel was carried to her lips.

"Is something wrong?" Camilla couldn't resist asking.

James coughed. He folded his napkin and set it down beside his plate. "Charlotte is tired. These routs and parties are a far cry from the quiet life we lead in Hampshire. She's not used to it."

"Or to the strain of wondering whether her 'cousin' is

going to call a peer by the wrong title or disgrace herself on the dance floor." Camilla smiled.

"Oh no, you're doing wonderfully." Charlotte reached out a hand and touched Camilla's arm. "I wish you were truly my cousin—or my sister," she said impulsively, a wistful expression in her eyes.

Camilla was touched. "I feel as if you were my family, too," she confided shyly. "You've been so kind to me—both of you."

James stood up. "This harebrained scheme of my brother's has turned out to be one of his better impulses all around. You've had a remarkable effect on him, Camilla. Philip is different these days. He's different when he's been with you."

"I don't know what you mean. I've tried to be his friend . . ."

"You've been a friend to all of us—particularly Charlotte and Jared—and Dorinda. You've brought laughter and ease and warmth to this house, and to Westcott Park. Before there was only strain. For that, both Philip and I are grateful to you."

She was stunned. "He told you that?"

James nodded. "He said so himself this morning." He added, somewhat under his breath, "I only hope that when he finally wins Brittany—and he will win her—he's very close to it, from what I've seen—that she'll bring half the sunshine you have into this family." Coming around the table, he lifted Camilla's hand to his lips and lightly kissed her fingertips. "We're in your debt, Miss Smith," he said softly.

Then he turned to Charlotte and planted a kiss on the top of her golden head. "I'll order the carriage brought round," he told her. "It's best we get to the workhouse and back before the rain worsens."

For the first time Camilla noted that the pale morning sunshine had faded to a swirling gray mist. The sky gleamed dull pewter outside the rain-spattered windows. Despite the gloomy aspect, her spirits felt lifted by the unexpected words James had spoken.

Alone in the dining room with Charlotte, she felt suddenly excited that her plan to help Hester and the other children was finally reaching fruition. "Thank you for delivering these things to the workhouse. Would you do something else for me?"

"Anything," Charlotte replied instantly.

"Please ask to see Hester alone for a few moments. Then you can tell her that I sent you, and that I also send my love." She tapped a finger on her chin. "As far as Mrs. Toombs is concerned, it is probably best if you tell her that the donation is from an acquaintance of Hester's dead parents," she said slowly. "That should increase Hester's standing tenfold—Mrs. Toombs will treat her like gold after this."

"She means a great deal to you—this little girl, doesn't she?" Charlotte asked softly. They were alone in the dining room now, with only the ticking of the mantel clock and the drum of rain on the windows echoing around them.

"She is very dear. When you meet her, you'll understand. I only wish I could see her again—or help her more than this. But . . ." Camilla folded her hands in her lap, forcing herself to restrain her enthusiasm. "The shoes and blankets will be a wonderful thing. And you must tell me about the expression on her face after she hears about it all."

"There," Charlotte said, almost to herself. "I must needs go with him, then—to bring you back all of these details. Men are so unaware of all the little particulars which we women find so important. If James went alone he would no doubt hand the basket and the document over to Mrs. Toombs and walk out without noticing so much as whether she said thank you or not."

"James didn't want you to go to the workhouse? I hope you didn't argue over that," Camilla said quickly, distressed that she should be the cause of trouble between them.

"Oh no. We didn't argue at all. It's just that . . . that . . . Nothing."

Camilla didn't want to pry. She could see that some great emotion quivered inside the blond girl, and she sensed the struggle going on within her. Charlotte wanted to confide in her, and yet felt compelled not to. Camilla didn't want to add to her dilemma, so she picked up her knife, buttered a roll, and said gently, "Dorinda seemed ever so much better this morning, didn't she?"

Charlotte appeared not to hear her. Her delicate blue eyes filled slowly with tears, and then the rest of her fragile composure crumpled. Her coffee cup overturned and her spoon clattered to the floor as she covered her face with her hands and began to weep.

"What is it? Dear Charlotte, whatever is the matter?" Instantly Camilla hurried to her side and put her arms around the girl's shoulders. Charlotte shook her head from side to side, tears splashing through her fingers.

"It was . . . the story . . . you told Dorinda," she said sobbing.

"What?" Baffled, Camilla tried to understand. "The story I told Dorinda last night—about the farmer and his wife? But why should that make you cry?"

Charlotte's shoulders shook harder. "I can't . . . talk about it. James won't want me to . . ."

"Come with me," Camilla said firmly, and led her to the little settee before the window.

"Charlotte, I don't understand," she said quietly. "Now I don't want you to reveal anything private, but if there is something I can do to help . . ."

"No one can help." She gave a gasping sob. "Camilla, I'm so unhappy. And when James and I heard the story last night, it brought the hurt home so sharply to both of us. I wish . . . oh, how I wish there was a gypsy who *could* sell a child . . . I wish more than anything . . . oh, God, don't let on to James that I told you. He doesn't like to talk about it . . ."

A flash of understanding swept over Camilla. She tightened her arms around the weeping girl. "You and James cannot have a child together," she said softly, not a question but a statement.

Charlotte dragged her fingers from her reddened eyes and nodded. "We tried . . . once. I lost the child . . . the doctor said if we were to try again, I would probably die, and the child with me." Her voice broke. Tears streamed down her cheeks.

"Charlotte, I'm so sorry."

"James says he doesn't care. He says we don't need children, we have each other. But I know he is heartbroken. He was so excited about the baby . . . and then . . ." Her lip quivered. "He has never complained to me, or blamed me, not once. But we both feel it . . . this loss, this need. We want to ask Philip if Dorinda could spend some time with us up in Hampshire. I know her place is at Westcott Park, and that Philip will make a good home for her with Brittany, but . . . it helps sometimes to hear her laughter, to see that beautiful little face, so young and vibrant. Of course, I know I'm only her

sister-in-law and not her mother, but . . . sometimes I
can pretend . . ."

Camilla's heart went out to her. It wasn't anger she
sensed sometimes between James and Charlotte, it was
sadness. Both of them hurting, neither wanting to burden
the other with expressions of their own pain. She stroked
Charlotte's hair and tried to speak comfortingly.

"James loves you. You have each other. You must try
to take solace in that," she murmured, knowing her
words were pale palliatives for the emptiness in Charlotte's heart. "And I'm sure Philip will let Dorinda spend
time with you in Hampshire. She adores you, Charlotte,
and it would be so good for her."

"Do you really think Philip will agree? When we first
came to Westcott Park James and I were both certain he
would refuse, that he would sneer at us and think that we
weren't to be trusted with Dorinda. He still thinks of
James as a careless boy who can't be depended upon to
use good judgment. And it isn't fair," she cried, dashing
the tears from her eyes as she reflected on Philip's unjust
opinion of her husband. "James is the most staunch, de-
pendable man I know. He—we—would take excellent
care of Dorinda!"

"I'm sure you would."

"Maybe Philip will consent." Bleak hope shone in
Charlotte's eyes. She groped in her pocket for her handkerchief and dabbed at her swollen nose. "He has
changed, you know. This morning he met with James and
Jared and actually talked to them as if they were intelligent beings, and not irresponsible troublemakers." She
took a deep, steadying breath and regarded Camilla
keenly. "Since you came, he is different. He's lost that
vicious edge that used to frighten me so. He could be so
cruel . . ."

"Philip has never been cruel," Camilla objected indignantly. "He is the gentlest, kindest man I've ever known."

Charlotte stared at her incredulously. "Philip?"

Camilla stood up, hands clenched at her side. "I won't allow you or anyone to say a word against him."

"I'm not, only . . ."

"You simply don't understand him!"

Charlotte's expression of astonishment vanished, replaced by one of slowly dawning horror. "Camilla—you're not falling in love with him?" she gasped. She jumped up and seized the other girl's hands. "Tell me it isn't true," she pleaded.

"It . . . isn't true. I value his friendship, I respect him, I am very grateful to him for all he's done for me but . . ."

"Oh, God, I can see by your face you don't mean a word of it! You love him! Don't you?"

"Ye . . . es." Camilla swallowed hard. The words came out, half-defiant, half-proud, before she could stop them. "I love him," she whispered.

Now it was Charlotte's turn to clasp her in her arms. But Camilla didn't cry. She held onto her dignity with rigid self-control.

"What are you going to do?" Charlotte asked, standing back and studying her in helpless concern.

"Do?" Camilla shrugged, her mouth a tight, grim line. "I'm going to do what I agreed upon in the first place. I'm going to see this charade through until the end, until Philip has made Brittany so jealous she stops toying with all the men in London and comes running to him, as he wishes, and then I'm going to leave."

"You can't return to life as a serving maid," Charlotte said quickly. She stared at Camilla's fine dress of delicate peach muslin edged in ivory lace, her gaze traveling upward to her friend's elegant chignon, and down to her satin-slippered feet, saying, "You don't belong in a tavern anymore, Camilla, as if you ever did."

"I don't belong here either." She met Charlotte's distraught expression with an air of crisp resolve that was far more calm than what she was feeling. "You don't need to worry about me, Charlotte. I've survived all these years on my own and I'm quite used to it. I'll be perfectly fine when I leave this house and Westcott Park. I'll miss you—all of you—I'll miss you terribly." She couldn't bear to think about saying good-bye, not now. Her chin lifted as she pushed all thoughts of parting from her mind. "But I'll make something good of my life, whatever happens. You won't need to . . . to pity me or to worry."

"I'm sure we won't." Charlotte smiled tremulously. "You're the strongest person I know, Camilla. I'll miss you, too. I wish—"

She broke off as James stuck his head into the room. "The carriage is ready."

"I'm coming." She turned back to Camilla with a misty smile. "I meant what I said before. I truly wish you were my cousin. Or that somehow things could turn out differently . . ." She bit her lip, shook her head sadly, and went out without another word.

Camilla walked slowly through the hallway to the petit salon. She sank onto the patterned sofa, stared at the crystal raindrops striking the windowpane, and tried not to think about the precious short time she had left in the role of Miss Camilla Smith.

Meanwhile, across town, within the dignified portals of the French embassy, the Earl of Westcott was being ushered into a handsome sitting room filled with books, paintings, and an official-looking desk and chair.

The ambassador, a tall, florid-complexioned man with snowy hair piled on a polished pink head welcomed him warmly and invited him to have a seat in one of the opulent wing chairs.

"Your lordship, a pleasure. How may I be of service to you?"

Philip stretched his long legs out before him, regarded the smoothly polite face of the diplomat for a moment, and pulled Camilla's golden lion charm from his pocket.

"Examine this for me, if you would, monsieur. I believe it may mean something to you." He saw the flash of recognition shine in the ambassador's shrewd eyes as he took the charm between his fingers.

"*Oui*, monsieur, but of course. Where did you get this?"

"All in good time, monsieur." Philip hid the jolt of excitement that coursed through him at the ambassador's recognition of the charm. He'd known he was right. If what he suspected was true, it would change Camilla's life forever.

He leaned forward and fixed his hard gaze on the other man's florid face. "We have much to discuss," he said coolly. "But first you will kindly provide me with answers to some very important questions."

21

"You have got your work cut out for you, my boy, if you wish to win Miss Smith away from Westcott," Lady Asterley remarked to her nephew as she surveyed her crowded ballroom where the Earl and his lovely fiancée were the center of attention. "Westcott has scarcely left her side all night."

"*His* affections may be fixed, Aunt Elizabeth, but that does not mean *hers* are," Lord Winthrop pointed out, his envious gaze following the couple in question around the marble-tiled dance floor.

It was a glittering assembly, all silks and satins and diamonds and pearls, but no one in the magnificent, chandelier-lit room dazzled with more splendor or attracted more notice than the broad-shouldered Earl of Westcott and his charming betrothed. All those assembled gazed on them with admiration, the women wistfully ogling Philip in his elegant black evening clothes, the gentlemen regarding Camilla with mingled desire and delight. She was a vision, in an exquisite gown of emerald satin spangled with gold lace, her burnished hair caught back from her enchanting oval face with emerald combs, and an emerald and diamond choker around her slender neck. The décolleté gown with the full sleeves and narrow band of velvet encircling her tiny waist accentuated the lush femininity of her figure, and she looked like a radiant goddess as she whirled across the dance floor in the Earl's very capable arms.

"She doesn't appear at all reluctant to dance with the fellow," Lady Asterley commented dryly, her beady eyes lingering upon the attractive pair.

"That's not the same as marrying him! According to Freddy, all is not entirely settled between them. It is common knowledge that Miss Smith has not officially agreed to the match. Certainly no formal announcement has been made."

Lady Asterley sighed and patted his arm affectionately with her fan. "They've scarcely taken their eyes off one another all evening. If this is not a love match, dear boy, I don't know what is."

"She isn't laughing."

"Odd creature, what's that to say to anything?"

"Miss Smith has the most enchanting sense of humor. If she were truly happy, she'd be smiling and laughing tonight. Instead, she looks far more serious than I've ever seen her."

Lady Asterley squinted her gaze across the room once more. Surprised, she was forced to admit that her often scatter-brained nephew had a point. Miss Smith did look rather somber. So did the Earl, for that matter. Perhaps there was a bit of a twist in their path to the altar after all. Perhaps Miss Smith, so newly introduced to London, had developed a tendre for someone else, one of the many eager suitors who'd begun pining for her after only one introduction. Perhaps even for dear Timothy. She glanced at him, and shook her head ruefully. "You young men. Only a few weeks ago it was that Deaville heiress you were all chasing after like a pack of wolves. Now it's Miss Smith." She gave her imperious head a shake. "If I didn't know better, I'd think you were smitten with whichever chit the Earl of Westcott takes a fancy to."

"Aunt Elizabeth, that is rubbish, ma'am," Lord Winthrop cried indignantly. He smoothed the lapels of his evening coat and then took a pinch of snuff from his enameled Sèvres box. "Lady Brittany has never paid me the least heed—she's always been too busy with Marchfield and Westcott and Kirby, and several other of her favorites. I knew I didn't stand a chance there. But Miss Smith is something else. No matter that she's become all the rage—she smiles at me as if she truly enjoys my compliments and admires the witty things I say—well, *she* thinks they're witty, even if my own family doesn't!"

"The truth, dear boy, is that she treats you as if she thinks you are witty. A very intelligent trait in a female, I always said. I find her a very pretty-behaved girl, I admit, and I would find no objection if you were to offer for her, but don't gamble on her accepting you—not with Westcott in the game."

"We'll see, Aunt Elizabeth," her nephew promised in a determined tone, and took his leave of her.

The strains of the waltz filled the air as Camilla and Philip, locked in each other's arms, whirled past the blur of onlookers. Awkwardness had existed between them all the evening, but their dancing was smoothly, impeccably in step. *Only our emotions are off-balance,* Camilla thought to herself as she counted the beats and prayed she would get through the dance without a misstep.

"It's strange to think that there might be a murderer in this room," she said at last. The silence between them

had gone on for too long, people would begin to notice. It
already felt as though every pair of eyes in the ballroom
was fixed piercingly upon them as they danced, but Camilla told herself that was only her imagination.

"That's a safe topic of conversation," he complimented
her. "I wish I'd thought of it myself."

She flushed. "What do *you* wish to talk about?" she
countered. "Our misadventure last evening?" She
couldn't resist the words, their flipness hiding her pain,
but instantly she regretted them.

Philip's arm tightened warningly around her waist.
"This is hardly the time or place to discuss that, Camilla.
Not that I blame you for being angry. I blame myself for
the entire misadventure, as you put it."

"Well, don't." She attempted a light, airy smile.

"I beg your pardon?"

"Don't," she replied more irritably than she'd intended. "I'm a grown woman, and I chose to be where I
was and to do what I did—what we did—so I accept my
share of the blame. I don't think we should dwell on it
anymore. It was a mistake, we both agree upon that, and
we'd best forget about it."

"A mistake? You feel that way, too?"

She cringed at the relief in his face. She kept her outward composure with rigid determination. "Oh yes," she
assured him. "It was . . . very pleasant, of course, but I
don't think we should dwell on it or let it interfere with
business."

"Or with our friendship, Camilla," he said quickly.
"That's what truly concerns me. I like you. I have a great
deal of respect for you. I don't want anything to ruin the
comaraderie between us."

Men. They were all idiots, she decided, wishing she
could howl with fury. "Why should it?" By sheer grit, she

succeeded in sounding indifferent. "Philip, I'm far more concerned about finding this murderer than I am about one reckless night."

He stared at her. She seemed to be telling the truth. But with a woman, he had had enough experience to recognize, you could never tell.

The waltz ended. As he led her from the floor, noting her flushed cheeks, he offered to bring her a glass of lemonade.

"Sit here," he commanded, indicating one of the three dainty gilt chairs clustered near a potted palm. "I'll be back in a moment."

He glanced watchfully around the room as he moved toward the refreshment table. It seemed absurd to think that one of these laughing, chattering guests might be a murderer, but he knew well that all too often depravity and secret ugliness oozed beneath even the most polished surface. That Frenchman, André Dubois, for one, had glittered among the ton like an elegant diamond until he'd shown his true nature to be more that of a filthy, rough-hewn stone. Who here among this throng shared that low nature?

Philip's gaze rested upon the urbane figure of Lord Marchfield. Beside Marchfield, her head bent to catch his whisper, was Brittany, one gloved hand resting lightly on his arm. As Philip looked at her, she suddenly glanced his way, and their eyes met. Even across the room, he saw the immediate flash of yearning in her gaze. She didn't look away but continued to gaze at him urgently. He realized she was sending him some kind of signal.

He guessed that she would seek him out, and he was right. No sooner had he reached the refreshment table than he felt a light hand touch his sleeve. He turned his head. Brittany gazed quietly up at him.

* * *

Charlotte and James slipped into the velvet-curtained alcove as the strains of the quadrille began. There, in privacy, they clasped one another in barely contained excitement.

"I simply must tell someone! I'm so happy! Oh, James," Charlotte cried, searching his sparkling eyes with heartbreaking eagerness, "Do you really want to do this?"

"More than anything. I can scarcely wait." He kissed her, and then traced a fingertip along the dainty line of her jaw. "When I saw that sweet, beautiful little child . . ."

"Yes, yes, I felt it instantly, too. Oh, James, it is meant to be! Can we tell Camilla tonight? And Philip, too. I want to tell the world!"

"I think we should wait a little while. Philip confided several things to me this morning, other than what I've mentioned already, and . . . he and Miss Smith have a great deal to contend with just now. I think it would be best if we were to save our good news until later."

"But you'll begin making all the arrangements immediately, won't you?" Charlotte asked anxiously.

He kissed her again. "On the morrow, I swear it."

She threw her arms around his neck and began to cry.

"Charlotte," James exclaimed in dismay, handing her his handkerchief.

"I'm just so happy," she gasped, and dabbed at the tears before they could fall upon her diaphanous yellow gown. "I suppose we must rejoin the party, but I can scarcely keep from jumping about like Dorinda when she is particularly excited about something."

"Try," James suggested dryly.

She grinned up at him. "What kind of things do Philip

and Camilla have to contend with? Other than that their deadline for the success of their plan is drawing ever nearer?"

"Shhh." James glanced quickly about. "You never know who might be about," he chided her, and took her arm. "Never mind all that for now. I'll tell you about it tomorrow when we're safely back at Westcott Park. Come, Char, let's find ourselves two glasses of champagne. We have reason to celebrate."

Yes, Charlotte thought, accompanying him back into the glittering ballroom, her heart full of hope and anticipation. *We do have reason to celebrate. And all because of Camilla. If only she could know one tenth the happiness James and I feel at this moment.*

She glanced quickly about for her friend in the crowded room and saw her surrounded by a throng of admiring dandies. Philip was nowhere near her side.

Charlotte took one look at Camilla's bravely smiling face and knew deep in her soul that it was all a lie. She saw that Camilla was pretending, she sensed even across the room the other girl's despair, and she fought the urge to seek out her awe-inspiring brother-in-law and box his ears.

"Philip, I must speak with you alone for a moment. Will you meet me on the terrace?"

For once the sophisticated gaiety was nowhere to be seen on Brittany's countenance. Magnificently gowned in low-cut gold taffeta, her hair curled into an elaborate chignon, Brittany's elegantly chiseled face looked young and lovely and full of desperate hope.

Philip's pulse quickened. "Where is Lord Marchfield?" he inquired coolly.

"I foisted him off on Florence when I saw the chance

to speak with you," she said in a quick undertone. "I've been trying to catch your eye all evening. But you've been most caught up in dancing with Miss Smith."

She sounded so put out Philip could scarcely contain a grin. He managed however to keep his expression indifferent. "That is as it should be," he remarked, half-turning away.

"No. Yes. I suppose it is, but . . . perhaps not. Philip, will you meet me?"

His eyes flickered over her without apparent emotion. "As you wish."

Inwardly, he felt the thread of satisfaction tightening. The game was won. He was the victor. She had come to him, surrendered, as he had known she would. He waited for the sense of exultation to overtake him, but it did not come.

Afterward, he told himself as he watched Brittany smile with relief. *After she has confessed her misery and exposed her true feelings.*

"Follow me in a moment," he instructed. "I'll wait for you near the fountain." He moved away with elegant grace and glanced toward the potted palms where he had left Camilla to wait for him. Satisfied to see her surrounded by admirers, with Kirby approaching even as he watched, he slipped out the terrace doors leading to Lady Asterley's stone-walled garden.

Camilla was safe for the moment, and he could afford to rendezvous with Brittany. Excitement quickened within him. His eyes glinted with the triumph of a hunter who has cornered his quarry. At last, the moment he had waited for. He would hold her in his arms, taste those sensuous rose lips. Hear her admit that she wanted to belong to him.

Philip moved noiselessly across the terrace and through

the stepping-stones leading to the fountain where water splashed in the cool night, and the scent of late-blooming rose blossoms perfumed the air.

He didn't have long to wait before Brittany slipped through the shadows to join him.

"This is highly unconventional behavior, Lady Brittany." He couldn't help teasing her. "Not for me, but certainly for you. It must be something urgent that would inspire you to meet a gentleman in a dark garden all alone."

"Don't tease me, Philip." She clutched at his coat. "Please, not tonight—I couldn't bear it. This is difficult enough . . ."

"What is?"

"Telling you . . . admitting to you . . ." She bit her lip and steadied herself. She gazed up at him with something of her old hauteur. "I've been a fool," she said. "I admit I've behaved like a spoiled little fool, but I can't bear to go on this way. I have to tell you—even though it means humbling myself before the great Earl of Westcott. Damn you, why do you make me go on like this? Don't you know what I'm trying to say?"

"It is always hazardous to presume to read a lady's mind."

"But you like hazardous activity—that's one of the things I find so irresistible about you," she murmured. "Much to my mama's dismay."

"This has something to do with your mama?"

"No, you know perfectly well it does not!" Laughing nervously, she snaked her arms up around his neck and stepped closer, her breathing light and quick in the rose-scented night. "Oh, Philip." Huge violet eyes searched his face as the beauty trembled in his arms. "Do you *truly* love that little hussy who has stolen you away from me?"

"Miss Smith," he said sharply, "is not a little hussy. Take care, Brittany."

"I beg your pardon." Tears shimmered in the brilliant eyes. "She is lovely, to be sure, and I can understand why you have developed a tendre for her, but, Philip . . . I thought *we* had something special between us."

"Did you? It is difficult to tell, Brittany, when you surround yourself with prattling suitors and evade me as you did at the masquerade."

"But I didn't . . . that's ridiculous . . ."

"Brittany." He caught her chin in his hand and tilted it upward so that she met his glinting gaze. "This is a night for truth, remember?"

Tears welled in her eyes. One trickled down her lovely cheek. "Yes, Philip, truth. The truth is . . . I *miss* you."

"You have many other gentlemen to entertain you."

"I don't care about them. None of them make me feel the way I do when I'm with you. I . . . I hate Miss Smith. It's awful to say that, but I can't help it. Every time I see you looking at her, dancing with her, I want to strangle her—what are you laughing at?"

"I always knew you were a passionate woman, Brittany, but you're absolutely on fire tonight. I do hope you'll refrain from exercising your violent emotions on Miss Smith—and turn them on me instead. I promise you I know exactly how to handle them."

"What will you do?" She smiled, her lips parting as she nestled closer against him.

"This." He swept her into his arms, and brought his mouth down hungrily on hers. It was a deep, demanding kiss, and Brittany responded exactly as he'd known she would. Her voluptuous form moved provocatively against his, her lips returned his kiss with ardor, and she gave a moan of pleasure as his hands twisted lightly in her hair.

* * *

"Miss Smith," Lord Winthrop said, bowing low over Camilla's gloved hand. "May I say how utterly ravishing you look tonight? Rubies, diamonds, and pearls would all be put to shame by your splendor."

Camilla's dimples peeped out as she smiled up at him. "Doing it too brown." She laughed. "But you are kindness itself, my lord."

"And you're also too late," Mr. Fitzroy added brutally, glaring at the newcomer who had wedged into place beside Miss Smith. "Miss Smith has already promised the next set to me—and the one after to Kirby. After that, you'll have to fight Westcott off."

"Where is Westcott?" Lord Winthrop inquired gloomily.

"Who cares?" young Mr. Seaton whispered fiercely in his ear. "This is the first opportunity any one of us has had to pay our compliments to Miss Smith. He's been guarding her like a dog over a bone all night. The devil take him!"

Camilla accepted a glass of lemonade from Alistair Kirby and tried to appear gay and carefree. It was difficult to hide her disappointment over Philip's disappearance. Naturally he had forgotten all about her the moment Brittany had approached him. She'd seen the entire encounter at the refreshment table, watching from the corner of her eye while appearing to flirt lightheartedly with Freddy Fitzroy. Indescribable pain had stabbed through her when she saw first Philip and then Brittany slip out the French doors leading to the terrace.

This could well be the moment Philip had been waiting for. Her role in his charade could be drawing to a close even as she now rose to dance with Freddy. A sense of unreality gripped her. This grand party, the magnificent

tiled ballroom and gold and crystal chandeliers, the
sumptuously attired men and women whose names and
faces she knew, who greeted her with cordiality and respect, all this was soon to be gone from her life. Her
gown, her jewels, the frothy ridiculous hat she'd bought at
Madame Modane's and worn to tea in Miss Drewe's parlor last week—all of this would soon be only memories of
the past. Her cozy morning breakfasts with Charlotte,
Mrs. Wyeth's now respectful greetings, the hours spent
curled on the settee with Dorinda beside her, listening to
stories, all would be gone. But the thing that hurt the
most, the thing that made her eyes sting with razor-sharp
tears was the thought that she would never see Philip's
face light with laughter again at some little joke she
made, never see him kiss Dorinda good night, or stride
into a room and draw everyone's glance. As Freddy chat-
tered at her and complimented her dancing, she was picturing Philip's mahogany bed in the flickering firelight
and the way his eyes softened when he stroked her, the
way his lips had felt when he kissed her, the way their two
bodies had twined and molded and fit together with such
unforgettable passion.

Tears blinded her.

"Miss Smith," Freddy Fitzroy gasped. He gaped at her,
the always effervescent beauty unexpectedly awash in
tears. It was shocking. People would think he'd done
something horrid to her. Aghast, he stopped dancing in
the middle of the floor. "What . . . what's the matter?"

She couldn't speak, couldn't possibly begin to explain.
Shaking her head helplessly, she broke free of Freddy's
limp arms and fled across the ballroom, her voluminous
emerald skirts gathered in one gloved hand.

* * *

It was a long time before Philip lifted his head.

"What's wrong?" Brittany traced his lips with her finger. "Philip, don't stop now . . . I've dreamed so often of this moment . . ."

"It's been more than a moment, Brittany." He heard his own voice as if from a long way off. The smell of roses permeated the night air. He felt vaguely ill. "We'd better get back."

She pouted, then smiled coaxingly, stroking a hand through his hair. "Don't tell me you're concerned about propriety. Or is it Miss Smith you're concerned about?"

He *was* worried about Camilla. He'd left her alone for too long. He'd promised to stay close by her side throughout the evening. It was damned ironic that he actually had Brittany in his arms, breathlessly kissing him, and his thoughts kept turning to another woman.

He took Brittany's arm and guided her back toward the house, moving quickly now through the shadows. "We must take care, Brittany. If you and I are to be together . . ."

"You'll have to disentangle yourself from Miss Smith. But, Philip, how are you going to do that?"

"Do you doubt my ability to accomplish whatever I set out to do, Brittany? If so, you will make me a very poor wife."

Those violet eyes glowed fascinatingly into his. "Is that a proposal, my lord?" she whispered eagerly.

"What do you think?"

"I think that I accept," she replied, and threw her arms around his neck.

He gazed down at her, wondering why he didn't feel more ecstatic. He had won, hadn't he? Brittany was his, she had agreed to be his wife, and he had won the bet with Marchfield with time to spare. He felt strangely flat and empty inside, and tried to fill the void by kissing her again, quickly, since they were now in sight of the windows. "Leave the rest to me. It will all be resolved without a hint of scandal. In a few days . . ."

"That long?"

He took her hand and pulled her toward the terrace. "Patience, my love, wins the day. Every time. Trust me."

They reached the doors. Brittany clung to his arm a moment longer. "Philip, you haven't told me yet—do you truly love me?"

He stared down at her. She was indescribably beautiful, but he felt oddly detached as she fixed those glorious eyes upon him, and sent him a look that a month ago would have melted his breeches. "I'm going to wed you, silly girl. What do you think?"

Her fingers closed sharply on his arm. "Philip, wait." A plaintive note entered her voice. "I think you are in an odious hurry for a man in love."

"Brittany, I told you. This is not the time . . ."

Lady Brittany Deaville was vain, self-centered, and spoiled but she was not a fool. Something was wrong. She'd felt it when he kissed her. Something had been missing.

When Lord Marchfield kissed her, there was a certain violence to his feelings, a need, a passion . . .

Philip's kiss had been powerful, but oddly empty.

"Tell me that you love me," she said, a strange expression coming over her face.

"Brittany . . ."

"Say it!" She sucked in her breath as he continued to stare at her in silence, his eyes confused, dark with tension. "My God, you can't, can you? Because you . . . don't love me," she whispered, stunned.

"Do you love me?"

"I don't know. I thought I didn't . . . and then I thought I did. I was jealous . . ."

They stared at each other, while from inside the ballroom, the strains of music and hearty laughter drifted out into the breeze.

She was beautiful, Philip thought, but her beauty didn't warm his heart or touch his soul—not the way another adorable, earnest little beauty did, a beauty with an infectious musical laugh and a gentle touch and a huge heart . . .

"It won't work, will it, Philip?" Brittany spoke slowly, taking it all in for the first time, adjusting to the idea that it truly was not meant to be. "You *do* love Miss Smith?" she asked incredulously.

"I do."

The truth shocked him as much as it did her. They stared at each other again.

"I see." Brittany took a step back. "Well, then . . ."

"Brittany, I'm sorry. I've been a fool." Philip didn't know what to say. When had all this happened? *How* had it all happened?

Brittany gave her head a small, dazed shake. "I wish you happy, my lord," she said in a strained voice, and added as she whirled toward the doors: "Lord Marchfield will be wild with worry for me. I must go to him . . ."

Philip stood outside in the chill night air a moment longer. How had he been so blind?

He followed Brittany inside and blinked at the brightness. Without waiting another moment he turned to find Camilla, wondering and highly doubting if that independent pixie was still waiting obediently where he'd left her in her gilt chair.

* * *

As all around her people sipped champagne and laughed and gossiped, Camilla slipped through the chattering crowd like a pebble skimming across water. Somehow she reached a curtained anteroom that led to a corridor. She rushed on.

Turning a corner, she thought she heard a sound. Was that a footfall behind her? She glanced back, her face wet with tears, but saw no one. She ran blindly on. She sought only a quiet room away from the throng where she could cry her heart out and then compose herself to a semblance of dignity. The sounds of her own anguished sobs and running feet echoed eerily around her. Dimly, she realized she was lost, that she had somehow wandered away from the main part of the house and was now in a maze of confusing corridors. Turning a corner, she abruptly found herself in a narrow passage at the end of which was a closed door.

She ran forward, praying it was a parlor where she could sit alone a moment and compose herself.

But when she flung open the door, she nearly tumbled down a steep flight of stairs leading into gloom. Her heart jumped into her throat at her narrow escape. She leaned against the wall for support, then quickly shut the door against the musty darkness. The wine cellar, perhaps. At all events, a dead end.

A rush of air sounded behind her. Startled, she started to whip about, but before she had time she was seized around the throat from behind. Strong arms clamped across her throat with brutal force, pinning her backward against a hard, unseen chest. All but helpless, unable to breathe, Camilla clawed frantically at the arms choking her. The pressure increased. Her skirts rustled with her frantic, helpless movements. Through shooting lights popping in her head, Camilla realized what was happening. Her attacker was edging relentlessly forward toward the door leading to the stairs.

Through the roaring in her ears, she realized his aim. Her struggles intensified. He meant to hurl her down those steep, winding stairs. She could do nothing against his overwhelming strength. She was going to die.

With ebbing strength, she kicked and scratched, fighting with a desperate drive to survive, but she could not budge the muscular arms cutting off her air, could not halt the deadly progress he was making toward that door.

Her vision clouded. The roaring in her ears became deafening. Black and purple darkness pinpointed with exploding lights swirled before her eyes. Suddenly, just as she reached the door, her knees buckled. Dimly, she heard voices. They sounded far away, disconnected.

The man holding her seemed to hear them, too. He tensed.

She heard him curse, a low, raspy whisper horrifyingly familiar. The whisper of the masked murderer in Room 203, she realized. His words from that night played again in her head: "An unfortunate entrance, my lady. Now I'll have to kill you, too."

But this time he said in her ear: "Next time, Camilla. Next time, you die."

The arms squeezed a moment longer. Then blackness swooped down upon her, the floor crashed upward, and she was swept into oblivion.

"Camilla."

Philip's desperate voice reached her through the depths of darkness imprisoning her, dragging her upward, upward through the murky swamp in which she was drowning. Philip? Blindly, she tried to reach him.

She surfaced in a blur of pain and pressure. Her throat burned. Her eyes throbbed. She couldn't open them.

"Camilla, open your eyes." His voice was commanding, with an underlayer of frantic tension. "Look at me. *Wake up and look at me.* How badly are you hurt?"

He was worried, she realized faintly. She tried to do what would soothe him.

A gasp whistled through her lips as she opened her eyes. The world swam in a blue mist. Through it, she saw his dark face, rigid with tension, looming over her. Strong arms lifted her, pressed her close against a warm, strong chest.

"Philip." Her voice sounded frightening to her own ears, a raw hoarse whisper barely audible through her dry lips. It was agony to speak, but she had to tell him. "It was . . . him . . ." Her eyes watered, she coughed. "He tried . . ." She swallowed and gripped his sleeve with taut fingers. "Philip, he tried to kill me . . ."

"I know, sweetheart, I know."

Philip smoothed a damp strand of hair from her eyes. He glanced up at James, who was staring at him in horror.

"What the devil . . ." his brother began, but Philip shook his head.

"Not now. I'll explain tomorrow. Now I've got to get her out of here—away from London. We'll leave straight from here for Westcott Park. Can you get Charlotte home all right?"

"What do you think? Tell me what you want me to do."

"First, get Charlotte out of here, and for God's sake, stay with her."

Pale and grim, James nodded. Philip continued as he held Camilla close. "Pack up and leave in the morning. I'll explain it all when you get to Westcott Park. In the meantime, you can express our regrets to Lady Asterley for our abrupt departure. Make something up. I don't give a damn. Anything will do—except the truth.''

"Philip, who did this to her? Do you know?"

"Not yet, but I'm damn well going to find out."

And with the words, he swept Camilla into his arms, and strode at a near run back down the corridor.

Fading in and out of consciousness, she choked back the whimpers that sprang to her lips. Everything hurt. But she didn't want to give in to the pain. She didn't want to worry Philip.

Cold air slapped at her as they left the house. Somehow, she was in the carriage, with Philip beside her, wrapping her in her burgundy velvet cloak. The cold air helped revive her; it also intensified the rawness of her bruised throat.

She sank her head against his shoulder and clung to the solid strength of him beside her. She couldn't stop trembling.

"Camilla." With his chin resting on the top of her head, Philip cradled the slender figure in his arms. "It's all right, we're going to Westcott Park. You'll be safe there. I promise you, my girl, you'll be safe." Sick fear filled him when he thought how narrowly she had escaped. Those bruises on her neck filled him with white-hot rage. If he and James had been a moment longer tonight . . . He couldn't bear to think what would have happened.

"Petersham, hurry!"

The carriage door slammed, the driver cracked the whip over the horses, and the Earl of Westcott's gold-crested carriage thundered off into the night.

They lost a wheel on the turnpike road two miles outside of London. There was a crash, a shriek from the horses, and then a resounding jolt, which roused Camilla from her dozing state in Philip's arms and brought the driver scurrying round to the door.

Philip had already swung it open and was helping Camilla out of the lopsided coach.

"There's an inn up the road," he told her as she fastened the velvet cloak around her and stared dazedly up at the dark, star-filled sky. "We'll have some refreshment in their private parlor while the wheel is repaired. Shall I carry you?"

"No." She held out her hands and managed a shaky laugh. "I'm feeling much better—I am perfectly able to walk. If you carry me about much more, my limbs will forget how to function on their own. Which way is this inn?"

It was true, she felt much stronger now that the bracing air was whipping round her, and Philip was close by. The terror had faded, and she felt strangely alert and keyed up. The fact that the murderer had actually made an attempt to kill her tonight proved one thing: he had been there, at Lady Asterley's ball. He *was* a member of the ton.

But all her thoughts of him were forgotten as she and Philip neared the inn, and she saw the painted sign hanging above the porch. The Green Goose Inn!

Philip led her up the steps and into the hall before she could stop him. Smoky light flickered in the hallway, and the stout, bald-headed landlord who had ordered her evicted on the night she'd fled London bustled out as a bell tinkled overhead.

Camilla wasn't sure what she expected. She thought he would recognize her, stare, and demand to know what she was doing back here darkening his door. But no. His beady gaze was fixed, not on her, but on Philip, resplendent in his evening clothes and many-caped velvet greatcoat, standing in the hall with an expression of impatience on his face.

"Yes, my lord? What can I do for you, my lord?"

The landlord was all obsequious servility, bowing until his bulbous nose nearly touched the floor.

Philip said curtly, "We require a private parlor and some refreshment while some repairs are made to our carriage. And a substantial fire, as well. The lady is chilled."

"Of course. A thousand pardons, madam." The landlord's eyes swept over Camilla, shining this time not with contempt but with admiration and eagerness to please. "This way, if you please, it will be only a moment. A substantial fire, but yes. Bessie! Bessie, quickly, you old cow! My lord, I beg your indulgence. It will be done in a twinkling."

As he ushered them into a dim, spacious parlor and bustled about lighting the sconces and kindling a fire, he continued to prattle on until his wife waddled into the room.

By now, the light was brilliant, illuminating a comfortable salon with gold-tasseled green draperies at the window, plump sofas and chairs, and a fire coming to life in the hearth. "Bessie, where have you been?" the landlord bit out between clenched teeth. "Can you not see that we have a gentleman and lady here and they are desirous of supper? Quickly, quickly—my lord cannot wait all night."

The innkeeper's wife dropped the pile of dishes she'd been about to put away in her pantry when her husband summoned her. They crashed onto the spotless wooden floor.

"Clumsy oaf!" the landlord exploded.

"Beg pardon, your lordship, your ladyship." The woman curtsied low, then knelt down and quickly began to gather up the scattered shards. When her husband ran out to fetch a servant with a broom, Camilla walked to the fire and stood with her hands stretched out toward the blaze.

She thought of that other night, when she was alone, exhausted and frightened, and had begged for a bed in the stable hay. How indifferently, contemptuously, had this pair turned her away, shooing her into the wet, chill night as though she were a fox come to raid their chicken coop. Now, because she was here in the guise of a "lady" accompanied by a gentleman of obvious wealth and position, she was treated like royalty, welcomed, pampered. Bessie had even curtsied to her.

The irony of the situation made her lips tighten. Something deep inside rebelled against the notion that her outward appearance and the eminence of the man by her side determined her station, her worth to these people. But they were no different from Lady Asterley or Mr. Fitzroy or Brittany Deaville, she realized bitterly. In every circle of society, whether high or low, a person, particularly a woman, was judged more by beauty, birth, position, and appearance than by her own character. Her worth was measured by the worth of her husband, or father, not by the quickness of her mind or the qualities that resided in her heart. Because she had been shabbily dressed that night, alone and in need, she had been turned away. Now, in circumstances far less desperate, she was coddled like some fragile porcelain doll, regarded with awe and respect. She now was considered their superior, while before she had been judged impossibly inferior. She shook her head, and turned to glance at Philip, who was stripping off his coat and pulling up a chair for her before the fire.

A sharp pang went through her. Only Philip had treated her like a lady from the very first. For all of his reputation for arrogance, for a harsh temper and sharp tongue, he had always treated her with respect, even kindness. And that was true of James and Charlotte and Jared as well, she realized. And Lord Kirby. They had all known the truth, but it had not prevented them from drawing her into their circle, making her feel at home. For a while they had been her family, she who had been alone and entirely self-reliant for so long. She knew then with painful clarity just how keenly she would miss them when this splendid masquerade was over, when she bade them all farewell and returned to being plain Camilla Brent, alone and adrift once more in the world.

And the time was coming sooner than she'd thought, she realized, remembering abruptly the way Philip and Brittany had slipped off together at the ball.

As Camilla sank into the chair Philip held for her, Bessie flashed a glance in her direction.

"I hope you're warm enough now, my lady." She bobbed her head forward. Her sharp, birdlike gaze flitted fawningly over the elegant young woman aglitter in jewels.

"Yes, thank you." Camilla stiffened, drawing in her breath. She wondered if despite her fine garments the woman would recognize her—then what would she do? But she saw immediately that this was not going to happen. Bessie's scrutiny revealed merely a pale, well-bred lady in a stunning burgundy velvet cloak, her hair twisted into an elaborate chignon, gems winking at her ears, and dainty satin slippers on her feet.

"Supper will be served in a trice, your lordship," she promised, her glance veering toward Philip's imposing frame, superbly impressive in his black evening finery. She recognized the impatience in his eyes and scooted out of the parlor with alacrity.

The door thudded behind her, and Camilla and Philip found themselves alone.

"You're feeling better now?" He poured her brandy from a decanter the landlord had produced and handed her a glass. As she unfastened the cloak, his gaze fell upon the red bruises on her throat both above and below her necklace. His jaw clenched.

"Oh yes, I'm fine now," she assured him. "It was only the shock of the experience. I'm not usually so weak and missish, I assure you."

"You're the least missish girl I know. That's one of the things I lov—like about you," he corrected swiftly.

Camilla's gaze locked with his. Her heart gave a painful lurch.

"Do you . . . have any idea who it was that followed

me?" she asked to cover her confusion. "Was Lord Marchfield missing from the ballroom when you returned?"

"Possibly. To tell you the truth, I didn't notice. I saw Fitzroy and Winthrop having a squabble with Seaton and heard that you'd left off dancing abruptly. Apparently Winthrop accused Fitzroy of having insulted you—they were about to come to blows when I arrived. Fitzroy told me which way you'd run off, and I followed. James joined me. But I was too concerned about you to notice Marchfield's whereabouts at the time. For all I know, he could have been the one to follow you, but I've no proof."

"So we're no closer to finding out the murderer's identity than we were before."

"We'll find out, Camilla." He drained his glass. "I've spoken to the authorities in London, and they're grateful for the clues you provided. Until they get to the bottom of this, or we uncover something else, I'll protect you."

"You don't have to do that," she informed him, crumpling the velvet skirt of her gown in tense fingers. "I'll be leaving soon enough."

His expression grew alert, watchful, as he studied her face, but he didn't say anything.

"You and Brittany—you've come to an understanding, haven't you?" Camilla asked slowly, staring down at her hands.

"Yes."

Somehow she pasted a smile upon her face. "I see. So she agreed to marry you?"

"She accepted, yes . . . but . . ."

Philip wasn't quite sure how to explain, how much to reveal before he knew more of her own feelings. And watching her face, he found it impossible to read her reaction.

"Camilla, if you're worried about your future, don't be," he said slowly. "I'm making some inquiries regarding you which might lead to something quite unexpected."

Quite wonderful, was more like it, he told himself, but he didn't want to say that yet, he didn't want to raise her hopes, on the chance that he was wrong. What he suspected was so wild, so seemingly impossible, that it would be cruel to suggest it to her, but pure gut instinct told him it could be true. All he said now though was, "You've become a friend to all of us, and we don't want to see you go back to your old life. We want to help you—at the very least help you become established somewhere . . ."

"Where, Philip?" She gave a hollow laugh. "Doing what? Being a shop girl, or a governess? Not in London, certainly, where I am known to the quality as Miss Smith, the same Miss Smith who is about to break off her engagement to the Earl of Westcott and to disappear back to her country home. I can't return to London, and there is no place for me at Westcott Park—Brittany would not fancy my staying on, I imagine. And how would you explain it to her? No," she said, rising from her chair with squared shoulders.

"I have managed quite well all these years on my own, and I will continue to do so. I don't need your help, nor anyone else's to get by, I assure you. There is no cause for you to worry about me."

He plunked down his empty glass on the sideboard. "Damn it, Camilla, you are the most stubborn, proud, infuriating woman I've ever met."

"Thank you."

The hint of a smile in her eyes made him grit his teeth. "It wasn't meant as a compliment."

He reached her side in two quick strides and grasped her firmly by the shoulders, meaning only to talk some sense into her. "What am I going to do with you?" he said in frustration. "Box your ears, take you over my knee, or . . ."

"Or what?" she whispered.

He was going to say "kiss you till you swoon." She looked so lovely, so damned kissable, gazing up at him with that saucy, sweet half-smile, her eyes like molten jade in the firelight, her shoulders soft beneath his digging hands, that he acted in a flash decision that had nothing to do with rational thought.

He crushed her to him, caught her sweet mouth with his, and kissed her fiercely. He breathed in her scent, tasted her lips, twined his fingers through the flaming cloud of her hair. The force of all the resulting sensations shocked him and raced like potent wine through his blood.

They jumped apart as the doors opened and the landlord and his wife entered followed by two servants bearing a multitude of covered dishes.

Camilla's cheeks flamed, but Philip didn't appear at all discomfited. While the landlord rubbed his hands together and waited, eyes alight with amusement, for the servants to leave, Philip strode to the fire and gazed into the dancing flames. Only he knew of the upheaval going on within. For all outward appearances, he was as cool as the moon gleaming palely outside the window, as controlled as the stars mounted in their predestined places in the universe.

The lackeys left. "Perhaps," the landlord said softly, cocking his bald head to one side and slyly regarding the lady his lordship had been caught kissing, "my lord would like a bedchamber for the night. We can offer you excellent hospitality and privacy befitting—"

He froze in midsentence, silenced by the thunderous frown on my lord's face.

"I beg your pardon, your lordship." He backed up, sweat breaking out on his brow as he realized his mistake. "I meant no harm, I only thought . . ."

"You didn't think—because you're not capable of thinking, you mangy, worthless dog." Philip advanced upon him with dangerous alacrity. "Get out and leave us to our supper."

"Of course, your lordship. At once, your lordship. Good evening, your lordship."

"Get out, damn you."

The door squealed shut upon his sweating, inanely smiling face and Philip stalked across the room to pull out Camilla's chair.

"Eat," he ordered, and stalked to take his own place. He realized he was furious because he would like nothing better than to take Camilla up to a room in this damned place, toss her down on a bed, and make love to her all night.

Who would ever have thought such a scruffy little ragamuffin walking down a deserted road could turn out to be such a mesmerizing little beauty, with a heart that could singe a man's soul and a laugh as enchanting as a song? Not he. He had once thought that what he felt for a proud golden-haired heiress was as close to love as he would ever get—but he knew with certainty as he sat across from Camilla in the Green Goose Inn and watched her taste a morsel of lamb that he'd never felt even a shred toward Brittany of what he felt for Camilla Brent.

His mood grew dark, restive. Now what was he going to do? Until he had determined the truth about her background, it would be unfair to tell Camilla how he felt. She might have choices she'd never imagined—how could he steer her toward what *he* wanted before she knew of all her opportunities. And besides that, he couldn't be sure exactly of her feelings. Oh yes, she had kissed him just now with a warmth and ardor that set his blood afire, and she had made love to him the other night with passionate abandon, but afterward she had said it was a mistake. She had never once given a hint of jealousy over Brittany, or seemed disturbed by his plans to marry her. True, she seemed sad to leave Westcott Park, but that could be merely because she was fond of the family. She cared for Dorinda, and Charlotte and Jared—but for him? As more than a friend? Her nature was warm, giving. But did her feelings for him go deeper than she had claimed, did they in truth come near to matching his own?

He sensed something else about her. She was proud. If she did care for him, she wouldn't betray it, not while she thought he was planning to wed Brittany Deaville.

He couldn't speak to her yet, however—not until he had settled this business of the charm. For once he wouldn't be reckless and impulsive, he vowed. He would wait, think. And how better to give himself time and distance to do that than by going to France, by finding out about that golden charm personally?

She'd be safe at Westcott Park while he was gone, with James to look after her. He realized in surprise that he no longer considered his brother an irresponsible boy. These past few weeks he had come to see James in a new light, and some of his old bitterness had gone. James would look after Camilla while he was in France. He was no longer the same youth who had been careless with Marguerite.

Philip relaxed at the knowledge that he could trust his brother. He even managed to smile across the table at Camilla.

"The wheel should be fixed by now. We'll be home within the hour."

She nodded. Home. His home, not hers. She was still warm from his kiss, but an aching hurt blistered through her.

She knew with certainty that Brittany Deaville would follow Philip to Westcott Park to seal her claim, and that her own excuse for being there was growing thinner by the day.

Westcott Park would not be her home for long.

"I have to go away for a few days on business." He broke into her thoughts as if he could read them. "James will keep you safe until I return. You'll be so involved getting ready for the ball I'm sure you'll scarcely notice."

Did he really believe that? Couldn't he guess how she felt every time he entered a room, or said good morning, or grinned that irresistible pirate's grin?

"Perhaps," she said carefully, "I should leave before the ball. We have two weeks. By then, you could formally announce your engagement to Brittany and . . ."

"No."

She regarded him over her wineglass. She clutched it tightly to keep her hand from trembling. "Why not?"

"We'll see this through my way. You'll stay through the ball. Then . . ."

"Brittany will surely never stand for that kind of delay."

"Won't she?" He pushed back his chair and stood. "Don't be so certain you know all the answers, Miss Smith. Life often holds some curious surprises."

"Like a madman trying to choke the life out of me at a party attended by all of my friends," she commented dryly, folding her napkin and setting it down beside her plate.

"Some surprises are more pleasant than others."

"What do you have in mind?" she demanded suspiciously. There was an odd, determined expression on his face, almost as if he knew something very important that he wasn't yet ready to share. He laughed as he came forward and placed her cloak around her shoulders.

"Wait and see."

"I don't like waiting. I'm not very good at it."

"I think you do very well at everything you attempt. Singing like an angel, dancing the waltz, conquering hearts . . ."

"Don't be absurd . . ."

"Winthrop, Fitzroy, and several others have lost theirs to your charms. I had no idea you were such a dangerous woman when I embarked with you on this little scheme. If I truly were your fiancé, I'd have to guard you night and day."

"You have been doing just that," she pointed out.

"Not very effectively," he said grimly. "If I hadn't left you tonight that madman wouldn't have gotten his hands on you."

His face looked so harsh she touched his arm. "It wasn't your fault. It was stupid of me to leave the ballroom. If I'd stayed with the crowd . . ."

"That's another thing. Why did you leave? Fitzroy said you were crying."

She turned away, fumbling with the pearl clasp on her cloak. She said the first thing that came to mind. "He stepped on my toe."

"That made you cry? You?" he demanded incredulously, turning her so that she was forced to stare into his face.

"Yes." There was nothing to do now but stick by her

story. "Who'd ever have thought such a charming man could be so clumsy?"

"You're certain there was nothing more? Tell me the truth—did he insult you?"

"Of course not." She gave a weak laugh. "No one could be more proper. Except, perhaps, Lord Kirby. He is always the perfect gentleman you know, except when he gets that mischievous light in his eyes and you know he is laughing inside at something ridiculous someone has said . . ."

"Stop babbling, Camilla." He put a gentle finger to her lips. She went still.

"Is that what you like in a man—that he is a gentleman? I wonder where that puts me?"

She gazed up at him quietly, sensing his bleak, restless mood, sensing he was casting about for something: comfort, encouragement, guidance. But why: with Brittany in his pocket, what more could he possibly want?

"You're more truly a gentleman than anyone I've ever known," she whispered, unable to play coy, unable to do anything but answer him with the forthright honesty that was so much a part of her. "A gentleman through and through."

"But also a man, Camilla," he whispered hoarsely, his hand gripping her nape. "And you're so very beautiful." He dragged her into his arms, his willpower dying before the luminous glow of her eyes. "When you look at me like that, what in hell's name am I supposed to do?"

She caught her breath. Their gazes locked, and she could feel his heart thumping beneath his coat, feel the whipcord sensual tension gripping him. In his eyes she saw a hungry tenderness that seared straight through to her soul.

Her own heart hammered wildly beneath her rich

gown. His nearness intoxicated her. Love welled up within her. She forgot caution, she forgot prudence, she even forgot pride. She reached up, cupped his rugged face between her hands, and lifted her lips to his beautiful, hard mouth.

She kissed him with all the love in her heart.

The velvet cloak slipped to the floor. His hands tightened at her waist and her nape, and his mouth crushed hers with a fierce intensity that exploded through them both like a tidal storm. Her hair tumbled from its chignon beneath his entangling fingers, cascading down her back in rippling copper waves. Philip crushed the fiery curls between his fingers. His other hand cupped her breast, and he felt the eager tautening beneath his exploring fingers. They sank down upon the sofa as the passion spiraled through them in unstoppable waves.

"You're so damned beautiful," Philip groaned, crouching atop her on the sofa.

"The landlord," she gasped, blushing fierily as he deftly worked to free her from layers of voluminous clothes.

"The landlord is not pretty at all," he panted, kissing the round swell of her breast.

Camilla laughed breathlessly. "If he comes in . . ."

"If he comes in, I'll kill him, so don't give it another thought," Philip assured her with that devil's grin. She laughed again and pulled him down on top of her as he struggled with his trousers and boots.

At last, partially nude, tangled amid clothes and each other's arms, laughing and gasping, they molded their bodies together upon the creaking sofa. Philip licked at her nipples, and stroked the damp triangle between her thighs, his own powerful body taut and straining for release. When he plunged inside of her, it was all Camilla could do to bite back a cry of joy, and she arced her back, drawing him closer, deeper, wanting him, wanting all of him forever and ever . . .

The fire crackled in the hearth. The room stopped spinning after a while, and Philip pressed a kiss to the delicate hollow in the base of her throat.

"Camilla, my little love. My precious beautiful love."

Her heart cried out for joy. *Did he mean it?* she wondered, hope blossoming like a flower bathed in sunshine. Or was this only the wild emotion and unthinking words of an Audley caught up in one more reckless impulse which he would all too soon regret?

What about Brittany? she wanted to ask. What about me? Surely you don't really want a serving maid to be your little love—not for more than a night or two at most? Surely not forever?

A sound in the hall broke the spell of dreamy enchantment between them. Suddenly Philip was businesslike again. He pulled on his breeches, picked up her gown, and grinning, tossed it to her.

"Camilla," he said as frantic moments later, both properly dressed once more, he tried to help her secure the pins in her flowing hair, "if we stay in here much longer we'll have the entire damn inn ogling us by the time we depart. We have a whole comfortable house waiting for us less than an hour's drive away. Come."

She straightened her gown and pushed the last pin in as neatly as she could, wondering what he had in mind. When he opened the door, she held her head high.

The landlord and his wife accompanied them to the door, bowing and smiling, each chattering louder than the other. If they had any suspicions about what had gone on behind the closed doors in the private parlor, they gave no sign of it in their eagerness to efface themselves before their lofty guests.

"I do hope everything was to your liking, your ladyship." Bessie curtsied as Camilla swept across the hall. Camilla paused on the same spot where that not so long ago night she had tracked mud in upon Bessie's spotless floor.

"Not precisely."

Bessie gawked at her. Her husband's face reddened, and he cast his wife an angry look.

"Why, wh-what was amiss?" the landlady stammered.

Camilla regarded her steadily as Philip paused at her side.

"Several weeks ago a desperate young woman came to your door and begged for shelter. You turned her away. You even warned her not to attempt to sleep in the barn, saying you would set the dogs on her. Do you remember?"

Bessie stared at the stunning, bejeweled creature before her. It . . . couldn't be. It *couldn't* be. Baffled, she at first nodded her head, then shook it vigorously.

"N-no, your ladyship, I don't recall . . ."

"You asked her if she intended to pay for her room with cow droppings."

Bessie gasped. Beside Camilla, Philip's face hardened and he started to speak, but Camilla placed a warning hand upon his arm.

"Now do you recall?" she inquired softly.

Bessie gulped and nodded. Her husband gave a cough.

"And you, sir—do you recall shooing her away like a pesky fly? In the future I would suggest you both remember that no act of kindness, no matter how small, is ever wasted."

Camilla gazed up at Philip and tucked her arm into his. "May we leave now?"

"Of a certainty." He frowned at the speechless couple who seemed frozen before them.

"When a lady offers advice, it is proper to thank her," he drawled.

"Thank you, your ladyship," Bessie cried, curtsying till her fat knee brushed the floor. Her husband echoed her words as sweat poured down his florid face.

Philip led Camilla into the bitter night where the carriage waited.

"Are you certain you're not a princess in disguise?" he asked as he handed her up into the coach. "You handled that as though royal blood flowed in your veins."

"Only anger flowed in my veins," she responded with a rueful laugh. "But then, maybe I should have thanked them. If they hadn't turned me away that night, I wouldn't have been out on Edgewood Lane when you were driving home, and we'd never have met."

"Who would have imagined," he said, "that such a pair of fools would have me in their debt forever."

Outside the carriage windows, the wind whistled through the ancient oaks. Plumes of smoke rose from the chimneys of cottages set off the road, smoky in the starlight.

"There is one thing you ought to know, Camilla," Philip said at length, watching as she sat so still upon the cushioned seat. "Everything is in a fine mess right now, but one thing at least you should know."

"Yes?"

"I don't love Brittany."

She clenched the folds of her skirt. Her breath caught in her throat. "But you said there is now an understanding between you."

"There is. An understanding that we are not destined to come together in marriage."

"But that's what you wanted. The reason we . . . you asked me to . . . you've been wanting that all this time . . ."

"I did."

She forced herself to stay calm. "Philip, I don't understand," she muttered, scarcely daring to hope.

"I thought Brittany was the right woman for me to marry. It was time for me to settle down, time to think about an heir. Brittany was the first woman ever to . . . resist my charms. She even appeared indifferent to me. I suppose that made her all the more desirable. But what I felt for her was never love. Only desire. She was a goal, a prize to be honorably won and possessed. It wasn't until recently that I realized I didn't want just a prize—however beautiful, however sophisticated and desirable. I want a woman, Camilla, a very special woman. She must have certain characteristics, or she won't do."

"Certain characteristics?" she asked doubtfully, her chest constricting. The rocking motion of the carriage suddenly made her feel light-headed.

Philip nodded. "She must sneeze when she's in the same room with a kitten for more than ten minutes. She must giggle adorably when she falls into a swamp of mud. She must care about little girls with cruel governesses and narrow-minded older brothers, break her heart over orphans who go without shoes, and outshine every other woman just by entering a room. She must be able to sing country ballads and sailors' ditties with equal aplomb, look like a duchess in diamonds and pearls, and see goodness even in the heart of a tyrant whose family has all but given up on him. Am I making myself clear?"

"P-perfectly."

"She must be courageous and foolhardy enough to venture into the rough streets of London at night alone

when she wants to know something and can't wait until
daylight, she must know how to handle bullies and cutthroats and aristocrats with equal grace, and she must
know how to drive me mad with desire for her every time
she comes within kissing distance."

He moved with lithe grace onto her side of the coach
and drew her roughly into his arms. "The only thing I
need to know about her is, will she have an undeserving
fool for a husband—if and when he can prove that he is
worthy of her?"

She reached up and touched his cheek with shaking
fingers. "Yes," she whispered.

His arms tightened round her. His eyes burned into
hers in the darkness. "Yes—just like that? No questions?
No doubts or hesitations?"

"One question, Philip." She threw her arms around
him. "Will you kiss me again—please?"

23 All of Westcott Park hummed with excitement as the day of the ball drew near. Less than a fortnight remained until the grand occasion, and there was much to do. Preparations for the hour when the first guests would arrive sped along with well-oiled precision. Menus were planned, flowers ordered, gardens manicured to perfection, and servants bustled about with efficient haste, while upstairs in the family apartments gowns and jewels and slippers and gloves were all selected as precisely as weapons in a military campaign.

One silvery afternoon when the sun glittered in a diamond-blue sky, Camilla wandered out upon the little terrace with a book, trying not to think about Philip's absence. He'd been gone three days, and there had been no word from him. She wondered what business was so important that it commanded his attention so urgently at this particular time, with so much unsettled. He had assured her it did not concern the search for the murderer, but would reveal nothing more.

She missed him sorely. She had been used to spending such a great deal of time with him that when he was gone, the world seemed dimmer, less vibrant and fascinating. Her eyes misted as she recalled his words to her before his departure.

"Soon this will all be behind us, Camilla. You'll be safe, and we can think about the future."

One lingering kiss, and he was gone.

She could scarcely believe that he cared for her and not Brittany Deaville, yet the expression in his eyes that night at the inn, and later in his bed at Westcott Park, had made plain his feelings. One moment she had been certain he was lost to her, and the next, he told her he loved her.

In the blink of an eye, your life can change.

She basked in the chill November sun, the book open on her lap, and tried to believe that it was all true.

She still couldn't quite see how it would work out. If they were to wed, he would be marrying disgracefully beneath him—although, if they were careful, no one outside the family would ever discover that.

It worried her, though. She didn't want Charlotte or James to think her a fortune hunter, but the vast differences in her standing and Philip's might be difficult for his family to accept.

If the reaction of Philip's family presented one problem, the murderer presented quite another.

He was still out there, somewhere, eerily close by. Philip couldn't guard her every day for the rest of her life. If whoever had killed Anders and Silas and tried to kill her at Lady Asterley's ball wasn't discovered and apprehended once and for all, she couldn't stay on at Westcott Park and endanger Dorinda, Jared, Philip, and everyone else.

A shiver ran through her. She remembered the madness in the murderer's eyes, the wild, dancing blue light. He would come after her again—and again—until he accomplished his goal. She knew that as surely as she knew the spelling of her own name.

Maybe she should just go away.

She pushed the thought from her mind, but it kept returning. An insidious voice inside told her that Philip would soon forget her, that he could marry Brittany after all, and his life would be far less complicated.

Her gloomy thoughts were interrupted by Charlotte and Miss Brigham, who came out to the terrace in search of Dorinda.

"But I haven't seen her," Camilla exclaimed, suddenly uneasy.

Miss Brigham seemed more exasperated than concerned, however. "Poor thing, she has been cooped up so long with the sniffles she just couldn't wait to get out for a while. But it is past time for her lessons and she has not returned. I thought she was only going to play in the garden, but she was nowhere to be seen on the path."

"I'll check the stables," Camilla offered, rising quickly and setting aside her book. "She may have gone to visit her pony—or to follow the grooms about. She loves to "help" them, as she puts it."

Charlotte offered to search through the maze, another of Dorinda's haunts.

"And I'll go down toward the lake." Miss Brigham began to look worried. "Although I trust she hasn't gone *there* alone."

"She may be playing house in the gazebo," Camilla told her, patting the governess's arm reassuringly. "I found one of her dolls there only yesterday when I was out riding."

"Very well. We'll split up and I'm sure we'll find her in one of those places," Charlotte declared.

Camilla set off at a quick pace toward the stables. Knowing Dorinda's fascination with animals and her idolatry of Jerome, the head groom, she felt optimistic of finding the child there.

Marmalade greeted her arrival in the stables with a friendly whicker. She smiled as she moved to the mare's stall and stretched out a hand to stroke the velvety muzzle.

"Not today, girl," she said regretfully.

Since her return to Westcott Park, she'd made it a point to ride nearly every afternoon. It wasn't Marmalade's fault there had been a burr under the saddle that day, and Camilla had determined she would not let one tumble keep her from learning to ride. Jerome, the groom, had been extremely helpful to her, even accompanying her on several of her rides, and Charlotte and Jared had also offered her the benefit of their instruction. She had a natural gracefulness and sense of balance, they all told her, and was improving daily. She would soon be proficient enough to try one of Philip's more spirited horses.

She found Jerome mending a saddle in the tack room. He assured her that Miss Dorinda had not been down to the stables all day.

"Is something wrong, miss?" He lifted his shaggy head and peered at her from beneath heavy black brows, his square face as unreadable as ever.

"No, no, I don't believe so, Jerome," she replied somewhat distractedly. Where *could* Dorinda have gone?

She left the stable, lost in thought. Suddenly she remembered something Dorinda had mentioned to her on her first day at Westcott Park, something about the Pirate's Cove, Dorinda's very favorite place to hide.

She turned and followed the path past the maze and the rose garden to the shrubbery Dorinda had described. When she parted it she indeed found a hidden path that dipped down a slight slope to the secluded glade Dorinda had told her about. And there, with Tickles prowling through the shrubs and her doll Agnes perched on a rock in the dirt, sat Dorinda, sketch pad on her knee, her little face screwed up in concentration as she drew Agnes surrounded by twigs, leaves, and brush.

"Oh, hullo. How'd you find me?" She smiled contentedly as Camilla came up beside her.

"I followed your trail of bread crumbs."

"But I didn't leave . . . oh, you're pulling my leg." Dorinda nodded wisely and grinned. "If you sit down, I'll sketch you, too," she offered generously.

Camilla shook her head. "Do you know that Miss Brigham and Charlotte and I have been searching for you for quite some time now? You've missed a good portion of your lessons, young lady."

"Oops." Dorinda looked genuinely startled. "I forgot," she confessed, and giggled. "Good thing Philip isn't here."

"He'll learn all about it if you don't hurry back to the house and tell Durgess or Mrs. Wyeth you'll be waiting for Miss Brigham in the nursery."

Dorinda frowned.

"And then," Camilla advised kindly, "it might be a very good thing if you were to get started on your lessons all by yourself, for perhaps then Miss Brigham will be so pleased with you, she'll overlook your thoughtlessness—this time."

"I'm sick to death of lessons," Dorinda grumbled, and

a pout began at the corner of her lips, but she caught Camilla's firm glance and capitulated with a most graceful shrug of her shoulders. "Oh, very well. One must do what one must do."

Camilla laughed.

"Are you coming back with me?"

"Well . . ."

Camilla peered around the delightful clearing, remembering what Dorinda had originally told her. This had been one of Marguerite's favorite places, she recalled, as well as Dorinda's. She felt an urge to spend a few moments in this idyllic spot where Philip's sister had loved to spend time. "I'll be along in a few moments. You run ahead."

She helped Dorinda gather up her sketch pad, pencils, Agnes, and Tickles, and watched her scamper up the path. Then she found a smooth stretch of grass beneath a giant oak and stretched out, spreading her skirts about her.

It was quiet, save for the occasional call of a bird, or rustle of a branch as some unseen wooded creature darted by. A brook babbled softly in the distance, she wasn't quite sure from where. She leaned back against the tree trunk and stared up through the gnarled branches at the sky. Several trees ringed the clearing, she noted, all of them old and knotted. Beneath one, she saw something white fluttering on the ground, snagged in a tree root. When she investigated, she found it was a linen napkin with the Earl of Westcott's family seal emblazoned upon it. Gingerbread crumbs clung to the cloth.

Dorinda. Obviously she'd stolen or begged some gingerbread from Cook and enjoyed nibbling the secret treat in her Pirate's Cove hideaway. Smiling fondly, Camilla folded the napkin in a neat rectangle and tucked it into the pocket of her dress. As she turned to head back toward the house, a carving in the tree before her caught her eye.

She leaned closer.

The letters *M* and *A* were carved within a heart upon the trunk of the tree. Marguerite and . . . who?

A . . . for Alistair? She smiled. Had the young, buoyant Marguerite nourished a secret infatuation with her older brother's friend? There was nothing else carved upon that particular tree. On an impulse she turned to the one nearest it. Nothing. But the third tree, the one under which she had at first been seated, revealed another carved heart. This time the initials inside read *M* and *M*.

Alistair's brother, Maxwell?

She gave her head a shake. Marguerite had apparently been torn between two secret loves. Had they truly been secret? She wondered if Philip or James or either of the Kirbys had even known of the young girl's infatuation with them.

Probably she would never know the answer. The very subject of Marguerite was so sensitive that it often seemed best not to even broach her name. Perhaps, after more time had passed, Philip would be able to look back and recall the joy of having had such a beautiful, vibrant sister, to treasure all of the happy memories, instead of grieving over the pain of her death.

She traced the roughly carved heart with her finger. And then she noticed it. Higher up, barely visible in the scarred and ancient bark, she saw what looked like a square block cut into the trunk of the tree. Camilla touched the edge of the square tentatively. To her surprise, it moved inward slightly beneath the weight of her hand. She realized with a little shock that it was a tiny hollowed-out opening, slightly larger than her hand from fingertip to wrist. Beneath her probing fingers, the square block of the tree trunk fell into her palm. Behind it was a gaping hole.

A shiver ran down her spine. Pirate's Cove. She had the feeling she was about to discover buried treasure. As she started to reach inside it suddenly occurred to her that of course Marguerite and James and Jared, and probably Philip as well, had all played here during the course of their childhood—any one of them might have carved the secret window and left all sorts of treasures tucked away inside. Like dead rats or spiders or beetles, she thought on a gulp of distaste, but curiosity got the better of her and she stuck her hand in and groped about.

Her fingers closed upon what felt like a book wedged tightly inside the opening.

She drew it out and discovered not an ordinary book, but a diary. A slim volume bound in dirt-encrusted red leather, the edges of the pages frayed and warped. She opened it carefully and stared at the bold, flowing lines.

This Diary Is the Exclusive Property of Lady Marguerite Audley—And No One Save Lady Marguerite Is Allowed to Read It!

Marguerite. She could picture the lovely, vivacious young girl sitting on the grass, writing those words. She drew in her breath. She had to give this to Philip. It would cause him pain, she knew, to see something so personal that had belonged to Marguerite, but he had a right to have it.

Something bulged in the center of the book and she turned to that page, strangely drawn to this long-hidden tome, not wanting to violate Marguerite's privacy, yet overcome with an odd urgency she didn't quite understand. A cloud had passed over the sun—and the Pirate's Cove was full of shadows.

There was a folded letter on the page to which she had opened the book. Her eye caught the graceful signature:

It read: *With all my love forevermore, Alistair.*

A jolt of shock rippled through her. A love letter? From Alistair Kirby? So the secret passion had not been quite so secret after all—and obviously not unrequited. A pang of guilt stabbed her. She was intruding into things that were none of her business. It was wrong. She closed the book with a thunk.

At the same time, she heard a footfall on the path, and glancing up, saw a dark figure approaching down the slope.

Instinctively, she dropped the book into her pocket. In the next instant she recognized Lord Kirby striding along past the rows of brambles.

She hoped she wasn't blushing as she hurried to meet him. He caught her hand and kissed it, his eyes twinkling at her.

"The mysterious Miss Smith—who vanished from the ball without a word to anyone." He grinned down at her. "I was sorely wounded. I never had the opportunity to claim my dance."

"I'm so sorry to have missed that pleasure," she assured him. "It's good to see you. But you know that Philip has left town?"

"I do, indeed. But you are the one I wish to see. I should first inform you, however, that I have not come to call alone. You may not wish to return too quickly to the house," he said dryly. "Brittany, Lord Marchfield, Fitzroy, and a small party of friends arrived from London last night to stay at Morrowing until the ball. They've come to call upon you and they're waiting for you at the house."

"Are they?" she asked in dismay. "Oh, dear, exactly what I did not wish to happen."

He studied her as she lapsed into thought, trying to think of how to deal with Brittany—and with Lord Marchfield. Of course, he would scarcely try to murder her in the gold salon with a crowd present, but she wasn't looking forward to facing over tea the man who probably had tried to strangle her.

"I suppose we'd better go back," she said, squaring her shoulders. She would simply have to behave as though she suspected nothing—but she would be sorely tempted to empty the pot of tea into his lap.

Kirby's chiseled features softened with concern. "Look, if you'd rather not, Camilla, I'll gladly keep you company. Let them wait. Perhaps they'll chat awhile with Charlotte and then go away, thinking I haven't found you."

"That's the coward's way out, I suppose, but it's worth a try." She laughed, relieved not to have to face either Brittany or Marchfield or Fitzroy just yet. Freddy would no doubt ply her with questions about why she had disappeared like that from the ballroom, and she was in no mood for concocting excuses.

Kirby began to stroll about the clearing, a pleased smile warming his face. "The Pirate's Cove—isn't that what Dorinda calls this place? James and Maxwell and I used to play Robin Hood and his Merry Men here. And Marguerite used to pretend to be the Sheriff of Nottingham and try to capture us all." He chuckled and sank down upon a tree stump. "Those were the grandest days," he said wistfully. "We were young, wild as wolves, and happily innocent as only children can be."

"Marguerite joined you in your games?" Camilla inquired curiously.

"Well, not when she was young, but as she grew older, perhaps nine, ten, she started to trot after us everywhere we went, like a puppy one can't quite shake off." He chuckled wryly. "Marguerite was special even then. Bright, active, as game as any boy you ever met. There was nothing that frightened her, nothing she wouldn't do on a dare."

He saw Camilla glancing at the tree behind him, where the initials were carved, and said without even looking behind him, "As she grew older, she developed schoolgirl crushes on both Max and me. You saw the initials carved into the trees? She brought us each here to this spot, separately, of course, and showed each of us the heart where our own initials were carved—then she tried to kiss us." A tender look crossed his angular features, dappled in sunlight and shadow by the shifting clouds. "We were horrified, naturally. We thought of her as our own little sister. Fortunately for all of us, she outgrew those infatuations quickly and we all went on being comfortable again."

He stood up and smiled at Camilla. "But that was all a long time ago," he said gently. "What concerns me more is what is happening now, today. Camilla, I'm fond of you. I admire you greatly. But I'm worried about you."

"About me? Why?"

He hesitated, then began to speak with careful deliberation, obviously choosing his words as tactfully as possible. "I see the effect you have had upon Philip in a very short time. Believe me, I marvel at it. He has become himself again, after all these years of closing himself off. You've brought back his joy in life, his patience, even his humanity. After Marguerite's death, he grew bitter,

harsh, cold. Now you've melted away that hard core and
he is much more like he was before: happy, able to enjoy
life and the people around him. You're a very special,
very lovely woman, Camilla—that's why I hate the
thought of seeing you hurt."

His words struck her like an ax blow. She stared at him
blankly. "Hurt? How . . . do you mean?"

He sank down beside her on the grass and touched her
hand. "I'm not blind, Camilla. My own pursuit, hapless as
it seems, of the magnificent Brittany has not obscured
from me the very obvious fact that you have fallen in love
with Philip."

She said nothing, but her heart began to thud. Kirby's
face reflected kindness and ready sympathy, which
touched her, but also filled her with a mute humiliation
that was difficult to bear. She bore it in silence, however,
hearing him out without comment.

"Every woman who meets Philip tends to fall in love
with him." He smiled ruefully. "Even Brittany, for all of
her protestations. I know full well she has only been leading him a merry chase, intending all along to capitulate in
the end, but his bringing you in as a rival for her was a
stroke of genius. You were fresh and beautiful and
charming enough to give her pause. And when you and
Philip were together, well, you appeared to truly delight
in each other's company. Everyone could sense it."

She swallowed. "What does this have to do with my
being hurt?"

"I'm afraid Philip played his part too well."

"Meaning what, Lord Kirby?"

She didn't want to hear this. She didn't at all like the
way the conversation was going.

Apparently he didn't either. His face tightened. "I'm

sorry, Camilla—damn it, this is as difficult for me as it is for you. The last thing I want is to see you hurt."

She forced herself to speak calmly. "I learned long ago that when one has something very unpleasant to say, it is best to get it over with as quickly as possible."

He raked a hand through his fair hair. "You're right, of course. Very well, then." He took a deep breath, then plunged ahead in low-voiced determination. "I saw Philip yesterday in London. I spoke with him and . . . he shared with me the trouble that is besetting him."

"Trouble having to do with me?" she managed to breathe.

"With you and . . . Brittany."

Her heart went very still. For a moment she couldn't speak. Then she whispered, "I see."

"Do you, Camilla?" He turned to her and grasped her wrist gently. "Philip has managed to become doubly entangled—and frankly, he doesn't know what to do. When I saw him, he was driving with Brittany in the park. They were talking very intently. After he drove her home, he met me at White's. We had a long conversation—about Brittany and about you."

Please, she thought frantically. *Let him have used the afternoon drive with Brittany to make one final break with her. Let him have ended matters between them, whether gracefully, clumsily—however he could. Let him come back to me.*

But the little voice of doubt that had nagged at her all along slowly grew to a roar. She wanted to clap her hands over her ears and block it out, but she only sat still as a mouse and waited for Kirby to finish slicing open her heart.

"Philip gave Brittany a ring yesterday—an emerald to pledge their betrothal. But he confided to me that he

asked her not to wear it yet—to keep their plans secret,
until he has had time to settle matters between the two of
you. I'm sorry, Camilla," he burst out, quick concern written across his features. "I don't mean to hurt you, but I'm
trying to help. To help you and Philip."

"Did he *ask* you to come to me and speak for him?"

She could scarcely believe that he would. Philip was the
most straightforward man she knew and he feared nothing. He would not hesitate to face her with the truth—at
least, she didn't believe that he would. But she had to
know for sure.

Kirby shook his head quickly. "God, no. He plans to
tell you himself as soon as he returns. You know, Philip.
But he was so unhappy. I knew how awkward it would be
for both of you. So I thought . . ."

"You thought it would be best if you broke the news to
me and spared me the painful scene."

He groaned and got to his feet abruptly. He began to
pace about the clearing. "You're angry at my interfer-
ence. Forgive me if I've overstepped my bounds. Camilla,
this is damned ugly business. But you don't deserve to be
hurt, and I thought I could spare you and Philip the humiliation of facing each other . . . I guessed some time
ago how deeply your feelings for Philip actually run."

How deep her feelings ran? She thought of his kissing
her in the Green Goose Inn, of the firelight playing over
his hard, handsome features, of his hands scorching her
skin, arousing undreamed of sensations. She thought of
his whispered words: *"You're so damned beautiful, Camilla."*

Impulsive. She'd always known he was reckless and impulsive. That night in the inn had been another act of
impulse, his words of love, his rejection of Brittany, all
brought on by the passions of the moment. Oh, he had

probably meant them at the time, she realized dully. Caught up in forbidden love, a daring liaison, combined with his noble sentiments of having to protect her—oh yes, his judgment had been clouded and he had done and said things that were rash.

Now he'd had time to think and he regretted them. He had gone to Brittany, and in her dazzling company had quickly realized his mistake. He'd sealed his future with her, even given her a ring as his pledge. And now, she, Camilla was nothing more than a dead weight around his neck, a burden to be somehow cast off—as kindly, delicately, and generously as possible, naturally—but cast off all the same.

Her chest hurt so much she could scarcely bear the agony of it. Without realizing it, her nails dug into the flesh of her palms, drawing blood. At that moment she hated Philip, hated Kirby, hated them all. But mostly, she hated herself for believing that dreams could come true.

"What is it you want me to do, Lord Kirby?" she burst out on a gasp of pain. "Leave Westcott Park before he returns? Run off like a frightened hare and never be heard from again?"

"Yes," he said quietly. "That is exactly what I thought you might wish to do."

Silence fell between them. Camilla fought back the tears that burned the corners of her eyelids. She would *not* cry. Not here, now, before Alistair Kirby, so that he would be obliged to tell Philip later, with pity in his voice: "Yes, the poor girl was terribly upset—what did you expect? Damned ugly business."

A bird twittered in a tree. The wind ruffled through the bright banners of fallen leaves. Camilla looked up into Alistair Kirby's worried face.

He was right, of course. There was no reason to stay a moment longer.

"Very well." She rose with an air of bleak decision, avoiding his eyes. "If you'll be so kind as to help me get away, Lord Kirby, I know exactly what I will do."

24 Late afternoon clouds scudded across the dreary sky as Lord Kirby's carriage plunged across the countryside toward Portsmouth with Camilla huddled disconsolately inside. The wind had picked up, rushing through the trees with wailing shrieks, like those of a terrified woman, and a downpour threatened. The handsome bay horses, responding to their master's skill with the ribbons, galloped at a headlong pace, which jolted the carriage considerably, but Camilla, drowned in her pain, scarcely noticed.

They had been traveling for several hours. In all this time, the turmoil had not faded from her thoughts. She kept clasping and unclasping her hands, smoothing her skirt, pushing back a loose tendril of hair behind her ear. She wondered what was happening at Westcott Park, if anyone missed her yet from the house. She wondered what they would all say at dinner, by which time her disappearance would surely have been discovered. She wondered if Philip would return on the morrow, no doubt having received word of her departure (for the more she considered the matter, the more she believed that James must actually know where to reach him and would do so immediately now that she was gone). She imagined, torturously, the reunion of Philip and Brittany, their joy and relief now that no impediments stood in the way of their happiness.

And she gritted her teeth and forced back the river of tears all too ready to overflow if she let her control slip for even a moment. She would *not* cry.

She had been stupid to think that he loved her. Stupid to think that what had passed between them had been anything more than an absurd fantasy—temporary, brief, and all too impossible to be real.

It had grown cold in the carriage. She was shivering. She thought of how she had slipped unnoticed into the house through the servants' door while Brittany, Marchfield, and Freddy chatted unknowingly in the parlor with Charlotte. She thought of the note she had left in her room addressed to James and Charlotte, that brief, formal note propped on her dressing table, explaining that she had gone to France as she had always intended. In the few brief lines she had scrawled in her haste to escape she had thanked all of the Audleys for their kindness to her and ended by wishing them well. She had not been able to write one single word to Philip, but that was hardly necessary.

He would understand and no doubt be relieved.

Her head ached with misery as she recalled the meaningless contents of that final correspondence. She had written as though writing to people she scarcely knew and didn't care about, fulfilling a civil obligation, nothing more. She had given no sign in the letter or in the neat, orderly way she had left the Blue Room of the wrenching pain tearing her apart. She had simply left, taking nothing but her cloak, a small traveling bag, and her reticule, disappearing into the clouded afternoon like a wraith, someone who had never belonged and would be all too soon forgotten, a vague dream creature of the night dissolving beneath the gilded light of a new day.

She felt cold. So cold. She pulled her cloak more tightly about her as raindrops spattered the roof of the carriage. As she did so, she felt something heavy in the pocket of her gown thud against her. Then she remembered Marguerite's diary.

The napkin crested with the Westcott Park seal was still in her pocket, too, she realized ruefully, as she pulled out the slim volume and turned it over in her hands. She was trying to leave Westcott Park behind, but tiny bits of it were haunting her.

Well, she would give the diary and the napkin to Lord Kirby when they reached Portsmouth. It couldn't be much further now.

Caught up in her own troubles, beset by a mood so dark it made the rolling storm clouds outside seem luminous by comparison, she absently began flipping through the pages of the diary, scanning them without really reading the passages. Until something caught her eye. The words: *He frightens me,* underlined three times, jumped out at her.

An eerie chill inched up her spine. She couldn't ignore those words. Perhaps it was curiosity, or perhaps it was a premonition, but something overcame her previous scruples about reading the diary, and her gaze swept to the passage above it.

Alistair does not—will not—understand. He writes to me daily, arranges that we should meet alone, all the while making it appear an accident. I wonder if I should tell Philip. Or James. But I don't want them to start asking me

*questions, for they always insist I am a terrible liar and
cannot hide anything from them. It's true, and I'm afraid I
will give away my feelings for Max. That would be disastrous, for Philip will say I am far too young to be in love and
forbid me to see him. I will die if I cannot see him!*

*Max tells me he can handle Alistair. But yesterday they
had a terrible fight. I cried when I saw Max's face, horribly
battered—because of me.*

*I have decided to keep the latest letter he has sent me—in
the event that I do tell Philip, and must show him proof that
I am not exaggerating. The letter will show Philip how determined Alistair is, even though he knows I love Max.*

*My greatest fear is that if Philip were to see that letter he
might well come to blows—or even a duel—with Alistair, his
oldest friend, and it would be all my fault. I see now that it
would be dangerous to show it to him. But at times I want to
let Philip handle everything. He would not let anything horrid happen to me or to Max, that much I know. And sometimes I long to let him take over and protect me. I've been
having the most terrible nightmares. It's childish, and yet, I
cannot stop them.*

*I never dreamed this side of Alistair existed. I don't know
what to do. He frightens me.*

But I won't tell Philip or James. Not yet.

The carriage was slowing. Glancing out the window,
Camilla realized that they had turned off the main highway and were jolting up a twisting lane to an inn. Its lights
burned like yellow cat's eyes through the thickly falling
darkness and drumming rain.

She stuffed the diary hastily into the pocket of her
cloak. Her brain was whirling. Alistair Kirby came to the
door of the carriage and opened it. Rain streamed in
silvery torrents from his many-caped greatcoat.

"I thought you could use a bit of refreshment before we complete our journey. It won't be much longer."

He spoke cheerfully, looked as well bred and handsome as ever, and offered her his hand with courteous solicitude.

Not frightening in the least.

But Camilla felt oddly reluctant all at once to leave the carriage.

Kirby's blue eyes glowed out at her through the darkness.

"Come along, I beg of you," he urged with a smile. "I'm getting soaked. Is something the matter, Camilla?"

"No, no, certainly not. I beg your pardon."

Her hand was shaking as she put it in his.

"A nice steaming cup of tea will fix both of us right up," he promised. And led her carefully, gallantly, across the puddled courtyard and through the entrance of the Dragon Tail Inn.

The Duke felt old and weary as he waited behind his desk in the firelit room. Ember-flamed shadows danced across the tall cabinets and bookcases, and illuminated the rich mahogany-carved arms of sofas and chairs. Scarlet draperies tassled with gold fringe adorned the huge mullioned windows. Beyond the château rolled the magnificent French countryside, a vista of breathtaking hills, twisting, fertile valleys, and a glint of pale blue lake.

Philip strode across the red and blue Aubusson carpet, his boots scraping loudly, seeming to echo up into the elaborately painted and plastered ceiling. The grayhaired man watched him approach, his pale green eyes alert within his still distinguished face. Yet for all their keenness, they looked somehow dead. Empty. Full of misery.

Philip studied him appraisingly. "Monsieur, I believe you know why I have come."

"*Oui.*" The voice was sharp, whiplike. Yet beneath it, and beneath the piercing eyes, Philip noticed what he had not noticed at first. Hope, a tiny glimmer of hope. The old Duke was not dead with despair after all, he realized. Beneath the stolid facade, this rigid, dignified Frenchman was clinging yet to a thread of hope.

"You have proof, monsieur? Proof that this girl is my daughter?" the Duke asked slowly, calmly. But his eyes shone.

"No." Philip met that glittering green gaze with cool directness. "No proof—only a story to tell. And, of course, this."

He had come to a halt before the desk, and now he reached inside the pocket of his coat and brought out the tiny golden lion charm. He placed it on the desk before the gray-haired nobleman, and watched the Duke de Mont de Lyon's face go pale as a winter sky.

"She wore this nearly every day on a chain round her neck, until it broke recently," Philip told him. "That is when I noticed it. That is when I began to wonder, to have my doubts about certain things."

"What things?" The Duke leaned forward eagerly, clutching the desk as if to keep from falling. But he would not fall, Philip realized, recognizing the strength that still lay in those long-fingered, elegant hands, the toughness in the lined, still-handsome face of this aristocratic nobleman.

"You must tell me everything about her—everything," the Duke commanded. "It is imperative. Sit, sit, young man. But do not keep me waiting. I am old, and I have waited long enough. I must know—I *will* know—if you have found my daughter."

25 The coffee room of the Dragon Tail Inn was nearly deserted on this rainy evening and Alistair Kirby had no difficulty in commanding use of the landlord's private parlor. The landlord, a thin, grave man with a head bald as an egg, had ushered them into the parlor, promised brandy, tea, and a veritable feast, and bowed himself out without fuss or fustian.

To Kirby's apparent surprise, Camilla asked for a glass of brandy and downed it in one gulp as she paced to and fro before the fire. She appeared distracted during supper, kept her cloak on, and picked at her food without interest. She ignored the landlady's blueberry tartlets, but drank her tea as if chilled to the bone.

When the meal was over, Lord Kirby asked her gently if she was regretting her decision to so hastily leave Westcott Park.

"No," she exclaimed, staring at him as if recalling his presence only at that moment. "I beg your pardon! I have been thinking . . . forgive me for being rude."

"You've been thinking about never seeing any of the

Audleys again—particularly Philip? I wonder, shall we go back?"

Camilla found herself staring into that fair, attractive face and wondering how anyone could be frightened of Alistair Kirby. Yet the words that Marguerite had written were stamped firmly in her brain. They had consumed her thoughts all during supper, haunting her, speaking to her —warning her.

She had tried reminding herself that Marguerite had been a young and impressionable girl when she'd written in her diary, and young girls were given to exaggerations and romantic fantasies. The jealousy she had hinted at could have been of her own imagining. And yet, something almost desperate in those long-ago written words would not allow Camilla to dismiss them as a schoolgirl's overly dramatic fancies.

"I don't wish to go back," she answered slowly, and rising from the table, she walked to the fire. She stretched her hands out toward the flames, wishing she could get warm.

"I know that my decision was the right one," she continued, her back still to Kirby at the table. "But I do wonder how all of them will get on. I mean, in particular, Jared and Dorinda. I know that I'll miss them," she added in nearly a whisper. She turned to peer anxiously at him. "You do think Brittany will encourage Philip to spend some of his time with them, don't you?"

"Brittany is not as selfless as you, Camilla." Kirby set down his cup in the saucer and rose from the table. "She'll want Philip all to herself, at least for a while. But don't worry, neither Jared nor Dorinda will suffer. I have already befriended Jared—he reminds me a great deal of Philip in his youth, did you know that? I'll take him under my wing. And as for Dorinda . . ." He paused, smiling quietly. "I will take care of her as well. Young as she is, she sometimes has the look of Marguerite about her. It's utterly amazing. Of course, she will have her own kind of beauty and spirit, no doubt, but . . . every so often, particularly when she is playing some game with that kitten, lovely little Dorinda reminds me quite strongly of Marguerite."

Camilla went very still. She moistened her lips. "D-does she?"

"Yes, indeed. But of course, no one can in fairness be compared to Marguerite. She was . . . incomparable."

Camilla stepped closer to him, struck by the intent, dreamy look on his face.

"Marguerite was very beautiful, I know. I saw her portrait in the gallery," she said softly.

"Her portrait!" Kirby snorted in disgust. His eyes blazed beneath his pale, aristocratic brows. "Her portrait cannot compare to Marguerite in person—it did not capture her spirit, her soul, her joy in life—" He broke off, flushing, and quickly poured himself another brandy. "I'm sorry. But I feel her loss keenly every now and then, as do all of the Audleys. I have been so close to them for many years . . ."

"And your brother's loss, too, I am sure. You do not often speak of him. I know that as your twin, the two of you must have been very close."

"Yes." He nodded, and now his eyes seemed to glow even brighter. "Max and I loved all of the same things, and we hated all of the same things. We were like two sides of the same coin. Nothing has been the same since he died. He and Marguerite died together, you know, as they deserved. . . ."

"Deserved?"

His eyes slowly focused upon her shocked face. "I

meant as was their destiny," he corrected. He stared down at the brandy snifter in his hand. "More brandy?" he asked abruptly.

"No . . . thank you, I've had quite enough." While before she had been cold, now she was growing warm. Her face felt hot. The heavy cloak with the diary stuffed in the pocket seemed to drag her down. She was having difficulty figuring out why he should say it was his brother and Marguerite's destiny to die together.

"I don't understand." Camilla wanted to unfasten the cloak, but it would take too much effort. And besides, they would be leaving in a moment, driving on to Portsmouth where she could catch the packet to Dieppe.

"You will," he said softly, smiling at her. "You will understand everything very soon. Are you certain you don't wish another glass? It will keep you warm on the journey."

His eyes . . . Camilla found herself gazing, transfixed, at his eyes. She had never fully noticed how dazzlingly blue they were. But now, in the flickering firelight, in this somewhat dim, shabby parlor, she saw them and was reminded of something else, something horrible . . .

Her brain felt fuzzy, full of cotton wool. She shook her head, trying to clear it. But perspiration beaded at her temples and dripped down her brow. It was unbearably hot and stuffy in here. She suddenly wanted to go back out into the cool, rainy night, to breathe deeply of the fresh autumn air.

And at the same time she didn't want to go anywhere at all with Alistair Kirby. Even through her befuddled brain, a warning bell was sounding.

"How . . . how long will it be until we reach Portsmouth?" she asked, stalling for time as he moved toward the door.

"Not long."

It was an effort to speak. She went on as calmly as she could. "Perhaps we should consider staying the night here. I am far more tired than I realized a short while ago. We could continue on in the morning."

"Ah, but I have a schedule, Camilla, which will not allow me to tarry here. We must go on tonight."

He gripped her arm. He was very strong, she realized suddenly. All at once, panic broke over her. She wrenched away, giving a nervous laugh. "Lord Kirby, I have inconvenienced you quite enough. Do you know what I think I'll do? I'll stay on here at the Dragon Tail this evening and allow you to return home. In the morning, I'll simply take the mail coach to Portsmouth. Thank you for all your kindness, but I realize I must not take advantage of your good nature a moment longer. I can continue the journey alone quite happily."

"I wouldn't think of it."

"But I wouldn't think of inconveniencing you another moment . . ."

He laughed aloud, a rich, amused bellow that sent shivers down her spine. "You know, don't you?" he said genially. "What gave me away?"

"I don't understand what you mean."

"Come, come, Camilla. It's obvious you've recognized me. And that you've guessed the truth about me and Max and Marguerite. Admit it," he urged pleasantly.

"Lord Kirby," she cried in desperation, her mind beginning to spin with spiraling terror. She clawed her way through the mist of overwhelming heat and dizziness and fear and tried to pretend nothing was amiss. "I must bid you good night. I am going to request that the landlord prepare a bedchamber and—"

"You'll do nothing of the sort."

He grasped her arm, spun her violently around, and sent her reeling across the room to land in a heap upon the sofa. Then he stalked toward her, his face now dark with purpose.

"You're coming with me. Don't argue any further."

"But I'm too weary to go to Portsmouth . . ."

"Portsmouth!" He gave a crack of laughter. It was a chilling, demonic sound. "We're not going to Portsmouth, you idiotic chit."

This wasn't happening. This was a nightmare. Lord Kirby was her friend, Philip's friend. "Then where?"

"Cornwall. My estate there. You'll find it charming, I know. Philip and James spent a summer there once with Max and me and our grandfather. It's quite picturesque, what with the sea and the cliffs. Only we've a rather long drive ahead."

"I won't go with you." She scrambled up off the sofa and tried to dart away from him, but her head swam. She caught the back of a chair for support and scooted around it, keeping it between her and Kirby. "Leave me here," she cried. "I'm staying at the inn! If you try to force me to go with you, I'll scream."

"You will do no such thing," he said, almost sweetly. He was smiling at her now, a wide, amiable smile so filled with amusement and gentle condescension it made her stomach roil with nausea. "The concoction I put in your brandy—and in your tea—will be taking full effect any moment now. You'll be fast asleep in a twinkling. I'll tell them you took ill, and we must hurry on our way." He consulted his pocket watch, every move calm and languid as Camilla's mouth dropped open, and her eyes glazed with horror. "You should sleep straight through until we reach Kirby Keep. Good night, dear Miss Smith."

"You're mad," she gasped in terror, and started for the

door on swaying legs. A scream began deep in her lungs, but before it could escape her lips a hand clamped brutally over her mouth and she was swept off her feet and into his arms. Her face was crushed into the buttons of his coat. The hot, stuffy feeling enveloped her completely, she was suffocating, perspiring, gasping for air, breathing in the leather and musk scent of his coat.

You're mad, you're mad, you're mad. She must have been whispering the words faintly in her stupor, struggling feebly against the effects of the drug he had given her, for her body felt weighted, her limbs heavy as anchors, and she could do nothing to free herself from his manacling arms.

She heard two things before she slipped into hot, drugged sleep. His laughter, soft and melodic above the hissing flames of the fire, and his quietly spoken, almost affectionate words.

"You're quite right, Miss Smith, as usual. Mad enough to kill. I killed Max and I killed Marguerite. Not to mention Anders and Silas. But I had very good reasons. *Very* good reasons, as you shall soon discover. I will not kill you before I've explained it all. I would have had you die in a riding mishap at that picnic, if it had worked out that way, or I would have ended your life at the Asterley ball, but I see now that either of those things would have been an injustice. You're a fine young woman even if you are a serving maid, and you deserve an explanation before you die. Sleep, Miss Smith, and do not fear."

The burning darkness sucked at her, closing over her like a fetid swamp. She heard his voice as if from a long way off, felt his arms enclosing her like iron fetters.

"I will kill you softly, Miss Smith," he promised a moment before she fainted. She knew he was smiling. "You will scarcely feel the blade."

26

"This isn't like Camilla. She isn't impulsive and she doesn't act in haste. *Why* would she leave? Why now?"

Philip's voice held steely calm, Charlotte noted, but his eyes glittered with a fierce urgency that spoke of supressed violence as he gripped the edge of the library table. His interrogative gaze swept over each member of his family assembled in the library—even little Dorinda huddled beside Jared on the sofa, her eyes red from crying.

"You saw her note," James grated out in frustration. He paced back and forth, scowling all the while. He had known Philip would blame him for Camilla's departure. And he wished to heaven he had seen her and been able to forestall her leaving. But she must have been stealthy as a thief. James was almost as upset as Philip. The house wasn't the same without Camilla. From the moment her disappearance had been discovered, it had seemed possessed by an eerie silence, a sad solemnity heavy as London fog. Charlotte had felt it, too. And it had been all

James could do to keep Jared from riding out pell mell after her through the thunder and the rain.

The note had been found the previous evening when Camilla didn't appear for dinner. It was now mid-afternoon the following day, only moments after Philip's abrupt return to Westcott Park.

He'd seemed to be in a state of stunned disbelief ever since James had broken the news.

But the depth of shock seemed overwarranted in James's view. Unless, as he had been suspecting for some time now, the irrepressible "Miss Smith" meant more to his brother than Philip cared to admit.

"Let's think about this calmly," he suggested, pausing before the mantel and surveying the tense faces in the room.

"I'm calm," Philip bit off. "Perfectly, damnably calm."

But a muscle worked in his jaw. And his mouth was a tight hard line in his face.

"Dorinda, run along to your room now," Charlotte urged quietly, leaning forward in her chair. Dorinda started to protest, saw her brothers' faces, and surprisingly, scrambled to her feet.

"Only if you promise me that Miss Smith will come back," she insisted, but the beseeching glance she sent all three of her brothers was at odds with her demanding tone.

Philip contained his impatience long enough to kneel down eye to eye with the little girl.

"I promise you, Dorinda. Camilla will come back. Just as soon as I track her down," he vowed through his teeth.

She put a dainty hand to his shoulder. "But why did she leave?" she whispered. "Doesn't she like us anymore?"

"I don't know. I truly don't know. But it had nothing to do with you—Camilla didn't leave because of anything

you said or did." He hesitated. "There may have been
some misunderstanding between her and me. But I'm going to get to the bottom of it and settle it once and for
all."

Dorinda stared into his glinting eyes, and her fear dissipated.

"Good." She smiled. "Then I'll go. Miss Brigham said
we could have lessons in the Pirate's Cove today. Let me
know when Camilla gets here," she called over her shoulder as she skipped out the door.

The remaining members of the family gazed bleakly at
one another.

"If only it were that simple," Charlotte murmured,
twisting a lace handkerchief back and forth through her
hands.

"I want to know everything that happened yesterday."
Philip stripped off his driving gloves and threw them
down on the table. He pulled up a wing chair and folded
his long form into it. "Everything," he repeated sharply.
"James, you begin."

When James had related to him the order of events,
Philip leaned back thoughtfully in his chair.

"So, Brittany, Fitzroy, Marchfield, and Alistair came to
call, but Camilla didn't receive any one of them."

"Right." James rubbed his bleary eyes. "And I kept my
eye on Marchfield the entire time. He wasn't left alone
for a moment."

"Lord Kirby went in search of Camilla," Charlotte put
in, explaining: "She had gone looking for Dorinda and
apparently found her in the Pirate's Cove. She sent Dorinda home to Miss Brigham and said she would follow
shortly."

"So we can assume that that is where Kirby met with
her," Philip said, frowning. "And during that conversa-

tion a decision was somehow reached for Camilla to leave Westcott Park. But why the hell would Kirby interfere with my business?"

"Perhaps Camilla had made the decision herself, and Alistair was trying to oblige her—and you." Jared suggested with a noticeable edge to his voice.

"What do you mean?" Philip's gaze swung to his youngest brother's flushed, accusing face.

"Well, it was plain to me—to all of us, I suspect—that Camilla was in love with you," Jared retorted.

Charlotte made a small sound, and clasped her hands in her lap. James nodded his agreement, meeting Philip's narrowed gaze without flinching.

Philip said nothing. Jared rushed on angrily: "You see, we all knew it. And everyone, including Camilla, knew you loved Lady Brittany and meant to marry her. So, perhaps, she was so unhappy she couldn't bear to be here anymore, and she simply decided to leave before you could come back and force her to continue with that stupid charade. And maybe Kirby was simply trying to help her save what was left of her pride, and help you to get on with your conquest of Brittany—without having to deal with getting rid of Camilla yourself. He was trying to do you a favor by taking her away to Portsmouth."

"Perhaps." Philip knew this explanation made sense— up to a point. Yet his heart rebelled. Camilla had known that he loved her, that he intended to make everything work out between them. Hadn't she? He thought of those tender moments they'd spent together, of the promises he'd made her. Had she changed her mind about her own feelings, or had she somehow begun to doubt his?

Oh, Camilla, you unpredictable, stubborn little minx. Are you truly running away from me or are you in trouble?

Cold fear sliced through him as he sorted through the

various possibilities before him. Despite the note, despite the indications that it was Kirby she had willingly gone off with, he couldn't shake off the feeling that something terrible had happened to Camilla, that this had to do with the murderer, and not Brittany after all.

"How do we know?" he asked James, trying to keep his apprehension at bay, "that she did go off with Kirby? No one saw them together. Isn't it possible . . ." He steeled himself to complete the sentence. "Isn't it possible that they might both have met with foul play?"

But James shook his head. "I wasn't taking any chances, Philip, after you entrusted me with guarding her against a murderer. I worked out a certain arrangement with Jerome, that he should keep an eye on Camilla when she was out of the house—riding, walking, whatever—any activity where she was not accompanied by someone from the family."

Philip stared at him. "Good man," he said slowly. "That was clever of you, James. I'm impressed."

James flushed with pleasure at the compliment. "It worked well, for she rode quite often, and Jerome was able to accompany her. And last night, after we found Camilla's note, I questioned Jerome. He was on the look-out, and he saw her slip into the house while Brittany and Marchfield and Fitzroy were still here. He also saw her slip out again through the servants' door."

"Did he see where she went?" Philip felt his muscles tense.

"He followed her to the road and saw Kirby help her into his carriage. No one else was about."

So it was true. She had gone with Kirby of her own accord. She wasn't in danger, she was running away from him.

She loves me, Philip told himself, stubbornly fighting

the doubts. *I know she loves me. But she doesn't believe in me. She doesn't have faith.*

Who could blame her? The way he'd made a fool of himself over Brittany all these months, when the real love of his life was right in front of him. He'd been blind. It was no wonder Camilla didn't have faith in his promises or his love.

But I have enough faith for both of us, my love.

He strode toward the door, oblivious of the baffled stares of his brothers and Charlotte.

"Durgess!" he roared, and the butler hurried from the shadows like a genie from a bottle.

"I want my light traveling coach and the bays harnessed immediately. I leave within the quarter hour. And tell O'Neill that if he's already unpacked my damned cloak-bag he had better just pack it again and be quick as the devil about it. And send for Jerome—I'll speak to him before I leave."

Mrs. Wyeth, who was coming down the stairway as his lordship sprinted up, exchanged alarmed glances with the butler. His lordship was in a rare taking. They both could guess why.

Pretty little Miss Smith—who'd gone off *most* mysteriously without a word to anyone.

Who would ever have thought a girl like that would have had such an effect on a household? But even Mrs. Wyeth, who'd had to eat all of her earlier doubts, couldn't deny that there was something special about the green-eyed young lady with the tinkling laugh and earnest smile who had made Westcott Park come alive. Neither she nor Durgess had time to think on the matter, however, for when his lordship was in one of these moods, heaven help anyone caught nodding. Mrs. Wyeth scurried down the stairs to inform Cook that, after all, his lordship would not be dining at home, while Durgess, stern visage intact, minced off to summon his fellow lackeys to do his lord- ship's bidding.

James and Charlotte were waiting in the hall when Philip bounded downstairs once more in his driving cloak and gloves.

"You're going after her? But, Philip, if she really wants to leave . . ."

"She doesn't."

Charlotte put in suddenly, "She didn't take anything but her cloak with her, and it's cool by the sea. I took the liberty of instructing Mary to pack some of her things—a muff, and her fur-lined gloves—and her velvet pelisse."

Philip glanced at the traveling bag his sister-in-law held out toward him, then at Charlotte's anxious face.

"That was very thoughtful of you, Charlotte. You have my thanks." Abruptly, he bent down and kissed her cheek. "I know how fond you are of Camilla. Don't worry, I'll bring her back to us safely—and soon. You may tell Dorinda that, as well."

Jared rushed in from the kitchen, with Jerome, cap in hand, following behind him.

The sense of urgency was interrupted by the knocker sounding briskly at the front door.

"Damnation." Philip swore under his breath. "Who- ever that is, I don't have time to talk to them. Kirby's had a good day's head start, and chances are Camilla's al- ready in Paris by now."

Portsmouth . . . Paris . . . He'd track her through all of France, if necessary. He'd not return home without Camilla. It wouldn't *be* home without Camilla.

He remembered the charm he carried. Now he knew its full significance, and Camilla had to know as well. He would tell her everything—the truth—the life she'd been cheated of, the place that was rightfully hers and that she had for so long been denied. Then it would be up to her to decide the future, both of their futures.

He turned toward the groom, shifting uncomfortably from foot to foot. Brawny Jerome looked as out of place in the high-ceilinged entrance hall as a boar in a gazebo.

"Jerome," he began, but the question on his lips was interrupted by the sound of the brass knocker rapping through the hall once again.

Philip's temper rose. Before he could lash out, Durgess whisked past the gathering in the hall and opened the door.

They all stared at the diminutive, bow-kneed man hovering on the threshold.

From that moment on, as Philip recalled later, everything seemed to happen at once.

27 The castle was dank and dim and drafty. Its endless stone corridors echoed with the murmurs of the sea and with the shrieks of wild birds upon the cliffs and with the futile whispers of Kirby ancestors long dead.

In a locked room in the tower, on a high, narrow bed, Camilla lay in darkness. Her hands and feet were bound by ropes to the bedposts, but she couldn't have escaped if she'd been free. The drug kept her dazed and dreaming.

Kirby came and looked at her from time to time throughout the night. He was as excited as a child on the eve of his birthday. He had found Marguerite's diary in Camilla's cloak when he'd tied her to the bed and he had pored over it as the hours passed with the glee of a pirate discovering a treasure trove of rubies and emeralds and gold. Marguerite's thoughts—her every feeling—were recorded for him to study and understand. Her foolish preference for Maxwell, her absurd fear of himself. All of it had confirmed for Alistair how necessary it had been to kill her, to kill them both.

He was grateful to Camilla for this unexpected gift. More than ever, he was determined that her death would be as painless as he could arrange. He certainly owed her that.

When the stars began to fade from the sky, he lifted Camilla's head in the crook of his arm and poured more drugged wine down her throat. He let her sink back down on the woolen coverlet, and touched the rose-petal softness of her pale cheek.

An excited shiver ran through him. So beautiful. So loved by Philip. He was ecstatic.

He couldn't decide how to kill her. Or when, precisely. The anticipation was a huge part of the fun.

He tiptoed away as a cool lilac dawn was breaking and slept in the bedchamber he and his twin had shared as boys. The wind whistled through the cracks in the high windows. The patterned floor creaked. He had beautiful dreams.

Today would be a very special day—a killing day.

He could scarcely wait.

Camilla awoke to the sound of waves crashing against the gray rock cliffs of Cornwall. Her body was numb with cold. Her mouth felt as if it was full of sawdust. There was a steady, throbbing pain between her temples. Fighting the grogginess and the bombarding cold, she struggled to think, to remember.

When she realized she was bound terror rushed back. So did the memories.

Looking around her as best she could, she saw that she was in a narrow tower room with a single barred window, and a granite door. Outside that high window, all she could discern was a square of dingy gray sky. It was daylight though, she realized.

And she was alone in a deserted castle high on the cliffs of Cornwall with a madman who intended to kill her.

She struggled against her bonds until her wrists and ankles were chafed and bleeding, but the knots held fast. She lay exhausted on the bed, shivering despite her exertion. The wind rushing in the open window came straight off the sea. It was chill and damp, tangy with salt spray. The tower room seemed to echo with every pounding roar of the waves.

Hours passed. Camilla thought of Philip, of the Audley family gathered at Westcott Park. Had Philip even returned yet from wherever he had been? Did he care that she was gone? As she lay there in helpless frustration and mounting fear she suddenly wondered if he truly *had* given a ring to Brittany, if he had indeed chosen Brittany over herself. All of those things Lord Kirby had told her in the Pirate's Cove had been designed to lure her away from Westcott Park with him. Perhaps, she thought on a choking sob of hope, they weren't true, after all. Perhaps Philip had not decided he loved Brittany, had not changed his mind.

A lot of good it would do her now. Even if Philip had wanted to come after her, and tried to do so, he would go to Portsmouth—and then, uselessly, on to Paris. By then it would be too late.

She knew little of Kirby's plans or his mad reasoning, but she did know he planned to kill her soon. She had sensed it in him before she lost consciousness in the Dragon Tail, sensed the blood lust, the urge to kill. He wouldn't be able to hold off long.

And even if he did, Philip would never come here, to Kirby Keep, in search of her. Why should he? In all these years, he had never once suspected Alistair Kirby of causing Marguerite's death. He had never suspected him of the murder in the White Horse Inn. He would continue to suspect Marchfield. And Kirby, when she was gone, would console him, and stand by and watch him marry Brittany. And . . . plan something horrible for Dorinda.

As surely as she still breathed, Camilla knew with sudden clarity that his insane obsessions were leading him more and more toward Dorinda, whom he considered the younger version of his beloved Marguerite.

A key scratched in the lock. Camilla's gaze flew to the door as Lord Kirby entered the tower room. Immaculate in a plum satin coat, embroidered waistcoat, and yellow-striped trousers, he looked for all the world like a handsome young lord out for a promenade in the park—except for the demonic diamond-studded black mask concealing his face.

"The hour has come, sweet Camilla. It is time. Don't be afraid."

She had been steeling herself for this moment for hours. But all her preparation couldn't prevent the icy prickle of horror that raised the hairs on her nape. She gazed back at Kirby with apparent composure, praying he couldn't detect the terror that was turning her blood to ice, and causing her heart to palpitate so furiously she could scarcely draw breath. Somehow she managed to speak with creditable crispness.

"Lord Kirby, I was hoping you would come. I wish to speak with you."

"Do you, Miss Smith?" An edge of mockery laced the brief words. And his glinting, mad blue eyes. She ignored it.

"Yes. My mind is full of questions, questions only you can answer. You promised me an explanation, if you remember."

"That I do." He approached the bed with light, exuberant steps and surveyed her as if she were an exotic flower whose petals he would tear off one by one.

"I never was able to explain to Marguerite—or to Max. That has bothered me considerably over the years. Of course, the others didn't matter. Henry Anders and Silas Tregaron were only dirty blackmailing maggots, they didn't deserve an explanation as to why they had to die. But I would have liked to have explained to Marguerite and to Max why they encountered their fate. Do you believe in fate, Miss Smith?"

"Indeed I do. Lord Kirby, is it my fate to die of extreme discomfort?" She sent him what she hoped was a prettily beseeching smile. "You have fastened these bonds with such excessive tautness they are cutting off my circulation. Couldn't you possibly loosen them a little? Or perhaps remove them for a while? Surely you are not afraid I will overpower you."

He smiled at her, a grinning demon's smile beneath that black mask. "Are you trying to trick me, Miss Smith?"

She regarded him with the frank look that characterized her. "Of course not. I'm trying to become more comfortable so that I can better concentrate on what you are going to explain to me."

He hesitated a moment, studying her face for a sign of insincerity, then shrugged and came forward so quickly it startled her. Out of nowhere he held a knife. "Allow me to oblige you, ma'am."

It felt wonderful to be free. She immediately began to rub her chafed wrists and ankles, trying not to glance toward the open door.

"Thank you. Is there perhaps . . . any food in this

castle? I . . . I could fix us some breakfast and we could chat in the kitchen, if you'd like."

He laughed, a merry, crazily echoing laugh that seemed to bounce off the confining walls of the tower.

"Don't push your luck, Miss Smith. You will not be hungry much longer. The hour for you to meet your ultimate fate is nearer than you think."

"Surely you won't make me meet it on an empty stomach?"

But her attempts at levity were beginning to irritate him. He made a quick gesture toward her with the knife. "Do you truly wish to understand your death—or do you simply wish to stall for time until . . . what? Philip rides to your rescue like Sir Lancelot to his Guinevere?"

"We both know that won't happen," she answered quietly, biting her lip.

"Yes, because I've outwitted him again. To think that I should outwit the great and splendid Earl of Westcott!" He laughed delightedly. He sauntered to the three-legged stool near the window and perched on it, his movements eerily boyish and seemingly normal in contrast to that chillingly demonic mask. "Philip always excelled at everything, you know. It all came easily to him. James admired him tremendously, so did Max. But I always knew of his other side."

"Other side?"

Crouched on the bed, Camilla tried to estimate the number of paces to the door. Kirby, seated near the window, was now on the opposite side of the room. He'd have to run round the bed to catch her. *Not yet,* she warned herself, tension rippling through every fiber of her being. *Wait for the right moment, when he's off-guard. It could give you a precious second's advantage.*

"Oh yes, indeed," Kirby continued, watching her face

as he talked. He still held the knife in one hand, casually, loosely, as if he had forgotten its existence. "Philip could be most autocratic, even as a child. He always had to plan the adventures, choose the games. He was a natural leader. And that made him think he had power over the rest of us, that he could determine our fate."

"I . . . I'm afraid I don't understand."

"Neither did I until the day Marguerite turned thirteen, and I discovered she had budded into a most enchanting young woman. I fell in love with her on that day, or maybe on the day I met her, I can never be sure exactly when—but by her thirteenth birthday I certainly did love her, and so did Max. Both of us were determined to marry her."

"You were jealous of him?"

"Of Max? Don't be ridiculous. Marguerite preferred me—she always did. But you see, Philip had once seen me talking to Marguerite, gazing into her eyes—she had the most beautiful eyes. And afterward, he told her that I was far too old for her, that she was to stay away from me. He never said a word about Max. But he came to me later and thrashed me for daring to look at his sister. We were supposed to be friends, Camilla, and don't friends trust one another? But he didn't trust me with Marguerite. He didn't think I was good enough for her. He always did like Max better."

His shoulders hunched, tensed beneath the plum coat. A rigid scowl froze upon his face. He gained control of the anger building inside of him and continued on with an effort, his tone one of false, teetering calm.

"But Marguerite loved *me,*" he insisted. "She wanted to marry me when she was of age—but she knew Philip would never countenance it, because he thought she was lovely enough to snare herself a duke or an earl. And I was only the youngest son of a viscount. Max was born two minutes before me, did you know that, Camilla? He inherited the title and the estates because of *two minutes.* So I was not deemed good enough for Lady Marguerite, even if I was Philip's friend."

The fury and uncontrolled bitterness rising in his voice frightened her. Gone now was every vestige of the calm, amused facade. A demon sat on that stool, shaking with wrath, his mouth beneath the hideous mask twisted with rage.

"I vowed then that Philip would pay. And you, Miss Smith, will be the instrument of my revenge."

"Me?" she whispered through stiff lips.

He nodded, and suddenly his hands tightened on the knife, his knuckles whitening. "If I wasn't good enough for Marguerite, surely you are not good enough for Philip." He giggled suddenly. "You thought I wanted to kill you only because you witnessed Anders's murder, didn't you? It started out that way, but now I have a much more compelling reason. Philip loves you. I could tell by the way he kept talking about you at the club that night before the Asterley ball. It could have been Brittany instead—I truly thought it would be. Instead, he chose you. I'm sorry, in a way. It would have been such a notable deed to kill the famous Lady Brittany and get away with it —but it will be so pitifully easy to do away with you. You have no friends, no family, no one who will persist in searching for you. Only the Audleys know your true identity. And they won't have a hint of the truth, because they think you've gone to Paris. It's too easy." He suddenly sounded almost plaintive. "I wish I could let him know you were dead. I'd like to see his face when he learned of it. But the risk would be too great. They'll all know you left with me. They must simply think that you've disappeared in France, never to be seen again."

"But if Philip does love me, you know he won't give up," Camilla said desperately. "We planned to marry, you know. He'll have the Bow Street runners searching for me, he'll make inquiries himself. You know how determined he can be."

"It won't do him any good. There will be no proof, no hint of my involvement. I shall beg his forgiveness for aiding your departure from Westcott Park, explaining that you begged me to take you away, that you couldn't face the prospect of becoming the Countess of Westcott. Yes, that's excellent—oh, it will be a most noble sacrifice you made. As a mere serving girl you didn't wish to bring disgrace down upon his family name—you fully recognized that the marriage would be a horrid mistake for him, a misalliance he would someday live to regret. And certainly you would not have settled for anything less than marriage. Philip will understand, believe me, and will love you more for your self-sacrifice. His loss will be deep and keen."

"He'll be furious with you."

"He will forgive me when I explain how distraught you were, how you begged my help, how I only had both of your best interests at heart."

He had begun pacing around the room as he talked, his boots scraping against the stone floor. He had reached the window, and paused for a moment with his back to her, staring out at something that caught his eye. Gasping, he leaned forward and pressed his face to the bars.

Camilla didn't wait to discover what had startled him. She saw her chance the instant his back was turned. With a leap, she sprang from the bed and toward the open door, her skirts clutched in one hand. As she darted through the archway she heard him shriek behind her and felt the rush of air as he lunged across the tower room in pursuit.

A long, dim corridor stretched before her. She plummeted through it, her feet skidding on the damp stone beneath. Suddenly, out of nowhere, a staircase zigzagged beside her, lit by a row of torches winding downward. She nearly missed it, stopped, and doubled back, fleeing down those steps with the desperate speed of a hare trying to outrun a pack of wolves. She slipped in her haste, and tumbled headlong. With a jarring jolt, she crashed into the rough-hewn stone landing some ten steps below.

For a moment, she lay there, dazed and shaken, the breath knocked from her. Her knee throbbed, and she had skinned her elbow on the stone. But there was no time to nurse her hurts—she heard the rapid pounding of footsteps from above, and terror sent her scrambling to her feet. She peered desperately through the gloom, trying to discern what lay ahead. She was in another dank corridor, nearly black but for the light of a single torch, which revealed twists and turns ahead. Kirby knew the castle; she didn't. How would she ever escape him? Yet with the human drive for survival flaming through her like a red-hot torch, she plunged on, running this way and that through the maze of passages, her eyes straining to see in the near-darkness, her breath rasping in tortured gasps in her throat.

At last, she darted to the right through a low archway and saw a door at the end of the tunnel.

"Stop!" Kirby hissed, not far behind her. His voice reverberated crazily from the black slabs of wall on either side. "You can't get away—you're trapped. If you stop now, I'll still kill you softly. If not . . ."

Camilla didn't wait to hear the rest. Her feet slithered

over the stone floor as she made for the doorway ahead. Choking back sobs, she prayed it wouldn't be locked.

She pushed at it. Locked! She pushed again, tears of frustration momentarily blinding her, and suddenly, the door gave beneath her grasp. She shoved her shoulder against its heavy weight and pushed with all her might, forcing it wide. She was in a cavernous entrance hall—the main hall of the castle, she realized—and straight ahead loomed the huge double doors leading outside to the cliffs and the sea.

She felt a whooshing rush beside her, felt a hand close on her sleeve even as she darted forward. She heard a tearing sound.

He panted and cursed and screamed as she whisked out from his clutching hands, but Camilla bolted with frantic determination toward the door ahead.

Please let it be unbolted, please let it be unbolted, she prayed as she pelted forward, past ancient suits of armor guarding the lofty portals of the entrance hall, past a huge arch leading to the darkened medieval rooms beyond. She reached the double doors, tugged at the huge bronze handles, and saw winter grass and buttressing cliffs ahead . . .

But before she could stumble through the doors, a hand twisted savagely in her hair, and Kirby jerked her head back cruelly. She screamed. The next moment, his arm clamped across her throat, and he held her fast against him. His grip made her gasp in pain, but no words could escape. Suddenly she felt the icy blade of the knife against her cheek.

"I was thinking of letting you drown peacefully in the sea, but now I'll slice you to ribbons," he hissed.

A quiet voice spoke from the shadows.

"Let her go, Alistair. She's nothing to do with this. It's now between you and me."

Philip emerged from the shadows of an adjoining aperture. He looked haggard, his chest rising and falling beneath his coat as if he'd just been running very quickly, and was out of breath. Though she dared not move, Camilla gazed at him in an agony of mingled hope and fear.

He looked exhausted. His eyes were ringed by dark circles, his face drawn and gray beneath a glaze of sweat. Yet there was iron resolve mirrored in the depths of his eyes, and he stood straight and tall despite his weariness. He was staring at Kirby with an air of cool watchfulness, his gaze fixed upon the knife that hovered alongside Camilla's delicate cheek.

She had no idea how Philip had found her or how he had known that she was in trouble; she only knew that he was here, that he had come to save her. But a heavy fear wrapped itself around her heart. Kirby would now try to kill them both.

"I don't understand." Kirby's voice went high-pitched with shock. She could feel his breath quick and hot as coals on her neck. "You can't be here. You were supposed to go to Portsmouth."

"I almost did. You nearly fooled me. You're very clever, Alistair. I congratulate you for that." Philip was measuring the distance between them as he spoke. At least twenty paces separated him from Camilla and Kirby. Plenty of time for Kirby to kill her if he tried to make a run for it. He felt perspiration beading on his brow.

Wait. Don't do anything rash. Better to try to talk him into letting her go, or dropping the knife—and if that fails, watch for the right opportunity to move.

He inched forward imperceptibly. He must keep his

voice level, keep all emotion from his face despite the
fear for Camilla gripping him. If Kirby hurt her . . .

But he mustn't think about that. He must concentrate
on getting her out of reach of that knife.

"Stand back! Don't move!" Kirby barked, noticing the
slight advance Philip had accomplished. He ran his
tongue over his dry lips in panic.

"How did you know?" he demanded, sounding almost
peevish. "Answer me! Tell me how you found out."

Philip moved not a muscle. "Easy, my friend. It was
Bow Street. A runner came to my door."

"A runner . . ." Kirby shook his head, as if trying to
clear his brain of its confusion.

"I had told the authorities what Camilla saw the night
of the murder at the White Horse Inn and relayed to
them the contents of the note you stole from her room.
The runner showed up at my doorstep as I was leaving for
Portsmouth. He came with the news that Silas Tregaron
had left a detailed letter hidden in his rooming house
quarters, explaining all about what you did to Max . . .
and to Marguerite."

Philip's voice broke off for a moment, and then continued, even more clipped and calm than before. Camilla
knew what that pretense of composure must be costing
him.

"The letter explained that Silas and Henry Anders
were drinking together in that cottage on your estate
when Max and Marguerite rode up that night. They hid
outside and watched. They saw them kissing, Alistair."

"Marguerite never wanted to kiss Max—it was me she
loved! But she thought you didn't approve of me . . ."

"They saw you rush in and stab Marguerite and Max in
the cottage that night and then set the place on fire."

"You're lying!" Kirby's fingers dug into Camilla's flesh

so hard she cried out. He ignored her, his masked gaze still fixed wildly on Philip, who was motionless in the gloom of the hall. "I searched Silas's room—there was nothing there—I would have found it . . ."

"The runners were more thorough. They found the letter stuffed inside an empty flask in the cupboard. I imagine you overlooked it. You must have been in the devil of a hurry."

"I glanced in the cupboard, I remember," Kirby muttered, half to himself. "But I missed it . . . the damn cupboard was stuffed with bottles and broken plates and cups. It was crawling with roaches. I never thought—"

Suddenly, he gave a peal of laughter. It was so loud, so strange and crazed that shivers ran up and down Camilla's spine. She fought the urge to break away, conscious of that keen blade resting against her cheek. Kirby was mad. He would kill them both. It was only a matter of seconds now . . .

"It's better this way," he gloated. "Oh yes, I see that now. Much better. I wanted you to know all along, Philip, my dear friend. I've been itching for you to know. I killed Marguerite. And Max. Because they betrayed me. But it really wasn't Marguerite's fault," he amended quickly, hysterically. "It was your fault, Philip. She turned against me because of you."

"That's right, Alistair. And you hate me for that—I understand," Philip agreed quickly, realizing that Kirby was rapidly losing whatever remnant of self-control he still possessed. "But Camilla isn't involved in this, you know. My groom, Jerome, saw you set your carriage on the road headed west, not south, so I figured it wasn't Portsmouth you were headed for at all. I knew if you were traveling west you'd be making for Kirby Keep, so I came to fetch Camilla. Let her go, Alistair, we don't need her. We can settle this ourselves."

Kirby went on as if Philip hadn't spoken. "I had to kill Anders and Silas, too—because they witnessed the whole thing and blackmailed me over it. After I paid them the first time, they left me alone. I thought it was over. But a year later they came back and wanted more. It took me a while to learn their identities, but by then they left the country. Anders had been working for Marchfield, I discovered, but he disappeared without a trace before I could get my hands on him. So did Tregaron. Just when I thought I was rid of them forever, they showed up again, demanding five thousand pounds. Only this time I found the greedy bastards and killed them instead."

He laughed suddenly, and the knife whispered along Camilla's cheek. "But you don't care about them, do you, Philip? You only care about Marguerite! Well, it's true enough—I killed her. Only because you were determined to keep her from me."

"Marguerite was young, Alistair. Too young for either you or Max . . ."

"Her diary is upstairs. I read it all. Marguerite wrote that she loved Max, but she didn't mean it. My darling girl didn't mean it. She only wanted me, but she was afraid you would find the diary and discover us, so she wrote that to cover up the truth. The truth was that we loved each other, and you kept us apart. You beat me to keep us apart."

"I never beat you, Alistair." Perspiration dripped down Philip's brow. That knife was too close to Camilla. He could sense her terror. How she managed to remain still and quiet he didn't know. It was a feat of unimaginable courage. He tried once more to break through Kirby's armor of madness, to find a chink of reason inside. "I told you once that Marguerite was too young to be flirted with," he said softly, "and warned you to leave her alone until she was old enough to be out of the schoolroom— but I never struck you or even raised my voice. I never took it seriously, Alistair."

"You thrashed me," Kirby cried. "You wanted Max to have her."

"Let Camilla go and we'll step outside and talk it over," Philip urged desperately.

"I had to punish you. And Max. Because he wanted Marguerite for himself. He tricked her into thinking she loved him—but all the time she loved me. So he had to pay. And you had to pay. It was the only way. But I lost Marguerite . . . only now Dorinda is the image of her. I see that already . . . I have only to wait and I will have another chance to be happy. . . ."

He suddenly seemed aware of Camilla, still frozen in his grasp. "And this will make me happy—killing your precious Miss Smith. You love her, Philip, don't you?"

"Miss Smith isn't involved in this. This is between us."

"She's beautiful, isn't she? And full of life. I'm going to kill her and force you to watch, Philip."

"If you shed one drop of her blood, I'll rip you in two," Philip warned with deadly quiet.

Silence, but for the sound of her own heartbeat pounding in her ears and the rush of the sea beyond the castle walls.

Suddenly, Kirby began dragging Camilla backward, through the open door. She tried to resist, tried to drag her feet, but his arm tightened cruelly across her throat, cutting off her air, and he suddenly sliced downward with the knife, making a slash across her arm.

"Don't!" Philip shouted, and lunged forward, but Kirby

instantly brought the knife back up to her throat, the blade prickling the delicate skin beneath her ear.

"Stop or she's dead," he snarled, and Philip froze in his tracks, fury, desperation, and anguish etched upon his face.

"Get ahold of yourself, Kirby!" Philip shouted, his fists clenched at his sides. "Hurting Camilla won't accomplish anything. It's me you want to hurt. Let her go and face me man to man. You were never a coward."

"Shut up!" Kirby shrieked. He was half-running, backward, dragging Camilla across the dead winter grass, through the fog swirling over the cliff. "Stop fighting me, Camilla, or I'll carve you up like a stuffed pheasant," he screamed at her.

Camilla knew that the insane urge to kill was consuming him. He wouldn't stop now, she realized with chilling clarity—he *couldn't* be stopped now.

They reached the jutting arm of the cliff within a stone's throw of the precipice. Below, the foaming waves of the sea glinted gray-green in the murky late afternoon light.

All of her senses seemed to have awakened suddenly, jarring her with their stinging sensitivity. A gull circled overhead, screeching as it dove for fish. The sharp salt tang of the sea filled Camilla's nostrils, making her bitingly, achingly aware of the life that was about to come to a crashing end.

"Not a step closer!" Kirby roared at Philip, who had followed them frantically every step of the tortured journey.

Philip halted, his tall form rigid with tension and fear. From the depths of his eyes burned a fierce determination. Camilla feared his effort to save her—and he would try to save her, she knew—would only get him killed.

I love you, she wanted to cry. But there was no air in her lungs for speech. Kirby's arm tight as a noose across her neck was slowly choking the air and strength from her body.

Suddenly, the death-grip loosened. She slumped, half-fainting, in Kirby's arms, her ears full of the fury of the sea. "It's time, Philip," Alistair Kirby said in a flat, almost dreamy tone. To Camilla he sounded far, far away.

"It's time to watch your precious Camilla die, Philip—and then I will kill you. Nothing can stop me, you see. No one. I am too clever, too strong. You always thought you were the strong one, the leader, but now you see the truth. The role of power belongs to me . . ."

Suddenly there was a blur of flailing bodies, sharp cries and grunts, the thud of blows. Camilla was shoved in the direction of the castle, and she fell to her knees in the grass. Philip surged past her, diving straight at Kirby. She looked up in time to see James and Jared locked in a frenzied struggle with Kirby for the knife.

Kirby fought as though possessed with the demon strength of ten men. He stabbed Jared in the chest before the boy could block the thrust. As James watched his young brother crumple to the earth spurting blood, Kirby sliced the blade straight at him.

"No!" Camilla screamed. "James, look out!"

Distracted for an instant, Kirby's arm hesitated no longer than it took to blink an eye. But it was enough time for James to react. His arm shot up in a flash and seized Kirby's wrist in mid-air. With ferocious strength, he wrenched the knife away.

At that moment, Philip hit Kirby in a flying leap. Both men went down in a rough blur of grunting bodies.

Camilla staggered to her feet, her hands at her throat. She ran to Jared and dragged him away from the fray.

The men were shouting, fighting, with James trying to help Philip subdue Kirby. Sick and dazed, she could only stare at the bleeding boy whose head she cradled in her arms.

Jared's eyes were wide with pain and shock, his breathing shallow. Blood gushed everywhere, and she knew only that she had to stanch the bleeding or he would surely die. With shaking fingers she unknotted his cravat, folded it and tried to stanch the wound. Then she remembered the napkin from Westcott Park, still in the pocket of her gown, and frantically she drew it out, and used this, also, to stem the river of blood. All the while she murmured: "It's all right, Jared, don't move. Everything will be all right."

But it wasn't all right. Kirby's madness seemed to invest him with uncanny strength. As Philip and James tried to pin him to the ground, he fought wildly. A gunshot rang out, and as she looked up in horror she saw James flop over on his side. Slowly, dazedly, he peered down at the hole in his forearm, then groaned and tried to stumble to his knees. Kirby had fired from a pistol hidden in his pocket. For one instant, he grinned with elation, and then with a burst of strength, tore free of Philip's hold. He scrambled quickly to his feet, even as Philip charged toward him yet again.

Like lightning, Kirby dragged his rapier from its scabbard and wielded it before him, holding Philip at bay.

"I could shoot you, too, Philip, but I want to kill you with my sword. Then I will have taken the lives of all the members of the Audley family. Except Dorinda, of course. I wouldn't hurt Dorinda for the world . . . I'm going to marry her someday . . ."

"Don't listen to him, Philip—Jared is very much alive," Camilla shouted over the clamor of the sea. "I'm trying to stop the bleeding now—and James is only wounded in the arm."

"I'll be . . . fine," James gasped, and tried to rise, but Philip spoke without taking his gaze from Kirby's masked face. Beneath the black, diamond-studded mask, Kirby's eyes glowed like twin bolts of lightning.

"It's down to us now, Kirby. You and me. That's what you really wanted all along, isn't it?"

A convulsive nod. Kirby's mouth twitched into a smile. "I want to kill you with my sword, Philip. Do you remember when we had mock duels as children? And fencing instruction as young men? I always won. It was the only sport at which I could defeat you. I still can, you know. I'm better than ever."

"Put the sword down, Kirby," Philip said. "There's been enough bloodshed. You're sick. I don't want to hurt you. I only want to help you. We must take care of Jared and James . . ."

"Very well, then—I'll kill Miss Smith—that will make you fight me!" Kirby choked out, impatient for his own ends. He darted toward Camilla, brandishing the sword before she had time to do more than glance up helplessly, still cradling Jared in her arms.

But Philip somehow sprang between her and Kirby, and in wonder she saw that he had drawn his own rapier, that he held it with the blade pointed at Kirby.

"I tried to warn you," he grated out. "Desist now, Alistair. Don't hurt anyone further, and I'll take you back to London alive."

"I have to kill you—all of you—it is your fate!" Kirby shrieked. "I don't want to—I didn't want to kill Marguerite or Max—but you forced me, Philip. You came between us. It's all your fault!"

He attacked with astonishing swiftness, his sword slicing forward with deftness and strength. Philip parried just in time.

He realized grimly that there was no longer any choice. He'd have to kill Kirby to stop him. The most grueling, desperate fight of his life was on.

Both men fought with fierce concentration, their breath coming hard, sweat glistening in great beads on their faces.

James picked up Kirby's knife with his good hand, and tried to get at Kirby, but Philip coolly ordered him to stand back.

"I'll finish this," he lashed out. "See to Camilla and Jared."

The three of them crouched together watching the battle taking place on the windswept cliff. Watching the duelists with her heart in her throat, Camilla's anxiety built to an unbearable pitch. She felt numb with tension at the ripping blades, the deadly intent of the fencers. Kirby, for all his insane blood lust, fought with supreme skill and cunning. Every movement was precise, strategic, potentially deadly.

Philip, who must have ridden all through the day and night to reach her, she realized, appeared at a disadvantage at first. He was caught up in defending himself against the rapid drive and thrust of Kirby's sword. But as the clouds scudded overhead and the sky changed from pewter to the softened sunset hues of violet and rose, his strength seemed to grow. His face was set with grim purpose, his eyes penetratingly alert in that lean, handsome face. He began to fight with savage energy, each stroke of the sword brilliant, quick as lightning.

He would never give up, Camilla realized. He would never allow himself to fail.

Philip drove harder and harder, the rapier cutting in

and out with dazzling speed and undeniable strength. Kirby's wrist seemed to have weakened, his grip kept slipping on his sword, and his mouth worked silently, frantically, beneath that eerie mask.

His desperation was a palpable thing. All at once Philip lunged at him, and Kirby's sword went flying from his hand. It landed in a bramble of thorns clinging at the tip of the precipice. So exhausted and desperate was he that he dove for it without thinking, and found himself skittering over the edge of the cliff. He saved himself just in time, grabbing the brambles, laughing hysterically. Stepping back to that perilous edge once more, he raised the sword over his head. Still teetering on the brink he faced Philip. His eyes glittered like shards of crystal-blue ice.

"You can't defeat me, Philip," he shouted. "I'm indestructible. Each time I kill it gives me the strength of a bull. I'm going to kill you all before the sun sets, I'm going to watch you die . . ."

The wind howled down suddenly with such ferocity that the castle itself seemed to shudder beneath its gale force, and the waves below swarmed upward in a foaming lather. Kirby, caught unawares by that sudden gust, lost his balance.

He toppled backward over the cliff's edge and as they watched in mute horror, plummeted straight down into the thrashing sea.

Philip ran to the escarpment and peered over at the tiny form bobbing far below. Kirby's body was swept from view, lost in the violent crashing of the waves, tossed up once more, then dragged under for several long moments. It never reappeared. Philip knew, as the sun glided across the pastel horizon, that he was buried forever in the flailing sea.

Philip turned away from the thrashing waves. He

stooped wearily beside Camilla, filled with dazed relief that through all the mayhem she had not been seriously harmed. He glanced into her pale face, then reached out and caressed her cheek with his fingertip. Tears of relief and happiness shone in her eyes. She clutched his hand and raised it thankfully to her lips.

Exhaustion tugged at him. He peered blearily down at his youngest brother's ashen countenance.

"Jared is going to be all right," James told him quickly. "The wound is not deep. But we'd better fetch a doctor quickly from the village."

"Yes, I'm going. Camilla?"

She tried to smile. "I'm fine."

"She's more than fine," James put in, wincing as he shifted position and jolted his wounded arm. "She stanched Jared's wound, and bound up mine. She's taken good care of us while you danced around with Alistair taking your own sweet time."

Philip grinned at his brother's dry jest, but his gaze lingered tenderly on Camilla's upturned face. "Of course she has taken good care of you. That's my girl," he said softly. And promptly left.

It was all she needed to hear.

Sunset gilded the Cornish sky as Philip rode hell-bent for the village. The sea crashed against the ancient stones, and blood splattered the land, but there was a singing happiness in Camilla's heart. With quiet joy she awaited her love's return.

28 The château rose majestically from the verdant pastures of the vine country, glimmering silver in the early morning light. It looked like a storybook place: enchanted and beautifully romantic with graceful spires and towers and stone parapets. A giant flagged courtyard ringed the castle, and there were fruit trees in the valley beyond. Closer, ornamental gardens with fountains and stone benches and magnificent statuary adorned the perfectly manicured grounds. The high walls and buttresses and towers, the stone parapets and mullioned windows and terraces all glittered with ancient grandeur beneath the sapphire-domed sky. Inside those towering walls, Camilla knew with awed certainty, would be tapestries and richly woven rugs, long halls and salons and banquet rooms filled with untold wealth and splendor.

"Why did you bring me here?" she asked Philip for the hundredth time as she peered from the window of the carriage he had hired in Paris, eyeing the castle with awe and misgiving. So much had happened since they'd left

Cornwall. Yet only a few days had passed since the duel at Kirby Keep. James and Jared had been transported home to Westcott Park to recover from their wounds, which, thankfully, had not been dangerous. It had been a joyful homecoming. Charlotte had welcomed Camilla back with tears of joy, hugged her, pressed her hands, and promptly stunned her with the news that Charlotte and James planned to adopt Hester and raise her as their own daughter. Yet, with all the excitement, and the grand ball that was to be held in a short number of days, Philip had nevertheless insisted on leaving Westcott Park with Camilla and five trunks of her baggage almost as soon as they arrived.

He was bringing her to France without delay, he said, but he wouldn't tell her why. All he would say is that he had solved the mystery of the lion charm.

"Well, tell me," she had urged, impatient to understand at last, but Philip had refused.

"It is not for me to tell," he had answered her, and kissed the tip of her nose. No amount of cajoling or insisting had moved him. "We leave at first light for Portsmouth and will make the crossing to Dieppe. Then, soon enough, my love, you will know."

Now here they were, crossing the bridge over the moat, approaching that imposing-looking castle, which Philip had informed her belonged to the Duke de Mont de Lyon.

And he still hadn't even given her back the charm.

What connection there was between the little charm her mother had given her as a child and this French château she could not begin to imagine, nor could she see any reason why a Frenchman had come in search of her at the workhouse, but Philip promised her all would be revealed shortly, and Camilla could do nothing but wait.

Aside from her burning curiosity, and a shivery feeling of awe at the castle she was about to enter, she was happy —happier than she had ever been. With Philip beside her, how could she be otherwise? The love and joy she read in his face every time he looked at her made her own contentment double and triple by the moment.

The knowledge that Kirby had lied about everything, that Philip had never gone back to Brittany with a ring, filled her with gladness. Yet every now and then, even when Philip kissed her and held her, she wondered about the wisdom of their marriage. It would disgrace him if ever anyone learned he had married a serving girl. No matter that she was of the gentry born—a squire's daughter was still far beneath an earl. She knew it didn't matter to Philip, or to his family, but it might someday—if the wrong people somehow learned of her background, or used it somehow against their children. . . .

"Come." Philip jumped down from the carriage and held out his hand to her. "There is someone waiting to meet you."

Yet before they entered the castle he pulled her abruptly into his arms. His eyes gleamed oddly down into hers. "Let me kiss my little serving maid one last time," he murmured huskily, and drew her close against him.

They jumped apart when a liveried manservant opened the castle door. "Mademoiselle Brent and the Earl of Westcott," Philip told the man. "I believe the Duke is expecting us."

Trepidation filled her as they followed a series of manservants through the enormous castle, up winding staircases, down endless carpeted halls, until they were ushered into a large, dark-paneled study where a thin, elegant man sat with bent head at a desk. He looked up

sharply when they entered, came to his feet, but said
nothing as Philip closed the door for privacy.

"Go on, Camilla." Philip gently pushed her forward, an
odd note in his voice. Camilla wondered why he himself
lingered behind. "Go to him, Camilla. Listen to him. He
holds the answers to your questions."

She knew with certainty that the man who had risen
with slow dignity from the carved chair was the Duke de
Mont de Lyon.

He was tall, straight-shouldered, and slightly built, with
iron-gray hair, a rather thin face, and handsome, distinguished features. His eyes were a striking shade of green.
His mouth was thin, unsmiling, firm, his jawline chiseled
in aristocratic elegance.

But it was not at the Duke that Camilla was staring as
she paused in the center of the room. It was at the painting on the wall behind him, a gold-framed painting of a
young woman with burnished hair and blue-green eyes
and a mobile, lovely face—a face so similar to hers that
she dropped her reticule to the floor in shock when she
gazed at it.

No one moved to pick it up. Philip remained in the
background, silent as a stone, and the Duke stared quietly at the stunned young woman before him.

As for Camilla, she let her gaze drop at last to the
Duke. He held her glance for a long moment, his eyes
kindling with an eagerness she did not understand. Her
heart began to race and she knew that something mo-
mentous was happening in this room. When he spoke to
her his voice was courtly and gentle—and filled with pain.
And were those tears in his eyes?

"My child, come. Sit down. What you see before you is
true. That woman in the painting—she could be your

twin. But she is your mama. Ah, *chérie,* you are as lovely as she."

"No!"

He came around the desk with surprising quickness for a man of his years. He reached for her hands, then stopped himself as she drew back. He collected his composure, set his shoulders, and continued as Philip at last came forward to stand by her side.

"My dear," the Duke said with slow precision, gazing firmly into her pale face, "this is a day for the truth. At last, at last, the truth. That woman was my wife, the Duchess Antoinette de Mont de Lyon—your mama, *chérie.* I am your papa."

He caught her by the shoulders as she started to back away. He spoke urgently. "It is a fantastic tale, but all too true. Listen to me, *chérie,* and I will explain about a very great tragedy that befell us all at the time you were born —eighteen years ago."

Camilla's lips trembled. She fought the urge to run from the room. Why had Philip brought her here, exposed her to these insane lies? Her parents were Squire Brent and his wife Matilda, not the Duke and Duchess de Mont de Lyon.

The Duke reached into his pocket suddenly and pulled out the golden lion charm on a shimmering chain. He placed it in her palm.

"The lion is our family crest. The design is the same one you may have noticed when you first came in. Like this."

He showed her the magnificent carved emerald ring on his hand. It was in the exact same shape of the lion, with a ruby in each eye.

She was shaking all over. Her throat ached with sobs she refused to let out. Philip's arm circled her shoulders, squeezing tight for reassurance. But she looked at the Duke, his face mirroring sorrow and hope, his eyes filled with unspeakable pain. Her own gaze was searching, wondering, needing to know. She said in a small, steady voice: "I will listen now. Please—Your Grace—tell me this incredible tale."

She sat in a garden on a carved stone bench, listening to the wind sigh through the poplars. It was quiet save for the thunder of her own thoughts, the whisper of the tears sliding down her cheeks. When Philip came out through the terrace doors and crossed the flagged stones to her, she stayed perfectly still. But the moment he paused beside her and said her name, she threw herself into his arms.

"It's true, it's all true, isn't it, Philip? The Duke truly is my father!"

She wept aloud then, and he held her close, stroking the silken curtain of her hair over and over, as if she were a child he could soothe. "I suspected as much when your necklace broke and I looked at the charm closely for the first time. I recognized it. But I couldn't understand the connection. When you told that tale to Dorinda, about the farmer and his wife getting a child from the gypsy, I began to have even more suspicions. But it seemed so wild, so . . ."

"Absurd," she supplied in a whisper. The memory of her mother—of Matilda Brent, relating the story to her so many times inside Brentwood Manor, filled her with strange emotions. Good, sweet, kind Matilda. She and the squire had never known that the child they brought back to England with them had been stolen. They had been dear, loving people, lonely people in want of a child to nourish as their own. They had been the only parents she had ever known, and she would always love them. . . .

More tears came then, so many tears, tears of loss and tears of discovery. Philip held her all the while, comforting her with his arms, his words, his strength. At last, she wiped her eyes with his handkerchief and gave her head a shake.

"That wicked woman who stole me for revenge," she whispered. "And her poor baby, that died with my mother on the ship—it's all so sad."

She thought of the Duke in his study, waiting patiently for her to return. How long had he searched for her? Ever since that doctor's daughter came to him with the truth she had discovered, he had been frantic to find her. Now he was waiting again, this time for her to come to him.

Her heart went out to him. She didn't know him—yet. But she wanted to. There was so much they had missed. So many things she needed to know. She was glad that there was kindness as well as nobility in his face. He seemed like a man she could respect. Maybe she would never love him like a father, as she had loved Andrew Brent—but who knew? If there was respect and friendship first, who knew what would come?

They had many years to make up for—and it would take time to learn to know one another. "I will see the Duke now," she said suddenly. "There are so many questions I want to ask him—about my mother, and other things as well."

"Wait." Philip caught her arm and she turned to him, resting her hands upon his broad chest.

"There is one thing you should think about, perhaps not now, but when you've had time to accustom yourself to the idea that you are a duke's daughter—Lady Camilla de Mont de Lyon.''

He said it so seriously, she found herself chuckling. "Yes?'' she asked, and reaching up, stroked his lean cheek with her hand.

"Camilla, I'm not sure how to say this.''

She paused, wondering at that cool, flinty gleam in his eyes, his hard tone. He was steeling himself for something —but for what?

"You have every right to cry off our engagement, Camilla,'' he said quickly. "No, listen to me,'' and well-considered purpose flashed through him as he grasped her arms and held her still. "The Duke wishes to present you to French society. You ought to seriously consider it. Your life is changing. It's very sudden. You have opportunities now.''

Her eyes narrowed. "I don't want them.''

"Think about it. Don't be rash. You don't need to marry an English earl. You're a Frenchwoman by rights, the daughter of a Duke, and one day you will inherit all of this. Many men will vie for your hand—you may have your pick among the finest of nobility. Many of these men can offer you as much as I—more, perhaps—and you should not be so quick to turn your back on what is rightfully yours . . .''

"And you,'' Camilla said softly, keeping her emotions in check with an effort. "What will you do, my dear Philip, while I am gallivanting through French society, seeking out this most superior match?''

"I will wait for you.'' His tone was stony. He was determined to be noble, she saw, and she wanted to shake him. "And should you decide, after you have been in society, that you still wish to marry me, I will be there for you.''

"I see. You'll wait for me. And if I choose another?''

His eyes went dark, frightening. "I will . . . I will . . ."

She grinned saucily up at him, watching the sudden struggle flickering through his face. His body was tense as a bowspring.

"If I decide I wish to kiss another man and sleep with him," she murmured, her hands sliding provocatively over his rock-hard chest, "to bear his children, and play with him in bed . . ."

"I'll kill him!" Philip burst out with violence, and Camilla grinned in delight as he seized her to him, and held her in the iron clasp of his arms.

"Since I do not wish to see you hanged for murder perhaps it would be best if we forge ahead with our plans and are married as soon as possible," she suggested sweetly, but her words were cut off by his mouth swooping down on hers.

The kiss was hungry, deep, and possessive. Philip's hands tangled in her hair, his tongue probed hot and searching into the depths of her eager mouth. He didn't let her go for a long time.

"You're right," he said at last. "Your fate is sealed. You're going to become the Countess of Westcott by special license before the month is out—like it or not, my lady."

She smoothed the dark locks back from his brow and cradled his face between her hands. Gazing lovingly into the gleaming depths of his eyes, she knew that all of her dreams were really going to come true.

"I think I'm going to like it very much, your lordship. And so, I'd wager, will you."

EPILOGUE

The day of the ball dawned bright and clear. All of Westcott Park hummed with a heady excitement, for this year the ball was also a wedding ball—and the Earl of Westcott and his bride were to be feted with a splendor that would make all the previous festivities at Westcott Park pale in comparison.

Wonderful smells emanated from the kitchen as Cook prepared a banquet supper fit for the Prince Regent himself. Maids and footmen scurried about the house and grounds at a mad pace, scouring, sweeping, trimming, polishing—readying everything for the arrival of the guests. The house shone like a diamond from top to bottom. The long, oval ballroom at the top of the marble staircase glittered like a huge glowing crystal. Musicians readied their instruments and played the first tentative notes of a waltz. A thousand brilliant orchids adorned the ballroom, overflowing from vases set upon gold-veined marble stands. A fountain splashed champagne into a fluted silver pool. Crystal chandeliers bedecked with a fairyland of glowing candles illuminated the gleaming checkered floor, the orchids' beauty, the radiance of velvet draperies, and white linen–draped tables heaped with sumptuous treats. All was ready for an unforgettable evening.

Jared, James, and Charlotte were all dressed in their finest attire and waited in the ballroom at the foot of the staircase for the bride and groom to make their appearance. The Duke de Mont de Lyon joined them, glanced around the flower-filled wonderland in approval, and kissed Charlotte's hand with smooth grace.

The seconds ticked by and the first guests were due to arrive any moment. Still there was no sign of the guests of honor.

James and Jared exchanged glances over the Duke's head; Charlotte fidgeted with her gloves.

"I can't imagine what can be keeping them," she said and promptly blushed.

The Duke said dryly, "Can't you, my dear? Well, they were married only this morning . . ." A tiny pause. "I do imagine they have many wedding gifts to unwrap."

Jared said nervously, "You don't think they'll forget about the ball, do you? It'll be devilish embarrassing if the first guests arrive and they're not here . . ."

"Durgess," James interrupted, stopping the butler who was gliding past them with an air of extreme importance while on his way to the kitchen quarters, "will you be so good as to knock upon my brother's door and see what is keeping him? He is about to be excessively late for his own ball."

"Me, sir?" Durgess's stiff face turned to him in horror. "Knock upon his lordship's bedchamber door? Surely, that would be highly improper . . . most inopportune . . . quite irregular . . ."

"Dash it, never mind. I'll fetch them myself!" James said irritably and sprinted up the stairs.

In the little green velvet salon that linked the two huge

suites of the master bedroom apartments, Philip and Camilla were clasped in a sensuous, spellbound embrace.

"Love, you'll crush my gown," she murmured at last in
faint protest, and promptly snuggled closer against him,
nibbling the corner of his lip.

"Then take it off," Philip suggested, his hand moving
to the dainty pearl buttons at the back.

"I've already taken it off—twice," she reminded him,
then gasped with pleasure as he captured her lips in a
hungry kiss that scorched her all the way down to her
toes.

"Once more," he urged, and lowered his head to the
swelling mounds of her breasts, which peeped tantaliz-
ingly up at him above her décolleté gown. "Camilla, I
can't get enough of you. It's not my fault you're so beautiful you drive me wild."

In the back of her mind she wondered what time it was
—surely it was nearly the hour for the ball—but maybe
not—maybe there was time for both of them to take off
these lovely evening clothes once again and celebrate
their marriage . . .

A knock at the door startled them apart. "Who the
hell . . . ?"

Philip flung the door wide to behold his brother in the
corridor.

"Bad ton to be late for your own wedding ball," James
shot at him in exasperation, noting his brother's tousled
hair, untied cravat, and burning gaze.

"Surely it isn't time yet . . ." Philip exploded, and
James gave a crack of laughter.

"Surely it is. We're all waiting downstairs for the first
guest to arrive—your papa-in-law is being most patient,"
James pointed out, "but it will be difficult to explain to

your guests that their host and hostess have not yet made an appearance."

"Oh, dear, how *scandalous*." Hurriedly straightening her gown, Camilla flew to the door and gave James a radiant smile. "You look wonderful, James. We'll be down in a moment, I give you my word. Philip, let me go, love, I must get my jewels." Laughing, Camilla broke away from him and floated off in a happy daze to the airy peach-colored suite where Mary and Kate had unpacked all of her belongings today after the wedding.

As she fastened the brilliant sapphires in her ears, and picked up the exquisite diamond and sapphire necklace Philip had presented her with as a wedding present, she heard James say:

"What is this card from Marchfield? Is he making trouble?"

"On the contrary," Philip answered, his voice carrying quite clearly to her in the adjoining room.

"He has made me a wedding gift of the bays I presented to him as forfeit for our bet. Quite handsome of him, really. I'll never like the fellow, but he wasn't guilty of murder or blackmail, after all—only of befriending that son of a bitch Dubois years ago. Maybe Marchfield and I shall call a truce yet. Or"—he shrugged—"maybe not."

"After all, you both ended up with exactly what you wanted. In my opinion, he and Brittany will suit admirably together. Perhaps it is time to let the past go," James concurred quietly.

"You know, James, it is far easier to do that when one can see the bright glow of the future," Camilla heard Philip say. "And I see that glow every time I look into my wife's eyes."

Camilla smiled at her own reflection, warming at his

words. How lucky she was. She had found love, a home, and a family. A short time ago she had been all alone—a serving maid eking out an existence without a single person to help her in a moment of trouble—now she had Philip and all of the Audleys to stand beside her, to love her and to let her love them.

She stared at the girl in the looking glass. All traces of the wretch known as Weed had vanished. The Countess of Westcott gazed wonderingly back at her. She was still amazed by her own transformation, always startled when she glanced in the mirror—and never more so than on this most special night.

Her coppery hair was a mass of curls caught up upon her head by a stunning sapphire tiara. In a low-cut ball gown of shimmering sapphire velvet, with satin slippers, a lace and velvet demi-train, and her jewels, she looked lovely, regal, her skin creamy and glowing, her eyes luminous with anticipation of the night ahead. Her father waited downstairs, the father she was only beginning to know. And soon, she would encounter Marchfield, Brittany, Lady Asterley, Miss Drewe, Miss Fitzroy, and Freddy . . . and all of the other members of the ton she had come to know during the past season.

Once the prospect had daunted her—now she greeted it with humor and pleasure. She could take kindness where it was given, recognize flattery for exactly what it was, smile to herself over the foibles and eccentricities of the aristocracy.

She was one of them now—and yet, she was also still Weed, the girl who knew how difficult and discouraging it was to toil for a living, how bleak it was to be alone, how uncertain to live at the mercy of an uncaring world. The girl who was once known as Weed would always savor each new luxury, whether it be silks and satins, diamonds and rubies—or the unbounded love now bestowed so generously on her.

Let me never take it all for granted, she prayed silently, and then whirled from the mirror as Philip strode into her room, followed by James.

"What's that?" her husband demanded.

She followed his gaze to the four-poster bed hung with flowing peach draperies and saw the edge of a yellow muslin gown sticking out from beneath the satin dust ruffle. At the same moment, she realized that her eyes were watering.

"Dorinda! And Hester? Come out from under that bed. If you've brought that kitten in here . . . how long have you two been hiding in my room?"

They emerged, giggling, and stared up at her without remorse. "Oh, we popped in just a moment before James knocked on the door. Don't worry," Dorinda assured her. "We didn't hear much kissing."

Hester, clutching Tickles in her arms and looking stouter and happier than Camilla would have thought possible, confessed: "We thought you had already gone down to the ball—we wanted to try on some of your hats and slippers."

"You did, did you?" James scooped Hester up into his arms and chucked her lightly under the chin. "Don't you know to ask permission before entering someone's bedroom?"

"I'm sorry," she began, obviously afraid she had offended her new father, but he immediately kissed her on the cheek.

"Don't tell a soul, but I committed far worse crimes when I was your age," he whispered solemnly.

"Tell her about putting the salt in the sugar bowl," Dorinda urged, eyes sparkling, but Philip interrupted with a frown.

"We're not talking about the past tonight. We're talking about right here and now. I think this is a punishable offense," Philip added severely, with a meaningful glance at his brother, but Dorinda, regarding him apprehensively at first, caught the glint of humor in his eyes and dimpled.

"You won't dare punish me—Camilla will get angry with you!" she warned.

"Achoo!" Camilla laughed helplessly and backed away from the kitten. "No, I won't be angry, Philip. Do what you want with the pair of them—only get that kitten away before I am forced to go down to the ball looking as though I've been crying for hours!"

"Aha. You heard her. We have permission to punish this pair as we see fit, James. Do you know what I'm thinking?"

The girls squealed with laughter as James bundled one girl under each arm, with Hester still haplessly clutching the kitten in her little hands.

"Take them away!" Philip ordered, unable to suppress a grin as he opened the door for his brother.

"Where are you taking us? What are you doing?" The girls shrieked with laughter as James bore them off down the hall, and Camilla sent a quizzical glance at her husband.

"There's a private gallery above the ballroom where they can watch the ball," he told her as he came up behind her and slid his arms around her waist. "Marguerite used to do it all the time. Charlotte has arranged for Miss Brigham to be there with a spread of tarts and lemonade for them. They should have quite a festive evening—

food, music, and the ability to spy on everyone below without being seen."

"Maybe we'll steal up there and join them," she suggested, leaning her head back against his chest. "It sounds ever so cozy. And I like to spy on my fellows as much as the next person does."

"Really—and what else do you like?" Philip asked softly, his hand sliding up to cup her breast.

"This," she breathed, and closed her eyes.

She felt so soft and sensuous in his arms. He wanted to strip the velvet gown off her and make love to her right now. In the mirror, he saw the passion flame in her eyes at his intimate touch, felt her body growing warm against him.

"And what else?" he murmured, licking inside the seashell curve of her ear.

"That, also," she whispered. "Oh yes, Philip, and many other things . . ."

They both heard the carriage at the same moment, the wheels crunching loudly on the stones below.

"Oh no!"

Her eyes flew open, and she stiffened with alarm. Philip's hands dropped disappointedly to his sides.

"Damn!"

But he was grinning as Camilla caught his hand in hers and pulled him, running, toward the door.

In the brightly lit ballroom the Duke, Charlotte, James, and Jared glanced at each other in chagrin.

"I thought they were coming," James muttered.

"What will we say . . . " Charlotte began in consternation, but just then they heard the sound of pounding footsteps and laughter on the stairs above, and the Earl and Countess raced into view, resplendent in their evening finery, breathless as children, as they raced full-speed down the garlanded stairs of Westcott Park to take their place in the receiving line. They were laughing like love-crazed fools as hand in hand they bolted into the ballroom only ten paces ahead of the first group of guests —Lord Marchfield, Lady Brittany, and Lord and Lady Marrowing.

"It's about time," Jared whispered, fighting back a chuckle. "You two have the rest of your lives for . . . whatever."

"That we do," Philip flung back, squeezing Camilla's gloved hand. "We have tonight, tomorrow, and forever after."

Forever after. How wonderful that sounded. She lifted her gaze to Philip's as the lilting music filled the room and let the love in his eyes fill her heart.